Korea

Book 11 in the Combined Operations Series

By

Griff Hosker

Korea

Published by Sword Books Ltd 2018
Copyright © Griff Hosker First Edition

The author has asserted their moral right under the Copyright, Designs, and Patents Act, 1988, to be identified as the author of this work.

All Rights reserved. No part of this publication may be reproduced, copied, stored in a retrieval system, or transmitted, in any form or by any means, without the prior written consent of the copyright holder, nor be otherwise circulated in any form of binding or cover other than that in which it is published and without a similar condition being imposed on the subsequent purchaser.
A CIP catalogue record for this title is available from the British Library.
Cover by Design for Writers

Thanks to Sooyon Sy Morgan for the help with the Korean names and places.

Contents

Korea 1
Prologue 4
Chapter 1 8
Chapter 2 22
Chapter 3 37
Chapter 4 52
Chapter 5 64
Chapter 5 78
Chapter 6 91
Chapter 7 102
Chapter 8 113
Chapter 9 129
Chapter 10 145
Chapter 11 160
Chapter 12 173
Chapter 13 182
Chapter 14 193
Chapter 15 202
Chapter 16 211
Epilogue 228
Glossary 232
Historical background 235
Other books by Griff Hosker 237

Prologue

When the war ended and I went home I did not know what the future held for me beyond marriage to Susan and a reunion with my mother and father. The war was over and my men, my brothers in arms, were able to attend my wedding. That day was a celebration. It was not just a wedding celebration. We had all survived. The Nazis had tried to exterminate the Commandos and they had failed. The German High Command had tried to destroy Britain and all that her people stood for. We had been too tough for them and we had survived. Their leaders would soon be on trial for their crimes but I knew that many would escape justice. The end of the war had been a confusing time. In their race to get to Berlin, the allies had been lax about security and I knew that many who should have been on trial would have fled with ill-gotten gains.

As Susan and I walked from the tiny parish church in Burnham on Crouch, the war was a million miles away from us. My men formed a guard of honour. The newly promoted Captain Poulson and the rest of my men wore their number ones and fresh, gleaming medal ribbons. That was a reminder of the years of hell but the rest of the day was a celebration of peace and hope. Only Polly Poulson and Gordy Barker would be remaining in the service. The rest of us would be demobbed. My wedding day was the last time that my section would be all together.

We meant to meet up again. We made promises to do just that. We even set dates. Many of us made the ones in forty-six and forty-seven. After that, it was just the occasional get together for those who lived close to each other. I was the only one who lived in Essex. When my men brought their girlfriends and wives to London, Susan and I would head up to town to meet them. It was not the same. No matter how much we tried we could not bring back the camaraderie of the war. No one was to blame. We had lives to pick up. I had been about to go to University when the war started. Susan still wanted me to go. Many men my age did so but it was not for me.

My father also left the R.A.F. He had been in longer than I had. He felt it was time for something new. We had sat in the garden of my new house overlooking the River Crouch sipping whisky when he had made his proposal to me. He had suggested that we use some of the money he had accrued over the years to buy one of the many Dakotas, the workhorse C-47, which were being sold for next to nothing. He thought to set up an air cargo service. He still loved flying and had contacts in the service. There were fitters and mechanics who would love to work for a hero like my father. He was one of the few aces from the Great War. I had nothing else to do and it deferred thinking of a career. Ever a procrastinator I joined him.

    We both knew that it would be some time before we would be making any money and were resigned to using our savings. Thanks to the Honourable Reginald St. John Brown of Burton Leonard, North Yorkshire, my father had a healthy income each month. Even if the business failed we would not be poor. When Lady Burscough had died she left money for both my father and for me. She had no children and whilst death duties accounted for much of the estate we were both well off. We bought an old trainer for a song. The war was over and the Government were trying to get rid of as many aeroplanes as they could. I was rusty and I spent every hour in the air while Bert and Norman worked on the Dakota.

    Mum and Susan got on well and they operated the office. Mum proved a whizz at finding business. Poor dad thought he was going to have a pleasant little business which would see him tootling around the skies and enjoying himself. From the moment the Dakota was airworthy she was flying every day. I was the co-pilot, navigator and engineer all rolled into one. I didn't mind. Dad and I were making up for lost time. We got to chat. Much of our business involved flying to France and Germany. In the months after the war, there were shortages of everything except, ironically, petrol. Bread might have been put on the ration again but petrol was now readily available. Despite our fears within three months, we had made enough money to buy a second Dakota and take on more staff. As the months went on we bought a third. We operated out of Southend Airport. I had been there when it was requisitioned in the war. Now it was a civilian airfield once more and eager for our company to be based there. It was handy for Dad and I. It was also close enough to London. Dad's network of service contacts meant that we found two more pilots to take over some of our work. As mum said we had worked hard all of our lives and did not need to work every hour that God sent.

    When Susan gave birth to our first child in March 1946 I had another reason to work less. My son, William, was a joy and both Dad and I spent as much time as we could with him. We managed to buy two more Dakotas before that source of buses dried up. We had more pilots and therefore were able to assign just one flight a week to ourselves. The business prospered. It helped to have two pilots who had each won a V.C. Businesses trusted the company.

My daughter Isabelle was born in 1947 and in 1948 my second son, Samuel. Had our world remained the same then I suspect I would have stopped flying within a year or two. We had a good reputation for efficiency and reliability. Our staff were all ex-servicemen and worked hard for good pay. With a fleet of five aeroplanes and business all over Europe, we were contemplating branching out into the burgeoning passenger business. All that changed in June of that year when the Soviets introduced a blockade on Berlin. The Berlin Airlift, as it came to be known, was the first conflict between the west and the communist world. That conflict would soon escalate. The R.A.F. no longer had enough aircraft. The Labour Government had been draconian in its military cuts. They had sold off her assets and allowed too many men to be thrown onto the scrapheap. We were one of the companies who were chartered to fly into Berlin.

The risks were great. By the time it was over sixty airmen had died. No company would insure us but we were lucky and we had all been in the service. We survived and lost neither aircraft nor crew. I was proud of our service. It showed me that there were still enemies out there. Although we were not in uniform we had done our bit. They were not Nazis. Now the enemies were Communists. They were not just in Europe they were all over the world. They were an enemy because they did not believe in live and let live. They believed in changing the world so that it was a Communist one. We had not fought two world wars to allow that to happen.

I was a reservist. I still had my uniform and my rank. I had been a full major when the war had ended and I kept the title. Until the Berlin Airlift, the commitment was not arduous. I had a couple of weeks a year when I would play soldiers with other commandos. Often, I had served with the men and the training became a chance to catch up and reminisce. We sometimes had a week of exercises. All they proved to me was how unfit I had become. That did not matter then but when the airlift ended in May 1949 I saw the red threat. Dad and I talked about it. We were both relatively young. Dad was still in his early fifties while I was not even thirty. If war came against the Communists then we would both volunteer. Dad knew that he would be a dinosaur. The pilots now flew jets but he understood the service. With me it was different. I had been at the peak of my powers just four short years earlier. We both agreed that I needed to become fitter.

I flew just once a week but every other day saw me running along the Essex lanes. We bought a couple of canoes and Dad and I would paddle along the Crouch and the Blackwater. The running built up my legs and the canoeing my arms. I quite enjoyed the canoeing as did my father. When my children were old enough then they could join in too.

Gordy Barker was now Chief Quartermaster at Bickleigh Barracks in Devon. As well as the trainer we had also managed to buy a Mosquito. She had been one of the last of her kind. I always thought it a great shame that they got rid of her and the Spitfire. I had never flown a jet and I had no desire to. There was an elegance about some of the aircraft developed to fight the Germans. For me, the Mosquito was one of the best aeroplanes of the war. She was perfect for a quick flight down to Devon. We now had enough contacts and knew of enough airfields to use the Mossy as an aerial taxi. The fact that it had two seats was a bonus. I flew down one weekend and managed to practise with the current weapons. Most were still the weapons I remembered but there were newer explosives. Gordy somehow coerced some of the NCO's to demonstrate the weapons. I enjoyed the break and it was good to catch up with an old comrade.

All of this meant that as 1949 slipped towards 1950 I was prepared as well as I could be to fight the Communists. When the war did come, however, it came from a direction I did not expect at all: the Korean Peninsula.

Chapter 1

On the 25th of June, 1950 everything changed when the Communist North Korean Army invaded the Republic of Korea. Dad and I knew what it meant but Susan, my mum and the children were blissfully unaware that this would change our lives forever. We were in the offices at the airfield and listening to the radio when we heard the news. The bulletin was on the radio on the Monday. It was at lunchtime that we heard. We would listen to the radio in the office. Mum liked to work in the morning and then head for my house where she would play with the children. She had already left for my home. She had just secured a new contract for us and left in high spirits. William would be at school within the next year and Mum wanted to spend as much time as possible with them. Bert and Norman were foremen now and they had six mechanics, riggers and fitters working for them. We were in the office discussing the work schedules for the next week when we heard the announcer, Alvar Liddell, on the BBC give us the news. We had all been in the service and knew what this meant.

"The Government will never stand for this, Mr Harsker! They will send soldiers in!"

My father smiled at Bert's words, "Not as simple as that these days, Bert. We have something called the United Nations now. They will intervene."

"Nah, sir, with due respect that won't work. We had it before the war, it was called the League of Nations. Did that stop Adolf, Mussolini and Hirohito? Did it buggery! The only thing that will stop these commies is us. Send a fleet, a couple of squadrons of bombers and Bob's your uncle! Problem solved! They aren't like Jerry. We'll stop them!"

I looked at Dad and shook my head. We had been reading such rhetoric in the papers for weeks. The United Nations had not stopped the Soviet blockade of Berlin. The American and British air forces had. But Norman was wrong. The North Koreans were a tough nation and they had a large army. From the papers I had been reading either the Russians or the Chinese would supply them with arms and aeroplanes. This would not be plain sailing. Added to that it was halfway around the world. When the two foremen had left us, we lit our pipes and talked about it.

"Of course things will be in place already. When there is an announcement like this those in the War Office have already decided who will be sent. We learned our lesson with Neville Chamberlain." Dad had been quite senior in the last war and moved in the corridors of power. He knew the secrets of Whitehall. He was probably right. "Do you think that you will be called up, Tom?"

I shrugged, "Commandos are good for working behind the lines and being a nuisance but we don't win wars. We open doors to make it easier for the big boys to do their job. I am ready to go if I have to but I think there will be regulars that can do the job. Bickleigh is full of recruits. If the United Nations sends troops straight away then they might have to use some of the older hands. We'll see."

"You will have to mention this to Susan and your Mum. I can't see either being very happy about it." He laughed, "When I went off to Russia after the Great War I thought your mum was going to have a Dicky fit!"

"They may not call me up but I will tell Susan the possibility tonight."

We all lived in the same small village. Mum, who ran the family like Sergeant Major Dean used to run the battalion, had spotted the house when it came up for sale. It had been just a month before the end of the war and she had bought it with her own savings. When we married we had paid her back but the house was perfect with a lovely enclosed garden in which the children could play. The four bedrooms were now full but we would worry about that if a fourth child came along. With a good village pub which Dad and I enjoyed my life was idyllic.

Aware that I might be leaving at some time in the near future, I stayed a little later than normal to make certain I left no loose ends. I knew that Dad would already be warning Mum of the implications of the announcement. Consequently, it was a little later than normal when I walked into the house. The sound of the car had alerted the children and the three of them hurled themselves down the hall with a collective scream of, "Daddy!"

I bent to sweep them up in my arms. Once it had been easy but William and Isabelle were now much bigger. Isabelle lay her head on my shoulder, "You are late, Daddy!"

William nodded, "We were hungry and Mummy said we had to wait for you!"

"Well, I am here now! I am hungry too! Come on. You two are getting too big to carry! I lowered my two eldest to the floor and looked at Samuel. He was almost two and a half. He could almost talk in sentences. "And how is my tomato picker today?" Samuel loved to pick tomatoes with me.

He nodded seriously, "Red ones are ready!"

"Then after we have eaten we will go and pick them. How does that suit?" He nodded vigorously.

We had a large dining room but we saved that for company. The large wooden table in the kitchen was where we ate most meals. I knew that Susan would not have been cooking. We still had rationing. As this was Monday we had the leftovers from the joint. There was little left. The children had healthy appetites. We were lucky that my mum and dad used their meat ration with ours. That allowed us to buy a joint. Sunday and Monday were now the only days when we ate meat. For the rest of the week, we had offal, which was no longer rationed, or rabbit. Dad and I were good shots and there were plenty of rabbits. As it was summer we would be having the small amount of meat left from the joint with the salad we grew ourselves, new potatoes from the garden and pickles which we also made. It was healthy food and we enjoyed it.

Susan knew that something was amiss. We read each other well. I knew that I had been lucky to marry her. She would not say anything while the children were there. She was a great believer in routine. After we ate we piled the dishes into the sink and all went into the garden. We made the most of the summer. We had a small lawn but most of the garden was devoted to vegetables and salads. That was a relic of war and rationing. We were still heavily rationed. The tomatoes had done well. I grew a bush variety called Tumbler Tom. The children found it amusing as that was my name. I grew them because they produced a good crop and I didn't have to nip out side shoots. Dad had managed to get the seeds on one of our flights. We just saved seeds each year and grew them that way. The children, especially Samuel, loved to pick them. They made it a competition. It had taken some time to persuade Samuel that he could only pick red ones. Our arms laden, we went to the outdoor tap to wash them. One of the reasons we had bought the house was because it had water inside and out. The indoor toilet was a luxury in the village. Only my parents and we had one. The rest still used the outdoor toilet. We washed the tomatoes. To the children it was a game; a wet game. Susan frowned and tutted but the giggling children turned her frown to a smile.

"Right, bath time!"

We had an indoor bath and, thanks to the range, we had hot water. I collected firewood each autumn. The constantly hot kitchen was a small price to pay for the luxury of hot water. I ran the bath while Susan undressed the children. Bath time was a wonderfully chaotic time. Inevitably both Susan and I would be as wet as the children but their laughter made up for that. While Susan dressed them, I put milk on to warm through. There was still milk rationing but we had a goat, Betty. Susan had named her after one of the women she worked with. We hoped that when rationing ended we might be able to make our own goat's cheese. When we just had William, we had made a couple of batches and enjoyed it. Now Betty's output was purely for the children.

Dressed in pyjamas and nighty the children trooped down to the living room and the huge settee. I put their mugs of Horlicks on the table to cool and said, "Now, do we want a book or a story?"

"Story!"

With my children cuddled in close Susan went to do the dishes while I told them a story. I normally made them up. There was little originality in them. They would involve knights, princesses and dragons. I made up for the lack of originality by doing voices. I was nowhere near as good as Scouse Fletcher. He could imitate anyone! However, I had learned from him and the children seemed to enjoy them. When Sam yawned then I knew it was time to bring my story to a close. They always gave a round of applause when I had finished.

Susan came in when she heard it, "Come on William! Give Dad a kiss."

"Night Dad!"

She took him from me and I lifted the two youngest. I would not be able to do this for much longer. As I climbed the stairs I made a game of it. I pretended I was a giant and they both giggled as I said, "Fee, Fie, Foe, Fum" up the stairs. Susan said, "Tom! It is bedtime! No silliness!"

I put on a Boris Karloff voice, "Yes Master!" It just made all three of them giggle even more.

The three each had their own room. Samuel had just moved from the cot in our room to the bed in the box room. I had had a carpenter move the door handles so that they could not reach them but, generally, they were so exhausted at bedtime that they just fell asleep. I lowered Izzy into her bed, "Night, night sweetheart! Sleep tight, hope the bed bugs don't bite!"

"Night, Daddy!"

Still holding Samuel, I leaned over and kissed her, "I'll be back in a minute to tuck you in."

Sam's bed was the one all of my children had used after progressing from the cot. The room was small and cosy. I handed him Teddy and Cat. They were two stuffed toys and he would not go to sleep without them. I held Teddy and spoke in what Susan called my sergeant's voice, "Now Teddy remember you are in charge here tonight. When I come tomorrow I want everything ship shape and Bristol fashion!" I did a high-pitched voice and pretended it came from Teddy. "Yes sir, Major Harsker!"

Samuel laughed and hugged his bear, "Night, night Daddy!"

"Night bonnie lad; love you!" I leaned over and kissed him. When I reached the landing, Susan had tucked Isabelle in and was closing the door. We walked down the stairs, inevitably making at least two of them creak. I kept saying I would have them repaired but never did.

Susan did not close the hall door. We never did. Even though it was unlikely that they would wake we still kept an ear out and talked in whispers. She sat on the settee and patted it. "No wireless tonight?"

"You are never late, Tom Harsker, and I saw that look in your eyes. What is up?"

"Nothing!" I saw her nostrils flare. "That is to say probably nothing but North Korea has invaded its neighbour."

"I know. I heard it on the lunchtime bulletin but what has that to do with you?" She was a bright woman. She had worked in Combined Operations headquarters. Realisation dawned. "No, Tom! You did your bit and then some. Not you again!"

I shook my head, "They probably won't want me it is just that I am in the Reserve and they could call me up. They still have conscription you know."

"And I know how many skivers avoided the call up last time and the decent ones went and got killed. You were almost killed. It isn't right."

"Like I said they probably won't want me and I will happily stay here in Blighty. All I am saying is that if that telegram comes then I will have to go and I will probably have to move a little sharpish too!"

She cuddled in, "I like having you at home. The children..." Her hand went to her mouth. "Think of the three of them! And your mother! Goodness me she will not be happy! She thinks that you and your father have done enough."

I said nothing and just held her tightly. She began to cry and I let her. This would probably come to nothing but I knew it was better to be prepared than not. After she stopped she lifted her head. "I must be getting soft. I didn't cry when the war was on! I will go and make a cuppa."

I picked up the newspaper and leafed through it. There was little sign of rationing ending. Bread and potatoes were back on the ration book. That had been down to nature. A couple of bad winters had wiped out the wheat and potatoes. We didn't mind the potatoes, we grew our own. As we could still readily get oats we made oat bread. The newspapers were full of the news that the Conservatives wanted to cease rationing but Labour were adamant that it would continue. With an election coming up that was big news.

I put the paper away when Susan returned with the tea, "And what about the business? Can your dad carry on alone?"

I laughed, "That is the least of my worries. I only have one flight a week. Mum and Dad enjoy being in the office and making the business grow. From what I can see it is a hobby that will give us and Mary an income."

Susan nodded, "And she is so far away too."

"She is." Mary, my sister, had been one of the many female pilots who delivered aeroplanes during the war. They were truly unsung heroines. She had met a Canadian just as the war ended. It was a whirlwind romance and now they lived in Dundas, Ontario. The last letter we had received said that Mary was pregnant. One advantage of an air business was that we could visit whenever we liked. So far we had not availed ourselves of the opportunity but once there were more grandchildren then I knew Mum and Dad would both be off.

I was about to turn on the radio when the telephone rang. My father and I were both lucky enough to have one. I often thought that it was a curse. I wondered if it was Mum. Like Susan, she seemed to be able to read her husband well. My father was a war hero but he always raised the white flag when Mum attacked!

It was Toppy Foster. When I had last seen him, at the end of the war, he had been like me a major. I recognised his voice immediately, "Tom! How are you, dear boy! Toppy here."

"Hello, Toppy. This is a call out of the blue." I glanced at Susan. She saw my face and then ran from the room. She knew Toppy. She knew him as Major Foster for he had been in command of the Headquarters. She knew what a phone call from him meant. "And I take it the call is not a social one."

"Sharp as a tack! Listen, I shall be brief. I am Colonel Foster now and I work at the War Office. As you can imagine we have been working on a South Korean scenario for some time. I can't say any more on an open line but General Wainwright wondered if you could pop up to town tomorrow and meet us at the War Office." I allowed a silence to develop. "Hello? You still there, Tom?"

"Yes, Toppy. I just wanted to make certain that I would be home on the evening train. I have a family now not to mention a business to run."

"Quite! Yes, of course. Just a little chat. Pick your brains and the like eh? After all, you have more experience than most men who are much older, me included."

"In that case, I will be there."

"Shall we say nine-thirty? Room twenty. You know the place. Bring your ID. See you then." And then he was gone.

Susan had recovered her composure. "I have to go to town tomorrow. I shall take the train. Toppy reckons I will be back by tea time."

"Major Foster's promises are not to be believed!"

"He is a Colonel now and sounds like he is quite proud of the promotion." I kissed her, "Sorry about this. I had better check that my uniform hasn't been eaten by moths."

"And the other equipment?" She gave me a pointed look. I had a steel cabinet in our bedroom. It had my Bergen and weapons. I had not used any of them since the war but they were all well maintained. I had German pistols, a Colt, a Webley. There was a Lee Enfield and my faithful Thompson. My commando dagger, toggle and garotte were all there too along with spare bits of kit I had acquired over the war years.

"I won't need it tomorrow. They said it was just for a chat."

"And I remember ringing up officers in the war to ask them to come in for a chat! Don't treat me like a child, Tom. We both know they want you for something and it won't be advice." She stood. "I will give your good jacket a sponge. You haven't worn it for a while.

As the train pulled in to Liverpool Street Station I wondered what on earth they could need me for. I had rung Dad the night before. He needed to know where I would be. All he had said was, "I will tell your mum but you owe me a pint and an ounce of Baby's Bottom from Standish the tobacconist!"

"It is a deal!"

London was stifling in June. I hated the city. At least it was not as grim as it had been in the war. There were no taped windows and much of the bomb damage had been repaired. New buildings were sprouting up all over. I had caught an early train and so, even though it was a long walk, I decided to stroll to Whitehall. It was a pleasant walk and half of it would be along the river. I smiled at the workers hurrying across the bridges. Offices and shops seemed to suck in people like a vacuum cleaner. I worked in an office but these workers looked like ants and they all had the same pasty look of people who never saw the sun. There was a tobacconist just opposite the Houses of Parliament and I called there to buy Dad some Baby's Bottom tobacco. I bought some Condor Bar. Bar kept longer than loose tobacco and I bought half a pound of it. Bill Leslie had shown me a trick of trickling Navy rum on the bar and letting it soak in. It kept the tobacco moister for longer. I had taken to doing this with whisky. While I was there I saw a good-looking billiard pipe. Made by Brigham, it was a quality pipe. I bought it. Dad's birthday was coming up and I was always short of ideas about what to get him.

Once on the street, I checked my watch. I hated getting anywhere late. I stepped out smartly and reached the War Office five minutes early. Security was tight and I had to show my ID three times before I was admitted to an antechamber. There I saw Polly Poulson. He would always be that to me even though his title had been Captain Paul Poulson. He was in uniform. He was still a captain. He still bore the scar he had suffered when bullets had sprayed splinters of rock into his face. He had been lucky not to lose an eye! The scar gave him a roguish appearance. He grinned as he stood to greet me. "I hoped they might ask you to be here too, sir! You are looking good!"

"The country air is good for me. And you? Married yet?"

He shook his head. "I was but it didn't work out. She liked the uniform when we married and then tired of it. She ran off with a salesman." He shrugged, "At least there were no children. I am happy enough. I have the service. How is the air business?"

"Doing well." He nodded. "Now the small talk is out of the way what is this all about? Korea?"

"That would be my guess. I was about to go on a training exercise in British Columbia when I was pulled off the transport. All my gear is downstairs."

We were saved any further speculation by the arrival of a sergeant from the Women's Royal Army Corps. We had known them as ATS during the war. This one looked to be of an age where she had served in the war. "Major, Captain, if you would like to follow me."

Korea

Instead of going into the office behind us she led us up some stairs and down a narrow corridor. It was a deserted part of the building. The cuts had not just been in servicemen, tanks, ships and aeroplanes. She opened a door and gestured for us to enter. When we did so the door was closed behind us. There were two officers in the room: Colonel Foster and General Wainwright. I recognised Toppy and as the other officer was a general then I took him to be the officer I was supposed to meet. The two civilians I did not know. Although, as I looked, one looked vaguely familiar.

It was obvious that Colonel Foster was the low man on the totem pole for he made the introductions. "Gentlemen this is Captain Poulson and Major Harsker of the Commandos. I served with both men in the war and I can tell you that they are the best in their field." He gestured with his arm, "This is General Wainwright who represents the General Staff. The Honourable John St. Loe Strachey is the Secretary of State for War and the last gentleman…well he is from MI6 and for obvious reasons his identity must remain a secret. You may call him, L." We both nodded, "Sit down, please. The Secretary of State will speak with you, briefly, and then he will leave."

I knew I had seen one of the civilians before. John Strachey had been Minister of Food and had been highly unpopular. Much as we all hated rationing we knew that it was necessary. He smiled, "First of all, Major, can I say what an honour this is for me. I served as an Adjutant in a Hurricane squadron in the last war. Your father was something of a hero of mine and I can see that his son is following in his footsteps." The smile went. "This war, half a world away, is not one sought by us but we have to obey the wishes of the world and fight these enemies of democracy. Already there are hundreds of ships heading for the region. We are sending seventeen ships and seven thousand men. We are mobilising men in India too but the North Koreans have driven so far south that soon little of South Korea will be in the hands of their own people. Major Harsker, you are a reservist but we are recalling you to the colours. We wish to fly you to Japan in the morning."

I flashed an angry look at Toppy. He must have known of this timescale when he rang me.

"You and the Commandos who will be with you will be amongst the first to strike back at the Communists." He smiled again. "I have to say, Major, that the Americans specifically asked for you. It seems you impressed them in Italy and then in the race for Paris. It bodes well for the future. Our two nations going forward together arm in arm against the red menace." He stood and walked over to us. We both rose and he shook our hands. It was a firm handshake. "God speed!" And then he was gone.

We heard his footsteps receding down the corridor. The man call L lit a cigarette and then said, as he blew smoke into the air, "Well thank God the politician has gone. We have wasted enough time already!"

Inside I was seething. Toppy had to have known that I would be whisked off without seeing my family. Had he done this deliberately? Even as I was thinking that the man from MI6 stood.

He rolled down a map, "South Korea. The Communists have planned this well. Seoul is already taken and we believe that by the middle of next month there will be very little left in South Korea which is not controlled by Communists. That is where you chaps come in. You are going to do what you did for much of the war. You are going to raid behind their lines and cause as much trouble as you can. You will have twenty-eight men with you but we want you to make the Communists think that there is a battalion behind their lines. You have to help slow up the North Korean advance." I had so many questions and doubts but he went on like the Flying Scotsman. "You will be operating under American command. Don't worry, Major, they will not restrict you but they have ultimate control. Major Max Hampton of the 5th Ranger Battalion is in command. His men are going to be operating behind enemy lines. You will be going in by sea. We have two MTBs and a Motor Launch heading from Singapore even as we speak."

He paused to light another cigarette and I took the opportunity to speak. "Sir, the last time I fought was at the end of the war. I am used to working with British commanders and not Americans, as much as I admire Americans. I have not the first clue how to speak Korean." I paused for breath, "And may I ask, with respect, sir, why is an MI6 officer briefing us?"

I saw Toppy and General Wainwright smile. Toppy said, "I told you he was bright."

The MI6 officer gave me a rueful smile and sucked on his cigarette. "I am here because there are Russian and East German agents operating in Whitehall." He waved his cigarette around the room like a priest with incense, "We have chosen this room because we know there are no listening devices and there is no one else on this floor. We are secure here. We have been compromised and that is why you will be working without communication with London. The boat crews who are joining you were helping to train Australians in small boats. The Commandos you will take have been on deployment in British Honduras. The only man who has been serving in England is Captain Poulson." There was a pause. "And Colonel Foster vouches for him." He smiled. "After today, Major, it is highly unlikely that you will ever see me again. I will go back to the murky world of spy catching. You are right, I need not have been here but now you will be even more vigilant and careful, will you not?" I nodded. "And I have met you and I will be able to tell the CIA that the commandos we have sent can be trusted and will get the job done." He stood. He gave a laugh, "It is like one of those Agatha Christie books isn't it? Ten little Indians." And then he was gone.

The General visibly relaxed, "Not the sort of chap I would want in my club but a necessary evil. I am sorry about this, Major Harsker. We would have liked to give you more time to get used to the idea but the Yanks asked for you. You must really have made an impression on them."

"Sir, I accept that but if Colonel Foster had only told me last night I could have brought my gear, said goodbye to my family…"

"Who says that you can't?"

I looked at Toppy. "But the chap from MI6 said we were leaving in the morning."

"You are, from Southend Airport. We have chartered two aircraft from a small company based there." He smiled. "You can stay at your home tonight and I believe you know your way to the airport."

I was stunned. "But how…"

Toppy couldn't help chuckling, "I spoke to your mother yesterday. I didn't say who I was, of course, I just said I needed to charter two Dakotas to fly to Basrah. From there we have a couple of R.A.F. transports waiting to take you to Japan. This way, Tom, we sneak you out of the country. L was correct. There are spies." He shrugged, "The way things are going there may be some here in this building or even in our battalions. I daresay that their spies will have reported a Reservist major coming here but they won't be looking for two old Dakotas flying out of Southend. The troop of Commandos and their lorries are on their way from Bickleigh. They will arrive at dawn. You will have to bring them up to speed when you are airborne."

I sat back in my seat. The General said, "Now let us get you chaps up to speed too!" He smiled, "Officially both the United States and the

United Kingdom are considering their responses. The reality is that we have been preparing for this for some time."

Someone had been working hard. We had folders with maps of the areas in which we would be operating. The Americans had been aware of a problem for six months and they had been gathering information. The folder contained all that we would need to know. The North Koreans were well armed. Their weaponry came from the Soviet Union. They had provided tanks and aeroplanes. I had known axis weaponry. Communist weaponry was new to me and I would have three days of flying to get up to speed on the differing types. They had huge numbers of men and, as far as I could see, the only advantage the allies would have was at sea. That gave me hope for we would be going in by sea. We would not have to run the gauntlet of E-boats as we had in the Channel. The North Korean navy looked to be non-existent. It took all the morning and into the early afternoon before we were done. The sergeant who had taken us in brought us a tray of sandwiches and a pot of tea. We had heard no one else. We were being kept isolated.

"What about the language sir?"

"There will be a liaison officer waiting for you in Pusan. I am afraid the situation is very fluid." The General gave me a wry smile as he filled his pipe. "It is one with which you will be familiar, Major. It sounds like 1940 all over again. The retreating South Koreans are being isolated and picked off piecemeal. This time there will be no Dunkirk. If we lose South Korea then we will have to have another D-Day."

Toppy nodded, "I was talking to Major Ritter at dinner last night and he told me that they are already planning one."

I cocked an eyebrow, "And what about these Soviet spies and moles?"

"They are everywhere. The war made out the Russians to be our friends. We were so desperate to get into bed with them we didn't think to look at their motives. Major Ritter and I go running each morning. I am trying to get half as fit as you were in the war, Tom. We can't be overheard. L was right, Tom, this is a serious problem. Any enclosed public areas are a potential danger zone. That includes pubs, trains, taxis. There are many Communist sympathisers. We don't know the extent of the problem yet. The Americans have a similar problem Stateside. They allowed many refugees in after the war. Without becoming paranoid check for the red under the bed. There are concerns that the atomic bomb secrets may have been leaked to the Soviets."

By one thirty we had finished. "Sir, how long is this posting?"

"How long is a piece of string, Major?" The General shook his head, "I don't know but I will try to get you back as soon as we can, Major. I am aware that you are in the Reserve. You have been chosen because of your record. You are going over to jump-start our efforts. We are trying to utilise the skills you honed in the last war. The team you take are a mixture of men who served in the war and those younger chaps who have joined up since. As much as anything we want you to build a team as good as the one that helped de Gaulle take Paris and stopped the rockets destroying London. When that is done we will get you back." He stood and shook my hand. "Good luck, Major."

He left the room and Toppy began to gather up the papers and remove the maps which festooned the walls. The WRAC sergeant came in to help. Toppy came over to speak with me. "Listen, Tom, I know that you won't be reporting to me but I will have an overview of what you are doing. The moment we think you have done what we want you to do then we will whisk you back home and you will be a civilian again. I know that Susan will be unhappy about this."

"That, Toppy, is an understatement."

He turned to Captain Poulson, "And you, Captain; I know that you see the Commandos as a career. You want promotion and you deserve it. This will be your next step up the ladder." We shook hands. I still found him hard to trust. The man who had picked me out in the retreat to Dunkirk had been changed by war. He was ambitious.

As we descended we said little. It was only when we reached the ground floor that we spoke. "I have my gear to fetch, sir."

"I'll give you a hand and as I am in civvies call me Tom. Remember that chap's words."

"Yes, sir... Tom."

We went to the porter's lodge. The sergeant was a world war two veteran. I saw the respect in his eyes when he saw the Captain's medals. "Kept a weather eye on your gear, sir! Will you want a taxi?"

He looked at me. I nodded. "You can stay with us if you don't mind bunking on a couch."

He shook his head, "I will come on the train with you, Tom, but I think I will stay at the airfield. The chaps may come in early and I need to get to know them."

"Right, sergeant, get us a taxi then and can I use the phone?"

"Of course, sir."

He left us and I rang the airfield. I asked for Dad. I was keenly aware that someone might be listening on the phone. I hoped that Dad would pick up from my voice that this was important. "Dad, I have a chum here and he is taking a flight from the airport tomorrow, early. I said he could wait in the office. That okay?"

"No problem, son. I have to be at the field early tomorrow. We have a couple of flights heading south. I'll have some food left and make sure that Harry knows he is coming." Harry was the night watchman. Dad had put two and two together. "Mum and I thought we would come around to your place for tea today. One of the lads brought back a couple of chickens. Your mum was going to cook them for tea."

"Lovely. See you later." I hoped that the conversation was innocuous enough to allay any suspicions from eavesdroppers. "No problem, Paul."

"Taxi is here, sir!"

The security issue meant that we just chatted about my family as we went first in the taxi and then on the train. That seemed safer than talking about Polly's failed marriage. I was aware that I would miss my children and it would be a wrench for all of us. The Captain would stay on the train once I got off. He would get a taxi from the railway station to the airfield. He would be there before Bert and Norman had finished. I suspect we could have talked for we were alone in our carriage. Rush hour had not yet started and few people were heading to Southend. The train would be full on the way back. It was summer and there were day trippers who would be enjoying the beach and the glorious sunshine.

When the train pulled into the station I shook hands with Polly. "See you soon, eh?"

"Yes Tom, and enjoy your night with your family. I envy you more than you can possibly know."

I was able to walk home. My papers were tucked under my arm. As I headed up the lane to the main road I took in all that lay around me. I would not take for granted that which I might never see again, the fields with ripening crops, the hedgerows with unripe fruit and a promise of an autumn harvest. As the lane rose I turned and saw a few boats on the Crouch. I had had almost five years of taking it for granted but now it was going to be snatched away from me. I was not the same as I had been at the end of the war. I had been single. There were no children. I was a different man. Would I be different when it came to the job? Once again, I would have the responsibility of men looking up to me to make the right decisions so that they, too, could have a future.

Chapter 2

"Daddy's home!"

The three hugs I received as I walked through the door meant a little more to me as I knew they would be the last for some time. When I had gone off to war before I had said just a goodbye to Mum and that was it. I saw Mum with her arm around Susan. Susan's eyes were red.

William pulled away. "Gran says you are going away! Why?"

I picked them all up and took them to the settee. "Well, children, in a country far away some bad men have taken the land from some other men. They want Daddy to go and help them take their country back."

Izzy said, "Like knights and dragons?"

"Sort of!"

William said, "We could come! We could help."

I nodded, "And that would be a good idea except that who would be here to look after Mummy and Gran? Granddad can't do it on his own."

Izzy said, quietly, "It will be like the stories won't it, Daddy? The knight will rescue the princess and come home safe and sound."

I looked up as Susan and Mum fled to the kitchen. "I hope so but sometimes stories don't turn out the way that we hope." I heard a car pulling up on the gravel. That would be Dad. "And here's Granddad. This a treat isn't it? A meal with Gran and Granddad! We are lucky ducks!"

Samuel jumped down and ran to the door as it opened shouting, "Granddad!" Dad was adored by all the children but Samuel especially so. If anything happened to me then I knew that the children would be looked after.

I heard him say, "And here's my little soldier! Come on Sam, show Granddad how well you can march!" With arms swinging Samuel walked in, head held high followed by my Dad also marching. His smile was for me, "Hello son. The Captain was settling in when I left." He shook hands with me. We normally did that when we parted but there was nothing wrong with it now. I felt his fingers squeeze hard around mine. He said quietly, "I will look after them. You know that."

"I know and it makes it easier!

Samuel shouted, "Tomatoes!" A stranger would not have known that was what he said but we did.

Korea

"Come on then and whoever picks the most gets the wishbone!" Dad knew how to make a game of everything.

Dinner should have been a delight. Indeed, with two chickens we knew that we were blessed. Certainly, the children relished the almost exotic meat. Of course, with two wishbones all three children got to pull them. The children were oblivious to the tension around the table. Susan's conversation was terse, to say the least. Mum and Dad did the dishes while Susan and I bathed the children. We all sat in the living room while I read a story. I did not want them to be reminded of knights and dragons and I played safe. I read Winnie the Pooh.

We went to Samuel's room first and William and Isabelle stood while I tucked him in. "Now when you wake in the morning I shall be gone so I will say goodbye now except that soldiers never say goodbye, they say until we meet again. So I will kiss you now, Sam and say 'Until we meet again.'"

I kissed him and I saw him concentrating. He nodded and said, very seriously, trying to get it all right, "Till meet again."

I thought my heart was going to break right there. The other two were easier. I am not certain why. The hug from Izzy almost stopped the circulation in my neck but I didn't care. "Goodnight princess!"

"Goodnight Daddy. The dragons don't stand a chance. They have the white knight coming for them!"

William was the most serious. "Are you going to Korea, Daddy?"

He surprised me, "Yes, how did you guess?"

"It was on the radio at lunchtime and when Mummy heard it she cried and turned off the radio. I will watch over Mummy. Don't worry and when I am old enough I will come with you. Will you be taking your guns?"

The children knew of the locked cabinet and what it contained. They knew that it was forbidden for them to open it. "Yes, and my uniform."

"Night Daddy. I like having a hero for a Daddy."

I closed his door and stood with my eyes closed and my back to the wall. When I had spoken to Dad, what was it two days ago, I had just thought about doing my duty. Now I was conflicted. I was no fool. I had seen too many good men die: Fred Briggs, Alan Crowe, Harry Gowland, Bert Grimsdale, Ralph Betts. There were many more but they had been next to me one minute and then dead the next. Would my rustiness bring about my death? I could not say no now. I could not back out. William liked me as a hero. I could not let my children down but if I made a

Korea

mistake then I could leave them fatherless. Mum, Dad and Susan would have to be a father to them, if that was the case.

The three of them were waiting for me in the sitting room. Dad had poured me a whisky. I suddenly remembered the tobacco and I went to my jacket to remove the tin. I would give Susan the pipe to wrap later. "Here Dad, I nearly forgot."

He smiled, "I didn't think you would have had time."

He handed me the whisky and I said, "Cheers!"

Mum shook her head after she had emptied half of the gin and tonic. "If I had known it was the War Office I would have refused the contract."

"They would have just got someone else. At least this way I know the pilots for the first part of the journey."

Dad asked, more to defuse mother than anything else, "How long will it take you?"

"Could be four or five days. Polly and I will need it to sort out the men. Neither of us knows them."

An awkward silence descended. I desperately needed to get my equipment ready but I could not leave my family. Every moment I could spend with them was precious to me. Dad must have given Mum a look for she said, "The children were sweet tonight."

I nodded, glad of the opportunity to speak of something safe. "They are always cute at bedtime. We are lucky that the three of them get on so well."

"Don't do yourselves down, son, you and Susan have done a first-rate job of raising them. I was halfway around the world when you and Mary were little. Your Mum had to do it on her own." Susan's hand went to her mouth.

Mum shook her head, "Bill Harsker! Think before you open that big mouth of yours. Fill your pipe and shut up!"

"Yes dear!"

"I dare say they will be censoring letters again."

I was pleased to be able to answer her, "And we will be working with the Americans. I am not sure how their system works."

Mum nodded, "Then we need a code. It always helps us, back here, if we have an idea of where you are and what you are up to. All we have is the BBC and the newspapers. The newspapers are just good for wrapping chips and the BBC... well, they are not what they were." I agreed with Mum. I never trusted reporters of any kind. I wondered if this news service, television, would be any better. Perhaps actual footage would help but I remembered British Pathé Newsreels from the war and they had been edited to give a rosy picture.

"How about this then. If I say how is Uncle Lumpy then you know I am in the north of the country. Has Dad been canoeing on the Crouch means the south. If I ask about the seaside then we are operating in boats and if I ask about the Lake District then I am in the mountains."

Susan asked, "And what if you are wounded? Or dead? What then?"

I took her hand in mine, "If I am dead then you will get a telegram and if I am wounded then I will be on my way home!"

"That should do, son. I am not sure this will last as long as the last one."

"Bill!"

"I am just saying! Unless the Chinese or the Soviets get involved then it should be over by the New Year."

Mum rolled her eyes. Dad was well-meaning but he kept putting his foot into his mouth!

They left at ten. After they had gone I just sat and cuddled Susan. She was now resigned to me going. If she had not worked at Headquarters then it would not have been so bad but she knew what Commandos did. She knew of the danger. She had had to type letters of condolence for Toppy to sign. At eleven I said, "I will have to pack. I need to be at the field by six. I will take the car and get Bert or Norman to bring it back for you." We had a Humber Super Snipe Mark Two and it was the best car I had ever had. I wanted one last drive in it.

"I will give you a hand. I know what you are like at packing." I had a soft kit bag and she packed my spare uniform and my Number Ones as well as the other items of clothing I would need. I was busy with my Bergen and my weapons. I took everything out and then repacked it. I had to take all of my ammunition for I was uncertain where I might get more of some of the more obscure cartridges. I still had some of the parachute cord we always salvaged. It did not take up much space and always came in handy. I had the home-made wire cutters which still worked. Just packing it into the Bergen brought back memories. I said, over my shoulder, "Don't forget to pack my winter coats, gloves and plenty of socks."

"But it is summer!"

"And soon it will be winter. I know the way the Army works." I packed my two cap comforters. I was not sure that I would even need my helmet but I packed it anyway. It was two in the morning before we finished. I loaded the Humber. I washed and prepared for bed. "Look I will say goodbye now and then I can just slip out in the morning."

She nodded. We kissed. One kiss led to another. Afterwards, she fell asleep in my arms and I disengaged myself and began to dress. It was three in the morning. There was little point in trying to sleep. I could sleep on the aeroplane. After I was dressed I kissed Susan. She smiled in her sleep. I had the landing light on and I peered in at my three children. I did not disturb them but I took a mental picture of each one. Closing their doors and descending was one of the hardest things I have ever done.

The guard at the field was surprised to see me so early. "Got an early flight Major Harsker?"

"Something like that."

He pointed to the offices and our hangar. "Harry has got the kettle on. I saw him waking the passenger you are taking."

"The rest will be arriving soon. They are soldiers."

"Soldiers? Unusual eh sir?"

I shrugged, "A contract is a contract."

I parked the car in front of the office and then unpacked the car. Leaving my bags in the reception area I went up to Dad's office and put the keys on his desk. I scribbled a note for him. I could hear laughter from the workshop. A whiff of cooking bacon hit me too. I opened the door and saw Harry and Captain Poulson having a fry up and a cup of tea.

"Any for me, Harry?"

He jumped to attention. He was an old soldier, the Guards. "Major Harsker sir! Very smart! Of course, sir. I won't be a jiffy."

Polly said, "You are up early, sir."

"Could say the same about you."

He nodded, "I couldn't sleep. The mission was rattling around inside my head."

I suddenly felt guilty for I had not given it another thought since I had stepped off the train. Captain Poulson was the professional and not me.

"We have, probably, a week to get to grips with what we have to do. This isn't like nipping over to St. Nazaire."

Harry came back and, after shuffling the bacon in the pan around, put another four slices in the pan. I recognised the pan. It was the kind squaddies used in the field. You could cook enough bacon for a whole section in one. This one had the blackened look of a veteran. Harry then poured me a mug of tea. I laughed. Harry looked offended, "What's wrong sir?"

"Nothing Harry. It's just that the last time I had tea like this Sergeant Major Dean was serving it up. You could stand a spoon up in this."

He grinned, "Aye sir, proper tea."

We went through what we would be telling the men. As we sipped the tea I said, "Did you bring your cold weather gear?"

"I did sir. I hope that this lot coming in did as well."

"They are coming in from Bickleigh." He looked puzzled. "Gordy Barker is QM there. He will have made certain that they were well equipped, especially once he heard where they were going."

"It's funny sir but apart from those couple of reunions, I haven't seen many of the lads since the war. I thought a couple were going to stay in and we might have seen them."

"They were all good lads. I hear Hewitt trained as a teacher. He works in the northeast somewhere. Beaumont went back to University and he is now a professor of engineering."

"They keep in touch then?"

"A bit like us, a couple of cards and letters. I am guessing they will dry up. I thought it might bother me but it doesn't now. I have a family and my life to get on with. I am just happy knowing that the lads we led are out there and England is a better place for having them in it. There is all this doom and gloom about but I remember that they did what they did for England and that can't be a bad thing."

The fry up was wonderful. Harry had dipped the bread in the bacon fat so that when we bit into the sandwiches the HP sauce and bacon fat dripped down our chins. I was wearing my oldest uniform. It was the most comfortable. A bit of sauce and fat would soon clean out. I would have to get used to doing my own dhobying. The Commandos, unlike the Guards, did not go in for servants.

Bert and Norman arrived at six with the rest of the ground crew. Having two buses in the air meant all hands on deck. Harry took our plates as they arrived. Their early arrival meant that he had an early one. "Good luck, sirs. I know that this must be hush hush but I shall read the papers and listen to the wireless. I shall follow you with interest."

I knew that Paul would not have said anything but Harry was an old hand. He could work things out. Two of the pilots arrived. Both were ex R.A.F. Jeremy had flown Spitfires and then Typhoons. Bill was a

Lancaster pilot. "We'll have to be on our best behaviour today, we have the boss' son with us!"

"Smooth take off and a landing which does not spill a drop of my martini is what I want!"

They laughed at my jest and went to file their flight plans while their crews did the last of the maintenance checks. I looked at my watch. The lorries were late. I had expected them before the pilots. I had hoped for an opportunity to talk to them altogether.

Dad and the other pilot, Jamie, an ex-Mosquito pilot, arrived together. Jamie had picked Dad up. He grinned when he saw me. "I thought you might need your car taking home. Jamie picked me up. He and I will be flying you, son."

"I wasn't certain you would be flying."

"Why? Because I had a couple of whiskies? In the Great War, we often had a nip before we went up. It used to be bloody cold in an open cockpit!" He looked around. "Passengers not here yet?"

"It is a long drive from Devon."

"There is no rush. We might have a tailwind. The flight from Basrah doesn't leave until six in the morning."

"And the flight to Basrah will be, what? Nineteen, twenty hours?"

"About that."

"Are you sure you are up to this? That is a long time to be flying."

"Do I tell you how to do what you do? No! I will be fine. We intend to have eight hours sleep in Basrah and then fly back. I am taking Norman with us and then he can check the buses out while we are on the ground."

Just then a Bedford lorry screeched to a halt outside and I heard a stentorian voice shout, "Right you shower, offload and I want the Bergens and your kit bags in neat lines! Don't show me up here!"

I nodded to Captain Poulson who went to speak with them. Norman was just heading to Dad to speak to him. He laughed, "That takes me back to the RAF and the regimental sergeant major. Used to scare me witless!"

By the time I went outside the Company Sergeant Major had the men at attention and ready for inspection. Company Sergeant Thorpe was a stocky man but he looked to be all muscle. He had a small moustache which was black and waxed but there were flecks of grey in his hair. He roared, "Attention! Commanding officer on parade."

Korea

I walked next to him and said, quietly, "I think, Sarn't Major, that the War Office wished us to sneak out the country."

He turned and gave me what looked like a slightly sheepish look. It looked incongruous. He said, just as quietly, "Sorry, sir but this is a shower! I don't think you picked them but whoever did obviously didn't meet them. We have a couple of right villains here."

"Why do you say I didn't pick them?"

"I was talking in the pub in Devon with Daddy Grant and Gordy Barker. They told me about you. When I found out you were the Commanding officer I was made up and then I met this lot."

The men were all waiting expectantly. I said, "Captain Poulson, divide the men up, will you? I would like to get us loaded as soon as we can."

"Sir."

The Sergeant Major looked at me quizzically, "Like me, Captain Poulson came up through the ranks. He can smell a bad 'un. This way they might try it on thinking he is young for the rank. They will soon find out that he knows his way around a Bergen. Come to the office. We'll have a cuppa and you can give me the SP on this lot. We do not have the luxury of time. A week from now we will be at the sharp end."

As we went in he looked up at the notice above the door, 'Harsker and Son Commercial Airline'. "This your business then sir?"

"My dad's. I just fly a bit for him. Not today though."

"Is he the one who was an ace in the Great War?"

"He is and he will be piloting us." Norman had made a fresh pot of tea and I poured a mug for the Sergeant Major. He looked surprised. "Now then give me the highlights."

"The NCO's and the specialists are good lads. There will be no bother from them. I reckon that the younger lads, with just a couple of exceptions, have potential. They are just green as grass. The bad 'uns are Blair and Marsh. Blair was in the last one and he has a chip on his shoulder the size of Portland Bill. He reckons he should be an NCO but he doesn't want to do the work."

"Why did he stay in?"

"No idea, sir. I met him two days ago. He was at Bickleigh but not in my unit. His sergeant filled me in on him. Proper little barrack room lawyer. A nasty piece of work and there is something about him I don't like. Can't put my finger on it."

I had met the type. "And Marsh?"

"Marsh joined after the war but he and Blair are oppos. Thick as thieves and the trouble is sir, they aren't thick. They have impressed two of the young lads, Evans and Carter. Evans is a Welsh lad. A rugby player and well-built but a bit of a thug if you get my meaning. Carter, I can't fathom. He is a proper loner and has latched on to Blair. Anyway, the four of them were awkward all the way here. I had them all in my lorry and they moaned the whole way."

"Right, Sarn't Major. We have Blair and Marsh on our aeroplane. I will have a word with Captain Poulson and see if we can't repair the damage of our bad apples."

"Sir they are in the same section as Blair and Marsh."

I smiled, "Sergeant Major, let us get one thing clear. This is my section. There is no one above me and I will decide on our formation and organization. I am happy to carry the can for any complaints but you and I, along with Captain Poulson will be running this team and we will do it our way. Unless these two characters impress me then they will be brought back from Basrah by my father."

I saw him brighten. "You'll do for me, sir, I had better go and help the Captain with the loading."

"What did the lads bring with them?"

"They all have two hundred rounds for each of their weapons. They have six Mills Bombs each and they have two week's field rations. Every one of them has their own basic medical kit and they have had their vaccinations."

"Good. I will let you get on with it then."

Dad had been leaning at the office door and listening. He smiled, "Nothing changes does it, son? We had characters like that in the Great War."

"If Blair and Marsh are the worst of my troubles then I will be a happy man. I will get the buses loaded."

It was going to be a fine day. The sun was already shining. I saw Blair straight away. He was a big man and he was arguing with Captain Poulson and Sergeant Major Thorpe. "Sir, this is not right. The Sarn't Major has had it in for me and my oppo all the way from Devon. He has no right to split up our section. Me and the lads get on. We are a team. That is what the Commandos are all about! Teamwork!"

I used my sergeant's voice. I had not used it for years. "Private Blair! On the double!" He turned to look at me and hesitated. "Private Blair are

Korea

you deaf? Or do you need my boot up your arse?" I saw Captain Poulson hide a smile.

The Private ran over to me. "Sir!"

"Come with me!" I strode quickly to the reception. I pointed to my Bergen and my kit bag. "Pick them up and take them to the aircraft!"

He looked at them and said, making no attempt to pick them up, "Sir, they are too heavy. I'll get Private Marsh to give me a hand."

I went close to him. "Are you a Commando?"

"Yes, sir. Six years now! I was at D-Day."

"I tapped the crown on my shoulder, "Then you recognise this insignia?"

He looked confused, "Yes sir!"

"Then you understand that when I give an order I expect it to be obeyed. I do not run a debating club. Now I carried both of these items from my car to here. You will pick both of them up and carry them." I went even closer. "You know the punishment for disobeying orders in time of war?"

"Sir we aren't at war!"

"Then when you are in the glasshouse you will be able to conduct a fine defence but either way I will not have to deal with a Bolshie little bastard like you so don't mention teamwork again to me because you have not the first concept of what it means but by the time I have finished with you then it will be abundantly clear."

I saw his mouth open as he thought to argue with me again. He would say I couldn't talk to him like that. Then he looked into my eyes and he picked the bags up. I did not open the door for him. He had to manhandle them through the door and it wasn't easy. Captain Poulson had loaded both aircraft. I saw Dad and Norman at the ladder of the leading Dakota. The other was already buttoned up. "There, the aircraft with the door open. You and I have a twenty-hour flight to get to know one another."

Norman said, "Here, I'll show you where to stow the Major's gear!"

Dad said, "I have a few large flasks of boiling water. Your lads can make tea. There are a dozen loaves and a few tins of bully beef. Norman's wife sent some home-made chutney." He grinned, "It will all go on the War Office bill!"

We had no seats inside the Dakota but there was a bench which ran along the two sides. This aircraft had been used at D-Day to drop the 101st Screaming Eagles. We had left them in because they were useful for lashing cargo to them. The latrine was a bucket. It could be emptied in flight. We had never had to do so before but I had a feeling that we would this time. The kit bags were behind a cargo net. There would just be a safety light once we took off plus small windows in the side and the ambient light when the cockpit door was open. I saw that Sergeant Major Thorpe had left a space for me in the middle of one side. Blair and Marsh were opposite. That had not been accidental. I put my leather satchel with the documents and maps beneath my seat. We had left in the seat belts from the days when it had dropped paratroopers and I fastened mine. I smiled as I saw the ones who had not already done so fasten them. I heard my father begin to rev the engines. He would be in command for the take-off. There would be little point in trying to talk until he was at cruising altitude. That would be at ten thousand feet.

I put my hands behind my head and closed my eyes. I preferred being in the pilot's seat when I flew. Dad knew that and was the reason he had the stick. I found myself nodding off. That was no surprise. I had had no sleep. Just before I nodded off I found myself smiling. I was back in the war. Then I had learned the ability to fall asleep and then wake instantly. I was becoming a warrior once more.

When I woke I noticed the pitch of the engines. Dad had cut the engines to their cruising speed. This would conserve fuel and save the engines excessive wear and tear. More importantly, I could talk. We would be flying level now. If there was turbulence ahead then Norman would open the door and tell us. We were flying towards the sunset and we would have a shorter day in terms of light. Ironically flying into the sunset also meant the flight would seem longer. Heading west always felt like you had built a time machine. I took off my seat belt and stood.

"Can you all hear me?"

All but Marsh and Blair nodded or raised their hands. As they were in front of me I knew that they were just being awkward.

"I am Major Harsker. I served with Number 4 Commando throughout the war. I am not a regular. I left in forty-five but I have been called back for this war." I stared at Blair defying him to argue with me. "We do not have long to get to know each other. These next four days in the air are it! Make the most of it. If I am not asleep then feel free to talk to me. I may relieve the pilots for a stint for I can fly but that apart I am here to get to know you. There will be no time when we get to Korea." I looked at them. "Questions?" There were none and I continued. "There are thirty of us in total and we will be operating under the Americans. They have asked for British Commandos and I take it as a compliment that they have done so. Our job is to do what we did for most of the last war. We will raid their coast. We will cause as much disruption as we can. There may be times when the whole troop attacks the same target. At others, we will operate in smaller groups. I trust all of my NCO's. I came up through the ranks. I was a sergeant once. No one has more respect for NCO's than I do."

I turned so that the ones behind me could see me.

"The difference between the last war and this one is that we will be fighting in a land where we do not speak the language and against a people who do not believe in the Geneva Convention. These are Communist fanatics. For those who fought in the last war, I would equate them with the S.S." I bent down and picked up my satchel. "I have the latest intelligence here and I am speaking with that in mind. This is not rumour, gossip or the ramblings of a journalist. If we are captured then it will go hard. You men who fought the Germans know of the Hitler order. This will be worse than that!"

Blair could not contain himself, "You aren't selling it very well, are you... sir?"

I smiled, "No Private Blair, and that is because I am not selling it. I am telling you the facts and, as you will learn, that is my way. You all took this mission because it meant more pay and, perhaps, promotion. If you get them then you will earn both!" Colonel Foster had given me some sheets with Korean phrases as well as sketch maps of the areas in which we would be operating. "Corporal Callow, would you give these out?"

"Sir!"

"Over the next few days learn these phrases and study the maps. They may save your life. That is all."

Private Marsh said, "What about a toilet sir? Food? Drink?"

I pointed to the curtain near to the cargo net. "There is your toilet. When it is full we empty it. I will show you how. As for drink? There are vacuum flasks with boiling water. There is tea, dried milk and sugar. Sergeant Major Thorpe will assign men to make some corned dog sandwiches at lunchtime. Apart from that, it depends on what you have with you."

"And what about smoking sir?"

"I am a pipe smoker, Private Blair, but I will forego that habit. You are flying in a huge petrol tank. It may be that a cigarette will not ignite the fumes but do you want to take that chance?" I needed to say no more.

Korea

No one smoked. I gave them ten minutes to come up with any questions. Some took out books and comics to read. Others looked out of the portholes. I went into the cockpit. There was a spare seat. It was there for a radio operator or navigator. Dad took off his headphones, "Everyone fine, son?"

"Yes, I think that some have never flown. They don't automatically give them airborne training these days. I am going to get my head down if you don't mind."

"Sleep away!"

I fastened myself into the seat. It was padded and more comfortable than the bench. I slept for four hours which was longer than I wanted to. When I woke I saw that Dad was also asleep and Jamie was the pilot. I waved to him and headed back into the main cabin. The majority of the men were asleep. I sat next to the Sergeant Major.

"You have a kip then, sir?"

"I learned that early on in the war. Sleep and eat while you can. You never know what is around the corner. Have you much experience in boats, Sergeant Major?"

He shook his head, "I joined just before D-Day." He pointed to Blair. He and Marsh had fallen asleep and their heads had fallen together, "Billy Bullshitter there wasn't at D-Day. I checked his record. He was at Southampton with the rest of the reinforcements. We landed at D-Day plus four. I wasn't with him but I was there with the rest of the lads. I was a lance corporal then."

"I did a lot in small boats: Dieppe, St. Nazaire, Walcheren. The Navy lads are good." He nodded. "The reason I mention it is that we have three boats. We may not need to use them all at once but if we do then you will have to take charge of one."

"Just so long as I don't have to sail one I will be fine, sir."

"Good. Then you can make your team unique to you and your boat. That will build esprit de corps."

"And with likely lads like these two, we will need that."

When we landed at Basrah it was like an oven. Dad had served there just after the Great War and again during the last one. He knew both the airfield and the approach. More importantly, he still had contacts and as soon as we had landed we were directed into the shade and shelter of a hangar. The air, as we clambered out, still burned the back of our throats but at least the sun was not beating down on us.

I went over to Captain Poulson, "Good flight?"

Korea

He nodded, "Informative and interesting. Did you know our friend Blair is a fully paid-up member of the Communist party?"

I didn't. A man's beliefs were his own and I would not judge a man for that but in the present climate that was a worrying thought. "How did you discover that?"

"Evans, the Welshman; he became a chatty little fellow when we got into the air. Doesn't like flying. Couldn't shut him up. Blair discovered that Evans was a keen Labour man. Does not like the fact that until they were nationalised the mine owners exploited the miners. He wants everything nationalised. He was easy for Blair to manipulate."

"And Carter?"

"He is a loner. An orphan from the war he joined because his dad had been in the Commandos. Died in Walcheren. He wanted to be like his dad but he has problems making friends. He will be alright."

"Then we have to watch Blair."

"We should leave him here, sir. He might be a liability."

"And have him infect another group of soldiers? No, we can watch him. His kind always makes a mistake and besides we have too few men as it is."

Dad came over and pointed to a couple of lorries which were approaching. Captain Poulson said, "I will get the lads sorted. It will give you and your dad time to say your goodbyes."

"Thanks."

Dad held out his hand, "Well son, good luck. Your mum and Susan aren't here so I can say keep your head down. You have done enough heroics already."

I laughed, "Hark who's talking. As I recall the last time you were here you almost won a second V.C."

He shook his head but he was smiling, "Don't do as I do, do as I say. You will have seats from now on and John Marshall is a good pilot."

"You know him?"

"I served with him here before the war. I spoke to him on the radio as we were approaching."

I took out my notepad and scribbled a note. "Dad, do me a favour when you get back give Toppy a ring. Tell him you have some information about someone in my section. His name is here. Toppy won't want to talk on the telephone." I lowered my voice. "This chap is a paid-up member of the Communist party. Well, that is the information I have. Toppy can check it out."

"I will take him back with me! You…"

"No, Dad, that might be putting you in danger and this way I can watch him. He can't do much for the next few days. We have another twenty-four hours in the air, don't we?"

He nodded and took the note.

Captain Poulson shouted, "Sir, the transport is waiting."

"You had better go, son." As he grasped my hand he said, "Now I think I understand what Mum went through every time I went off to war. I think I will take both of them a bunch of flowers."

I forced myself to turn and run to the lorry. I knew then that one way or another this would be the last time that I donned my uniform to go to war.

Chapter 3

The Handley Page Hastings was a four-engine transport. It had been introduced just two years earlier and was state of the art as far as military transports went. I had seen some operating when we had been on the Berlin Airlift run. We had been at Berlin-Tegel Airport last July when one had lost control during take-off and crashed. I would not mention that to the others. They had the aircraft on a quiet part of the airfield. I saw one of the crew in the cockpit while one of the pilots and the flight engineer looked up at the number four engine. There were two Ercs there ready to load the bags. As I knew correct loading was vital.

I jumped out and said, "Sarn't Major, have the lads form a human chain and give these Ercs a hand."

"Yes sir, come on my lovely lads!"

"Sarn't Major I am busting for a pee!" Private Hope looked in agony.

The Flight Engineer turned and pointed to a hut which stood nearby, "Over there, Sergeant Major." He grinned, "Like everything out here it is full of flies."

"Thanks, Flight Sergeant. Right lads, baggage first and then you get to pee!"

The officer, a grey-haired squadron leader held his hand out, "Squadron Leader John Marshall, you must be Major Harsker." We stood under the shade of the wing but I could still feel the sweat seeping down my armpits.

We were the same equivalent rank and had no need to 'sir' each other. "Tom. You knew Dad."

"He saved my life and my arm out there in the desert. This is the first time I have been back since then. Strange eh?" I nodded. "I see he has his own company?"

"We set it up together."

"Then how come I get diverted to take you to Japan?"

"Diverted?"

"I was on my way home having taken troops to Aden. We were sent here to pick you and your chaps up. Korea?"

I nodded. "I can't say any more."

"No need to. You are commandos and you have the V.C." He shook his head, "They did the same to your Dad after the Great War. Well, we shall get you there in one piece. We fly to Bombay first. The flight time should be ten hours or so. We have eight hours on the ground. I believe they have some cots and food ready for you. Then we fly to Formosa."

"China?"

"General Chiang Kai-shek and his Nationalists are keen to do all they can against the Communists but we will not stay long. That will be a two-hour stay. Enough time to refuel and for your lads to walk around the aircraft. Then a short three-hour flight to a small airfield in the south of Japan. That will be the hairiest part. I have never landed there. I believe that the Americans will take over from there on."

I laughed, "By then we will have no idea what day of the week it is. If I don't get another chance thanks for this."

He looked surprised, "Just doing my job, old chap."

I pointed to Dad's aeroplane, "I think you will be going out of your way to make this as smooth a flight as possible."

"Ah well, you could be right. It is not just the old boy's network. When you have served with a man he becomes closer than your family. Anyway, you best get aboard. The bags are loaded. There is a galley and hot water. I know you lads will do it but just a heads up, we have no cleaners on board. Your lads make a mess then they clean it. There are sandwiches. They should be good for a few hours and there will be a hot meal at Bombay. There is a toilet on board. When we get to Bombay if you could have a couple of your chaps help to empty it and again at Taipei."

"Will do."

I clambered up the steps. The inside was cooler than the outside but not by much. There were fifty seats and I saw that the men had spread themselves out. I spotted that Captain Poulson had sat next to Private Carter while Sergeant Major Thorpe had seated the section medic, Lance Corporal Pike, next to Evans. I had spoken with the Lance Corporal on the flight from England. He was a veteran from the war and he had been at D-Day. He was married and acted much older than his thirty years. He was a northern lad and I had learned he was keen on Rugby League. Ken must have realised that and put the two together. Blair and Marsh were at the back. No one was within four seats of them and they reminded me of the naughty boys in school!

I sat opposite the Captain. The Sergeant Major was walking down the aisle ensuring that everyone was accounted for. I gestured for him to sit on the seat in front. "When we get to our cruising altitude we might as well have a chat about the mission."

"Sir!"

The aeroplane smelled new. That was a good thing. I just hoped that they had ironed all of the kinks from her. Once we reached cruising speed and the engine noise diminished I took out the papers I needed. I was acutely aware that Private Carter could hear everything that we said. It was deliberate. He was a loner. When we stopped in Bombay he would be assaulted by others asking for word of what we had said. There would be no secrets. This would help him to fit in and let all of the lads know that Captain Poulson and I knew our business. I intended to keep Blair and Marsh away from the rest.

"So we need to divide the men into three teams. The two sergeants will be with the Captain and me. I will have Curtis and the Captain, Grant." They both wrote the names down on their notepads.

Polly said, "He is Daddy Grant's nephew."

"Small world eh? Sergeant Major, who do you want as your number two? You know them better than we do."

"Bob Lowery and I have served together. We get on. If you don't mind, sir."

"I want teams that can work together. Mates always work better. I will have the charm twins, Blair and Marsh." I saw the look Carter gave me. It was one of surprise.

"I don't mind having them, sir. I'll knock them into shape."

"We haven't got the luxury of time. I am in command and they will be my responsibility. Now the medic will be with me as will the radio operator."

"Lance Corporal Williams. He is a good lad too, sir."

"That leaves Swift with you, Captain, and Callow with me. Captain, you take the mortar crew and Sergeant Major the Bren gun. Do we have any anti-tank guns?"

"No, sir."

"Then Captain, when we land see if you can get a couple from the Americans."

"Now it's just the others to sort out. Do you know who is mates with who?"

Ken said, "Some. How about you Private Carter? Do you know who are oppos?"

"Some Sarge but…"

Captain Poulson said, "Excellent then you can be in my section. Your knowledge will be useful. We will start with your list and then let Sergeant Major Thorpe fill in the blanks."

It was as easy as that. The more Carter spoke the more his confidence grew. I saw Ken Thorpe smile. He leaned in and said, "The Captain is good isn't he, sir?"

"He is one of the best and I can see that we might have a good team here but time will tell. You take Evans."

"Yes, sir."

In the end, I had ten men, the Captain had nine and the Sergeant Major had eight. The Sergeant Major thought we should have even numbers. I shook my head. "I have the radio and the medic. I have fewer fighting men than the pair of you. This will be fine. Mine will be squad one, the Captain's squad two and yours, squad three."

We spent an hour or so going over the standard operating procedure and then the Sergeant Major went to tell the men the good or, in the case of Blair and Marsh, the bad news. Sergeant Major Thorpe sat next to Lowery and I was able to get my head down and sleep.

That was the pattern for the next two or was it three days? I had changed my watch so often that I had lost track of time zones. We ate when we were hungry but as we only had sandwiches and tea it didn't really matter. The exception was Bombay where we were served a curry. I liked curry but, inevitably, Blair and Marsh complained. They had to make do with rice, naan, and chapattis. No one had any sympathy for them. As I had hoped my ploy to have Carter next to us paid dividends. The younger hands flocked to him to get what they saw as privileged information. As the two naughty boys were emptying the chemical toilet he was not harassed. I saw Pike and Evans chattering away, as they ate with another northerner, Bernie Collins, who played the same code of rugby as Evans. I had a short time to mould a team and I was using every means at my disposal. I spent every waking hour going over every piece of paper I had been given. It was like cramming for an exam. The difference here was that failure could result in someone dying.

On the flight from Bombay, I got to see a sunrise from the cockpit. It was spectacular. Knowing I could fly I was given the co-pilot's seat and the cans while the co-pilot rested. I had little to do other than mirror the pilot. I chatted to John Marshall.

"Where to after you drop us off then?"

Korea

"We had a message waiting for us in Bombay. It seems we are going to be used to ferry troops around. I am not sure if there will be much of Korea left by the time we get there. It seems we are holding on to the Pusan peninsula and little else. You are getting here the quick way. The Argyll and Sutherland Highlanders and the Middlesex Regiment are on their way to Korea. They won't be there until the end of August. I fear it will be the Yanks and the South Koreans who have to bear the brunt of the fighting."

I smiled, "Makes a change. Normally it is us waiting for them to arrive."

"Well, they are mobilising fast this time. They are worried about the Communists and I don't blame them. The Berlin Airlift should have been a warning."

It was almost as though he was echoing the thoughts of my dad and me. Did people not realise the threat? There was a red block of countries and they were now within bombing distance of England. Thanks to the Labour Government's cuts, what had once been an Air Force and Navy of which we could be proud we were now scrabbling around to call up reservists like me!

Once the co-pilot had had an hour or so of rest I returned to my seat. There were impromptu card games while those with foresight read comics, books and magazines. The exceptions were Blair and Marsh who sat at the back of the aircraft. I would not be able to rely on them in a firefight. Luckily having so many men under my command meant that I could use them to fetch ammo and take away wounded. As I sat down again I took out my notebook. I had veterans who had fought in the war. There were thirteen of us and six were in my section. As one of those was Blair it was an unduly heavy weighting. Until the others had been given an opportunity to learn I would rely on the twelve of us who had real experience. We had all faced death. At least six of us had been wounded and the majority of us had killed. I suspected I had killed more often. I had made it clear to them that capture would probably mean death but to those who had not fought in the war that would mean little. It was probably still a game to them.

I looked again at my orders. All of our equipment, save for the weaponry we had brought with us, would be provided by the Americans. They had good gear. Corporal Callow and Private Green were our explosive experts. Callow was married and had three children. He had the dourest face I had ever seen. He rarely smiled. Perhaps that was his trade. Messing around with explosives was not something most soldiers chose to do. Len Green was young and keen. He had had a place at University but his parents couldn't afford for him to go. He had plans to go there when he had saved up enough money. I admired him for that. I felt a little guilty. I had had a place and my parents could afford for me to attend but I had chosen the army. Len had been forced to choose the army. After another short sleep, I woke and went to the galley to make some tea. Blair and Marsh were asleep. Godfrey Pike, the medic, was there. "Thanks for chatting to Evans." I gestured behind me with my thumb, "I think we can keep him on the straight and narrow."

"He's a good lad. Just a bit daft, sir. We all go through a phase like that."

"You know you will be on your own once we are in Korea?"

"Yes, sir."

"Well see if you can find a couple of volunteers amongst the young lads. It would be better if they were in the other two sections. I can get more medical kits from the Americans but just give them some basic techniques. You were in the last one. You know the drill."

"Aye sir, how to stop bleeding. If we had a doctor we could save more. I would tell them about the last resort."

"That would be wise." The last resort was an overdose of painkillers. Commandos were often far from help. A wound which needed a hospital could not be treated. Medics, after speaking to the C.O. would become God. I had not had to give such approval but I knew that if I had to then I would. By the time I had finished speaking with him, I felt as confident of him as I had been about John Hewitt.

Formosa, although a republic, was the avowed enemy of Mao Tse-tung and the Communist Chinese he led. When we landed there to refuel we were applauded like heroes. Blair did not de-plane. That was significant.

The last flight was a relatively short hop. When we had been in Taipei I had taken the opportunity to shower and change into a cleaner uniform. I had no doubt that I would have to meet Americans when I landed and I wanted to make a good impression. As we came into the small, former military airfield in the south of the country I saw that the land was very rural. Ōmura airfield had been used in the war. We were close to the site of one of the atomic bombs, Nagasaki. It was late afternoon when we arrived. I saw the sunlight reflecting off the sea. That would be our next mode of transport.

Korea

I had to ask the Flight Sergeant for the date. He grinned, "Second of July sir. Bit of a bugger flying east. It is easier going west. It just takes a day to get home but you are still in the air for more than thirty hours. Funny eh? Like having a time machine!"

As the Squadron Leader taxied I saw two large American trucks and a jeep waiting for us. We were expected! The Japanese ground crew were a model of efficiency. The trucks and the jeep drove as close as they could get to the parked Hasting. Sailors jumped from the cabs and the driver of the jeep climbed out. He had a cigar clenched between his teeth. He was a barrel of a man! I was the first one down the steps and he snapped to attention and growled, "Petty Officer First Class Flynn, sir. You would be Major Harsker?"

I learned that the growl was his normal voice. "Yes, Petty Officer. I take it we have not yet completed our journey."

His face broke into a grin, "I can see this is going to be a real pleasure, sir. I sure love the English accent. You sound like Errol Flynn! He is a hero of mine." I didn't like to point out that Errol Flynn came from Tasmania and was, therefore, an Australian! "Yes, sir. We are going to a little bay a few miles north of here. It is nice and secluded. We won't be there until dark."

"And our boats?"

"Arrived this morning. Major Hampton is over at Pusan but he will meet us tomorrow at your new base." He lowered his voice, "If the Koreans haven't driven us back into the sea before then."

"As bad as that?"

"Worse sir. At least we can get out on your PT boats!"

I turned, "Sarn't Major, have the trucks loaded."

"Trucks sir?"

I sighed, "Lorries!"

"Righto, sir."

"I will take my Bergen and weapons with me."

"Yes, sir. Bob fetch the Major's war gear!"

The Petty Officer said, "And you have to wear these, sir." He handed us blue armbands with UN on them. They legitimized us. I took one and gave the others to Captain Poulson. I slid mine up my arm. We were now fighting for the world!

I waited until the trucks were loaded before I dumped my guns and Bergen in the back and sat next to the Petty Officer. Polly clambered in the back and held on to his Bergen too. "Whenever you are ready, Petty Officer!"

In answer, he jammed it into first and spun us around.

Polly laughed, "Reminds me of Normandy sir. Remember Emerson? He loved his jeeps!"

"He loved anything with four wheels!"

Petty Officer First Class Flynn rarely removed his cigar from his mouth. "You officers serve in the last one then?"

"Yes, Petty Officer Flynn. I was at Dunkirk and was there when the Germans surrendered. And you?"

"I was over here. I was in the Navy before the war. I was in the PT boats. Remember the movie, 'They Were Expendable'?"

"John Wayne and Ward Bond, right?"

He seemed impressed, "Yes sir, well that was my unit. The director filmed us. I spent a year in the Philippines with the guerrillas and when I was repatriated I went back to little boats."

"Most of my war was spent going ashore in small boats."

"I think you will find it a little different here, sir."

"How so?"

"The language and as I found out in forty-two some of the locals are two-faced little sons of... let us just say sir that some of them change sides more often than my grandmother changes her sheets."

I had not thought about it but it made sense. The North and South Koreans would look identical. They might understand and recognise different dialects but I would not. I asked, "What about the uniforms? How do they differ?"

"The South Korean Army has American style helmets. The North Koreans like caps. If they have helmets then they will be Russian style. They have Russian weapons too. Sometimes they have Thompsons with the drum magazine. The South Koreans use our weapons."

I gestured to the back seat, "I still have the Thompson I was issued in nineteen forty."

"You look after your own weapons then, sir?"

"A soldier who doesn't do so will not last long in our line of work."

"Good sir. That is what I like to hear. Too many officers delegate that kind of stuff. I have no time for them."

"You are outspoken Petty Officer. I don't mind but I am guessing that there are some officers who would not approve."

He laughed, "Maybe that is why I was sent as your liaison, sir. I tell it the way it is, sir. To be honest this is my last tour. My enlistment is up in January. I think that this way my old boss figures that I might keep my pension. I have been busted back to seaman a couple of times."

"Don't worry about me, Petty Officer. I came up through the ranks. If I think you have overstepped the mark then you will know it."

"That is good to know sir. I think we will get along." He nodded, "If you don't mind, sir, I will concentrate on this next section. It can be a little tricky."

There were no lights on the road and the jeep's feeble bulbs barely lit a few yards in front of the jeep. The road twisted and turned. I found myself gripping the windscreen and seat to keep me stable. After thirty minutes of the roller coaster ride, I saw lights ahead.

"Nearly there, sir. We will be pushing off pretty much as soon as we get there. Major Hampton was keen that you get under cover while it is still dark. The crossing to Dongbaek-Ri will take about four and a half hours."

"Dongbaek-Ri?"

"Yes, sir, our own little home from home. It is a sleepy little fishing village or at least it was until the North Koreans took most of their country. Now it is crammed full of refugees. Best keep a good deck watch, sir. They don't have much and they will steal anything they can get their hands on!"

The road continued to twist down through the dark. I saw buildings take shape. They looked like fragile little shacks. Faces peered out as we passed and then disappeared. The petty officer laughed, "Scared witless of us! It is like driving through West Virginia. Most of these folks have never left their own village."

I nodded, "We have a couple of places like that in England: little places at the ends of roads."

I saw the sea for there were lights running from a generator and I saw the three vessels. One was the larger Fairmile. I had been told a Motor Launch but now I saw we had a larger vessel. The Fairmile was perfect for it packed twice the firepower of the MTB. It had two quick-firing six pounders, four Oerlikons and a few Brownings. It even had depth charges. It lacked torpedo tubes but we would not be needing those in any case. I saw seamen scurrying over them as they prepared for sea.

Petty Officer Flynn spun the jeep around as we neared the edge of the wharf. It was a spectacular piece of driving. "Here we are, sir. I will let you introduce yourselves to the Navy and I will go and give your Sergeant Major a hand!"

As we grabbed our gear Polly said, "Quite a character."

"He is. I think colourful was the word you were seeking!"

An officer wearing a pair of overalls strode down to meet us. He had a pipe in his mouth. It made me realise that I had not had a pipeful for four or five days! He held out a hand, "Lieutenant John Drake, Royal Navy. Commander of MGB 523! Thanks to you chaps she has a reprieve!"

I shook his hand, "Major Tom Harsker formerly of Number 4 Commando and Captain Paul Poulson. Reprieve?"

"Yes, sir, we were taking the three of them to Papua New Guinea. They were going to become part of the New Guinea Navy; probably a large part of it I should imagine. We were to hand them over and then head home. A shame really. I like the old girl. We have been together since forty-five." He looked at me and saw my shoulder flashes. "When I saw your name I thought I recognised it. Were you the chaps who used to pop across the channel in Lucky Lady with Alan Jorgensen?"

"We were."

"He was a good chap. Or so the old skipper told me. The old man used to go on about you and Jorgensen when we met up in Harwich. Shame about him and his crew."

I nodded. "He was a good chap. The American Petty Officer says we have to get a move on."

"Afraid so. We are the old lady here and we can't manage much above twenty-nine knots. Cloak and dagger stuff eh?"

I nodded, "Captain Poulson if you take that boat there, 527 and ask Sergeant Major Thorpe to take 256."

"Righto, sir."

Once they knew their boats the men worked quickly. They had had enough of aeroplanes. Here they could lie down. It might be on a wooden deck but it would be almost like a bed. I felt weary beyond words. There was no way we could go into action any day soon. In my view, it would take four or five days. How long would the North Koreans give us?

When the last man was aboard Petty Officer First Class Flynn hopped aboard. The Chief Boatswain shouted, "Get that cigar out Mr Flynn! This is a Royal Navy vessel we are not some Mickey Mouse navy!"

The American glared at the boatswain and then tossed the stub over the side. Lieutenant Drake laughed, "Chief Petty Officer Jennings is old school. He should have been retired a couple of years ago but the Royal Navy is his life. They only met this morning and yet the two do not get on. Ironically, they both have the same high standards!" I turned to go below decks. "Stay on the bridge if you like, sir. With your baggage, equipment and men it will be a little crowded below decks."

"Thanks, I would like that."

He spun the wheel, "All ahead, half!"

The helmsman repeated, "All ahead half. Aye, sir."

We edged from the wharf. There was nothing before us save the entrance to the harbour but Lieutenant Drake took it steadily. He kept glancing astern to make certain his consorts were on station. Once we had cleared the harbour then I felt the motion. A couple of my men had obviously not experienced small boats and Campbell and Green came hurtling up to hurl the contents of their stomachs over the side. The matelots gave them no sympathy and laughed at their discomfort.

When the other boats were clear the captain said, "All ahead full!" He turned and gave an apologetic smile, "Not exactly the rush of power the other boats could manage but she is an old girl and has done her bit and more. Still, if we can let her serve her country one more time then it won't be a bad thing."

"What is our new billet like?"

"Not a clue old chap. We arrived this morning and have spent the whole day preparing for you chaps. We lost the radio on the voyage from India and didn't know how many men we would have until we reached here." He smiled, "Got to hand it to the Americans. They get things done. We had the radios fixed within the hour. Marvellous." He turned to the midshipman who had been hovering nearby. "Right Middy, over to you. You have the course?"

"Yes, sir!"

"Then don't get us lost. I have heard of angry Commandos who eat Midshipmen for breakfast." The Midshipman looked as though he might believe the joke. "The Major and I will be on the other wing. Have Wilkinson bring us a couple of mugs of cocoa eh, stoker's cocoa!"

"Aye, Aye sir."

We went to the lee side of the bridge. That was Captain's privilege. "So Major, what exactly will we be doing?"

"From what I have been told pretty much the same as we did in France and the Low Countries in forty-three and forty-four. Annoy the hell out of the enemy. Hit behind their lines. Damage shipping and facilities. Stop them feeling comfortable. You will drop us off. We head inland. We do a bit of damage and then you take us home."

He laughed, "You make it sound so simple."

"Believe me it is anything but. There is so much which could go wrong. Standing orders from me are that if we do not make a rendezvous then you go. We are quite good at improvising. It isn't as though we have to swim back to Japan. So long as we are in Korea then we can always get home."

"These Commies are a little brutal you know."

"We had the Hitler order in France. If we had been caught then the S.S. would have had us and then we would have been shot. If you are a Commando then you accept that."

"A little rough though, sir."

"As you say a little rough. I was caught by the S.S. once." His mouth opened and then closed. "Oh, don't worry me and my sergeant escaped. It is remarkable what the thought of impending death can do to your thought processes."

"You are a reservist though aren't you, sir?"

I nodded, "England is still my country and if she needs me then…"

The cocoa arrived. It was laced with rum. I put it on the fiddle which ran around the bridge. "Would it upset the Chief Petty Officer if I had a smoke? It will be my first in a few days."

He laughed, "Go ahead and I will join you."

I took out my pipe and cleaned it with my penknife. I sucked and then blew to make sure it was clear. I took out my pouch and cut a few slivers of the whisky infused tobacco. The Lieutenant sniffed and then laughed, "That is an old mess deck trick."

I nodded, "Bill Leslie showed me that." I saw the Lieutenant looking curiously at the bar of tobacco. I handed him the pouch and my penknife. "Help yourself. I have plenty."

"Thanks, I will try it." He sniffed. "Whisky?"

"Bells. Just not worth a malt."

"Of course."

I rubbed the tobacco until it was shredded and then carefully packed it. Ducking below the bridge I struck a match and warmed the tobacco. This would take three matches. The tobacco was moist. I drew on the pipe. The match and the pipe went out. I struck a second. This one drew for a few puffs and then it sighed and died. The third one had it drawing well. I tamped down the tobacco with my finger and finally got to enjoy the pipe. Those few days without one made me appreciate it even more. After a couple of puffs, I drank some of the cocoa. It tasted even better. The Lieutenant handed me the knife and the pouch. He soon had his going. There is something about smoking a pipe which negates the need for chatter. More often than not idle words just fill the silence. We smoked. We drank and we watched the sea. I felt I knew the thoughts of the Lieutenant. He glanced over to the midshipman and the helmsman from time to time. He looked at the sky and he looked at the horizon. All was well and where was the need for words?

The pipes lasted almost forty-five minutes. The breeze from the sea fed them else we might have had a full hour. The Lieutenant tapped his out over the side. "I shall try that. Damned enjoyable what? Can never understand these chaps with cigarettes. They are a habit. A pipe is a hobby!"

After another hour he said, "Righto Middy, get the charts and then see if you can contact our American friends. Find out if Petty Officer Flynn can be of assistance eh?"

"Yes, sir."

When he had gone he said to the helmsman, "Are we still on course, Killick?"

The Leading Seaman grinned, "Aye sir. Mr Brown is alright. A little green but willing."

"I'll go below deck and see how the chaps are."

"With the exception of Campbell and Green, the rest of my men were all asleep. There is something about the motion of a boat which induces sleep. They looked at me guiltily as I stepped into the mess deck they had commandeered. "Don't worry lads. You will get used to it and so long as you hurl over the side then Navy doesn't mind."

"Sir!"

"If you want some advice." They nodded. "Get on deck and fix your eyes on the horizon. The fresh air and the steady line will make you feel better than this." They looked dubious. "I will tell you what, let's make that an order eh?"

"Sir!"

Sergeant Curtis chuckled, "I remember my first time on a little boat. It was Walcheren and I hurled for England. They will be alright."

"And the others?"

He glanced at Blair and Marsh. They were away from the rest. It spoke volumes. "With a couple of exceptions, I reckon they will be alright. They bitched and moaned but I expected that." I nodded. "You were at Walcheren weren't you sir?"

"I was."

"That was a cock-up alright and no mistake!"

"Yet we won and that was because of lads like Green and Campbell." I lowered my voice. "This may not go smoothly, Sergeant, but we are commandos and we deal with whatever is thrown our way. That is what we do."

For some reason that cheered him up. "I will pop to the galley. See if they have any cocoa. Fancy a mug sir?"

I smiled, "I have just had stoker's cocoa!"

He shook his head, "Officers! They get all the perks!" It was said without rancour and I smiled. It was a beginning.

Korea

Chapter 4

We reached Dongbaek-Ri well before dawn. My heart sank when I saw it. It had obviously been a small fishing port but the huge influx of ships at Pusan had made it suddenly become far more important. The refugees were already crowded on the wharf. There was just one ship tied up there; an American minesweeper. The refugees were looking for a way out of this war-torn country and as we approached the expectant faces rose like a false dawn.

"This does not look, good Major!"

"Slow down, Lieutenant. Sergeant Curtis, have the men stand to with their weapons."

The voice came from below decks, "Sir, yes sir! Come on ladies, shift yourselves! Weapons out and on safety!"

I took out my Colt. I held it before me. It was a big gun and I wanted the crowds to see it. "Edge in if you please Lieutenant."

"Sir."

I walked to the port side. The crowd were pushing against the six American soldiers who were guarding our berth. As we bumped alongside the mob surged forward. The soldiers were young. I raised my Colt and fired two bullets. I had tried to learn the phonetic Korean phrases I had been given. I shouted, "Stop or I will shoot!" I had no idea if I had pronounced the words correctly but they all stopped. Just then a couple of trucks and a jeep screeched to a halt. Korean soldiers rushed out and pushed the civilians to one side.

Behind me, I heard the Chief shout, "Secure the boat to the dock!"

Holstering my pistol, I stepped ashore. A Ranger wearing a Major's insignia stepped towards me, "Major Harsker you have a well-deserved reputation. Welcome to Korea. My name is Max Hampton of the 5th Ranger Battalion."

I shook his hand, "And thank you for arranging such a warm welcome."

He shrugged, "The poor sons of bitches have been chased for hundreds of miles. They just want away from here. They have no idea where they will go but they are just petrified of the Commies!"

I heard a grunt of disapproval from behind me and I knew that it was Blair. I would deal with him when I had time.

The Major pointed to a Nissen hut, "We have a Quonset hut for you. It will be, what do you guys say, cosy? Still, you can always bunk on the boats. I will be leaving a platoon of these guys here. You won't be troubled again."

"It isn't a problem Major."

He flashed me a disdainful look. "Hell, I am not worried about you guys. You can look after yourselves. I need the wharf keeping open. If the Commies bomb Pusan then this will be the secondary option for getting men in or," he added ominously, "for getting men out."

"As we found out at Dunkirk if you can hold on to a little piece of land then it makes life easier when you retake the country. Remember Utah Beach?"

"Good point. If you get your chaps to the hut I will take you to Headquarters and give you the picture. It is very fluid!" He turned and began to give orders in Korean.

I turned, "Captain Poulson, those are our digs! Get the men sorted. I am off to Headquarters with the Major."

"Sir!"

Corporal Callow leapt ashore. He handed me my Bergen and my Thompson. "The Sarn't Major thought you might need these, sir."

"Thanks, Corporal Callow." Once again, I went on a jeep ride. The difference was that this was shorter. The ramshackle buildings that made up Dongbaek-Ri soon gave way to countryside. I saw a military compound ahead. There was wire all around it and I saw tanks. They were all World War Two vintage. I saw Shermans and Chaffees. The Major saw the direction of my gaze. "They are Korean. Our stuff hasn't arrived yet. We have boots on the ground and a few squadrons of Mustangs and Twin Mustangs but that is all. The North Koreans can outgun these World War Two relics. The T-34 has an eighty-five-millimetre gun. The Chaffee is fast but the T-34 has a shell that can tear through it like tinfoil. That is why they have made such rapid gains. When the M26 Pershings get here then we can beat them."

As we pulled into the compound I said, "Things seem a little hairy then."

He laughed, "I love your understatement. If you mean are we hanging on to this peninsula with our fingertips then you are right. When we asked for you it was to help us to retake what the Koreans have lost. Now you will be asked to help to defend what we still hold."

As we walked into the concrete building I knew that it would be fruitless to ask for explosives and equipment. It would be like the last war. We would have to scavenge and improvise. There was an officer's mess and it was filled with both Korean and American officers. There was a fog of cigarette smoke above their heads.

They all stopped talking when we entered, "Gentlemen, may I introduce the first of the British contingent, Major Harsker of the Commandos."

There was a cheer and a couple of young American officers began singing 'Rule Britannia' but they soon ran out of words. I raised my hand in acknowledgement.

"Come on we will see the General."

General Smith was in his office with his adjutant. He was not a Ranger. He was army. He smiled when he saw me. "Glad you made it, Major. I am guessing you have no idea what day of the week it is eh?"

"Something like that, sir."

"I am not sure if the Major explained but you have to hit the ground running. I knew Colonel Darby in Italy and he told me that you were the most resourceful officer he had ever met. Well, we need you to be. We do not have the luxury of letting you become acclimatised to Korea and then doing that for which you were trained. We need you to be a battalion for a little while! Joe, get the map." His adjutant got out the map. "Here, twenty miles to the north of us is a small pass. We hope that the North Koreans won't use it but they might. I have the rest of our men and tanks ready to meet them on the main road from Daegu. Intelligence has their main armoured thrust heading from there. There is a Korean Brigade at Yangsan but if that falls then they could come through the back door. I am ready to repel an attack along the main road to Yangsan but I need you guys to hold the pass here. We are getting men ashore as quickly as we can but the main battles are to the west of us. The North Korean gains are even more spectacular there."

I looked at the map. The names were all in Korean and I could not read them but I saw a small village nestled between what looked like woods and high ground. "How about here?"

"That would do." The General paused. "That is it? You don't have a hundred questions and requests?"

I smiled as I faced him. "Sir, I was in the retreat to Dunkirk. This sounds similar. If you have transport and ammo then we would appreciate it and, of course, supplies. If not then we will improvise."

Major Hampton said, "I have Rangers north of Yangsan. They are trying to slow down the enemy by using hit and run tactics. They will be your first warning of trouble. Captain Rogers has almost forty Rangers.

Korea

They went up country three days ago. We lost radio contact yesterday." I heard the concern in his voice. "The roads are a quagmire. We have just had the monsoons. The mountainous nature of the land makes communication difficult. All you need to do is hold for a couple of days until we can get more men to you."

I wondered why the Major was not doing more. Then I realised that he was admin. He was not a fighting Ranger. He did not have the lean look that I remembered from Colonel Darby's men in Italy. He was a man who studied maps. I nodded, "Do you want us to leave right away?"

The General shook his head, "Your men will need a good night's sleep. Tomorrow will do. I have a couple of trucks for you and you can have one jeep. I will leave Petty Officer Flynn with you to liaise. I have a Korean soldier, Sergeant Bo-yeon Heon. He is a sergeant whose battalion was all captured close to Seoul. He will act as your interpreter. He is getting his gear now. He speaks good English. I think that he was some sort of teacher. He is not a commando but he is the best that we can do." He stood and shook his hand. "We did not bring you here to act as a backstop but I appreciate you helping us out." His adjutant gave me the maps and papers I would need.

"You are welcome, sir." I turned to the Major. "Will this sergeant know his way back to the port?"

"I will come back with you. I will be spending the night there. We have more Rangers arriving in the next few days. They are the rest of the Rangers I will be coordinating. I want to get them into the war as soon as possible. They will be your relief and I will get them to you as soon as we can. We will talk about your real role when this crisis is over."

The General stood, "Good luck Major. We appreciate this cooperation."

"Of course, sir. Glad we could be of help."

Sergeant Bo-yeon Heon was waiting at the jeep. He was older than I was expecting. As we neared him the Major said, "He is an English teacher from Seoul University. He is in the reserves. If we hadn't taken him as your interpreter then he would probably either be dead or in a camp. His family are behind enemy lines now and he was quite cut up about that."

The sergeant snapped smartly to attention. "Sergeant Bo-yeon Heon of the Republic of Korean Army, sir."

"At ease Sergeant. I am Major Harsker. Put your gear in the back and we will get to the barracks." I turned to the Major, "Do you mind if I drive back? I ought to get to know the roads around here."

"No problem."

As I put it into gear I said, "How about weapons and ammo, Major?"

"Until the ships arrive from Japan with the men it is just what you brought or what you can scavenge."

"The old hands may well have .45 ammo but the younger lads will have the .303."

"We have crates of those on the ship. The North Koreans struck a damn sight faster than we expected! We can let you have the .45 ammo."

"Sergeant do you know the area south of Yangsan?"

"Sorry, sir. I am a city boy from Seoul."

"And can you fight as well as interpret?"

"Oh yes, sir and I am eagerly looking forward to killing as many Communists as I can!"

His English was slightly less formal than I had expected. It did not take us long to reach the wharf. The Koreans had cleared the refugees from what I had optimistically named the barracks. I saw that the three boats all had guards at the gangplanks and all had one machine gun manned. I pulled in next to the hut. "That is how we will be going to war. Are you a sailor?"

"I have seen the sea, sir." Enigmatically that was all he said but I took that to mean that he was no sailor. So long as he could interpret then I would be happy. I had just reached for my Bergen when I heard the wail of the air raid siren. I looked up at the Major. "North Korean fighters. Best take cover."

I looked at the refugees who were, largely, in the open. "What about them?"

He shrugged, "There are no shelters."

I gave my Bergen to the Sergeant, "Get inside the hut!"

I ran towards the Fairmile. The crew were still, largely, below decks. Only the machine gun was manned. I shouted to the sentry, "Can you load an Oerlikon?"

"Aye, sir. Can you fire one?"

"It has been some time but let's give it a go. What is your name seaman?"

"Able Seaman Gordon Tyreman sir."

"Right, you spot and load!"

Lieutenant John Drake appeared on deck. He had been in the middle of a shave. He had a vest on and half of his face was covered in shaving soap. I strapped myself into the Oerlikon. It had been five years since I had fired one. I saw that this one was belt fed. We would not have to change the magazine. I leaned back into the harness with my hands on the triggers. I said, "Where is he Tyreman?"

"Coming in low sir from the northeast."

Lieutenant Drake shouted, "All hands on deck! Man the guns!"

I swung the twin Oerlikon around. It had been a single one I had fired. Next, to us, the minesweeper's guns fired. They were using tracer. I had no idea what this ammunition would be. The tracer from the Browning on the minesweeper showed me where the Russian built Yak 9s were coming from. They were just fifty feet above the sea. I saw the flames from their guns as the two cannons and a single machine gun in each aeroplane ripped into the minesweeper. I pulled the triggers. I expected the twin Oerlikon to kick but it didn't. The result was that my first burst was too low and I quickly corrected. My second was more accurate but the Yak was just a hundred yards away when the twenty mill shells smashed into the belly of the aircraft. There was armour plating there. Then it was over me and I shifted to the second. This one was firing at me. I heard Tyreman throw himself to the deck. It was the sensible thing to do. I fired in short bursts. This time I began to hit the wings and, I think, the propeller. The Korean pilot made the same mistake I had done and his bullets went too low. They hit the water. I felt at least two hit the hull and then he was gone but there was smoke coming from him. As the machine gunner had also been firing I could not take all the credit. The third one was just coming into my sights when the Brownings on the minesweeper hit something vital and the aeroplane exploded just a hundred yards from us. The concussive wave of heat and air hit me. It was lucky that Tyreman had taken cover or he might have been blown over the side. Only my harness saved me.

And then it was over. With one aeroplane smoking and one destroyed they headed north-west. I heard, from the minesweeper, "Medic!" They had taken casualties. I unstrapped myself and turned around. I saw that the refugees had also been hit; at least thirty of them.

Tyreman stood and grinned, "You are a game 'un sir!"

John Drake said, "If you ever want a berth as a gunner then you are more than welcome. Your reactions put us to shame."

I shook my head, "I had just arrived from headquarters and I feared for the refugees." Major Hampton approached from the safety of our hut. "Major Hampton, you had better get those refugees shifted. There is no cover here."

"I know. I hoped that the Koreans would have done something but I think this invasion has knocked their confidence! Leave it with me. Nice shooting."

I nodded and turned to the naval lieutenant, "John, me and my chaps will be away into the hills tomorrow. Keep an eye on the barracks for us."

He nodded, "I think we will all have repairs to make anyway. I will have a couple of the lads sleep ashore. And I guess we will have to act as anti-aircraft batteries too."

"It is a good job they don't appear to have bombers."

"You can say that again. A nice welcome eh, sir?"

Captain Poulson and my men were outside now that the all-clear had been sounded. The attack had been useful in one way. It showed that we were in a war zone. "Are there cooking facilities, Sergeant Major?"

He looked at me as though I was speaking Korean. "What sir?"

"We will need to eat. If there are no cooking facilities then we will have to improvise them."

"Right sir. No there are just cots and lockers. We have rigged up some curtains so that you and Captain Poulson can have privacy."

I looked around. I saw some discarded oil barrels. "Sergeant Heon, do you know where there is cutting equipment? I want to cut these barrels in two and make some field kitchens and we will need food."

Major Hampton scratched his chin and said, "There was supposed to be supplies laid on. Come with me, Sergeant Heon. Sergeant Major give me four reliable men."

"Corporal Swift pick three men and go with the Major. The rest of you let's give these people a hand!" The six of them headed off into the village.

The Korean soldiers had risen like wraiths from their places of hiding and were just standing around. Without an interpreter, we could do little but perhaps my men's example might stir them. I went into the barracks. It was functional. I saw that there were no curtains on the windows. If there were air raids then we would need blackout. I took out my notebook and wrote in it. I would need to remind myself of what was needed. We needed a quiet area for my office. The men would also like some privacy. The Sergeant Major had used what he had to hand but we needed more curtains. We needed a shower rigging up. My men would like to be clean. It would not be hot water but it would be water and we were commandos.

By the time night fell we had two barrels cut in two. We had lit wood in them to burn off the oil residue. The minesweeper had had oxy-acetylene torches and they had been glad to help us. My resourceful men had found and rigged up curtains so that we could have lights at night. After managing to take supplies from the Korean soldiers the Major had gone to the minesweeper. They would be able to house and feed him.

I waited until we had eaten before I gave my men the unwelcome news that we would not have the luxury of a few days to acclimatize. I gave them the bare bones of our mission. "We leave before dawn. There is a village we need to occupy. Our task is to hold up the enemy until we are relieved by the Americans." As I had expected Blair and Marsh groaned and pulled faces. "You should know that there are Americans just like us, Rangers, and they are up country. Those who served in the war know what it is like to be behind enemy lines. Headquarters has lost touch with them. We will be their only hope. By the time they reach us, they will be out of ammunition and food. This is not why they brought us here but we are commandos and we know how to improvise."

Sergeant Major Thorpe said, "Don't worry sir. We won't let them down." He glared at Blair and Marsh.

"I know. We can leave our kit bags here. Take your Bergens. Take all your ammunition and your rations. Your winter weather gear can stay here. We travel light. We have transport there but if we have another air attack then who knows. Williams, have you had a chance to test the radio yet?"

"No, sir."

"Then do it now. Who is your number two?"

"I haven't got one, sir."

"Then get one. If you cop one then we are up the creek without a paddle." His face fell. "It is a fact of life, Williams. If I fall then Captain Poulson will carry on. No one is indispensable."

"Sir."

"Now check your Bergens and your weapons. That air attack was just the warning we needed. We are in a war zone now!"

Korea

Paul Poulson came over to me and smiled, "I don't think you need worry that you are rusty, sir. You thought of more things than I did. You haven't lost it."

"I am worried, Paul. This has all the hallmarks of a disaster. The North Koreans and their main army are less than eighty miles away. The General is ready to block a major attack along the main road but our little band of Spartans are all that stand between the enemy and this port. If they get here then it will be far worse for the civilians than three aircraft."

"Sir."

I followed my own advice and checked my weapons. I would leave my Lee Enfield, Webley and nine millimetre on the Fairmile. That way I would only have .45 ammunition to take. I pared the Bergen down to the minimum. I would wear my cap comforter and take my battle jerkin. I had eight Mills Bombs and, thanks to the war, I still had four German grenades. I was not sure if they had deteriorated in storage but I hoped not. They were perfect for booby traps.

Sergeant Heon came into the barracks. "Sergeant I want you to have a word with our two drivers. I need to know how reliable they are."

"Sir?"

"I will be blunt Sergeant. I don't want them running when things get sticky."

"Sticky sir?"

"Dangerous. Sorry, it is an English idiom."

"I will speak with them but you need not worry. If they try to run then I will shoot them myself. If more of our men had stood and fought then my family might not be behind enemy lines."

Petty Officer Flynn wanted to come with us but I did not think he was fit enough. I spared his feelings by giving him a job to do. "Petty Officer, we will be away for just a couple of days. If this is going to be our billet we need it making homelier. Can I leave that in your capable hands?"

"Of course, sir, and this tub of lard won't slow you down!"

"Never crossed my mind Petty Officer."

He grinned, "Horses for courses I believe you guys say. I prefer ships. I can help the guys with the boats. The camouflage is all wrong. I will make us invisible!"

"Thanks, Petty Officer."

We slipped away before dawn. I managed six hours of sleep. Lieutenant Drake had his men stand watch for us and that helped enormously. Captain Poulson drove the jeep. Williams rode in one truck with the Sergeant Major. We would use the radio on the Fairmile to communicate. It was safer that way. We only had twenty miles to go along a narrow and winding road. Sergeant Heon told us that the name of the village we were heading for was called Sason-Ri. He told me that the word Ri meant a small village. From his description, it sounded as big as the one in which I lived. As dawn broke we saw that there had been refugees on the road. As in the Low Countries they had been strafed. Bloated bodies of people and animals lay in the ditches at the side of the mud-covered road. It took almost three hours to cover the twenty miles. We could have run it faster. We had to clear bodies from sections and others were so muddy that the men had to push the trucks.

The village was deserted. Perhaps the bodies we had seen had been the villagers. The road from Yangsan descended to the village and we could hear the sounds of combat from the distant town. The Korean Brigade was still defending the town. There were no signs of fighting in the village and that was a relief but the North Korean Airforce had done a good job of destroying it. After Corporal Callow and my men had searched the village and found it empty we began to make it defensible. We placed the trucks at the southeastern end of the village in case we had to get away quickly. Captain Poulson and his men used some of the wrecked carts and wagons to make a barricade across the road. The Sergeant Major had his men move rocks to make emplacements. The Bren was placed where it would have a good field of fire. We dug a mortar pit and put some wooden beams from a wrecked house around them. Haynes and Barton used their entrenching tools to pack mud between the wood. If it did not rain and the sun continued to shine it would harden and give them more protection. They used camouflage nets to disguise it. We all had them and I had them spread out to disguise our positions. I sent Corporal Callow with three men to find water. Everything which could be used was incorporated into our bunkers and gun pits. We would have a perimeter less than a hundred yards in length. I had the two flanks angled back and secured against the remains of two buildings.

I had Williams set up the command post close to the mortar in the one building which had avoided complete destruction. Like the others, it was a single-story building but it still had its roof. There was nothing inside save for a table. The radio was placed beneath it to give added protection from an aerial attack. I sent the rest of my men to scavenge for food and to see if there was a water supply. I walked forward to examine the ground. I paced it out so that I could judge the range better. I saw where the enemy could use features to attack us and how we might counter them. I walked back slowly and took it all in.

When they came back Corporal Callow told me they had found a stream on the edge of the trees which lay to the northeast of us. "Sir, if they come through the trees they can outflank us." He pointed to the other side of the road. "And there too!"

I went to my Bergen and gave him the four German grenades and four of my Mills bombs. "Do you still remember how to rig these as booby traps?"

He grinned, "Potato mashers! Haven't seen these since the war. Aye, sir you never forget."

"Then I want you to place them in the woods. It is just to give us warning of men moving in them."

"Right sir. Come on then my lovely lads! Time for a bit of mischief and you young lads are going to get a practical lesson in sabotage! No charge!" He laughed at his own pun.

The aeroplanes came in the early afternoon. This time they were the Lavochkin La-9. This was a faster and heavier armed aeroplane. There were two of them. I shouted, "Hold your fire and keep still!" I hoped that travelling at over four hundred miles an hour they might not see us. I forgot about the trucks. They flew over the village and then, seeing the trucks, climbed to return for an attack. As soon as I saw them bank and climb I knew we were going to be strafed. "Prepare to fire! Those with automatic weapons use short bursts. We have limited ammunition and stay in cover."

I wracked my brains to try to remember what I had read about the guns. I seemed to remember that each cannon only had seventy-five rounds. If the pilots were experienced then they would husband their ammunition. As they screamed in from the east for their attack it became obvious that they were novices. They both fired all four cannons and their target was the same truck. It was, as the Americans might say, a rooky error. They blasted one truck and the exploding petrol tank threw pieces of debris into the air. I saw one of the aeroplanes begin to smoke. A piece of debris must have hit something vital. I did not fire but my men did. I heard bullets hitting the metal-skinned aircraft and then they were gone, heading north and west. They would go back and say they had destroyed American trucks.

Korea

"Are there any casualties?" I saw the two Korean drivers emerge from beneath the second lorry. They had been lucky. "Sergeant Major, move the other lorry and get it camouflaged!" I cursed myself for the oversight. I should have hidden them before. "See if you can salvage anything from the wreckage."

I walked with Captain Poulson to view the road north. I took out my binoculars. I could see nothing but the column of smoke would tell any North Koreans close by what had happened. The two pilots would, no doubt, be telling their base that there were soldiers in Sason-Ri. We were no longer a secret.

Chapter 5

It was dark before the lorry fire was extinguished. As darkness fell we could see, to the north-west, fires burning. Yangsan still held out. The longer they held the more men General Smith could bring to bear when they tried to advance south. We ate cold rations augmented by the little food we had found. We had camouflaged the lorry and we would use that as a first aid centre. The two drivers slept there as well. The rest of us slept at our posts. Each section took a four-hour watch. So long as there was fighting in Yangsan then I hoped that we would be safe from attack. My section had the middle watch. Williams had reported to the boat and they knew of the loss of the lorry. It was not a disaster. If we had to then the men could all fit in one lorry. I went around my section to talk to them and to get to know them. It was easy with all of them. Blair and Marsh were the two hardest.

"So Private Blair, what made you stay in after the war?"

He gave me a sullen shrug, "I had no other prospects. School didn't prepare me for anything worthwhile. Now we have a proper education system then kids like me have a better chance. I wasn't rich and privileged like some." He meant me of course. "My uncle, Michael, he is the clever one. He is an MP." He said it as a threat. It did not worry me.

"And do you want to be a politician?"

"I might. It would be a way to stop the rich from getting richer at the expense of the poor. Wealth should be distributed fairly. Why should those who have money keep it? It should be shared around equitably."

I did not rise to the bait. Marsh was leaning against the wooden beam which gave them protection. It would be cosy for the two of them in this little nest. "And you Marsh, what about you? Why did you join?"

"I thought it would be a chance to see the world and was more exciting than working in the steelworks in Sheffield. I wanted to be an actor but there was no chance of that in Sheffield."

"Then you should be happy. You are halfway around the world already."

He shook his head, "I want to see more than this."

I noticed that they had not once used, 'sir'. I could have been a martinet and pulled them up about it but this was just a casual chat. I did not want to build up even more barriers. At least it had been a civil conversation and I knew a little more about them. Blair was driven by politics but Marsh wanted adventure. I could see why he wanted to be an actor. He had the brooding looks of a young Tyrone Power. It was a chink of light.

I noticed the fighting cease in the middle of the night. The shelling ceased and I could just hear small arms fire. The last pockets of resistance were being eliminated. I was no longer confident about the time but that seemed about right. I found Sergeant Curtis. "The fighting has stopped. Let's get a dixie of tea on. I think things will hot up once dawn breaks."

"Aye, sir. A man fights better with a mug of tea inside him." He turned, "Harris, go and get the dixie from the lorry. Fill it up with water!"

One of the items we had saved from the lorry was a jerrycan of petrol. I had no idea why it had not exploded. We had kindling and half burnt wood already. I poured some petrol on it and threw a match into it. It almost exploded into life. Ken Thorpe, who had the next watch, woke. "Sorry Sarn't Major, just getting a brew going. The fighting has stopped in Yangsan."

He stood and stretched, "Then they could be here by morning. I am not sure if I am on English time, Arab time or Indian time. I have had enough sleep."

Private Harris struggled with the dixie. Sergeant Major Thorpe shook his head, "Time was I could have carried two dixies like that! Getting soft these young recruits. Here son, let me give you a hand."

The older hands in Thorpe's section came to. They would have been on duty in half an hour anyway and old hands had a clock in their head. The water was bubbling just below boil when we went off duty. "Wake me in two hours Sarn't Major."

"You sure sir?"

"If there is no bother then I will let the lads sleep but I would rather be up."

"Righto, sir!"

I curled up in a ball close to the radio under the table. Williams was wrapped around it as though he was protecting it. As I knew I would I fell asleep straight away. Thorpe had barely touched my arm and I was awake.

"Still quiet sir but you said two hours."

"Thanks. I'll have a mug of tea please."

I went outside and relieved myself. We had a bucket we had found and it was full of river water. I sluiced myself down and felt wide awake.

Korea

I took my toothbrush from my Bergen and using some salt, cleaned my teeth. I rinsed with river water and felt better.

I took the mug of tea from Thorpe. "Quiet?"

"Yes, sir. We heard the sound of lorries heading south. I reckon the Korean Brigade has legged it. We heard an occasional bullet. They must have left snipers to slow down the enemy,"

"Who have we got who is in sniper class?" His silence was eloquent. "I have a scope for my Lee Enfield and I am not a bad shot. When we get back I will be the sniper."

We drank our tea, "Sir, do you mind me asking?" I nodded for him to continue as I cleaned out my pipe. "Why did you leave the service? You are a natural. I thought I had good officers before but you seem to have it all. You are good with the men. You know your stuff and the fruit salad on your chest tells me that you are no coward."

"A bullet which nearly ended my life and the love of a good woman. I enjoy flying too. I have a perfect life."

"And yet you came back, sir."

"I am in the Reserves."

"And we both know that you could have refused. This command could be led by Captain Poulson. They asked for the best and you came running, sir."

I smiled, "It must run in the family. Dad served from nineteen fourteen until forty-five. I just did six years. Maybe I thought I owed the service a few years."

He stood, "Well I, for one, am glad you are here, sir. I'll just go and ginger the young lads up."

I got my pipe going and thought of Susan and my three children. I missed kissing them goodnight and tucking them in. I missed playing with them, reading them stories, collecting tomatoes with Sam. I missed them. I watched the dawn. The sun came up from the east and bathed the hills ahead in a pale blue light. It was beautiful but I knew that the enemy would be contemplating their options. The two aeroplanes would have reported us here. Would that deter them? They had to know that the American General and the Koreans were waiting for them down the main road. Would they try an outflanking manoeuvre? I would have.

Everyone was roused before dawn. Blair complained. In many ways, I would have been disappointed had he not. He chuntered about having to do what Americans were paid to do. Sergeant Curtis told him to shut up and get more water from the river. It was cold rations but there was still stewed tea and British soldiers could fight all day on a decent pot of tea. I walked to the cart barrier across the road. The villagers had only left the cart because one wheel was broken. It was the most substantial part of the barricade. We had augmented it with some beams from a wrecked building.

"See what else you can find to make this a little sturdier eh lads?"

I took a couple of stones I had found and placed them strategically next to the wheel of the cart. The rest of my section did the same. They found more next to the stream. The stone wall was rising by the hour and affording us protection. I walked back to the burned-out lorry. It was cold now. I found the two doors which had been blown off and I waved over one of the Korean drivers who had just had a pee. I gestured for him to help me and we picked up the two doors and carried them to the cart barrier. I used some stones and a couple of pieces of broken beams to prop them up and I found I had a shelter through which I could observe the road. This would be my bunker. At a pinch, it could hold three men. I took my binoculars and wriggled underneath. I laid my Thompson on the ground and then used the binoculars to scan the road and the woods in the distance. Reassuringly I saw nothing.

Captain Poulson joined me. "Nice little nest, sir."

"If those aeroplanes return then I will have the illusion of protection. Those cannon shells could tear through this. My only hope is that all the pilots are as bad as those we saw yesterday."

"They hit the lorry, sir!"

"My mother could have hit the lorry! You fire short bursts with one gun. It wasn't as though we had anti-aircraft, was it? No, the danger we have to face is armour. If tanks come we will have to hope that there are tank-busting aircraft close by. If not then we will have to, as the Americans so eloquently put it, bug out! We will cross that bridge when we come to it."

"And the Rangers who are out there?"

"I am hoping that they make it here sooner rather than later. We both know that they are already beyond the time they were expected to survive. Go around the lads and tell them to keep their eyes open for Rangers. The young lads will be jumpy enough as it is. Have a good lookout on the roof of that one building which is left."

"Yes, sir."

I took out two grenades and laid them on the ground. We could not booby trap the road for the next ones down it might not be the enemy but either Koreans or Rangers fleeing. Corporal Callow brought me a mug of tea. "Here sir. I have checked our lads. They are all in position. He shook his head, I gave Blair and Marsh the safest part of the line. They are guarding Williams and his radio."

"What do you make of them Corporal? You were in the war."

"I can't figure them out. That Blair doesn't seem to want to be in the Commandos. Why stay in? And Marsh? He joined up yet he doesn't seem to like the life. He is always combing his hair and he wears stuff on his face that smells like perfume! Not right in a commando!"

"You are married, aren't you?"

He grinned, "Aye sir, two kids."

"What does your wife think of this?"

"Her dad was a soldier. We make the most of the time when I am at home. To be fair sir, this is the first posting away from England since the war started. She might be ready for a break."

Captain Poulson peered into the improvised bunker. "I have been around them all. I put the Korean Sergeant as a lookout. He knows the difference between South and North Koreans. Wouldn't do to make a mistake."

"I'll get out of your way sir." Corporal Callow slithered out backwards and Captain Poulson came in. I heard the Corporal say, "Sir If I shovel some soil on the top of the lorry doors it will disguise them and give you more protection."

"Thanks, Corporal."

I sipped the hot sweet tea. I had given up sugar. Sugar was rationed and Susan and the children had a sweet tooth. I suffered the tea. I would have to tell the men my preferences. Sugar in my tea was a waste. I had finished the tea when Sergeant Curtis appeared, "Sir, that Korean sergeant says there are North Koreans heading up the road. He says he has seen them in the woods to the north and south too. He couldn't see tanks. He has good eyes."

"Tell the lads to stand to."

"Yes, sir."

I turned to Captain Poulson who was slithering out of the bunker to return to his section. "They are trying to outflank us. You watch one flank and ask Thorpe to watch the other. If Callow's booby traps work we should have warning. Tell them to wait for my command to fire! Have Williams join me."

"Sir." He slipped out.

Lance Corporal Williams appeared. "You wanted me, sir?"

"You will be here with me. Anything come through from the boat?"

"Just that they have been attacked again and this time there were more aeroplanes. Lieutenant Drake said he had heard that there was a column heading down from Yangsan towards the port."

"It looks like we are on our own."

I cocked my Thompson. We had a good field of fire for three hundred yards. We would not open fire at that range. It would be a waste of bullets. Williams had a Lee Enfield. "I see from your record that you are a good shot."

"Aye, sir. I used to go hunting with my brothers before I joined up. I had a .22 and we made up the rations with rabbits. Mam would give me what for if I hit the rabbit anywhere but the head!"

"Good, then you aim for the officers and sergeants. This Tommy gun can keep the heads of the others down."

"How do I know which are which?"

I had spoken to Sergeant Heon and knew a little more than I had. "They have epaulettes; officers and sergeants. If they have a pistol then they are an officer."

"Right sir."

It seemed an age before we saw them. They came in a ragged line and they darted from what little cover there was to the next piece. I had chosen this as my defensive position because there was little cover ahead of us. I saw that they had a variety of uniforms but none wore helmets. Grenades would cause more casualties. I saw that there were two men with submachine guns and, after peering through my glasses, I saw that they had epaulettes. They were sergeants. I handed the glasses to Williams. "The sergeants have machine guns."

He peered through them and handed them back. "I could hit them from here sir!"

"No, we wait. Track them and drop them when I shout fire. I want as many hits in the first attack as we can manage."

They were just one hundred and fifty yards from us when the grenade booby trap went off in the woods to the north. They were close enough for me to see their faces. The officer was young and he looked north. They did not take cover and that was a mistake. "Fire!" I squeezed the trigger and fired a burst of eight bullets. I managed to hit the officer in the leg and he rolled into the ditch. Another bullet winged a soldier with a rifle. Williams managed to hit the two sergeants with two of the three

Korea

bullets he fired. All along our line came the sound of firing. The Bren's distinctive sound seemed to punctuate the cacophony of rifle and Tommy gun bullets. The mortars whistled and then exploded behind the Koreans. The flying shrapnel scythed through them. I fired another short burst and then another. The smell of cordite filled the air.

The Korean officer shouted something. The Koreans began to crawl backwards, seeking cover. I saw eight bodies across the front of our line. One tried to crawl and then simply stopped. The ones retreating fired as they fell back. They were wild shots and I heard them zipping above us. They were too high.

When they had fallen back two hundred yards I shouted, "Cease fire!" An eerie silence descended. "Anyone hurt? Section two?"

"No, sir."

"Section three?"

"All fine sir."

Just then there was the sound of bullets from the woods to the north and the south. Sergeant Major Thorpe shouted, "They are firing from cover, sir." There was an explosion. "And it looks like they are still tripping Corporal Callow's booby traps."

The problem would be nightfall. So long as we could see then we had a good field of fire. "Williams, get on the radio and tell the Lieutenant the position. Leave your Lee Enfield here."

"Sir!"

The sporadic gunfire from the woods continued. Occasionally a Lee Enfield would bark as one of my men spotted a target. Williams came back. "I told him, sir. He said the Koreans were pushing hard towards Pusan." They would still be fifty miles short of the major port but General Smith would have his hands full to hold them.

I wondered what they were up to. This was obviously an attempt by the Koreans to outflank us but why had they not sent armour? Had we stopped them? If so we had been incredibly lucky. We had caught them by surprise. They had known we were here but thought, perhaps, they could simply roll over us. Perhaps the pilots had claimed more damage than they had actually caused. Dad told me that sometimes pilots exaggerated their successes. We had our answer twenty minutes later. Three Yak 9s came screaming down the valley. They came in line astern and their cannon shells and machine gun bullets zipped and ripped through the village. I heard shouts even above the cacophony of noise. Then the bullets stopped and I heard the engines of the three aeroplanes as they climbed. I turned and poked the Thompson out of the back of my bunker. "You watch the Koreans, Williams!"

The three aeroplanes roared in and they were low. They fired early. I gave them a burst with my Thompson. I heard the Bren and the other Thompsons as they neared us. The bullets from the leading aircraft stitched a line towards me. When his nose rose I breathed a sigh of relief. He stopped firing for he did not want to hit his own men. And then they were gone.

"Keep watch, Lance Corporal." I scrambled from the back of the bunker. I changed my magazine. It was not empty but I would prefer a full magazine. I saw that the lorry was intact but I saw Pike rushing to a huddle of my men. When I reached them I shouted, "If you are not wounded then get back to your positions. The Koreans will be coming soon."

They dispersed and I saw Pike binding the leg of Private Blackwood. The medic looked up. "Lucky sir. The bullet missed everything vital. He won't be able to move though."

"Put him in the radio shack." I looked down at the body next to him. It was Sergeant Curtis. The Walcheren veteran had been torn in two by cannon shells. His death would leave a widow and a son.

Just then Williams shouted, "Here they come again!" I grabbed the wounded man and Pike and I manhandled him the thirty yards to the radio shack. I heard the Korean bullets as they opened fire. "Keep your heads down!"

I kept my head low and cocked my gun as I raced back to the bunker. I dived inside. Williams was working his bolt as fast as he could. I jammed my Thompson through the opening and gave a short burst. The mortar whumped and then the Bren kicked in. Once again, the Koreans had overestimated the effect of their attack. If they had had dive bombers then they would have killed us all. Trying to strafe so close to their own men effectively damaged their chances. That and the fact that they had used all of their bullets and shells up in two passes. I fired again and then peered out. There were fresh bodies but the Koreans were not retreating. They were using their dead as barricades.

"Sir, they are getting closer to the stream."

"Blair and Marsh, reinforce Captain Poulson." They were my only reserve apart from the two Korean drivers. If we suffered more losses then I would have to use them as well. This attack was prosecuted a little more forcefully than the first. I fear we might have come off worse had

Korea

not Haynes and Barton managed to drop four of their mortar shells just behind the Korean line. They were protected from our bullets by the dead bodies of their comrades but the shrapnel had no such obstacle and I heard the Korean officer shout an order. We managed to hit another two as they wriggled and slithered back down the road and out of range.

"Williams, go to the radio shack. Give them an update. Blackwood is there and he is wounded. Give him a crash course in the radio. He is now your number two." The last retreat had given us an hour of peace. If they summoned the aeroplanes again we would have another hour in which to prepare.

"Right sir."

I climbed out after him. "Sergeant Heon!"

He stood from his foxhole ten yards away from the bunker, "Sir!"

"What did the Korean officer shout?"

"He just said, 'fall back and regroup'."

"If he says anything different then tell me."

"Yes, sir."

"Go and get the drivers to make a brew. The lads will need it. I may need them as riflemen soon."

He shook his head, "They are drivers, sir, for a good reason. They are no damned good as soldiers!"

"We are two men down. If we lose more we may need them."

"Sir."

I shouted, "Anyone else hurt?"

Ken Thorpe shouted, "Not so far. They are still more than a hundred yards away. We haven't had to use our Thompsons yet."

"Captain Poulson?"

"They are bellied down in the dead ground close to the stream."

"Haynes and Barton, shift your mortar and see if you can clear them. The rest of you, repair your defences and be ready for another attack. They are not finished with us yet."

"Sir."

I knew that we had brought two boxes of mortar shells with us on the lorry. That meant thirty-six shells. I had not been keeping count but there could not be many shells left from the first box. I hurried over to Captain Poulson's position. He was using the wrecked remains of three houses for cover. I crawled next to him. Using my glasses, I could see the felt hats of two of the Koreans. A sniper might have hit them but they were safe from the rest of us. The stream was two hundred yards away.

Barton said, "Ready sir!"

"I will spot for you. Let's use our ammunition wisely."

I heard the pop of the first two-inch shell. It was a ranging shot. The mortar had a range of five hundred yards. It must have hit the stream for the water fountained in the air. "About ten yards too long."

"Sir!"

A moment or two later the second shell exploded and I heard screams. "Bob on! Four more shells."

Captain Poulson shouted, "They will shift soon enough be ready to pour it into them." I picked up my Thompson. The mortars could fire eight rounds a minute. The four shells landed in rapid succession. The nature of the weapon and the way it was fired mean that they did not land at exactly the same spot. As the third shell hit it became too much and the survivors stood and ran. We all opened fire at the same time. Eight survivors reached the woods. They would not try that again.

"Well done mortar crew. Realign your mortar. How many shells left?"

"Just the one box, sir."

"Then use them well."

I clambered up on to the pile of stones which Sergeant Heon had used to keep watch. They obviously had some significance for the village as they had been chosen carefully and were laid on top of one another. Perhaps it was a religious thing. It meant I was four feet higher than anything else. I risked a Korean sniper taking a pot shot but so far, I had not seen evidence of a sniper. I used the glasses and scanned the road ahead. The Koreans were beyond mortar range. I saw they had medics dealing with the wounded. I saw the antenna of a radio. I could see heavy machines guns. So far they had not brought them up. I estimated it to be a large company. I scanned the woods on our flanks. I saw movement in the woods but they were a thousand yards away. They were waiting for dusk. The mortar had kept them at bay but once darkness fell then they would come closer. I had a contingency plan for that. I lifted the glasses to look towards Yangsan. I could still see smoke rising from the town and hear the occasional crack of small arms fire. There would still be some units trying to fight their way south. I wondered where the Ranger detachment under Captain Rogers could be. Their job was to disrupt the enemy advance. By now they would have neither food nor ammunition. They were Rangers and as good as commandos. They would find some way to survive.

I used the glasses to look at the bodies which littered the ground between the lines. The Koreans had made no attempt to recover either weapons or bodies. Our Lee Enfields and the mortar would discourage that. I saw at least one officer and three sergeants amongst the dead. Their command structure would be weakened. More importantly, there were three submachine guns with the dead Koreans. Their firepower was damaged too. I switched the glasses back to the Korean Company. There was a huddle of men around the radio. When one of the officers pointed in our direction I knew what was coming.

"Stand to! They are going to attack!" As I hurried back to the bunker Sergeant Heon handed me a cup of tea. "Thanks, you come to the bunker with me and Williams. It will be cosy but I might need you to translate their commands."

"Yes, sir."

This time the Koreans came more cautiously. For some reason, they had no mortars of their own and so they resorted to smoke grenades. The wind came for the north and when they were three hundred paces from us they used grenade launchers to send smoke grenades. They landed just sixty paces from us. It did not completely hide them but it made it harder to see movements. They were planning on bringing up their heavy machine gun.

Captain Poulson shouted, "Should we drop mortar shells on them, sir?"

"No, save them. They will move men and the machine gun up in the smoke. Use rifles."

"Right sir."

Sergeant Heon had the .30 M1903A3 bolt action rifle. I was familiar with it for I had used one in World War Two. It was a good weapon. "How much ammunition do you have for that?"

"Forty rounds sir."

"Good, then when I tell you, begin to fire down the road. You will see nothing but imagine that you are firing at someone two hundred yards away; aim low. Just fire regularly and slowly. Move the rifle barrel ten degrees each time you fire."

"Yes sir, but I will miss more than I am likely to hit."

"They will be trying to set up a machine gun. There is a road which slopes upward. Your bullets which are short will ricochet and a ricochet can do as much damage as a hit."

Korea

All that we saw were shadows in the smoke. Soon the sun would set behind us and they would be silhouetted by the sun. We had to slow them as much as possible. I had to estimate their speed and position. A heavy machine would slow them down. The rest of the line would move at the speed of the machine gun.

"Open fire!"

I took out my glasses and stared through the smoke. Williams and Sergeant Heon began to fire into the smoke. The men to my left and right joined in. I saw the muzzle flash from the enemy guns. I did not worry about them. They would be as blind as we were and we had cover. They had none. I heard cries and saw a couple of shadows fall. We were winning. Before the smoke had fallen I had spied the only cover that there was. The ditch which ran alongside the road ran close by a wrecked shed. It might have been a home but there was little left of it. However, it afforded the best chance of cover. It was two hundred paces from our lines. They would have placed the machine gun here. From the Intelligence I had studied the machine gun they would be using would be the 7.62 Degtyarev DPM. It was popular with the Russians who had used it in the war but it's one drawback was its magazine. It used a forty-seven-shot drum magazine. At five hundred rounds a minute an operator had to use his ammunition wisely.

Our harassing rate of fire seemed to have an effect. It was the muzzle flashes of rifles I saw through the smoke. When the machine gun chattered I spotted it straight away. They were in the place I had suspected. The gunners fired short bursts. My men were hunkered down but I heard the bullets crack into the wood, metal and mud with which we had built our bunkers. Bullets skittered across the metal doors which protected our heads in my bunker.

"Haynes and Barton, drop four shells two hundred yards from our position and in the centre of the road."

"Sir!"

The road surface was not the best but any shells which exploded on it would send their fragments to the side. Even if the Koreans had protection at the front the side and rear would be exposed. Our rifles continued to crack. We were using up our ammunition but it was having an effect. I would worry about resupplying when we reached our boats. The two men on my mortar were good. They sent their four shells so quickly that the Koreans had no time to react and take cover. They spread the shells and I heard shouts, screams and the sound of metal on metal as the shrapnel struck the Korean weapons. There were shouts and screams and then the gun fell silent. The smoke began to thin and, as it did so I saw the Koreans dragging their wounded back down the road. I heard orders being shouted and I turned to Sergeant Heon.

"He said to fall back and dig in. I think we can expect another air strike, sir."

I looked out of the back of the bunker, "Not today. The light is too bad. They would have to fly low and that is risky. Unless these pilots are really good they would not risk a night attack. There is too much chance of them hitting their own men. Will these lads risk coming over at night?"

"They might, sir. There will be pride at stake. We have hurt them. They would have expected their flank attacks to work." He smiled, "I have an interest in military history. I have studied the campaigns against the Japanese."

"Then we will eat. Have the drivers make more tea and then boil up some water to make soup." We had bouillon cubes. The men would eat their cold rations but soup would make them feel like they had had a meal. The lads who had fought in the last war would put some of their rations and crackers in the soup."

"Sir."

"Williams, get on the radio and give Blackwood another lesson. Find out what is happening."

"Sir!"

I stepped out of the bunker. The air felt cooler but the smell of the smoke and gunsmoke hung in the air. From the west came the sound of artillery and tanks. There were other noises which could have been small arms fire but it was so far away as to be irrelevant. If the General lost then they would tell us and we would high tail it back to the sea. Going downhill I felt sure we could do it in less than two hours. "Captain Poulson, all sergeants, officers' call!" I hurried to the radio shack. It was further away from the North Koreans. I was relieved when all three of them appeared and looked unscathed. "How are we doing? Any casualties?"

Sergeant Major Thorpe said, "The machine gun sent some splinters of stone into our bunker, sir, but Pike dealt with the cuts. Nothing to worry about."

"Ammo?"

Captain Poulson said, "That is the problem. We have fourteen mortar shells left and the men are down to just over half of their .303 ammo. We have more Thompson ammo as we haven't used much."

"Sarn't Major, the Bren?"

"We have another six magazines. Just one hundred and eighty bullets, sir."

"Not enough. We will have to husband what we have. Sergeant Heon thinks that the North Koreans might come over tonight and I agree. We use small arms." The Bren gun crew and the mortar crew each had a Colt. Officially they were not supposed to have such weapons but Gordy Barker knew how useful they were and they had been surreptitiously issued. "Have the men paired up. One sleeps and one watches."

I looked over to where Sergeant Curtis' body had been. Sergeant Major Thorpe saw me looking and said, "I had the Korean drivers move Jimmy's body into the lorry sir. I have his tags."

"Thanks, Sarn't Major."

"You will need a sergeant, sir."

I nodded, "I will make Callow acting Sergeant."

"He is a good lad, sir." He paused, "So was Jimmy Curtis."

I nodded sombrely, "Yes Sergeant Major, we have had our first casualties and, unless help comes soon, we will have more."

Chapter 5

The steep-sided valley meant that nightfall when it came, descended far quicker than just down the road at the coast. It took me by surprise. After we had eaten I went around the men. I was still getting to know them. I smiled and made jokes where I could. I asked about equipment. I examined the dressings of those who had been wounded.

When I reached my section I said, "Williams, you and Blackwood to man the radio. One of you must be awake all night."

"Sir."

"Corporal Callow you are now an acting sergeant. I want you with me. We will buddy up. One of us will be awake throughout the hours of darkness."

"Sir, thank you, sir."

"The Koreans may try to attack us while we sleep. We haven't the luxury of booby traps. We will have to use the tins from the rations we had. String them together and, when it is completely dark, slip ten yards or so from our front and rig them. If they are the slightest bit careless then we will hear them. You hear any noise and be ready to fire."

Blair said, "Shouldn't we fire first and ask questions later… sir?"

"There may be elements of the South Korean Army and Rangers coming down this road. There is rough country to the north that they could use. The Rangers are experts at moving through rough country. If they can save South Korean troops they will. I will have Sergeant Heon stay here at the bunker. I will decide when we fire. If I am asleep and there is a noise then Acting Sergeant Callow will wake me."

I had the second watch. I dozed for an hour and then when I woke, I relieved Callow. I had my Colt ready as well as my Thompson. My commando knife was in my battle jerkin along with two grenades and my sap. I did not think I would need the sap but it was not very heavy and who knew when it might come in handy. "All quiet, sir, but you can have another couple of hours if you like."

I shook my head, "I have had enough sleep."

After he had slipped into the bunker I walked down my section of the defences and made certain my men were alert. They nodded as I passed. I relieved myself at the small latrine we had dug and returned to the bunker. I rested my hands on the lorry doors which made up the roof and I listened. There was little to see for it was pitch black. The sky was overcast. I heard nothing save a couple of Sergeant Major Thorpe's section chatting quietly. I could smell the dead bodies of the North Koreans but there was something else I could smell. I took out my Colt and my knife. I sniffed again. It was a human smell but not the smell of my men. I knew, from my time fighting Germans and Italians, that a man smelled of what he ate. This was not the smell of my men. I hissed, "Sergeant Heon!"

The Korean must have been cat napping for he rose like a wraith. "Sir?" It was a whisper. I tapped my nose with my knife and sniffed. He nodded and sniffed. I saw him frown. He mouthed, "K-O-R-E-A-N".

I said, quietly, "Callow, slip down the line and wake the lads. There is someone out there."

I put my head close to Sergeant Heon's. "Soldiers or refugees?"

He shook his head, "Not certain."

I placed my knife on the bunker and took out a Mills bomb. We needed a Very pistol. I should have brought one from the Fairmile. It was an oversight and it might cost us lives. Acting Sergeant Callow returned and nodded. He was a World War Two veteran and he had a Mauser HSc pistol. He took it out and, like me, placed a grenade before him. I was sure that I saw a movement.

Sergeant Heon said, quietly, "Let me try something, sir." I nodded. He spoke a few words in Korean. There was silence. He said, "North Korean!"

I took the pin from the grenade and tossed it high. I counted to three and shouted, "Grenade!" The three of us dropped down. The grenade exploded twenty yards away. I heard screams. "Open fire!"

Captain Poulson threw his own and shouted, "Grenade!" as my men opened fire with their pistols. I did not drop all the way down as the Captain was on the flanks. I saw, as his grenade flashed, that the Koreans had been caught crawling towards us. Even as the grenade took out four men close to the Captain a Korean face loomed up just five feet away. I brought up the Colt and the bullet almost took off his head. Callow's Mauser had an eight-shot magazine and he quickly fired four bullets into the surprised Koreans who, just a short time earlier, had been almost close enough to attack us. Muzzles flashed in the dark. Sergeant Heon picked up my Thompson and emptied half of the magazine. He had obviously never used one for although he aimed at the middle of the Koreans the kick made him fire higher. It proved an effective accident. They fled.

"Cease fire."

"Sorry, sir. I had no pistol and…"

"Don't worry, Sergeant Heon, you did alright although when time allows I will give you a lesson in how to use one. What did you say to them?"

He smiled, "I said, '*We have plenty of water and food. Come in.*' If they had been civilians they would have answered me. I just confused the soldiers. When there was no reply I knew. That and the fact I heard a pistol being cocked."

"Anyone hurt?"

Lance Corporal Pike shouted, "Private Marsh didn't duck quick enough. He has a piece of shrapnel in his cheek."

"Take him to the radio shack and ask Williams to tell the boat of the attack."

"Sir!"

"Acting Sergeant Callow watch here. Sergeant Heon, let's check the bodies." I holstered my Colt and slid my dagger into my boot. We clambered over the top of the barricade. The first ten bodies we found were all messy. A .45 bullet makes a large hole at close range. I took the pistols and ammunition from all of the dead. I found a rucksack on the back of one of the men and after emptying it I used that to carry the booty. Sergeant Heon went through their pockets for papers. We stopped when we were forty yards from our lines. There were fewer bodies there. I tapped Heon on the shoulder and we headed back to our lines. I counted twenty-two bodies. Some had been killed earlier but, along with the men killed on the flanks unless they were reinforced, they would not have enough men for a second attack.

Heon held up the papers he had taken. "These men were from the Fifteenth Division. They are the Forty Fifth regiment. They were only formed in March. It explains their youth and their lack of experience."

"Well done. You keep hold of that. Intelligence might find it handy." Captain Poulson and the Sergeant Major were waiting for me. "We have hurt them and I don't think they will come back again tonight. We will keep watch, just in case." I held up the bag I had brought back. "I found some pistols. They are either the Tokarev 68 or the North Korean version. They have the same ammunition but I don't think it will fit any of our weapons. Distribute them to the NCOs. We may need the firepower. Captain, go around and make certain that the chaps know this is not over yet. I will go and speak with Williams."

"Sir. We have been lucky so far."

"And I am not sure that luck will last. I have no idea how the battle is going to the west of us. We have heard no sounds of firing since it became dark. I need to check with base."

Blackwood was asleep when I entered. The Lance Corporal said, "He is a fast learner sir. I managed to get a couple of hours kip." I nodded. "Anyway sir, the General has held the attack up. A ship came today with troops. Not many and they have been rushed to help the General. General MacArthur has been appointed the commander of all the U.N forces in South Korea." It was news but it did not help us overmuch. "Task Force Smith, an American Division, is heading to somewhere called Taejon. They are trying to stop the Koreans there."

"Then it is unlikely that we will be relieved any time soon."

He nodded, "Yes sir. The lads on the boats are worried about us."

I smiled, "So am I, Lance Corporal Williams, so am I. Let me know if there is any more news. I will be in my bunker."

As I walked back to the bunker I began to wrack my brains for anything else we might do. I had one idea but it was a little gruesome. Captain Poulson was chatting to Sergeant Heon. "Well, sir? Any sign of relief?"

"Not in the short or medium term. We are like a boxer just waiting for the end of the round. I have a job for the lads on watch. It is not a pleasant one but it may help us in the long run. If we take the trousers and jackets from the dead North Korean soldiers we can fill them with soil and make them into sandbags. The soil is still wet from the monsoon."

"Good idea sir. It will keep them occupied."

"Sergeant Heon, we will keep watch a little further out. You have good senses."

"Thank you, sir. I don't know how I acquired them. I am a city boy!"

We stopped just twenty paces from our wooden wall. We could hear the Koreans even though they were a good six hundred yards from us. They had learned to respect our mortars. There were the moans of the wounded mixed in with what sounded like radio chatter. "Can you hear what they are saying, Sergeant?"

He shook his head, "The occasional word only sir; it sounds like they are calling in reinforcements."

That made sense. If the main assault was stalled then they had the opportunity to send men this way and outflank the main Republic of Korea forces.

Captain Poulson came along fifteen minutes after we had begun to watch. "Sir, all done. I had the men stack the bodies in front of the barricades." He shrugged. They are past caring and their bodies can slow down bullets."

"A little grim, Captain, but a good idea."

"Not mine, sir, Corporal Lowery's."

We were just turning to head back when Sergeant Heon hissed, "Sir, there are men coming. I can hear their boots. They are from the north."

I turned. I could see nothing for the night was still black. Yangsan lay to the north-west. The north was the woods. Was this the reinforcements? I shouted, "Stand to!" We hurried back over the barricade and I grabbed my Thompson. If this was reinforcements then we had to use every means possible to slow them down.

There was silence. Acting Sergeant Callow said, after five minutes where we had heard nothing, "Perhaps Sergeant Heon was hearing things, sir. I can hear nowt!"

"It won't hurt to wait. The sun should be up in an hour or so."

I peered into the dark. I saw a shadow moving and I cocked my Thompson. A voice said, quietly, "American Rangers coming in. Hold your fire!"

The voice sounded American but I remembered the fifth columnists in the war. "Come in slowly and hold your weapons above your head." I crept out of the back of the bunker. "Hold your fire but watch them!"

Eight shadows rose. I saw their rifles held above their heads. One said, "Jesus, there are bodies here!"

"Harris, shut up!"

"Yes, Captain!"

I recognised the signs of exhaustion as the Rangers climbed over our barricade. They looked thin. Their fatigues were both dirty and bloody. It was obvious that they were not Koreans. "Pike!" I shouted for my medic. "Captain Rogers?"

The officer leading them lowered his rifle and took my outstretched hand. "The very same. Jack Rogers. How did you know?"

"Major Hampton warned me. I am Major Harsker of the British Army."

He saluted, "Sorry sir."

I shook my head, "Let's not bother with that nonsense. I am a commando; we speak the same language. Sergeant Major, get a brew on and find some food for these chaps."

"Yes, sir. Collins, Miller, go to the lorry and see what you can dig up!"

"Sit down Captain you look all in."

"Yes, sir. I left fifteen men north of here. We ran out of food and ammo three days ago. We have been avoiding North Koreans. The South Koreans must have bugged out faster than my brother when the check arrives."

I saw Sergeant Heon move away. "My interpreter is South Korean Captain."

"Sorry, sir. I am tired. Do you have a cigarette? I could kill for one."

"Sorry I am a pipe man."

Sergeant Callow threw a packet at him. They were Capstan Full Strength, "Have these, sir, Jimmy Curtis won't be needing them."

The Captain caught them and looked at me. "One of my men bought it yesterday. The bodies you clambered over were the North Koreans who have been attacking us all day. There was an air strike and that was when we took casualties. Did you do what you were asked?"

He nodded as he took a deep drag on the cigarette, "Yes sir, blew up bridges, ambushed convoys but there were just too many of them and not enough of us. I left a lot of good men behind."

"I am afraid there won't be much relief here either. The main advance has stalled south of Yangsan. The North Koreans know how few men we have here. They will come and come in force."

Sergeant Major Thorpe said, cheerfully, "Tea up!"

"Tea!"

"Harris, drink it and be grateful!" He shook his head. "Moans like you wouldn't believe but a helluva fighter."

I pointed to the south of our position. "There is a lorry, sorry, truck there. You will find blankets and the like. Get your heads down when you have eaten. I will send a message to the Major that you are safe,"

He shook his head, "Some of us are safe! Tell him that most of my command are dead or prisoners."

We took them to the truck and Pike continued to tend to their wounds and injuries. I put my head into the radio room. "Get in touch with Major Hampton. We have Captain Rogers and seven of his men."

"Right sir!"

Captain Poulson was waiting for me. "We have more men to feed and they don't look to have ammunition."

"I know. There are still some rifles and machine guns out there. We will take those."

"Not much ammunition though sir."

"So long as they have a magazine each then it is more than we have already. Have the men collect what they can but go carefully. Dawn is coming and if the North Koreans called up reinforcements then we could be in trouble."

"Right sir. Sergeant Grant, have the men collect any weapons and ammo from the dead Koreans."

One of the Korean drivers came up to me and, bowing, handed me a cup of tea, "Thank you." He beamed. As I sipped the hot sweet tea I looked east and saw the first light of dawn. Sergeant Grant found two usable machine guns with forty rounds in two magazines, six rifles and a hundred rounds for them. They also found two Russian hand grenades. I gave those to Callow. He could work out how to use them. By the time the sun was up we were all in position. Our men had managed to make a few more sandbags. If we were not attacked then we would continue to make them. Dawn came and there was no sign of the enemy.

At nine a.m. a single Mustang flew overhead. He waggled his wings as he headed north and west. There was some desultory fire from our Korean neighbours but they missed. As he flew over Yangsan there was a burst of anti-aircraft fire. When he came back he headed south and then turned to fly low north and east across our front. Sergeant Major Thorpe said, "What is he up to?"

"Just a guess, Sergeant Major, but I think he is going to strafe the Koreans. It is what the Yaks should have done yesterday. It minimises the chances of us being hit."

The Mustang pilot knew his business and his guns ripped through the Korean camp and defences. I suppose we could have followed up and taken the camp and the Koreans but I had too few men as it was. I could not guard prisoners and defend the pass. The pilot waggled his wings as he banked to head back to Pusan. We had finished our improvised sandbags and eaten when Williams shouted, "Sir, I have a message from the base."

I saw Captain Rogers climb down from the back of the lorry. The few hours sleep appeared to have done him the world of good. As he approached me he said, "Now some OJ, a cup of coffee and steak and eggs would make me feel like I could go to war again!"

I laughed, "We can manage soup, spam and crackers." He shook his head. "Headquarters has been on the radio. We might have a better idea of what is going on."

Williams was busy writing something on a pad. His handwriting was not the best. As Williams said, "Out," he switched off the radio.

I looked at the scribble, "Williams, your handwriting is like the meandering of a drunken epileptic spider!"

"What sir?"

"Just tell me the message eh?"

"Oh, right sir!" I saw Captain Rogers smile. I suspected he had men like Williams too. "The General said that four companies of Rangers were expected." He stared at the word he had written and then said, with a question in his voice, "imminently?" My nod reassured him. "He hopes to relieve us in two days at the most. The Mustang reported a column heading from Yangsan. It looked to be half a regiment with two light tanks. That was it, sir."

"Thanks." Captain Rogers and I left the shack. "I have some captured Korean weapons for you and your chaps. I have nothing that will reload your M1 carbine. If you have any Colts or Thompsons then we have some of that ammunition." He nodded. "Officer's call!"

My NCO's and Captain Poulson joined us. Lance Corporal Pike handed a cup of something hot to the Captain. He smiled, "I know you don't like tea sir, this is Bovril! Put hairs on your chest sir."

Captain Rogers sniffed it and then sipped it. His eyes lit up, "Beef tea! Just what I needed!"

I gave the others the information I had received. They just nodded when I had finished. "So, we have to endure an attack by up to four hundred men. There will be tanks."

Sergeant Major Thorpe said, "We will have to save the mortars. We need to use them where they will do the most damage."

"Acting Sergeant Callow anything we can do with Mills bombs and those Korean grenades?"

He shook his head, "Sorry sir, both work on the principle of small charge and a case which easily breaks. We save them for when they rush us. I can, however, make some Molotov cocktails. The lads found some jugs and bottles. They were all empty but we have one spare jerrycan of petrol. I checked the lorry yesterday and we have more than half a tank left. We can make petrol bombs. The trouble is we have to be close enough to throw them."

Captain Rogers said, "I have just the man for that. Ranger Harris is a pitcher."

My men looked blank. I explained, "Baseball."

Sergeant Major Thorpe nodded, "Rounders for blokes!"

Captain Rogers gave an irritated look and then continued, "And he played quarterback at school. He has a good arm. He could send one forty yards."

"Then he can be the ace in the hole. We let them get close before we open fire. Their Yaks will have given them our numbers. They don't know we have reinforcements."

Captain Rogers laughed, "Kind of you to call us that!"

"If they have half a regiment then they might well try to flank us again. Your extra men will make the difference." I saw the despondent looks on all their faces but Captain Poulson's. He looked calm. "Look, light tanks mean a forty-five-millimetre gun. It means thinner armour. If this had been a T-34 then I would have jumped in the lorry and headed down the road. They must be saving their bigger armour for the General. We have a chance. It is a slim one but the Captain and I have been in worse positions in the last war. We don't have long. Captain, bring Ranger Harris to Acting Sergeant Callow. Callow, you decide the best place from which to attack the tanks and the time."

"Sir!"

I turned to Captain Rogers, "Sergeant Major Thorpe will give you and your men weapons. You decide where they go. Sergeant Grant, we need the wounded, the radiomen and the two drivers to be ready to fight. I want them as a mobile reserve under your command. If the Koreans get close and look like they are breaking through then you plug the gap. You better have Sergeant Heon with you to translate. When the threat is gone go back to the shack and regroup."

"Sir!"

That done I went to my Bergen to bring the rest of my ammunition. I laid the magazines out in the bunker. I still had two grenades and I put them within easy reach. That done I went outside and filled my pipe. I couldn't remember the last one I had smoked. As I lit it I remembered the pipe was one Mum and Dad had given to me just before the end of the war. I had brought it because it had a good bowl and was an easy smoker. It was well worn in. As I puffed on the whisky soaked tobacco I realised that I had had no time to think of England or my family. I suddenly felt guilty. They would be worried sick about me and I had not

Korea

given them a second thought. I was back to being a soldier and that drove all other thoughts from your head. Those who retained them did not last long.

I had almost finished when Sergeant Major Thorpe shouted, "Stand to! Enemy ahead!" He pointed down the road and I saw the T-70 tank as it trundled down the slope. It was an old tank and the Russians no longer used them. They were slow, had thin armour and a small gun. They were good enough for their Korean allies and, to be fair, stood a good chance of rolling over us. On the positive side, we now had more protection. The improvised sandbags would slow down shells. My men had also used more of the burned-out lorry to add a roof to their bunkers and fox holes. Only the mortar crew were exposed.

"Williams, tell base there are tanks and we are under attack!"

"Sir!"

Captain Rogers slipped into the bunker with me. Sergeant Callow and Harris were with Sergeant Grant and the reserve. My bunker was actually on the road. Not only that it was the centre of the road. The whole of the front of the barricade which crossed the road was made up of four beams from the houses of Sason-Ri. The houses may have been flimsy looking but they had sound structures. Callow and Williams had found rocks on the first day and they were also behind the sandbags and before the wood. Captain Rogers patted the wood, "That looks solid enough."

"It will need to be. Those two tanks will be coming directly for us."

The Captain had one of the captured submachine guns. He had just twenty rounds for his newly acquired weapon. I gave him two of my magazines for his Colt automatic. We had spoken of the problems of ammunition while we had eaten. He had not been in the last war and he listened with interest when I told him how we had made a point of getting hold of as many weapons as we could. As we waited I told him about my nine millimetre back on the boat. He nodded appreciatively. "Nice weapon."

I nodded, "A little bigger than the Tokarev but reliable as any weapon I have ever used. This one has never jammed and does not kick. The trouble is ammo."

Our conversation was ended as the leading T-70 opened fire with its main gun. It was a crack. The gunner had not allowed for the fact that he was on a sloping road and I heard the shell whistle over our heads. The crew compounded their error by opening fire with their machine gun. At a range of eight hundred yards, it wasted bullets. They only had a thousand per tank. I wondered if they were trying to unnerve us. I took out the glasses and saw that the Koreans were crowding behind the tanks. "Haynes, when the tanks are three hundred yards away give them four rounds."

"Sir."

"The odds on hitting the tanks are slim, sir."

"But the men around the tanks will be concentrated together. A perfect target for a two-inch mortar. And, if these crews are inexperienced then shrapnel cracking into their hull will worry them a little."

The bullets from the tank's machine gun finally began to hit the sandbags. We felt each one as it struck but none penetrated. It became clear that the main attack would be up the road and behind the tanks. If this had been the last war I would have used my numbers for a flank attack but then I had been fighting against some of the best soldiers in the world, the Germans. The gunner corrected his aim and one shell hit the barricade close to where Evans and Black were. There were moans.

Ken Thorpe shouted, "Pike, get Evans and Black to the radio shack. Hope and Wilson fill the gap."

The Korean tank's machine gun shifted to the left to fire at my men who were rescuing their wounded comrades and repairing the barricade. The Korean soldiers also wasted their ammunition. They were four hundred yards from us. I saw the muzzle flash from the Korean tank stop. It was either jammed or out of ammunition. As its consort was twenty yards behind they could not bring their gun to bear.

We had been here long enough to know yardage. Each time I had been beyond the barricade I had paced it out. Haynes and Barton had done the same. Captain Rogers was not expecting the mortar shell but I was. Their first, ranging shot was about ten yards too long but, even so, it still landed between the tanks. It tore through the men there. The next three came in rapid succession. Without looking I knew that the two crew would have dived back into their foxhole. They were not on the road and they had a nest in which to hide. Even as the three shells landed between the tanks to slice through flesh and to ping off the tanks' armour I saw the main gun swivel to take out the mortar crew. When I heard the explosion, I knew that it had hit behind us. I heard the half-demolished building on the right of our position disintegrate as the shell hit.

Even at the sedate speed of the old Soviet tank, they were still drawing closer. Had they not used all the bullets from the tank's machine gun then we would have had to endure a fusillade which might well have hurt us. The mortar shells had made a hole between the tanks and men had to race from the second tank to fill the gap. All the time they were drawing closer to us and were only able to fire the main gun. The second tank began to fire too but it had to fire to the side of its consort. My men there were well dug in and their defences had yet to be tested. The leading tank fired at the Sergeant Major's men and the other at Captain Poulson and his men. The result was that although the tanks were coming for us there was little firing in our direction.

Acting Sergeant Callow had been in World War Two and his experience showed through. I heard him say, from behind the bunker, "Right Harris, follow me. Remember I light 'em and you chuck 'em!"

The New Yorker said, "With you Sarge! Let's give these sons of bitches hell."

Ranger Harris was a big man and the roof of the bunker banged alarmingly as he used it to jump forward. I aimed my Thompson towards the tank which was now one hundred and fifty yards away. I had it set to single shot. The two seemed to bear a charmed life as they ran towards the tank. Then I saw the hatch of the T-70 open and a head and machine gun appeared. I took aim and squeezed off three quick bullets. One must have hit for the gun clattered off the front of the tank and the body and head lay half out of the turret. I saw Callow stop and light the first of the Molotov cocktails. The tanks kept coming. Ranger Harris hurled his first one as Callow lit the second. The first exploded just five yards in front of the tank. The flames leapt up and over the tank. It did no damage that I could see but the driver must have panicked for the tank began to turn. The second bomb hit the tank on the side. I saw that there were two bombs left. Harris and Callow threw them even as the second bomb engulfed the light tank. I saw Callow grab Harris' arm and physically pull him away from the burning tank. Inside I could hear shouts for Callow's bomb had hit the sloping front of the tank and the burning petrol had hit the driver's side. Ranger Harris stumbled over one of the Korean bodies we had left. Callow picked him up and threw him over the barricade to our right. As he dived to safety the fire ignited the petrol tank of the T-70. The tank seemed to rise in the air. I pushed Captain Roger's head down as I ducked. The wall of hot air and fire roared towards us. Had we not ducked then we would have been burned.

I heard Ken Thorpe shout, "Haynes, four shells, rapid fire. Section three open fire."

"To my left, I heard Captain Poulson shout, "Section Two rapid fire!"

I lifted my head. My men had no target. We had a burning tank a hundred and twenty yards from us. It had slewed to the side. We would be wasting bullets. The mortar shells caused mayhem for one managed to hit the second tank. The bullets from the two sections hit the Koreans who were trying to escape the inferno that was the T-70. The open hatch had allowed burning petrol to enter the interior. Shermans were called Ronsons but it looked as though the T-70 ran it a close second.

The second tank began to fire blindly. I heard the shells striking behind us. Ken Thorpe shouted, "Cease fire!" The smoke and the fire meant we were wasting precious bullets.

"Cease fire!" Captain Poulson's voice silenced the rest of our guns.

The only sounds were the burning of the tank, the moans of the wounded and the crack of the tank's gun. Sergeant Grant's voice roared, "Incoming! Mustang! Take cover!"

He and the reserve were well back from the barricade and he must have seen the flight of Twin Mustangs as they roared in. The second tank was almost two hundred yards away from us but the pilots were good. The first four rockets hit the second tank and it exploded. The other two used their machine guns to strafe the Koreans. I saw them bank and come in across our front. The second three used their rockets on the trucks the Koreans had brought. I could not see them until they exploded. Then the Mustangs waggled their wings as they soared south and east down the valley. Unlikely as it was we had survived a tank attack!

Chapter 6

Captain Rogers looked at the Korean gun. "And I never even had to fire my gun!"

"We were lucky and it was thanks to your aeroplanes!"

We crawled out of the back of the bunker. I saw Pike attending to Ranger Harris. His face had been struck by flying shrapnel. He had an ugly wound. Sergeant Thorpe and Captain Poulson emerged from their holes. I saw Evans and Black. Evans had a bandage around his head and Black had his left arm in a sling. He was smoking but they were both laughing. Evans had changed. Taking him away from Blair had been a good move. I saw that Sergeant Grant was bending over a body. There was no sign of Williams. Had he been hit? As I neared the Sergeant I saw that it was Private Marsh. He had taken the full impact of a forty-five-millimetre shell. Sergeant Grant shook his head, "It was quick sir. He didn't duck quick enough."

The rest of my men were emerging. Blair pointed an accusing finger at me, "That was murder! He was wounded and shouldn't have been asked to fight."

"Blair, back off and cool down before I put you on a charge!"

In answer, he bunched his fists and ran towards me. Evan's leg darted out and tripped him. He landed in a heap. Sergeant Grant and Sergeant Major Thorpe ran to him and lifted him to his feet.

Sergeant Grant put his face close to the commando, "You are on a fizzer my son!"

"Stick him in the lorry, Sergeant Major. We have not got time for this nonsense right now." I confess that I could not understand Blair's reaction. I turned. The North Koreans were hurrying back to the original Korean camp. We knew where it was for they stopped moving but we could not see it as it lay in dead ground. The tanks continued to smoulder and burn. The bodies nearby were charred lumps.

Captain Rogers shouted, "Sergeant Steinla, take some men and collect any weapons and ammo from the Koreans. Watch yourselves."

"Sir!" With the exception of Ranger Harris and Captain Rogers, most of the Rangers appeared to be short stocky men. Sergeant Steinla was no exception.

"Captain Poulson let's rebuild the defences. They may be back. Williams, tell base what happened and thank them for the air strike."

"Sir."

One of the Korean drivers, I had learned their names now and he was Private Ha-ram Kang, brought me a cup of tea. He grinned and said, "No sugar!" I saw Sergeant Heon smile. He must have told him of my preferences. We were building a unit. Would we survive another attack?

Captain Poulson came over. "It is fortunate they didn't send a T-34. It would have been all over."

I pointed to the sky, "And we have not had the Yaks back today. They will come. Had they coordinated their attacks we might have suffered." I looked at the body of Private Marsh, "More than we did."

Sergeant Heon was close by, "Excuse me, sir, but I think the North Koreans surprised themselves by their rapid advance. They are now fighting Americans and English." He smiled, "We fought a guerrilla war against the Japanese. You fought a war against tanks and it shows."

I nodded, "Have Sergeant Major Thorpe check on the rations. We have more mouths to feed now."

Captain Poulson nodded, "And any food they were carrying is now toast!"

The enemy had not returned by early afternoon. Williams got in touch with the Fairmile and discovered that there had been another battle fought to a draw on the road from Yangsan. The troops who had landed were being fed into the line there. We were a sideshow. As I lit my pipe and surveyed the detritus of the battle I realised that we had a problem. There were two burned out tanks less than a hundred and forty yards from our lines. We had, unwittingly, given them cover.

Captains Rogers and Poulson joined me. "My guys are happier now that they have weapons and ammo. Do you think they will come again?"

"You are the ones who have been in Indian country. What do you think?"

"I think they are in the end zone and there are just minutes left. Yes, sir. I think they will try to push us out. We are hanging on by our fingertips."

"Then we have a long couple of days. You take over here, Captain Poulson. I had better go and speak with Blair."

"What was that guy's problem, sir? I thought he was going to hit you with a haymaker!"

"I don't honestly know. One of his mates was killed but his reaction?" I shrugged, "I will try to find out."

Sergeant Grant was sat with Blair who still glowered. His weapons had been taken from him. The bodies of Curtis and Marsh were covered in some material my men had found in one of the deserted houses. "Have Private Black come to act as a guard."

"Sir." Sergeant Grant stared at Blair, "Whatever the Major does, Blair, you are finished. No one threatens an officer."

"Arse licker!"

I thought Sergeant Grant was going to hit Blair, "That will do, Sergeant."

"Yes sir, sorry sir."

As he descended I said to him, "We won't need your reserve section. Put them on the line. I will keep Sergeant Heon with me."

"Yes, sir."

When he had gone Blair gestured after him and said, "That's what you toffs like isn't it? The poorer classes knuckling our foreheads and saying yes sir no sir, three bags full sir! It makes me sick. I thought when we had a Labour Government then all that would end! We need a stronger Government to put the likes of you in their places; beneath the working man!"

I ignored the rhetoric for that was all it was. "You are in serious trouble, Private Blair, and I would like to find out what prompted it."

He leaned back against the side of the lorry and lit a cigarette. He had a sly look on his face. "I never touched you... sir."

I leaned over and flicked the cigarette from his mouth, "I didn't give you permission to smoke! I have witnesses and they saw your threatening behaviour. You can't wriggle out of this one but there may be mitigating circumstances."

He glared at me, "I am saying nothing! I will sit here and do my porridge while the other daft buggers get killed and for what? To support a pathetic little regime from those who should rightfully rule it!"

He was spouting Communist propaganda. Black arrived, "Watch him, Private Black. He only leaves here to go to the toilet. We will have his food sent."

"Yes, sir." I saw that Black had armed himself with a captured Tokarev pistol. It would be easier to keep Blair covered. I did not think he would try anything but Black was being cautious and I liked that.

The North Koreans came again in the late afternoon. They used their numbers this time. They came in a long line and they darted from cover to cover. There were now tanks and bodies littering the ground. They used classic light infantry tactics. One ran while the other fired his weapon to give cover. The bullets did little or no damage for we were behind cover and we did not return fire. We needed to conserve our .303 ammunition. The handguns we had taken had a good rate of fire but they would be for the time they closed to within forty paces. The submachine guns we would fire at a hundred yards. Until then we endured the bullets which zipped over our heads. We had ten mortar shells and they would be used judiciously.

When they reached the tanks, they set up a machine gun. It began to chatter and the bullets slammed into the sandbags. The fact that we did not return fire seemed to encourage them. A Korean voice shouted and Sergeant Heon said, "They are going to charge, sir!"

"Prepare to fire!"

I heard safeties clicking and bolts loading bullets. The Koreans came at us in a double line. They wasted bullets by firing while they were running. I heard Captain Poulson shout, "Mortar crew, target the machine gun. Four rounds of rapid fire!"

I had to judge this well. I remembered reading about the Imperial Guard charging the British at Waterloo. The five rapid volleys had been timed to perfection and the French had hit a wall of lead. I wanted the same effect.

I waited until they were just over a hundred yards away. "Open fire!" I had my Thompson and I emptied a magazine. Captain Rogers emptied his Soviet weapon and then I grabbed my Colt and emptied the magazine too. Finally, and with the Koreans just thirty yards away, I pulled the pin from a grenade and shouted, "Grenade!" Captain Rogers dropped his Tokarev, pulled the pin on my last grenade and just lobbed it five yards. We ducked down. The first explosion deafened us and pieces of shrapnel pinged off the roof of our little fort. When the second one went off, much closer this time, the shrapnel was worse and the concussion so bad that my ears hurt.

On our flanks, the other two sections and the Americans attached to them continued to fire. I slowly raised my head. Before me was a charnel house. I peered out into a silent world for I could hear nothing. In my ears was a whistling. The grenade sent by Captain Rogers had completed the work begun by mine. I took out my Colt, reloaded it and looked for targets. One Korean officer had miraculously survived although I saw blood coming from his right ear. He picked up a submachine gun. He was less than fifty yards from me. Resting on the wooden beam and holding my pistol in two hands I squeezed off a single shot. I hit his nose and he fell backwards. The Korean machine guns had been silenced. The mortar crew had done their work.

Even as my hearing returned I saw the Koreans pulling back. Their flanks had fared better but they had still lost men and the massacre on the road had weakened their resolve. "Cease fire! Conserve ammunition." In truth, we had few targets. The Koreans headed for the two tanks and the woods. Bullets would have been wasted.

"Lance Corporal Pike see to the wounded. Captain Poulson and Sergeant Major Thorpe, command bunker. Williams, tell the boat we have repelled another attack."

I crawled from the back of the bunker. This time we had been hurt. I saw not only Pike tending to the wounded but anyone who had been close to friends tending to those who had been hit. Billy Kenny was bandaging Ben Burrows hand. Harry Evans, himself wounded in an earlier attack, was bandaging John Carter's head. The two had been under the sway of Blair and now they were mates. It was a strange world. Captain Rogers emerged. I shook my head, "You are a mad bugger, Captain!"

He grinned. "It worked didn't it, sir!"

"When I get my hearing back I will let you know."

"Who did we lose?"

"Hutchins bought it and we have six wounded." Sergeant Major Thorpe said, "Sir, two of your men bought it." He handed over the dog tags. "Sorry. They didn't keep their heads down when the machine gun started."

Captain Rogers looked at the tags, "Kaplinsky and Wagner. Both were good guys. I can think of others, back home, who weren't. They are alive and two heroes are dead."

I nodded, "It is in the nature of war, captain. It is the good ones who go to war and the ones who sit at home reap the benefit. Exactly the same as in England."

"This is my first war, sir. I am learning."

"Have the men fed. Clear the weapons and ammo from the enemy. We will leave their bodies there."

Sergeant Grant shook his head, "Sir, it stinks now. It will only get worse."

I shrugged, "We have men who are tired already. Lugging the dead around, Sergeant Major might be the straw that breaks the camel's back.

I want one man in three on watch tonight. I will go and check with Williams and then Black."

"It is a waste having Blair watched, sir. Where can he go? We could use Black on the line."

"Nevertheless, Captain Poulson, we will go by the book. Blair is a barrack room lawyer. I want to give him no grounds to wriggle out of this." As I headed to the radio shack I reflected that I could do without the distraction that was Blair. "Well, Lance Corporal?"

"I told the boat. They said that the main column has held the Koreans but the General was waiting until Task Force Smith arrives. They have battleships and their shells can reach the east coast supply route to Yangsan. The Ranger ship is unloading now. There is little transport sir. The lad on the radio reckons that the earliest they could be with us is tomorrow afternoon."

"Then we hold until then. Blackwood, are you ready to go back on the line?"

"Yes, sir. I can work the radio now but I would rather do my bit with the other lads."

I headed to the lorry. The back flap was down. That made sense for with shrapnel flying around it would give some protection. When I lifted it I saw Private Black. He was lying on the floor and his Tokarev had gone. "Lance Corporal Pike, Sergeant Grant!" I put my hand on Black's neck. He was alive but the wound looked to be a bad one. There was a great deal of blood. I saw the weapon Blair had used to effect his escape. It was a piece of the pallet on which we had brought the rations. The rest had been used to light a fire under the dixie.

Pike appeared first. He pulled himself up and then opened the back flap to allow in more light. Sergeant Grant arrived a few moments later. "Blair has gone. Organise a search for him."

"He will be long gone, sir."

I shook my head, "Think about it, Sergeant. Where would he go? This is Korea! He can't exactly hitchhike home."

"Sir."

As he ran off I turned to Pike. "He will live, sir, but Blair tried to kill him. Black is a popular lad. If Blair is found…"

"If he is found he will be taken back to the boat for a court-martial. We may be fighting with the Americans but this is not the Wild West!"

He smiled, "No sir." He continued to work on the young Commando.

"You are the medic, Godrey, what made him do what he did?" The medic was silent. "Come on Lance Corporal. Do not hide it from me. Spit it out."

He looked at me, "Sir, I don't want to get anyone else in trouble. He is gone and good riddance. I hope he steps on a land mine and does us all a favour."

"Lance Corporal!"

"Sir, being a medic is like being a priest. You find out stuff which is private."

I realised that I was being unfair. Pike was not being insubordinate. I modified my voice as he finished bandaging Black's head. He laid him on his side, gently. "If this has nothing to do with the military efficiency of the troop then it will go no further."

Pike's eyes were sad, as he said, "And what about the law of the land sir?" I took out my pipe and began to fill it. When I had it going, I nodded. "Sir, Blair and Marsh, they were, well, a couple. Do you understand me?"

Suddenly it all became clear. Blair's reaction had been that of someone losing a loved one. Their relationship was against the law. Attitudes were not as harsh as they had been. It did not bother me but there were others in the troop who would be unhappy. "But Marsh is dead and Blair has done a runner. Who else could be affected?" He said nothing. Sometimes just smoking a pipe clarified the thought processes. "There are others in the troop."

Black began to stir, "Like I said sir being a medic is like a priest. I have broken no confidences and if you ask me more, sir, I will respectfully decline to answer."

I stood. "You are a good man, Pike, and I respect your views. I would not dream of invading a man's private life. Good God, my job is hard enough as it is."

I headed back to the command bunker. Sergeant Grant and Sergeant Heon approached. "Find him?"

"Sort of. Tell him, Sergeant Heon."

"Sir, when the battle was raging Private Ha-ram Kang, went to get more ammunition from the truck. He saw Private Blair running from the vehicle."

"And he ran down the road to the coast?"

"No sir, he ran to the Koreans. Private Ha-ram Kang saw him surrender to them."

I had already had one shock and this one seemed too incredulous to believe. I nodded, "Thank you and thank Private Ha-ram Kang for being so observant."

I reached Captain Poulson and Sergeant Major Thorpe. "Blair has surrendered to the Koreans." Their silence was eloquent. "Keep it to yourselves. It won't do morale any good to make it public knowledge but it will get out. The only good news is that we don't need to worry about him anymore. Private Black will recover."

Captain Poulson said, quietly, "But he knows how little we have in terms of men and ammunition. If the Koreans bring up more armour then…"

I shrugged, "We can't do anything about that. Has everyone been fed and watered?"

"Yes sir, although the tea is getting low!"

I smiled. The British soldier could endure almost anything and bear all manner of hardship but deprive him of his tea and his world would come to an end. "Eke out what we have. What Blair does not know is that we should be relieved by tomorrow. Rangers will be marching up the road. We hang on until then. Make sure that everyone has plenty of ammo. We need to make it last just another sixteen hours."

"Sir." Ken Thorpe handed me a Lee Enfield. I knew before he gave it to me that it was Blair's. "Sir when we took Blair's gun I examined it. There is still grease from the factory. He never fired it. I looked at Marsh's. He didn't either. Maybe they were both going to desert. They certainly didn't defend the camp with the other lads. If I could get my hands on him…"

"He is long gone but if we do catch him then I want him to face military justice. Understand?"

"Yes, sir."

"Yes, sir and one more thing?"

"Yes, Captain?"

"Get your head down. Go and have a nap now, sir. You need it."

"Yes sir, the Captain is right. You have a plate full and that's no error."

"Perhaps I will. Take command, Captain, and I will be in the lorry."

Evans, head bandaged and smoking cheerfully waved as I passed him and Carter, "We showed the buggers eh sir? They can come again and we will send 'em back again."

I nodded, "You did well. You both did well." I saw Evans swell with pride and Carter give me a shy smile. Suddenly so much became clear. Pike's words made sense. I should have seen it myself. Perhaps that clarity of vision helped me to understand Blair. As I climbed into the back of the lorry I could see the sequence of events. Perhaps Blair had always intended to defect for that was what this was, a defection and not a desertion. The words of L in London became clear. There were Communist agents in England at the War Office. Why should they not have infiltrated the army? Marsh and Blair would have had a much better and safer life in a Communist country. Marsh's wound and untimely death had spoiled their original plan. I would not put it past the Communists to have planted the two men in my troop to sabotage our work. If L was right then there were men high up in the War Office. How easy would it have been to slip two agents in with the rest of my men? I needed to send a report to Major Foster. I curled up and with unpleasant thoughts racing around my head I dozed.

I was woken by Acting Sergeant Callow. "Sir, the Captain sent me. There is movement out there."

I looked at my watch. I had been asleep for four hours. "Why did no one wake me?"

"You were tired sir. There was nothing happening. You'll be better for sleep." He handed me a mug of tea.

I drank as I hurried to the command bunker. Captain Poulson said, "We have everyone on the line." He did not add the reason. That would not help our men. The Koreans would try to overwhelm us.

"Get to your positions. Where is Captain Rogers?"

"He said he would fight with his own men as he has so few left. The dead men hit him hard sir."

"Thanks, Paul."

Acting Sergeant Callow said, "I have cleaned and loaded your guns, sir. There are just eight grenades left and I have spread those out along the line. The Korean Sergeant is with his mates."

"Thanks, Roy. It is like the Alamo. Men are fighting with their mates because they think we won't survive."

"Perhaps but we aren't done yet, are we sir?"

The early warning system had long been destroyed by shell, bodies and fire. Nature and the time of year came to our aid. The nights were still relatively short and there were no clouds. Acting Sergeant Callow nodded, "There will be a moon tonight, sir."

"You could be right Acting Sergeant and if there is then we have a chance."

I cocked the Thompson. My thoughts were still on Blair and the damage he had caused. Men could die now. That would be on me. I had had the chance to leave him in Basrah and I had declined the opportunity. Now my act of forgiveness had come back to haunt me. At least I had saved Carter and Evans. I would have to concentrate on the positives.

Darkness fell as did silence. The battle on the road to Yangsan could still be heard. Occasional eighty-five-millimetre shells and the crack of small arms was a background noise which I tried to filter out. I was listening for the creak of shoes. The scrape of a gun over metal. I was trying to hear the breathing of a Korean who was trying to get close enough to lob a grenade into my bunker. I would need fast reactions. If a Korean was faster then I would be dead and my children without a father.

The noise, when it came, was close to the Rangers. They were in the gap between my men and Sergeant Major Thorpe's. I had had the largest section but I now had just six men under my command. The sound was a strangled cry. Was it one of Rogers' men or a Korean? No one shouted, 'open fire'. We waited.

Then I heard, "Grenade!" from the direction of Captain Poulson's section to the left of my position. I dropped so that my eyes were level with the opening. I saw the flash and the Koreans highlighted by it. They were forty feet away and had been crawling over the dead bodies.

"Open fire!" I aimed the Thompson towards the ground and fired short bursts as I traversed from left to right. Acting Sergeant Callow had a submachine gun too and the two of us cleared the ground before us. As I clicked on empty I dropped the submachine gun. The Koreans were now close enough to throw grenades. I heard one bounce off the metal roof of the bunker. We both dropped to the ground. Pieces of metal zipped over my head and my ears rang with the concussion. I picked up the Colt and as I raised it I saw a Korean sergeant just thirty feet from me. He was arming his grenade. It was an RGD 33. He had to twist the cap to arm it. The action took longer than a German grenade or a Mills bomb. I aimed my Colt. I knew when he had armed it for he pulled back his right arm. I fired two shots into him and he fell back. There was a slight delay and then the grenade exploded. He must have had a fragmentation sleeve fitted for pieces of the grenade rattled off the wood of my bunker.

Korea

Acting Sergeant Callow had fitted a second magazine to his Russian gun. He sprayed to the left, closer to Captain Poulson and his men. The moon finally rose and bathed the battlefield as though it was daylight. The Lee Enfield rifles were more accurate and they began to pick off the officers and sergeants. A whistle sounded and they began to fall back. We had beaten off another attack. As it was night time we did not move. I just shouted, "Hold our positions. They may come again!" I reloaded my guns and saw that we had no more grenades and I was down to one magazine for each of my guns. One more attack would finish us off. We waited for the final attack.

In the end, they did not come. We stood to all night but as dawn broke a flight of Mustangs flew over and strafed the Korean position. We had survived despite the traitor.

Chapter 7

We had lost more men. David Miller had been killed. We had more men wounded than not. Even Sergeant Major Thorpe had a shrapnel wound. It was not the Rangers who relieved us but the 7th Infantry. They marched up into the village in good order despite a night march after a sea voyage. Lieutenant Burbank, who led the advance guard, saluted, "Sir, the Colonel's compliments. He wants us to scout ahead."

I said, "I would go carefully, Lieutenant, there is half a regiment up there."

He looked around as my men, dirty and dishevelled, appeared from their holes. He looked at the burned-out tanks. "You stopped them with just these men, sir?"

Captain Rogers shook his head, "Lieutenant, we are the Commandos and the Rangers. We stopped them but we paid a price."

"Sorry, sir. Sergeant, skirmish order. Jones, run back to the Colonel and tell him that there are Koreans ahead of us."

"I should warn you that there are lots of dead Korean bodies ahead. Some of your younger lads might be in for a shock."

"Sir."

As they hurried off Captain Rogers said, "Jeez what did they expect?"

"To be fair, Jack, they are just off the boat and if you were told that a detachment of men were holding a small village then you would not expect this would you?"

"I guess you are right. I have been here for ten days and it feels like a lifetime. I have a lot of letters to write when we get back to base."

"And it never gets easy. I have four to write too." He nodded, "Sergeant Major Thorpe, we will be heading back soon. Get the lorry packed. It will be crowded. The Captain can come with me and Williams in the jeep. Sergeant Heon can be in the lorry."

We had bodies to transport. We would want our dead buried properly. "Sir. Sergeant Grant, come with me."

"Lance Corporal Williams, you will be in the jeep. Put the radio there now."

"Sir."

I turned as the American infantry began to open fire. They had grenade launchers and the Lieutenant showed that he was not as green as he had appeared. As the grenades landed his automatic weapons began to fire. He had the luxury of ammunition. I heard the sound of boots pounding up the road. It was a company, led by a Captain and they were running. We stood aside as they ran by. The Captain threw a hurried salute at me. Our men were heading down to our lorry. I saw some of the younger ones looking at the place they had called home for a few days. Private Collins had a particularly thoughtful expression. He and Private Miller had shared a foxhole. Miller was dead and he was alive. I knew that feeling. It brought a man's mortality home to him.

The Lieutenant Colonel was about my age. He and his adjutant, along with a veteran Sergeant Major, stopped and saluted when they reached the two Captains and myself. "Colonel Franklin." He held out his hand, "You did a damned fine job, Major."

I nodded, "Your air force saved our bacon sir." I pointed north, "There is a stream there for water sir and very little else." I gestured with my thumb behind me. "Your Lieutenant is assessing the opposition!"

He laughed, "This is our first deployment, Major. We are all learning how to go to war. Major Hampton said you were in the last one; won a V.C."

"Yes, sir."

He nodded, "Lucky you were here then. Sergeant Major, let's start to make this home. Secure the perimeter and set up headquarters."

The Sergeant Major had as gravelly a voice as I had ever heard, "Sir."

Looking at me the Lieutenant Colonel said. "We offloaded at that little port of Dongbaek-Ri. Our heavy gear is being landed at Pusan. Those twenty or thirty miles helped us. Our tents and artillery should be with us by the morning. We will have to rough it for a day or so." He laughed, "Why am I telling you this? You guys rough it all the time. Sorry Major, you guys look like you need some R & R."

"I don't think our North Korean friends will allow us time, sir. I am guessing we will be off again in the next day or so."

He seemed to see Captain Rogers for the first time and he nodded, "I forgot what your day job was." He stood to attention and saluted, "Good luck guys!"

We returned his salute and then he hurried up the road with binoculars already in his hand. Williams was already at the jeep. He had managed to use the rope to secure the radio behind the back seat. He had tied his Bergen above it. I saw the men loading the lorry. Acting Sergeant Callow waved, "I have your Bergen and guns sir!"

"Thanks!"

Captain Poulson climbed in the back after tying his Bergen to the bonnet. I saw Captain Rogers throw him a look of curiosity. "When we used jeeps and Kubelwagen we found that a Bergen acted as a little piece of protection and gave a little more room in the jeep."

Williams said, "Sorry sir. I like cars and the like. I was worried we might overheat the engine."

"You know engines then?"

"Yes, sir. Like fiddling with them."

"Good. That may prove useful." I smiled as I started the jeep. "Don't worry Lance Corporal you will learn all these little wheezes and if you know engines too then that is a bonus."

I overtook the lorry and waited until Sergeant Major Thorpe waved at me. We set off down the road. Overhead the flight of Mustangs returned.

Captain Rogers said, "The Lieutenant Colonel said that you had a Victoria Cross?" I nodded. "A hero then?"

I shook my head, "Captain Poulson served with me for most of the war and he will tell you that there are more dead men who deserved a V.C. than those who were given the award. It is all luck and sometimes they give a medal to make a disaster seem like a victory."

"Captain, the Major is being a little self-effacing. He is a hero. He never asks one of us to do something he wouldn't but he is right about one thing, we left many friends in France, Germany and the Low Countries and a lot of them deserved more recognition than they got."

"Then how do you guys do it? I found it hard to watch my guys die."

"And when you get back, Jack, they will replace the men you lost and they will have to learn from scratch. Learning costs and some of those replacements will also die." He looked at me. I glanced at him and saw that he had not thought that far ahead. "Your question is a hard one to answer. I suppose you begin to do it for the guys you lead. I have three children at home and a wife I adore but since we arrived in Korea the guys in the lorry have become my family. The politicians and the writers of newspapers talk about King and Country, right and wrong but when you are at the sharp end of a firefight then it is the chap next to you who makes you fight and not run. You don't want to let them down. It is not heroism, it is friendship, it is loyalty to your team."

We were silent for the rest of the journey back to Dongbaek-Ri. I knew that, despite my words to Captain Rogers, my thoughts were back in England and my family. I would be back in harm's way soon enough and then they would be driven to the far recesses of my mind and tucked safely in my heart but for the rest of the journey I kept their faces in my head and I smiled.

Dongbaek-Ri had changed in the days we had been away. It was now a military compound. Our three small boats, not to mention the minesweeper, were dwarfed by the ships which were unloading vehicles and supplies. Captain Rogers shook his head, "The North Koreans don't know what is going to hit them. When Uncle Sam flexes his muscles then, brother, you had better watch out."

I knew what he meant. I remembered the build-up to D-Day. The roads around Southampton had been clogged with lorries and tanks heading to the port.

We headed for the compound first. The Rangers were using that as their base. Major Hampton saw our approach and we were allowed in before the convoy of supply trucks. "Sergeant Steinla, have the guys take their gear to the barracks."

"Sir."

We had all fought together and there were handshakes and goodbyes. I saw some exchanging addresses. Most would never be used. The intentions were good but the reality was that life often got in the way. Captain Poulson and I went with Captain Rogers to the admin building. Major Hampton grabbed Captain Roger's hand, "You and your guys did a great job, Jack."

"It cost me most of my men."

"But you saved this corner of Korea. If you and the Major here had not slowed down the enemy then the ships you saw landing men might still have been offshore. Replacements for you are on their way and we will try to give you a couple of weeks to bring them up to speed. Already the North Koreans are pulling back to a more defensible line further north. Taegu is where the fighting is now."

Captain Rogers might have gone into Indian country an innocent but he was now worldly wise. He nodded and said, "Yes sir!" but I knew that he was a little more cynical than he had been. "Sir I would like to put all of my men, but especially Ranger Harris, in for a decoration."

I said, "I concur, Major. Ranger Harris displayed great courage and but for his heroics then we might not have defeated the tanks."

Jack smiled his thanks at me.

"Well, we could sure do with some good news to give to the newspaper boys." This confirmed my view of the Major. He was a career officer. He was an American Colonel Foster.

Jack turned to me, "I daresay we will meet again. Thanks, Major. I learned a whole bunch of stuff from you guys. I hope I am a better soldier for it."

"You did well, Captain, and we might not have survived but for your men and their skills."

When Jack had gone the Major picked up a file. "Thanks for what you did but this," he tapped the manila folder, "is where the real work begins. Here are six targets for you. All have a priority next to them. We would like you to begin as soon as you can."

I handed the folder to Captain Poulson. "Sir, my men have had very little sleep for the best part of five nights. We have virtually no ammunition left. Six of my men have wounds. I do not think that you can expect us to begin to go behind enemy lines any time soon."

He smiled. It was a smile I had seen before. When Colonel Foster had been our master he had adopted it often. It was the smile which said I am your friend but I am going to give you an order which you won't be able to disobey. "There is ammunition, weapons and supplies on board your boats and you do not need to take all of your men. The first mission requires just one boat and a handful of men. So long as you have eight fit men it can be accomplished. The U.S. of A does not do things in half measure. Your barracks now has supplies, curtains and extra bedding." He smiled, "Winter will be here soon enough. There are explosives, .303 and .45 ammunition in abundance. We have more mortar shells and a PIAT on their way. For the first mission, you just need 523, your explosive expert and you."

I saw in his eyes that he had me. I was under his orders and had to obey them. "Very well, sir. We will be on our way then." My cold tone made his smile turn to a frown. I was too long in the tooth to be taken in by false overtures of friendship. I was here to do a job. We would do it.

Once outside Captain Poulson said, "No rest then, sir."

"There is for you and the rest of the men. I will take my section. You get the rest ready to go to war again." I tapped the folder. "Study the other missions and when I return you and Sergeant Major Thorpe can have them planned."

"But sir…"

I tapped the crown on my shoulder, "I am the leader. I get paid to lead." I got behind the wheel and we led the lorry back through the congested streets of Dongbaek-Ri to the barracks. "Get the men in the barracks. The Major said there were supplies. We need to give the men a shower and a hot meal. Rig up a shower. Today they do nothing. I will go and see Petty Officer Flynn and Lieutenant Drake. Williams, take my gear in for me."

"Yes, sir."

"Oh and get in touch with the Major. Our chaps and the Rangers need burying. They deserve a decent send-off."

"Of course, sir."

Picking the folder up I strode to MGB 523. Leading Seaman Wilkinson was on sentry duty. "Morning sir, good to have you back. It has been a bit quiet."

"Good to be back. I have missed the cocoa!"

"Skipper is in the mess with the Middy and the Yank!"

"Good!"

The three of them were poring over charts when I entered. Their faces showed the relief that I was back. I plopped the folder down on the desk. "No rest for the wicked, I am afraid. Our lords and masters want me out again ASAP!"

Midshipman Brown said, "That is not fair, sir. You have been at the front!"

Lieutenant Drake shook his head, "You will learn Middy that those above us see the bigger picture and we are just cogs in a war machine. Run along to the galley. Hopkins is on duty there. Get him to make a pot of tea for us and jug of coffee for the Petty Officer."

"Sir!"

"Coffee?"

Petty Officer Flynn grinned, "My prayers were answered, sir. Our supplies arrived two days ago!"

I nodded, "We lost four men, including Sergeant Curtis. I will be taking out a pared-down section. Callow is acting sergeant. The Major seems to think we can do the first job with minimum men. Let's see. He said the missions were prioritised." In the folder were six files. Each one was stapled to maps and there was a large number written on each one. I smiled as I took the one with #1 emblazoned in red letters two inches high. As I took out the staple I said, "No mistaking this one!"

There was a map and I recognised a bay some sixty miles north of us. There was a port there, Pohang. I pushed it across to Lieutenant Drake. He nodded, "As I recall it was a base the Japanese used for submarines during the war." He stroked his chin. "And as I recall there are South Korean forces just ten miles south of there."

I nodded as I read the brief. "That looks to be the target then."

The Lieutenant frowned, "But the North Koreans don't have any submarines."

I ignored him and read. The Midshipman came in with a tray and began to pour. I reached the bottom of the page. "No, but they have torpedo boats. There was a sea battle on the second of July. Your cruiser, Petty Officer Flynn, cruiser USS Juneau, the Royal Navy cruiser HMS Jamaica, and the Royal Navy frigate HMS Black Swan fought four North Korean torpedo boats and two mortar gunboats. The enemy were all destroyed. The chaps upstairs do not want them to be able to use the submarine pens to protect any other small craft."

I sipped the tea. We had been down to reusing old leaves at Sason-Ri. This was proper tea and I savoured it. Brown pushed over a plate of toast. I would have said hot buttered but I knew it would be margarine. Still, it would do. As I ate I watched the Lieutenant and the Petty Officer frown. They were sailors and I knew what problems they had seen. I ate a round of toast while looking at the aerial photographs and washed it down with tea. I smiled, "I know what you are thinking. Heading into that bay would be suicide. There are guns on the headland and in the port. 523 would be matchwood." The Skipper nodded. I jabbed my finger at a point to the east of the port. "From the aerial photographs, I think there are a few houses here and fishing boats. They will be South Korean. As far as I can tell the north has not fortified it. There is no road south. If this was taken in the last few days then it looks to me as though the villagers did not flee. We land there." I used my fingers on the map to estimate distance. "There is a small road here. It looks little more than a track. It is five or six miles from the base which is on the west side of the bay. They have an anti-aircraft battery here." I pointed to a point on the headland. "I can't see another military installation. We march there; plant the explosives and then toddle back to the boat. We can do that in four hours."

"It is an hour and a half up there, sir. The nights are not that long."

"We will have to leave in daylight. I don't want to risk being caught on the road in daylight."

The American looked dubious. "Two hours to march over unknown country, plant bombs and then escape? Seems a tall order to me, sir."

"And if I had not done this half a dozen times in France then I would have said the same. The difference then was that the Germans had men all over. Here the North Koreans are too busy trying to take South Korea to worry about consolidating what they have already. We can do it."

I pushed the map over so that the two seamen could see it and work out a route. I poured myself some more tea and then took out my pipe. I saw that the Petty Officer was desperate for a cigar. He glanced at the Lieutenant. Lieutenant Drake did not appear to look up but he murmured, "If you must then go ahead but not on deck, Mr Flynn!"

The American beamed, "Of course not sir."

"When do you want to leave?"

"The Major would want us to go now but the men need rest, food, a shower and then we need to re-equip. Tomorrow before dusk."

"Middy, see what the weather will be like and get the chief to check the fuel. I will tell Sub Lieutenant Guttridge that he is in temporary command. That will thrill him!"

Petty Officer Flynn sucked deeply on the cigar and gave a satisfied sigh. "What will you need, sir?"

"Explosives and detonators. Find Acting Sergeant Callow and ask him."

"Anything else sir?"

"We are all out of .303 and .45 ammo not to mention grenades."

"They didn't send Mills bombs sir, just U.S. issue grenades. They are good, sir," he added defensively.

"Of that, I have no doubt. They will do."

He nodded and slipped out of the mess. The Skipper sat back and lit his own pipe. We smoked in silence for a few minutes. It gave us both the chance to think. He said, "There is a good chance we will run foul of their aeroplanes. They have come here two or three times a day. So far we have only shot down one."

"Then, when we sail north, if your chaps open fire as soon as you see them then they might think that you are hunting them."

"They might at that. Good idea sir." He looked at the map again. "And what happens if you are not back in four hours, sir?"

"You leave an hour before dawn even if we are not back." Middy's mouth dropped open and I smiled, "If we are late then you go and we will make our own way back."

"Sir! Sixty miles through enemy territory?"

I nodded, "Yes Middy. Although there will be friendly forces closer than that. I have done it in France, Italy and Africa. It is all part of our training."

We spent an hour going through the details and then I yawned. The Lieutenant said, "Look sir you need some rest. I will go over the route and the terrain. We will pop over to the barracks at around seven." He smiled, "I have a bottle of whisky."

"Where from?"

"I did not ask Petty Officer Flynn but let us say he is resourceful. I am glad that he will be on the 523 when we sail."

I picked up most of the papers leaving just the map for the sailors. I had to brief my own men. I looked at my watch. They had had a good three hours. Some would be asleep but they would have eaten, shaved and showered. I only needed number one team along with the Captain and the Sergeant Major. As soon as I walked in I could see that they had begun to make it homelier. The curtains over the windows helped and there were more tables and chairs. We would all be able to eat around a mess table. Photographs of loved ones as well as football teams were on their lockers. The Sergeant Major would ensure that nothing was untoward. Half a dozen of my men were asleep. The NCOs and Captain Poulson were sat around the table. Only Acting Sergeant Callow was missing. I wondered where the rest were. Almost as though he was reading my thoughts Captain Poulson said, "Sergeant Heon and the two drivers offered to show the lads around Dongbaek-Ri."

"Dongbaek-Ri? That should take them about two minutes."

Polly shrugged. I put the folder on the table and pulled up a chair. "Number one section goes out tomorrow tea time. We have a mission sixty miles up the coast. We have to land, trek across six miles of enemy territory and then blow up some old sub pens."

They nodded. None of them would be on the mission but I know that they appreciated being told the details. Captain Poulson picked up the folder with the other targets. He scanned them and I lit my pipe. "It looks like this is the next one and that is in North Korea."

I roughly measured it. "That is almost two hundred miles!"

"Yes, sir. Quite a problem for three boats, especially as the 523 can do barely thirty knots."

"That will be something for you to wrestle with while we are up the coast. What are the other targets like?"

"Few are as far north as that sir." Captain Poulson held up a report. "The good news is that the North Koreans only have minesweepers and patrol boats. None are as well armed as an MTB. If we meet one, or even four or five we should be able to handle them. The problem will be the aircraft."

I nodded, "And the closer we are to North Korea the more likely it is that we will come under attack from their jets. They have a couple of MIGs and they are more than capable of blowing us out of the water. We cross that particular bridge when we come to it."

The door opened and Acting Sergeant Callow and Petty Officer Flynn struggled in with cases of explosives and detonators. "Wouldn't they be better on the boat, Acting Sergeant?"

"I need to check them over first sir and sort them out. I was going to put some on Captain Poulson's boat. If anything happens to me then all the eggs are not in one basket. I have Len Green working with me but Ronnie Black is keen and he is learning quickly. The more we have who can handle explosives the better."

"Good thinking Callow. We go tomorrow."

He grinned, "I know, Errol here told me."

The Petty Officer said, "Errol, you know sir, like Errol Flynn." Petty Officer Flynn patted his huge girth. "You can see the similarity can't you sir?"

We all laughed.

Later that evening the laughter was absent as we stood with the American Chaplain and buried the commandos and rangers who had fallen at Sason-Ri. They were simple graves and one day would have a stone. For the moment they had simple crosses with names carved by their friends. When I had spoken with Lieutenant Drake I would write my letters. I would have to write one home too although I was not in the right frame of mind for an upbeat letter.

The Lieutenant sat with my team and we planned the raid. I broached the issue of the raid to North Korea. He seemed sanguine about it. "That is not a problem. There is an island called both Ulleungdo or Dagelet dependent upon whom you speak to. It is a hundred and thirty miles from here and roughly the same distance from the north. We use that as a halfway point. The North Koreans don't have much of a navy and there is nothing military on the island. We can reach the mainland in three hours or so."

"Then I can leave the planning of the second mission with you chaps."

Our men had returned from their visit around the tiny town and were already preparing to crawl into bed. I said, "I will walk you back to your ship."

He gave me a curious look but nodded. He pointed to the whisky. We had consumed half of it, "I will leave this for you chaps. I am sure Mr Flynn will find another."

As we walked I told him about Blair. "I have kept it from the Americans. I am uncertain if there are any other agents. My gut tells me not but…"

"And you want me to give my men the once over."

"If you say they are all trustworthy then that is fine but I just want you to think about each one."

"It seems a reasonable idea. You know you will have to tell the Americans."

"When we get back."

Once back in the barracks I wrote the letters. It was as I was writing to Jimmy Curtis' family that I knew I had to force myself to write a letter home. What if this was my last mission? What if I failed to return? The letter would be all that they had. I lit my pipe and poured myself half a glass of whisky. When I had the pipe going I wrote the letter.

Chapter 8

The next morning, we had a visit from Max Hampton. My men were busy loading Bergens with ammunition and supplies. Acting Sergeant Callow spread the explosives and detonators around everyone's Bergens. It made sense. My bag was already packed. I had the silencer for the Colt and I would leave my machine gun and Lee Enfield in the barracks.

The Major frowned when he saw that we had not left. "I told you, Major, that this mission was urgent."

"And my men were in no condition to leave. Tired men make mistakes. They are still not fully ready but at least we have a fighting chance, sir." He did not look convinced. "The job will be done tonight and personally I don't think that patrol boats are a threat. We have a navy out there with destroyers, cruisers and battlewagons."

"You don't decide policy."

"No sir we carry it out. We pay the price of someone's clever idea."

"I expected something different, Major. I thought with all your medals…"

"That I was gung ho and a glory hunter? Well, I am not."

An awkward silence hung like a sword in the empty barracks.

He nodded, "I came to tell you that the 7th managed to hold Sason-Ri. The North Koreans brought up heavy tanks but they held them. The North Koreans had pulled back to a line thirty miles north. I don't think they are finished with us yet."

"Is this your way of telling me that the war is not going as well as the analysts in Washington predicted because if so I am not surprised."

"We will win, Major. Do not worry about that."

"Did you give Captain Rogers and his men some R & R?"

"They will be going out again tomorrow. Not that it is any of your concern."

"Then that is a mistake and it is my concern, Major. We fought together and became brothers in arms. They are good men and deserve a chance."

"We have to use what we have."

"Then do not abuse them. Men like Rogers and his Rangers are not easily replaced." I felt confident about talking to the Major in that tone. We were of equal rank. He could, of course, use the General to censure me but I did not think he would do that.

His mouth tightened into a thin line and he bunched his fists. Rangers were tough men and I guessed that he wanted to hit me. In the end, he said, "Well good luck, Major and I will see you when you return."

I had planned on giving my letters to the Major. Now I decided to ask Captain Poulson to do so.

Sergeant Heon did not know the area but one of the drivers, Private Seung-Ji Hwang did. He spent the morning discovering as much as he could about the village and the people. The two drivers were now permanently attached to our unit. They would act as sentries when all three boats were at sea. The battle of Sason-Ri had made them feel part of the troop and my men liked them.

We boarded 523 at three p.m. There were fewer of us and the boat was the largest of the three. We occupied the mess. Petty Officer Flynn was almost part of the crew and he ensured that we were as comfortable as possible. He had, on his hip, a Colt .45 revolver. His holster was a western one rather than a military one and hung low over his hip. I suspect it was not an affectation, a belt would have struggled to stay above his mighty girth. Lieutenant Drake had told me that the Petty Officer liked his steaks. He had brought a huge tray on board. With rationing in England, the crew had never seen so much meat and while the English divided the twenty-eight-ounce steaks into three, Petty Officer Flynn consumed a whole one himself. He was a man with a prodigious appetite. To give the men more room I shared the tiny officer's mess with the Lieutenant and the Midshipman. As they shared the watch there was room for me and I could continue to read up on the target as we journeyed north.

We left port at five p.m. We all stayed below decks to give any spies the illusion that the boat was just going on patrol. We headed towards Japan until the coast of Korea was below the horizon. Then the Lieutenant opened up the engines, turned north and we came on deck. I wore my war gear already. I would not be wearing my battle jerkin. Instead, I had all that I needed in my Bergen along with some explosives. I had my rubber-soled shoes and cap comforter on my head. We had, as the lads used to say, 'gone Al Jolson' and blacked up to disguise our face and hands. Private Harris surprised us by doing a good impression of Al Jolson singing, '*Mammy*'. When he came to the last lines, '*I'd walk a million miles for one of your smiles, my mammy!*' The whole boat erupted into spontaneous applause. It was a good sign and I saw Petty Officer Flynn nodding his approval. He brought some cocoa to me and said, "You have some good boys here." I nodded. "What happened to the big mouth, sir?"

He had a perceptive look on his face. I kept my face non-committal and said, "Missing in action is the term, Petty Officer."

"Good riddance then, sir. These guys are tighter without him. You'll be okay!"

I joined the Lieutenant on the bridge. With a crew of sixteen, he had enough to keep a good lookout. One was at the bow while two of them were on the tiny bridge. "Jenkins, go to the stern and make room for the Major."

"Sir."

One of the lookouts squeezed past me and went to the stern. Lieutenant Drake tapped the barometer. "Should be good weather there. Coming back, it may get a bit naughty but a little rain might keep us hidden."

"Sergeant Heon has the names of the village elders. With luck, he can introduce them to you and it may make life easier for you."

"Or worse for them, sir?" He turned to the Killick, "A couple of points to port if you please, Wilkinson."

"Aye, aye, sir."

"I mean that the North Koreans are ignoring the villagers at the moment. When we destroy their submarine pens they may seek retribution." I had not thought of that. "We'll just anchor and I will put a guard to stop them escaping. That way they have plausible deniability."

I laughed, "You sound like a lawyer!"

"I did a year of training, then my brother was killed at Walcheren and I joined up. I can always go back to it. I thought, when I joined up, that this would be an exciting life but all I have done is peace time patrols. Forty-five, when I was a Middy, was all about the war in Europe and not at sea. This voyage to hand over three boats is the most exciting thing I have done. And now to be actually doing something to win a war, well it is a dream come true, sir."

I drank my cocoa and thought about the effect the war had on us all. It changed all of us. I think it changed me for the better but Blair had been someone for whom war had brought out the worst. What would it do to Drake? Would he stay in and seek action or would he go back to University with the memories of an adventure to fall back upon? As night fell I went below. The lookouts had seen nothing and that was a good thing. I supposed that the North Korean air patrols were busy watching the Americans and supporting their armour. The rest of my men had gone below earlier. The veterans were checking their weapons and the younger ones were emulating them.

I waved over Callow and Green. "Once we reach the pens we are in your hands. I will watch the perimeter. Just make sure that they can't be used again. What fuse do you intend to use, Sergeant Callow?"

"We don't know how many guards there will be, do we sir?"

"Could be two or three or it could be a platoon. If there are boats there then a platoon."

"In which case, we need as short a fuse as possible. I was going to go for ten minutes sir and then run like hell."

"That suits me."

The road we will be using sir, is it a busy one?"

"Again, Callow, I am not certain. From the photographs, I would say that it was rarely used. Weeds were growing over the edges."

"When it goes up, sir, then we will be followed. I was going to leave some booby traps. We will have to lay them on our way to the pens so there is a risk to civilians."

I nodded. "We take that risk. I do not think that it will be civilians who are chasing us."

He looked relieved, "I didn't want to make that call, sir. We'll get on with the charges now."

Only Henry Harris and Stuart Campbell would have submachine guns. The rest of us would have handguns. I went to them next. "You two are the ones who will have to keep watch and keep the North Koreans off our backs if this goes pear-shaped!"

"Sir."

"I want to avoid gunfire if at all possible. If you are able then use your sap or a knife."

Harris looked at Campbell, "Don't worry, son. You will be able to use your knife when push comes to shove. It is just the thought of it that makes you nervous. Don't think about it."

I had forgotten what it was like to be nervous about killing someone. I had been doing it for so long that into longer bothered me. Or perhaps it did and I just put those thoughts deep inside me. Doubts could kill. I was responsible for these men.

The duty cook came in with a seaman carrying a dixie. "Grub up. Jack put it down there. Fetch the pot of tea." He pointed to the shelf with the fiddle running around it. "Plates and mugs there. Just this once we will do your dishes but from now on lads, you are on pan bash!"

Len Green asked, "What is it, Cookie?"

"Corn beef stew. The green stuff is what passes for cabbage over here."

Sergeant Heon said, "Pak Choi. It is good."

They looked at it dubiously. The British were ever wary of what they deemed to be foreign food. I lifted down a plate and ladled some into the bowl. I took two of the pieces of bread and went back to the officer's mess. I had shown willing to eat it and they would be more likely to now. It was good and I could not determine a taste in the Korean cabbage.

We maintained radio silence as we headed north and west. This was not like Europe where a town could be clearly seen from the lights. These were rural people who rose and slept with the sun. A good landfall depended upon your navigators and the Lieutenant was good. Able Seaman Tyreman popped his head around the curtain. "Coast a mile ahead, sir."

"Thanks, Tyreman."

I slipped my Bergen on my back. I checked that I had my canteen and my pipe. It was unlikely that I would get the opportunity to smoke it but it was comforting to have it. It was a reminder of home. I turned out the light and slipping out of the officer's mess, headed to the main mess. I peered in through the curtain. They had already dimmed their light to help with night vision. "Ready Sergeant."

"Right lads. Quick look-see and make sure you haven't left anything."

I headed to the deck. The air was much cooler. We were moving along at a fair rate of knots. If this had been the last war then we would have crept in to ensure there was no bow wave to give us away. Sergeant Heon was already on deck and was peering at the darker line which marked the coast. Midshipman Brown turned and gave the thumbs up. We were on course.

"Sergeant, you are here to translate. You did well at Sason-Ri. Here you need special skills. Stay out of the way and keep silent. Once we reach the target I should not need you and so you can help my team. Stay with Harris and Campbell."

"Sir."

Petty Officer Flynn appeared. He had a Thompson in his hand. I glanced at it and he smiled, "I figure that if I had it then I wouldn't need it!"

Sailors were superstitious.

I climbed up to the bridge as the rest of my men came on deck. I saw that the crew were all closed up. They wore, as did the Lieutenant and the Midshipman, their steel helmets. This was their first mission and they were doing it right. Without turning Lieutenant Drake, who had glasses on the coast said, "Fifteen minutes, tops. I can see the fishing boats and the headland. I have had Chief Jennings have the dinghy prepared but if we can land you at a jetty then I will do so."

We had seen, on the aerial photographs, what appeared to be a wooden jetty. The altitude of the aircraft and the angle of the sun made it difficult to determine the exact size. I took out my glasses. It was the terrain I was more interested in. The maps and the photographs were one thing but they were views from above. We were at sea level. I saw how steep the land rose behind the village. It would make it a hard slog up but, when we returned, it would be downhill. I saw the lighter patch which indicated the road. It looked to be straight and that helped too. If we were pursued then the launch would have a good field of fire.

As we neared I brought the glasses down to the boats. They were drawn up on the beach but, just to the left of them, I saw a flimsy looking wooden structure. There was a jetty. That would make embarkation quicker, easier and much safer. I heard the Lieutenant say, to himself, "Good!" He turned to me, "Right sir. Five minutes and we are there. I will land you from the port side and then turn the boat around while you are off."

I nodded, "See you in a few hours then."

"Good luck!"

Petty Officer Flynn and my men looked up expectantly as I approached. "Port side. Sergeant Heon, I want you first ashore. Have your hands empty. No guns. Get into the village and allay their fears. I will be right behind you."

"Sir!"

It was obvious we had been seen as we approached for I saw faces appearing. The Lieutenant had been with the boat for some time and he knew it well. We nudged next to the jetty and even as Hopkins jumped on to the jetty I had pushed Sergeant Heon and said, "Go!"

I landed at the same time as Hopkins and Heon and I ran down the jetty towards the huts. Two men stepped out. They were unafraid. One was white-haired and looked to be the village elder. Heon stopped before him and gave a slight bow. As they chatted I took the opportunity to look around the village. No one ran but the only faces I saw were those of men. That was to be expected.

Sergeant Heon turned and said, "This is Ji-hoo Kang and his son Jung-woo Kang. He says that this is Haejeon-Ri. I have told them who we are and they are happy to be of any help they can."

I shook my head, "Tell them that I do not wish to bring disaster upon their village. Tell them to tell the North Koreans that we kept them prisoner." Sergeant Heon did so and I saw the elder of the two nod. "Tell them that the boat will remain here overnight." He did and they nodded again.

Leaving the Sergeant, I hurried back to the road we had passed. I saw now that it was just a stone road covered with gravel and rough rocks. It would be little used. I saw no signs of vehicles except for a couple of bicycles. They would, I guessed, use their boats to sail around the headland. Petty Officer Flynn was with Acting Sergeant Callow. "The Koreans will give you no bother, Petty Officer. I told them to say that we held them at gunpoint. It might help the illusion if you sit at the end of the jetty as though you are their guard."

He nodded happily, "And I get to smoke a couple of stogies!"

"Sergeant Callow, bring up the rear. Harris, you are behind me. Sergeant Heon can be in the middle." This was where I missed my old team. Hay, Beaumont, Hewitt and Fletcher could all scout as well as any Commando I had ever met. This was our first patrol behind the lines and until I knew how they would cope then I would have to take it on myself. I turned and began to walk up the slope. We would run but I would wait until we had the grind of the upslope behind us. We ran through conifers. When we had been at Sason-Ri the trees had been mainly maples and poplars. The conifers presented a unique challenge. The pine needles were ever present. It made for sneaking through the forest difficult. The road turned to head due west. My runs had prepared me for this but I heard Harris and some of the others struggling behind me. I had not had any time to either assess or improve the fitness of my men. No matter what the Major said I would insist on at least forty-eight hours for my men to recover. When we reached the summit, I stopped and listened. Part of it was to allow the others to reach me and the second was to listen for activity. It was midnight and there should have been no activity at all. It was silent. I turned and said, quietly, "We run on this downhill section. Harris, watch for my signals."

"Sir."

Korea

I knew, from the maps, that I had roughly two and a half miles to go. I set off at a run. It was not a hard run. It just covered the ground quicker. The road suddenly twisted so that we looked north and west. I saw the port. Alarmingly there were lights and I could see activity. It looked like they were building something. In light of what we had seen it would probably be anti-aircraft defences. We were in the dark and would be hidden but lights and activity made our job that much harder. We were about half a mile from the water when I spied the hut. I held up my hand and then stopped. Pounding feet, even those clad in rubber-soled shoes, might still wake whoever lived within. We had passed no other houses and so I backed up the hill until I reached Callow. I pointed to his rucksack and took out a piece of parachute cord from my battledress. He nodded. He would make a booby trap. I made sure that everyone knew where it was. The wire he used was almost invisible and it was at ankle height. The grenades he used would clear an area of ten to twenty yards around the path. I pointed to my eyes and then the booby trap. They all nodded.

We turned and I drew my Colt and fitted my silencer. I led the section down the slope. We passed the hut in silence. I could now hear, from across the bay, the sound of construction. It was obvious that they were building a gun emplacement. They were trying to deter our aeroplanes. It was ironical that had we not sent air reconnaissance aircraft they would not have worried about putting in anti-aircraft guns. I knew that when we reached the water we would have to turn right and head along the road to the pens. The trees stopped two hundred yards from the water and there were buildings. I guessed, and hoped, that they were unoccupied but we had to pass them in any case. I saw, at the end, what looked to be some sort of guard post. There was a machine gun and it faced across the bay. I took the section through the gaps between the buildings. We were camouflaged and in the dark but I did not want an eagle-eyed sentry at the machine gun or on the other side to spot us. We were behind a building when I heard the patrol boat in the bay. I was working from a map in my head. By my estimate, we were less than two hundred yards from the pens. We had to head towards the water.

I walked slowly and headed closer to the small harbour. The air was cooler closer to the water. I heard the engine of the patrol boat recede in the distance. I reached the last building and peered right. The pens were there just fifty yards from me. They had been built in the cliffs. It looked like they might only have accommodated a couple of subs but they could hide ten or more patrol boats. The gaping mouths led into the bay. I had no doubt that they went deep under the headland. Even one of the bombs which had destroyed the dams in World War Two would have had little impact. I saw now why they wanted them eliminating. I pointed to Lance Corporal Williams. He did not have the radio to worry about. He nodded and as I slipped around the corner he followed me. I flattened myself against the wooden building which was between me and the pens. I moved along it. It was the glow from the sentry's cigarette as well as its smell which gave him away. He was leaning against the pen. I gestured for Williams to follow me. We moved close enough to smell the smoke from the man's cigarette. He was five yards from us. If he turned then he would see us. The patrol boat and the work meant that this was no longer an easy job. I handed my Colt to Williams. The building had given way to the concrete of the pen. I moved along the wall and I listened. I could only hear the Korean's breathing. Was he alone? I slid closer to him. His hand suddenly flicked the cigarette butt towards the bay. I grabbed his arm and, swinging him around, smashed his face into the cliff wall. His nose erupted, blood poured and he began to drop. I grabbed him.

Taking my gun from the Lance Corporal I hissed, "Tie his hands and gag him." I stepped out and waved to Harris. My men crept along the wall to join us. Running would draw attention to them. Although they would feel exposed walking was the safest option. With my gun before me, I stepped into the pens. There were neither boats nor men there. However, I could see that they had begun to put stores there. The one boat I had seen would be the first of many. My men hurried in.

"Williams, bring in the North Korean. Sergeant Heon, stand where the sentry was and pretend you are on guard. Take his cigarettes and light one. Harris and Campbell, on watch. Sergeant Callow, do your magic!"

They did not bother with 'sirring' me. They just raised their hand and nodded in acknowledgement. While Green and Callow began to search for the best places to place the explosives I examined the equipment which was already in there. There were the obvious ropes and spares for engines but there was also a large tank of fuel. I turned the spigot and the fuel began to spread across the floor. The explosion would ignite the fuel and complete the destruction of the pens. Leaving Callow to organise his men I went to the entrance.

Harris pointed as the patrol boat began its turn. I quickly took the field cap from the unconscious Korean. I jammed it on Heon's head and said, "Wave when they pass!

"Sir!"

"You two, back in cover."

The boat came back down. It was obviously doing circuits of the bay and then turning at sea. As it passed someone on the boat waved and Sergeant Heon responded. I hoped that the dark and the distinctive North Korean field cap would deceive the enemy.

"When we leave you two carry our Korean friend. We will dump him close to the hut. He should be safe enough there."

All of my men except for Callow and Green joined me. The patrol boat was at the harbour mouth. "Right, head back to the road. Take the Korean with you. Williams, you are in command. Wait for us there. Remember the booby trap."

"Sir."

They slipped away leaving me and my two explosives specialists. I took a drink from my canteen. I looked at my watch. It was ten minutes shy of three a.m. We would be sailing in daylight. I saw that the patrol boat was on the far side of the bay close to the work on the gun site. Private Green arrived, "Sergeant Callow is just setting them, sir."

"Good. Cut along after the rest of the men."

It seemed an age before the Sergeant ran towards me although it was less than thirty seconds. "All done sir." He smiled, "The petrol! Nice touch!"

We slipped out of the pen. I saw the slick of petrol on the water. Ahead I saw Green as he ducked into the little alley we had used. It was at that moment that fate intervened. There had been no one at the machine gun and guard post but one chose to come out just as Green was turning. Green was fifty yards from him and could be clearly seen. The young commando did the right thing, he ran up the little alleyway. I saw the Korean reacting. We both ran. I cocked my Colt. The Korean turned to the guard house and shouted. By that time I had reached the alley. I knelt and, taking aim, fired a pair of bullets at the Korean's legs. I hit him and he fell. A second man came out. He had his back to me and I fired another two shots into the back of his legs. I waved Sergeant Callow forward and we ran up the alley. There was the sound of an air raid siren. The cat was out of the bag. I had deliberately wounded rather than killed the Koreans. Dead men would have been ignored. A wounded man could be questioned and given medical attention.

Behind us, I heard the sounds of the patrol boat as it gunned its motor to race across the bay. Vehicles also roared into life as they sent men to see what had happened at the machine gun post. Even as I was running I worked out that there would only be four or five men at most in the post. My silenced bullets had given them no indication of where we were. The wounded man would point towards the pens. If they ran towards them then the explosion would take them out. I saw, ahead of me, my men. They had laid the Korean down and they had their weapons ready. Williams looked relieved. I looked at my watch, five minutes had elapsed since Callow had set the charges.

"Sergeant Callow lead them home. Harris and Campbell with me. We will be Tail End Charlie!"

"Sir!"

We all carefully stepped over the trip wire when we reached it. The North Korean soldier was sheltered by the hut a good sixty yards from the booby trap. We reached the trees and darkness enveloped us. This time we had the slope against us and we did not run. Every ten yards I stopped and listened. I checked my watch. The timers were not totally accurate. Thirty seconds or a minute either way was common. The bomb should have gone off. I heard the sound of a motorcycle. It was coming from the bay. It made sense. They would have known we had not passed through the town and short of walking on water or climbing the headland our only escape route was the road. I turned to run up the slope. Suddenly there was an almighty roar and explosion from behind me. I whipped my head around and saw the fireball race across the bay. The petrol had ignited instantly. A second explosion told me that the patrol boat had been unlucky enough to be in the path of the explosion. We had got the job done. If we could escape without injury then it would be perfect.

Suddenly I saw Callow ahead. He was bending down. "What is wrong, Sergeant?"

"Nothing sir. I put Williams in charge and I am setting a second booby trap." At that moment I heard the motorbike as it gunned its engine and then there was another explosion as he tripped the booby trap. "All done, sir. Step over it eh, sir!"

"And we had better run. Your handiwork will annoy them just a tadge, Sergeant!" We ran. We were just half a mile from the summit and soon we would be running downhill. We began to catch the others. "We all run!"

We settled into the easy jog we had all learned in training. I put the safety on my Colt and jammed it into my battledress. It made running easier. The water I had drunk had hydrated me. I suspected the young lads would not have taken the opportunity to drink. That would be my fault. There were so many things I had taken for granted. We had covered perhaps half a mile when we heard the second booby trap. That would slow them up. It had been clever of Callow to think of it. The first hint of dawn appeared in the eastern sky as we neared the bay. We had covered the five miles in an hour and ten minutes. It was not the quickest time but it would do.

Lieutenant Drake had the engine going on the launch. Petty Officer Flynn stood at the end of the jetty with his Thompson. I spied the glow from his cigar. Behind me, I heard the sound of a vehicle. The surface of the road did not allow for high speed and that had saved us. Harris, Campbell, turn and take cover in the trees. "Sergeant Callow get the men aboard." I took out my Luger. It had a full magazine. "Spread out and wait for my command to fire. Go for the tyres and radiator."

"Sir!"

I clicked off the safety and rested my right elbow on my knee. I supported the gun with my left hand. Obligingly the truck which lumbered towards us had its lights on. I saw it bounce down the poorly surfaced road. They would see the ship for it was highlighted by dawn's early light. We, on the other hand, would be almost invisible. I waited until it was just fifty yards from us. Then the lights would pick us out anyway.

"Fire!"

As the Thompson and Lee Enfield sent their bullets towards the tyres and radiator, I emptied the eight-shot magazine into the cab. The nine millimetre had a fast rate of fire and as soon as the last one was emptied I took out a grenade. The truck was already slewing around. Either a tyre had been hit or the driver.

"Run! Grenade!"

I hurled the grenade and ran after my two men. Bullets zipped after us but the dark, the trees and the bouncing of the slowing truck saved us. The twenty-millimetre Oerlikon on 523 opened up too but then the grenade exploded. It must have been close to the truck. Either the grenade or the twenty millimetre ignited the petrol tank and the truck exploded. We clattered down the rickety wooden jetty. Eager hands pulled us aboard and Petty Officer Flynn untied the launch and we roared away from the bay.

I looked at Callow, "Anyone hurt?"

He shook his head, "Sir, you three were the only ones in danger!"

"Good. Get the men below. Navy has a job to do now."

"Sir. Come on my lovely lads. Time for a cup of Horlicks and a bedtime story from your Uncle Roy!"

As they trooped below decks I went to the bridge. Lieutenant Drake never took his eyes from the sea. "We saw the explosion. Did you destroy it?"

I shrugged, "I hope so but we didn't hang around. Sorry, it took so long!" I waved a hand to the east where the sun was now bathing the sea in light.

"It couldn't be helped and besides we got to fire our guns in anger!" He turned and smiled, "You look all in. Get your head down. I will wake you if there is trouble. The cook has bacon and eggs on the go. I am afraid it is streaky bacon. The Americans don't seem to understand the concept of back bacon. Still mustn't look Petty Officer Flynn's gift horse in the mouth! And we even have HP sauce!"

"Then I am in seventh heaven already."

I went into the officer's mess. It was empty. I took off my Bergen and laid my guns on the table. Taking off my battledress I went to the officer's head and washed the blacking from my face and hands. I could smell the bacon frying and my mouth began to water. The reassuring throb of the Hall and Scott engines powered us south to home and safety. I reloaded my guns and then put the silencer back in the pocket of my Bergen. It was probably my single most valuable weapon. If I had not had it then the Koreans would have heard the bullets when I shot their men and might have caught us. I took out my pipe. I had not managed a smoke but now seemed appropriate.

Lance Corporal Pike brought me in a mug of tea. "Here you are, sir. I was excess baggage this trip."

"Lance Corporal I am more than happy for that to continue. It means we did not come close to losing a man."

He nodded, "The young ones are learning. Green and Campbell now know to drink as often as they can. They barely made it down the last slope."

"Was that North Korean lad alright? He smacked his head pretty hard."

"Yes, sir. He came to just before you arrived and Sergeant Heon asked him. He nodded." He gestured with his thumb, "Bacon and eggs will be ready in five minutes, sir!"

Korea

The pipe was going well and so I sat on the bench and sipped my tea. The lads could have first crack at the bacon and eggs. They had done well. Our first raid and, I hoped, we had achieved our objective and not suffered casualties.

Sergeant Callow popped his head through the curtain, "Sir, if you could come and get something to eat." I cocked an eyebrow. "The lads don't want to appear greedy sir and it is getting cold!"

I smiled and laid the pipe on the ashtray, "Of course. How rude of me."

When I went into the mess I saw that no-one had touched the food. I picked up a plate and said, "Looks and smells good cook!" I slid one egg and two rashers of bacon onto my plate. I picked up one piece of fried bread. I went to the far end of the table to dollop some sauce on the bacon. I picked up a piece of dry bread. "If you don't mind, lads, I will have this in my quarters. I don't want to cramp your style!"

"Stay sir!"

"Thanks, Private Green, but I have a report to write. I might as well use the time now. Enjoy the food and don't let it go to waste." As I left I saw Petty Officer Flynn and Sergeant Callow exchange a knowing look. I wondered what it meant. Once in the officer's mess, I devoured the food. It was delicious. I wanted to take more but I knew how much it meant to the men in the section. It was not often they got to enjoy such treats. Nor had I been lying. It was always better to write the reports while they were fresh in your mind.

I wiped the plate clean with the dry bread. I finished off the tea and then relit the pipe. It was still half full. I felt relaxed and I began to write the report in draft form. I would make it grammatically correct later. For now, I wanted the sequence of events to be right. I had just put the pipe down when the klaxon sounded. I knew what that meant. We were under attack. I grabbed my Thompson, spare magazines and ran out of the mess. "Grab your weapons and get on deck! We are under attack!"

I was the first one on deck and I saw that the skipper had put the wheel hard over. The gun crews had already been closed up and I watched the barrels of their guns as they tracked the two Yak 9s which were approaching from the west. I cocked the Thompson. It was a relatively close-range weapon but I had learned in the English Channel that if you threw a wall of lead into the air one lucky shot could bring down an aeroplane. As a pilot, I knew how fragile they were. Lieutenant Drake was turning the MGB so that we could bring all our guns to bear.

It was a brave act for the safest option for the men on the bridge was to have them attack across the bows.

"As soon as he opens fire I will turn west."

There was a chorus from the gunners, "Aye sir!"

I braced myself with my back to the bridge. It would give me a more stable platform. It meant I would have to turn when the ship did. I looked down the sight at the two dots which began to descend. They had done what I would have done. They had gained height so that when they came they would have the maximum speed. The time of day precluded them using the sun and they would be an easier target for us. Travelling at almost four hundred miles an hour they were fast and with two machine guns and a cannon packed a deadly punch. As I watched them come into range I tried to remember how many shells they had. It came to me. They had just one hundred and twenty cannon shells. Any one could do us serious damage, especially below the water line. But more would be wasted hitting the water. I saw the two six-pounders tracking the aeroplanes. The Oerlikons and the machine guns would fire as soon as the heavier ordnance had let rip.

The two aircraft appeared like dots. They were low and they were small. Lieutenant Drake shouted, "Stand by!" His orders were for his crew. My men would wait for my order. They had taken whatever cover they could. The first Yak opened fire. It was too soon. The captain turned the MGB and most of the bullets and shells missed. Perhaps he was nervous or had never fired at a ship. Sixty of his two hundred rounds hit the water. Then the Lieutenant shouted, "Open fire!" The two six-pounders cracked rapidly. They were deafening. The Oerlikons and the machine guns seemed to underscore the larger guns. It was almost musical. I felt cannon shells hit the hull. It was along the side.

I shouted, "Commandos, open fire!" I led the Yak and fired a short burst. I tracked it as I fired. The second Yak's bullets and shells hit the superstructure. There was armour near the bridge and I heard the shells strike metal. I felt my cheek scored by a piece of plywood. I fired a continuous burst for I knew that I would have time to reload. I saw the second one judder. It could have been anyone's shells or bullets. Each of us would think that it was our bullets which had brought down the enemy.

The second Yak peeled off and headed west. Smoke was pouring from it. The first Yak returned to avenge its consort. This time it would be attacking from bow to stern. I turned so that my left shoulder was against the bridge. I changed magazines as it came in even lower this time. Perhaps he was not inexperienced. By coming in low he negated the effect of the aft six pounder. Petty Officer Flynn knelt with his Tommy gun at the bow. He was a huge target and I wondered how he survived. He seemed to bear a charmed life as bullets hit the deck, the hull, the six pounder and the bridge. Petty Officer Flynn was hurling curses at the Korean pilot. I felt the machine gun bullets strike the hull. The American must have had a serious lucky charm. The six-pounder shells were almost parting his hair. The end, when it came, was dramatic. The pilot must have taken hits and he reacted by pushing his stick forward. His right wing tip caught the sea and his aeroplane cartwheeled in the air before plunging beneath the waves. In a heartbeat, it was over.

"Middy, damage control! SBA Laidlaw, see to the wounded."

My Lance Corporal was already preparing his dressings as I shouted, "Pike help the SBA."

"Sir!"

"Anyone hurt?"

I watched my men as they rose. All were intact. I knew that we had been fortunate. Sergeant Callow summed it up, "Petty Officer, you are a mad bugger and how they missed that carcass of yours I will never know!"

He pulled out the stump of a cigar and, lighting it, said, "Good living I guess!"

Chapter 9

Two of the crew were wounded. One, a stoker, was badly hurt and would have to be flown to Japan. We had been lucky. 523 would need repairs. Even if Major Hampton wished it we could not sail for a few days. Dongbaek-Ri was busy as we approached the port. Lieutenant Drake was already concerned about his wounded men and there appeared to be little order. We had passed a convoy of ships heading for Pusan from Japan and other ships had chosen to land at Dongbaek-Ri. It took until almost eleven for us to finally berth. There was an ambulance waiting to take off our wounded. The rest of our men and the other crews were waiting anxiously as we docked.

"I take it you will be seeing Major Hampton, sir." Lieutenant Drake's face was filled with concern. He suddenly looked old.

I nodded, "He will need my report."

"Then you had better let him know the damage. It isn't just the holes in the hull. The cannon shells damaged some of the machinery. The chief will need spares."

"I will tell him." I sought out Petty Officer Flynn. "Petty Officer, Major Hampton will know that we are returned and he will be anxious for my report. Take the jeep and tell him that I will visit later this afternoon with my report."

He nodded, "Do you want him to know how it went, sir?"

I waved at the holed hull of 523. "Give him the highlights eh Petty Officer."

"To be fair to the Major he is a Ranger."

I shook my head, "If you are behind a desk then you are no Ranger. Believe me, Petty Officer I have seen how a desk can change a fighting man into an accountant."

"Yes, sir." He brightened, "And I will see if there are any more supplies which have been sent to the wrong place!"

He took out a cigar as he strode down the gangplank. We would be eating well again. Private Green appeared with my Bergen and war gear. "Sergeant Callow asked me to bring these, sir."

"Good man. Take them to my bunk, would you?"

"Sir."

Sergeant Heon emerged with the rest of my men. "Sergeant Heon when you have time I would like to chat with you about the village."

"Yes, sir."

I had been on enough raids to know that the intelligence you brought back was often as important as the mission itself. I would make certain that the Americans had as full a report as possible. The Captain and Sergeant Major were eager for news of the mission. "Good to have you back sir. I put the kettle on when I saw you approaching. Billy Kenny will have it just the way you like it."

"Good man."

As we walked towards the barracks Captain Poulson said, "No wounds and no dead men. Well done sir."

I shook my head, "We were too slow. The men need to be fitter. They were camp ready but not war ready. The ship was jumped by aeroplanes because we were caught in the open in daylight. 523 needs repairs. We will need to rethink this mission in North Korea." As we sat around the table, I smoked my pipe and gave them the details of the raid. I evaluated the success and what I deemed to be the failures. "Captain Poulson, I want you to take the men out and give them a good ten-mile run. Full packs and carrying weapons." He nodded. "We can't go out again for at least two, perhaps three days. Tomorrow I will join you and we make it fifteen miles."

Sergeant Major Thorpe said, "And Sergeant Heon? He is not a commando."

"If he comes on the raids then he is. I will run with him. You will lead, the Captain and I will be at the rear to assess the weaknesses. Now get the maps out for this mission and let us see what exactly they need us to do."

I had paid scant attention to the next raid as I had been preoccupied with the first. The other two knew it better than I. However, my fresh eyes and my experiences in Pohang gave me a better insight into the practices of the North Koreans.

Captain Poulson had obviously read everything numerous times. He rarely had to refer to the folder. "The coastal highway runs all the way from Wonsan down to South Korea. Just south and east of Daegang-Ri it enters a tunnel and that emerges in South Korea. They want us to blow up the North Korean entrance to the tunnel. The North Koreans have men there guarding the entrance at both ends. There are lots of other ways from north to south but most are further west. I can see why they want this destroying."

I nodded and looked at the aerial photograph of the defences. "There is an anti-aircraft gun and machine guns. That does not need three boats."

"Perhaps, sir, they are ensuring that the job will get done."

"Perhaps, Sergeant Major, but three boats are more likely to be seen than one." I tapped out the ash from my pipe and laid it on the table. Ken Thorpe poured me another cup of tea. The aerial photographs had been handy. We could see the gun emplacements and defenders clearly. "I can see the beach where we could land but the three boats would be exposed. We would have to land at night. We would not have as far to go as we did on the first mission and, barring a disaster, we should be able to deal with the defenders we will meet. Sergeant Callow knows his stuff." I turned to the Sergeant Major. "I am going to make his promotion permanent. I will send the paperwork back to London. Who knows there may be some nice back pay when he gets home."

"He is a good lad. His family will appreciate that, sir."

I nodded and sipped my tea, "So we can get the job done but the tricky part will be getting home. They have plenty of aeroplanes and while the Yak might not be able to dog fight with our jets it can make a mess of our wooden ships. We use this island." I jabbed my finger at Dagelet. "If we can make it there unscathed then I intend to sail as close to Japan as we can and take a longer route home. Navy will have to make certain that they have enough fuel."

"Will you be seeing Major Hampton today, sir?"

I nodded, "I will give him my report, tell him about the damage and then give him all the bad news in one day. I will tell him about Blair."

Sergeant Major Thorpe said, "The lads all know about it. They won't mention it outside the barracks but they know."

"Well, I have a report to write and you have a run to organize."

Having all my notes to hand helped and I quickly wrote my report. I made suggestions for future operations. This was not like Combined Ops where we had a system in place. This was a new venture. I wanted the ground rules to be established. Petty Officer Flynn came in to the barracks. The men who had been on the raid were all asleep. I needed sleep but it would have to wait.

"Sir, Major Hampton's compliments and he asked if you could meet with him and Captain Rogers around six. He said he knew it was later than you asked but he would feed you at the base, sir."

I could tell that the Petty Officer did not like being a go-between. I smiled, "That will not be a problem Petty Officer. Are you going to get your head down too?"

He shook his head, "No sir, 523 needs work. I am a sailor at heart. I will go and give my buddies a hand."

When he had gone I went to the shower we had rigged up and cleaned myself up. I dressed in a good uniform and then I lay on the cot for an hour. It was what Mum called a Granddad nap. I was never fully asleep but when I rose I felt refreshed. I shaved before I left. I was just tidying my shaving kit away when I heard the rest of the troop return from their run. The men from my section were playing cards and reading. As the weary warriors staggered in they gave a cheer. I shouted, "Don't worry, lads. You get to do it tomorrow but it will be a little longer!" That silenced them.

Sergeant Major Thorpe said, "This was a good idea, sir. They are not as fit as they should be. To be fair the long flight didn't help but no excuses. We will get them up to speed." He seemed to see my smart uniform for the first time. "Off to see the Major?"

"Yes Sergeant Major."

"Some of the lads have been wondering about mail, sir. With the moving around England before this tour and the like it is almost a month for some of the married men."

"Will do. I should have thought of it myself."

"You have a lot on your plate, sir. See you later then."

When I reached the jeep Petty Officer Flynn was in the driver's seat. He had on a good uniform. "Thought I ought to earn my pay, sir. You might need someone to take notes."

"Thank you, Petty Officer. I appreciate it."

The base had grown since my last visit. I saw Sherman tanks as well as the Chaffee. There did not seem as many as I might have expected. The sentry at the main gate looked like he was going to be awkward until Petty Officer Flynn growled, "I was here this morning sweetheart! I have not become a Commie since then. Lift the barrier and stop embarrassing me in front of this English officer."

The sentry coloured and nodded for his companion to lift the barrier. Flynn shook his head, "You know, sir, they always put the guys on sentry who have never fired a gun in anger. A veteran would have waved us through! I despair of this man's army."

He pulled up outside the admin building. He took a space which I suspected was intended for someone of higher rank. I was learning that rank meant nothing to Petty Officer Flynn. The duty sergeant had a reassuringly large number of medal ribbons on his uniform and he must have met with Petty Officer Flynn's approval.

"Yes, Major Harsker, the Major and Captain Rogers are expecting you. Petty Officer, take the Major to the conference room."

"Yes Sergeant."

Sergeant Steinla was seated next to the Captain and as well as Major Hampton there was a uniformed female stenographer with a notepad. She was a stunning redhead. With her looks, she could have played Maureen O'Hara. She had her hair up and glasses perched on the end of her nose. Her red lacquered fingernails tapped on the notepad. I smiled to myself. After my last outburst, the Major was taking no chances. There would be witnesses and a record. Captain Rogers and his sergeant gave me a beaming smile. I had allies.

"Sit down, Major, we have much to talk about. Is that your report?"

I handed it over, "Yes sir."

"We sent a camera Mustang over this morning." He handed me the photographs. "You did a perfect job." I studied the photographs. I could see that half of the headland had slid into the bay. I saw the wreckage of the patrol boat. "Our lords and masters are pleased." I nodded noncommittally. "Now I understand that you need time to repair 523?"

"Yes, sir. She is holed and machinery was damaged. In addition, my men need time to recover too. We could send out 256 and 527 if you like."

The Major looked at Captain Rogers and shook his head. "I am afraid that we need all of your boats. Perhaps this enforced delay might actually help us." I did not like these games. I wanted him to get to the point. He rose and went to the door to make certain it was closed. "This next mission is an ambitious one. I can't go into details but there is something big on the horizon. D-Day taught us a great deal, gentlemen. We played all sorts of mind games with the Germans so that they had no idea where we were actually going to land. You both have a mission behind enemy lines and they are connected. Sergeant Aitkens here also works in Washington and is a liaison with the CIA and Hans Tofte."

I had heard of the CIA but not the officer he had named.

"Sergeant Aitkens is more than a stenographer. She has a higher clearance than anyone in this room."

I looked again at the stunningly beautiful woman. I had thought he had brought her to distract us. Now I knew differently. She was slightly built with a bun on her head. She had old fashioned glasses perched on the end of her nose. However, when I looked into her eyes I saw steel. She was playing a part.

"Your two units are going to make the North believe that we are going to invade on the Japan side of North Korea. The tunnel you will blow up is important but it will be the fact that Captain Rogers will have blown up a communication centre just twenty miles inland which will add to the ruse. Over the next two days, we will bomb the roads and bridges of eastern North Korea. Their ports will be attacked. When they discover that Rangers and Commandos are operating in their back yard they will switch forces to the east coast."

Captain Rogers looked up from the notes he was making. I had not yet told Petty Officer Flynn to write anything down. We did not need to. "Sir, do we parachute in?"

"Yes, Captain and you will exit with Major Harsker. These begin as two separate missions but combine once they are completed."

I looked up. I did not mind carrying the Rangers but this added greatly to the element of danger not to mention a higher risk of failure. "Sir, how do we coordinate this? I cannot believe that the North Koreans will allow three boats to wait off their coast. They will send aircraft and ships."

"The ships they have are no threat. That is why we need three of them. You are more than capable of defeating anything they can put on the water. But you are right. The Rangers will take off two days before you leave here. So, Major, when will you leave?"

I felt sorry for Captain Rogers. He was being asked to drop behind enemy lines. I had done that and there were so many things which could go wrong. "Major Hampton, we cannot leave until the sixteenth at the earliest. The spare parts have not arrived yet."

I saw the Major glance at the stenographer. Sergeant Aitkens gave the slightest of nods. She was not a sergeant. She was a ranking operative. "That is acceptable. Captain Rogers, as you know, the communication centre is in an underground bunker. Its defences lie in the concrete which protects it from air attack. I do not envisage losses but you have twenty miles of mountainous terrain to traverse. Can you do it in the time we have given you?"

"I guess so. The trick will be to arrive before the tunnel has been blown. Major Harsker will want to skedaddle as soon as it is blown up." The Major nodded as though that was self-evident. "The risk is that we are pursued."

"Then you will have to deal with that eventuality, both of you."

It was at that moment that I realised we were two pawns which they were happy to sacrifice. In fact, it might suit them to have us captured. It would add credibility to the story. I decided not to tell them of Dagelet Island. I did not trust Major Hampton nor the CIA. I had an idea that this grand plan would involve some sort of amphibious landing somewhere on the west coast. That explained why we were going to be a nuisance on the east coast. I caught Captain Rogers' eye. He nodded. We would set up some sort of radio code. There would be no secrets between us.

I smiled at the Major as did Captain Rogers. "Now all that remains is to give you the code words for your signals back to base. This time you will be communicating with this base." He handed me a folder. I wondered if the marks the sergeant was scribbling in the notebook meant anything at all! We spent an hour going over the details of the two raids and our signals. It became clear that there would be as much ordnance, supplies and fuel as we wished. They wanted us to succeed. After the raid was another matter but they wanted to ensure that the communication centre and the tunnel were blown up.

The Major leaned back and looked at his watch. "An hour before we eat, just time for a drink in the officer's mess. I am certain the Petty Officer and the sergeant will be accommodated."

I said, "Before we go down sir I have to tell you something."

"Yes, Major."

"One of my men, Blair, deserted when we were at Sason-Ri. I say deserted but I think it is more likely that he defected."

I had surprised both the Major and the CIA lady. She took off her glasses and said, "What makes you think he defected, Major?" Her voice showed that she was no mouse.

"His political views led me to think that he was a sympathiser and that was confirmed by the fact when he ran, he ran directly towards the North Koreans. We did not find his body and that led me to believe that he had defected."

"And why did you not report this sooner?"

"I was giving him the benefit of the doubt, Major. He was one of my men. He had been upset by the death of a friend. I thought that he might reconsider and then return. And, if I am truthful, I was looking for confirmation that he had defected." The Major looked quizzical but I saw that Sergeant Aitkens understood my reasoning. "If he was a prisoner of war then the North Koreans would have made much of it. If he was a defector or," I looked at Sergeant Aitkens, "an agent then they would keep that information to themselves."

Sergeant Aitkens nodded, "You have done the right thing, Major. I can see that you are a thinker rather than just a supremely efficient killer. We are aware, as are our colleges at Six that there are foreign agents planted in the military. This would make sense. Blair, you said?"

"Yes, Sergeant Aitkens."

"I will have my London liaison pull his record. The rest of your men?"

"Are loyal. I was just surprised that Blair was so obvious. I would have thought that he would have kept a low profile."

"Perhaps he was relying on the fact that the British love an underdog and give people as many chances as they need." She looked at the Major and nodded.

"Right! The bar calls I believe." As we reached the door the Major said, "Social time eh Major? Captain?"

I smiled. I could play this game too. "Of course, sir."

As we walked across the compound to the Officer's Club I asked, "You have replacements then?"

"Yes, sir. I will be taking nineteen men with me. For some, this will be their first landing under fire."

"Captain!" The Major snapped at him.

"Sorry, sir."

I nodded, "Let me tell you of my experiences then. As they were in the last war they are public record." Captain Rogers smiled. "No matter how well-intentioned the pilot, and I speak as a pilot, they can never get you as close to the target as the planners hope. Added to that with so many men in the stick your first and last man could be a mile apart. I used to let my NCO lead and I was always the last man out. That way there were two leaders and two men who knew the mission. We always cut our parachute cords and took them with us after we had landed. Whenever possible we took our chutes too. In winter they make great camouflage." We had reached the club. "And although there will be no parachutes for my team we are going to run every day until we are needed. You can never be too fit."

When we entered the bar, it was as though it was nineteen forty-five all over again. There was a great deal of jollity, merriment and loud laughter. It was always the same. Most of those in the bar had not yet fought. Many would be nervous, almost fearful. Others would be excited at the prospect. Until you had come under fire then you could not know the effect it would have. No amount of training could prepare you for that first moment when you knew that the men who were firing were not trying to frighten you. They wanted to kill you.

The Major was buying and I did not stop him. I made sure, however, that I just had two drinks before we ate. The meal was steak, potatoes and sweet corn. I ate more in that one meal than I would have eaten in a weekend at home. I knew it would come back to haunt me when we had our run the next day. I just enjoyed it. I chatted to Captain Rogers. I discovered that he was newly married and had no children. He saw himself as a career officer. The reason became obvious. He had been a sportsman at high school and focussed so much on football that he had neglected his studies. When a knee injury ended any chance of a career in football he chose a career which was active.

"You can always go back to school you know. I thought about doing so but then we set up the air freight business and…"

"You are lucky. I have a wife to support. If I stay in the service then with promotion will come financial security."

"Perhaps but you will be away from your family for long periods and in danger."

"Barb understands. Her dad was a soldier. He was killed at Omaha."

We compared our lives at home and realised that while we spoke the same language and fought for the same causes they were as different as could be. After the meal, we retired to the bar. I saw Petty Officer Flynn seated in the jeep and smoking a cigar. I had the chance to leave. I leaned in to Captain Rogers, "Pop by tomorrow evening and have a look around the boats. We need to set something up."

"Of course sir, and thanks for the advice. I will heed it."

I waved goodbye to the Major. He was in his cups and I am not even certain he saw me leave. I was about to get in the jeep when Sergeant Aitkens ghosted next to me. Her hair was down and she had taken off the glasses. I now knew that they had clear glass in them. "I have been in touch with London. That matter we discussed is in hand. I discovered that you are a man with hidden depths Major." She put her soft hand on mine. Her nails pressed slightly into my flesh. It was erotic. "Be careful!"

As we drove back Petty Officer Flynn said, apropos nothing, "Well she was a surprise, sir!"

I shook my head, "The war is hard enough without distractions like that."

I was up at five the next morning. Part of it was annoyance with myself. I should have said something to whoever Sergeant Aitkens really was but I had been taken by surprise and not thought quickly enough. I could come with responses in an instant if lives were in danger but I never understood relationships and women were a complete mystery to me. I wished for no female entanglements.

I put on my old uniform and my fully loaded Bergen. I took Sergeant Heon's helmet and began banging the table. "Up and at 'em! Rise and shine!" They were commandos and they were awake instantly. "Anyone who finishes today's run behind me is on pan bash for a week!"

I don't think that was the incentive which worked. It was more that I was dressed and ready to run. They had all been in bed when I had returned and they would know that I had had less sleep than any of them. I left the barracks and ran on the spot outside. Sergeant Major Thorpe was first out. He grinned at me, "Sneaky sir! I like it." He turned as the others threw themselves out of the door. "Come on you shower! Move yourselves!"

Captain Poulson emerged. "Right Captain lead them off!"

The rest of the men came out like rabbits being chased by a greyhound. I put my head in the door and saw that only Sergeant Heon was left, "Come on Sergeant!"

"Sorry, sir. I am not used to this!"

The nearest man to us was Private Campbell. I settled into an easy rhythm. Sergeant Heon tried to catch Campbell. "Slow down and lengthen your stride. Breathe!"

"Sir."

"Relax and use your arms. We have a long way to go."

Campbell had set off running too fast and we gradually reeled him in as he tired. After two miles of running along the circuit devised by the captain, the three of us were running together. I talked to them as we ran. I told them how to breathe. I made them relax and, gradually we caught up with the others. Lance Corporal Pike had gathered some of the young men around him. As we caught up with them he said, "Private Green has a stitch, sir."

"No easy way out of this, Green. Suck it up and run through it."

"Sir!"

Korea

In the end, there were eight of us at the rear. I could see Captain Poulson. He was a good two hundred yards ahead of us but no one had dropped out and that was a good thing. I had not done the run before but I recognised some of the landmarks from the journeys in the jeep. When we were a mile away from the barracks I could smell the sea. The men were flagging. I began to tell them the story of how my father had almost fallen from the front cockpit of a Gunbus.

I began to sing the song when I had finished.

Once I was happy but now I'm forlorn
Like an old coat that is tattered and town
Left on this wide world to fret and to mourn,
Betrayed by a maid in her teens

The girl that I loved she was handsome
I tried all I knew her to please
But I could not please her one quarter so well
Like that man up on the Trapeze

He'd fly through the air with the greatest of ease
A daring young man on the flying Trapeze
His movements were graceful, all girls he could please
And my love he purloined away

This young man by name was Signor Bona Slang
Tall, big, and handsome as well made as Chang
Where'er he appeared the Hall loudly rang
With ovation from all people there

He'd smile from the bar on the people below
And one night he smiled on my love
She winked back at him and she shouted, "Bravo!"
As he hung by his nose up above!

He'd fly through the air with the greatest of ease
A daring young man on the flying Trapeze
His movements were graceful, all girls he could please
And my love he purloined away

Korea

Her father and mother were both on my side
And very hard tried to make her my own bride
Her father he sighed and her mother she cried
To see her throw herself away

'Twas all no avail she went there ev'ry night
And would throw him Boquets on the stage
Which caused him to meet her, how he ran me down
To tell you would take a whole page

He'd fly through the air with the greatest of ease
A daring young man on the flying Trapeze
His movements were graceful, all girls he could please
And my love he purloined away

One night I as usual went to her dear home,
Found there her father and mother alone
I asked for my love and soon they made known
To my horror that she'd run away!

She'd packed up her box and eloped in the night
With him with the greatest of ease
From two stories high, he had lowered her down
To the ground on his flying Trapeze!

He'd fly through the air with the greatest of ease
A daring young man on the flying Trapeze
His movements were graceful, all girls he could please
And my love he purloined away

Some months after this I went to a Hall
Was greatly surprised to see on the wall
A bill in red letters which did my heart gall,
That she was appearing with him

He taught her gymnastics and dressed her in tights
To help him to live at his ease
And made her assume a masculine name
And now she goes on the Trapeze!

She floats through the air with the greatest of ease
You'd think her a man on the flying Trapeze
She does all the work while he takes his ease
And that's what's become of my love

He'd fly through the air with the greatest of ease
A daring young man on the flying Trapeze
His movements were graceful, all girls he could please
And my love he purloined away

I knew every word because it was my father's party piece. Some of the older men knew some of it and joined in but the younger ones and Sergeant Heon could only join in the chorus. As we ran towards the barracks the crews of the three boats and my men all applauded. It was silly but that little song became our song. Men would whistle it in the barracks or hum it while we marched. I had not been to officer's school but I guessed they did not teach that. It worked.

When we left Dongbaek-Ri the men were fitter and we were all closer. Silly that a music hall song could bond us together. We had our signals and codes ready to use when Captain Rogers and his men joined us. We, of course, left earlier than I had told the Major. We were sailing first to Dagelet Island. We would reach there in the afternoon. Some of the boats' crews could have a little sleep and we would all have enjoyed a few hours of rest. I spent most of the voyage with the Lieutenant on the bridge. I knew that this mission was balanced on the edge of a commando dagger. There was more likelihood that things could go wrong than things might go right. Captain Rogers and his men would already be heading for their target to strike at dusk and then march the twenty miles to reach us and we were still a hundred miles away.

Dagelet was a haven of peace. We headed to a deserted beach on the west coast. We moored in the bay and the Lieutenant put a third of his men on watch while the rest slept. There would be little danger to us. I sat on the bridge and smoked a pipe with the Lieutenant. We saw the first squadron of B-29s as they headed to Korea to bomb military installations pass overhead.

The Lieutenant said, "The Americans have so many aeroplanes that they could bomb the North to a cinder."

I nodded, "And that might just make either the Soviets or the Chinese take sides in an active way. I don't know about you but I do not want an atomic war. Those kinds of wars are not about soldiers, sailors and airmen they are about politicians and I do not trust any politician; even Winston Churchill!"

"You may be right." He tapped his pipe out over the side. "These American Rangers, do they have any chance of reaching us before daylight?"

"They are good chaps and I think they have an excellent chance but like all these things there are more things which could go wrong. My men have a better idea of how to fight aeroplanes and they are the real threat to us and not ground troops. The nearest military units are twenty miles up the coast. The biggest problem will be if they are pursued. I know how hard it can be to load a ship while under fire."

He nodded. "It is fortunate that we have Mr Flynn with us. Our replacements are still on their way from England. He has helped enormously."

"He is a good chap. Everything repaired below?"

"They are, sir and we have taken precautions. The more vulnerable areas, such as the engine room, now have an added layer of insulation. It won't stop bullets and the like but it will slow them down. It was Chief Jennings idea. He is another one who earns his money many times over." He looked at his watch. "Well sir, we leave in an hour. I will go and wake Middy. He can have an hour to watch."

"I shall stay here and go over the plan again. I managed a nap on the way up here."

I cleaned out my pipe. It helped me to think. We had had intelligence that, probably as a result of our raid, the Koreans were putting mines in their harbours. That would not harm us on this mission but it might in the future. I had seen the next four missions and all were based around a port or harbour. Although three were small ones one was large enough for mines. How would we deal with that? This raid would necessitate us landing on a beach. In a perfect world, we would use a landing craft. We did not have one and so we would have to go ashore in a rubber dinghy. Getting ashore would not be a problem it would be embarking under fire which would. I looked west. The Rangers would be at their target. They had a far harder task than we did. Twenty miles across enemy territory in the dark would not be easy. When Captain Rogers and I had met on 523 I had suggested that he steal Korean vehicles. I told him of the times we had done that in France and the Low Countries. He had not thought of it. One of his men loved engines and cars. He had a ready-made mechanic. As I had told him there had to be a vehicle near the communication centre to allow the men there to be relieved. If they did steal a vehicle then it increased their chances. The problem we had was that we had to give them the maximum time to reach us. Once the tunnel was blown then troops would come rushing from the north.

The Middy arrived and handed me a cup of tea. My pipe was ready to fill. I saw that he had a sidearm. It was a service, Webley. "Thanks, Middy. Excited?" I started to fill my pipe.

He nodded, "And, after the other raid, a little fearful. Those aeroplanes could have hit any of us. I knew we were lucky to just have two men wounded and it could have been so much worse."

I struck a match and drew through the pipe. I tamped it down and lit a second match. When it was drawing well I said, "It doesn't do to dwell on your mortality, Middy. It doesn't do any good. If you are worried that you are going to die then you are not concentrating and this job is hard enough without self-doubt."

"Yes sir but, with respect, it is easy for you. You are a hero."

I laughed and drank some of the tea, "A hero?" I shook my head. "It is Roger isn't it?"

"Yes, sir."

"Well Roger, these medals do not make me a hero. They make me a survivor. You think I don't get scared?"

"You said not to dwell on your own mortality sir."

"Good, you were listening. I was caught once, by the S.S. I was about to be shot. We were in North Africa and far from help. I thought I might die and so I did something about it. I escaped. You just do your job as best you can. If there is a bullet which hits you," I shrugged, "that is in the nature of war. If it is any consolation to you all the time we sailed on *'Lucky Lady'* in World War Two we lost just a couple of the crew. The odds that you will survive are in your favour."

He was silent for a while. My pipe was drawing well and with a benign sea and sky, I was at peace. After a while, he said, "Lieutenant Drake said *'Lucky Lady'* and all hands were lost in action."

The peaceful moment was shattered. I swallowed the last of my tea. "Aye, she was. And that is war. There is no promise of survival no matter how noble the cause or how much a man deserves to live." I looked at my watch. We would be leaving in forty minutes. I tapped out my pipe and descended to the mess deck. It was time to put on my war face.

Chapter 10

I did not want to disturb Lieutenant Drake and so I went to the mess where Sergeant Callow and my men were waiting. There was the inevitable game of pontoon. I saw that Petty Officer Flynn was playing with the four young soldiers. Sergeant Heon was watching. Williams was fiddling with his radio and Pike his dressings.

"Everyone okay, Sergeant Callow?"

"Aye, sir. They'll do alright. I reckon it is the others who will be more worried."

I knew what he meant. We had been blooded. We had been behind the lines; the section had landed at night, done their job and escaped. This mission was similar. While we took out those protecting the tunnel the other two sections would be preparing defences. While we were busy demolishing the tunnel, they would be waiting. Waiting was always harder.

"The Koreans have made it easier for us by having their nearest troops ten miles away. You just need to set your charges to go off as close to dawn as you can. We have to buy Captain Rogers and his men as much time as possible."

"This would be easier if we just had the one job to do, sir. This feels like our hands are being tied."

He was right. Captain Poulson and I had spoken at length about this. We had both worked for a Major Fleming who had used us in the Med. We had been a stepping stone to his promotion to Colonel. I did not think that Major Hampton was doing that. He wanted this war over quickly but he was using us as bait. Tying us to the Rangers made it more likely that the Koreans would find us. The planners were using us to draw the Korean's eye to the east.

"If we can make it back here to this little island then we have a good bay and can defend ourselves. The Korean fighters only have a range of four hundred and twenty miles. The nearest airfields are eighty miles inland. They can reach here, that is true, but they only have enough fuel for one attack. I am hoping that they will not expect us to head east after the attack. We can rest here and sail home in the dark."

"I am not complaining, sir. The brass always keeps us in the dark. I appreciate you taking us into your confidence. The lads like that. The last raid gave them confidence. Greeny will not be as nervous this time.

Campbell has actually fired his rifle at an enemy and thinks he is Wyatt Earp! We are lucky that we have so few young lads in the section."

"Aye well, best start getting ready." Above us, I heard Chief Jennings shout, "All hands prepare to leave harbour!" I smiled at the term harbour. We were in a sandy bay in the lee of a hill. I heard feet as they ran along the deck. Midshipman Brown would be signalling the two MTBs and we would soon be heading across the stretch of water to the North Korean mainland. Now that the Lieutenant was on deck I could use the officer's mess. I went to get ready. I would not need the Bergen. I would just use the battle jerkin. My weapons of choice were my two handguns, sap, grenades and dagger. If we could then we would capture the Korean guards but I would not risk my men. If they resisted then we would shoot them. Sergeant Heon would call on them to surrender. The rest was up to them. I would not black up yet although the men did. Private Harris gave them his rendition of 'Mammy' and they all joined in. I could see this becoming a ritual. Dad had told me that in the Great War pilots had used rituals before they flew. If they returned safely then it confirmed their belief that the ritual had worked and if not… then their number had been up.

I put the silencer in my battle dress pocket and my two automatics in their respective holsters. The sap and garotte wire went in the other battledress pocket. I ensured that the grenades were safely attached and donned my cap comforter.

"See you chaps on deck."

I needed nothing else. When the Lieutenant found the landing site then I would not need a map. Captain Poulson and Sergeant Major Thorpe had the longer-range weapons. We were doing what commandos did the best, we were utilising the skills of the whole team. Williams, with the radio, followed me on deck. I stood by the bridge and he stood in its lee. He looked at his watch. He sat and watched the sea.

"Too early?"

"Yes, sir. Tomahawk won't transmit until they have achieved their objective sir. That will be after dark. I will begin to listen in an hour. He is just going to transmit one word. We thought to keep it simple. Sitting Bull means they have blown the target and Crazy Horse means that there is a problem. If they send Geronimo then they are aborting the mission." I knew the code words but it did no harm for Williams to repeat them. His sole job would be to guard the radio and to be the link to the Rangers. He just had his service Colt and dagger. He did not even carry a grenade. As I looked west I saw the sun beginning to get lower to the horizon. As I looked astern I saw the other two boats in close attendance. Both were far faster than we were and if there was any threat to us from a vessel they would use their speed. We were the most heavily armed. I saw the rest of my troop on the two boats. The MTB was a smaller boat and they would be crowded. I knew how lucky we were. Petty Officer Flynn was wearing fatigues and a field cap. He would be our beachmaster. We needed someone to organise the embarkation. When the Rangers arrived, it would help them if it was an American voice telling them what to do.

My men emerged and they spread themselves on both sides of the boat. We would use the dinghy. The radio would have to be kept dry but most of the men would jump into the sea and wade ashore. I saw that it was Leading Seaman Wilkinson on the helm. I climbed up the ladder to join him and the Skipper. Lieutenant Drake pointed ahead, "The sea is getting up. I hope it doesn't cause us trouble at the beach. From what you tell me these Rangers could be all in by the time they reach us."

"They will be but they are as tough as my men. They will get aboard."

As the sun set Lance Corporal Williams checked his watch. He fired up the radio. I heard Williams as he spoke into the radio. "Tomahawk, this is General Custer authenticate over. Tomahawk, this is General Custer authenticate over. Tomahawk, this is General Custer authenticate over." There was silence. "Tomahawk, this is General Custer authenticate over." There was silence. I had been on many missions and knew that timing was fluid. We had decided on a time to blow the communication centre but a million and one events could have happened and the mission delayed.

I said, "Take off the cans, Williams so that we can all hear."

"Sir."

All we heard was static. "Tomahawk, this is General Custer authenticate over."

This time we heard, "General Custer this is Tomahawk I authenticate over."

"Tomahawk, this is General Custer I authenticate over."

"General Custer, this is Tomahawk, Sitting Bull, I say again, Sitting Bull, over."

"Tomahawk, this is General Custer out."

He looked up. "They did it, sir."

Korea

"So it seems." I turned to Lieutenant Drake. "Now we need to fulfil our side of the bargain; blow the tunnel and rescue them." He nodded. What the message did not tell us was if they had managed to secure transport.

When night fell I relaxed a little. I had worried that there might be some air patrols over the coast. Obviously, all of North Korea's military might was occupied trying to take the last corner of the south. They had missed their chance. Once America and the Commonwealth began to send troops in large numbers along with aircraft and ships they had no chance. We were in the hands of the Lieutenant and his midshipman. We were helped by the radar we had fitted. It did not have the range of a larger vessel but it would show us the coast and we would be able to make an accurate landfall. I knew that the Lieutenant would be worrying for much rested upon his navigational skills.

The Killick was relieved and Chief Jennings took over for the last part. The Killick fetched us cocoa. There was a tot of rum in it. With the Chief at the helm, the Lieutenant took the opportunity to smoke a pipe and drink his cocoa. I smiled. The Chief did not object to the Skipper smoking on deck!

"How much longer Lieutenant?"

"Forty-five minutes or so." He pointed to the radar repeater. I could see the coast ahead.

I nodded, "When I have finished this cocoa I will black up and then get the men organised."

I took the mug back to the galley and then went to my Bergen. I took out the burned cork and began to rub it on my face and the back of my hands. Sergeant Steinla had given me a tip. He said that it was just as effective if you put stripes on your face and hands. It broke up the outline and was easier to wash off. I looked in the mirror. I looked like a zebra or monochromatically challenged tiger! I checked that the flaps on the holsters were closed and went back up on deck.

"Sergeant Callow, you and Green go with Williams in the dingy."

"Sir."

"Lance Corporal Pike you lead Campbell and Harris starboard side. I will take Sergeant Heon port side. You and Petty Officer Flynn take charge on the beach until the radio is landed. Sergeant Heon and I will scout out the defences."

"Sir."

"From the aerial photographs, which were a week old, we had seen that they had sandbagged gun positions. The four machine guns faced both north and south. There was a second position with an anti-aircraft gun. The tents were higher up the slope, further west. We had studied the photographs after we had had our meeting with Major Hampton. Sergeant Heon had been a mine of information. He ascertained a crew of fifteen for the machine guns and ten for the anti-aircraft gun. That was more than we had been told but it made sense. I erred on the cautious side. We might have thirty men to deal with. It would make sense for them to have a night watch. I estimated five men; an NCO and four sentries.

I turned to Sergeant Heon. He was fitter now and I did not doubt his skills as a soldier. What I needed from him were the skills of a commando. We had managed to get him some rubber soled shoes. They had been Private Marsh's and they had been in the barracks when he had been killed. He also had a cap comforter but we would need him to wear his field cap. "Remember, Sergeant, we get as close to them as we can to assess numbers then, when my men are in position, you must use an authoritative voice to demand their surrender. We will shoot them if we have to."

"Yes, sir, I understand. I hope that my lack of skills does not jeopardise the mission."

"Just do your best eh?"

"Yes, sir. It is an honour to serve with you and your men. I look forward to the day when I can return home to Seoul and tell my wife and children what I did. There will be much honour in the telling of the tale."

Midshipman Brown appeared, "Sir, Skipper says he can see the beach ahead." He pointed. I saw that the land had suddenly grown and was a blacker mass than the sky.

"Stand by." I went to the bow and stood with Petty Officer Flynn. He pointed. "See there, sir, about eleven o'clock. I can see a light. I think they have a fire for their sentries."

I looked at where he pointed and, at first, I could see nothing. Then the light appeared. It was a dot but it was a fire. There must have been one of the Koreans walking in front of it. That made it easier for us. The sentries would be night blind. As we watched the land get closer I saw the waves breaking upon the beach. Able Seaman Hopkins appeared and lay down. He would signal the Lieutenant when he should reverse his engines. He did not want to become grounded. We were barely making way.

Petty Officer Flynn had his Thompson. He was a head shorter than I was. If he jumped too soon then the gun could drag him under. I said nothing. Petty Officer Flynn would have worked that out for himself. I saw the beach ahead. It was about forty yards away. With a draught of under five feet, we could get quite shallow and with the engine at the stern, the bow would ride a little higher anyway. Suddenly Hopkins' hand shot into the air. I leapt into the sea. I landed five feet from the bow. The water came up to my chest. I heard a splash behind me and turned. The Petty Officer was completely submerged. I reached down and grabbed the back of his uniform. I dragged him with me as I waded ashore. Sergeant Heon had seen the fate of Flynn and he made a prodigious leap to land almost next to me. As Petty Officer's face spluttered above the surface I let go. He coughed and spluttered but waved me forward. The surf would mask the sound of his cough and besides, we were half a mile from the position. Once we had secured it the three boats would drift down to us. Sergeant Heon and I ran across the beach and up the sandy and rocky slope to the road. This road had a good surface. I listened. The only noise I could hear above the surf was the wind which had gradually increased as we headed west. It seemed to wail. Harris and Campbell along with Lance Corporal Pike joined me. I took out my Colt and fitted the silencer. Until Captain Poulson joined us I was the only one with a silencer and so all three of them had a Thompson. We were going for firepower.

Captain Poulson and his men, minus the mortar and its crew, would join us. Sergeant Major Thorpe would set up a perimeter closer to the boats. Williams and his radio would be with them. We ran down the road at first. I could now see the brazier and at least three men with their backs to me. Our rubber-soled shoes made no noise on the tarmac. Harris was next to me with Heon close by. Harris had done this sort of thing in World War Two. Pike was on my left shoulder next to Heon. When we were two hundred yards from them I held up my hand. We stopped and I listened. I could hear them speaking. I waved to my right and Pike led Harris and Campbell up into the scrub so that they could cover the tents. I turned around and saw Captain Poulson leading the nine men from the other two sections. Sergeant Grant was with them. When they reached me, I waved to my left and Sergeant Grant led four of them towards the beach.

I pumped my arm twice and we headed towards the sandbags. I could make out the words but not the meaning. I relied on Sergeant Heon warning me if their voices displayed any anxiety. We crept closer. We moved in a half crouch and we were spread out in a semi-circle. Sergeant Heon was on my right and Captain Poulson to my left. I identified four men. Three were stood and one was lying on an elbow near to the brazier. I could smell the cigarette smoke. All of them were smoking. If Heon was correct then there had to be a fifth man but I could not see him. We had three sides covered. The only place left to run would be into the tunnel. That would not be disastrous. We moved even closer. It was now or never. I tapped Heon on the shoulder. I knew what he said for we had discussed it but I did not understand a word.

"Drop your weapons. You are surrounded by United Nations forces!" We all stepped forward as he spoke. That was partly as a threat but mainly to put our bodies between us and Sergeant Heon. I think they might have surrendered had the sergeant, who had been emptying his bowels, not risen less than ten yards from us, and shouted something. Captain Poulson fired one shot at him and his head disappeared. The other four made the mistake of going for their weapons. Private Lowe was a veteran and he swung his Thompson and smacked one of the Koreans in the head. Two turned their guns on Heon. Lowe's movement had left him exposed. The two men were just yards from me and I fired four shots at their legs. They collapsed in a heap. We had managed to do all of this without making a sound. Private Carter showed his inexperience and he fired his Thompson at the last man. I suspected that the men in the tents were already alerted but the five shots Carter fired guaranteed it. I heard shouts from the tents and the sound of a Tokarev. Then there was the chatter of Thompsons.

"Heon, shout for them to surrender."

Heon shouted as I said, "Cease fire! Cease fire!"

I think the shock of the submachine gun fire had the desired effect. Lance Corporal Pike's voice came from the dark. "They have had enough, sir. They are surrendering. They have wounded."

"Deal with it. Captain Poulson take charge here. Sergeant Heon, go and help Pike. Callow! Front and centre!" Sergeant Callow and Private Green ran to me. They were encumbered with explosives and cord. "Come on."

We ran the fifty yards to the tunnel. Green had a torch. He switched it to reveal the rough-hewn walls of the tunnel. As he played it along the walls Callow said, triumphantly, "Excellent. I can see the marks where they placed their charges. We don't need to drill. Green, the ladder!" Private Green had a little folding ladder and he took it from his back and quickly extended it. "You can leave this with us, sir. How long have we got?"

"Until the Rangers get here. Could be an hour maybe more."

"Right sir, we can do a good job then!"

I turned and walked back to the Korean gun emplacements. I looked at my watch. It was still at least two hours until dawn. Williams would have his ears glued to the headphones listening for a transmission from Tomahawk. Until that happened we would be in the dark. I reached the sandbags. Captain Poulson had sent the machine guns up to Sergeant Major Thorpe. "We have spiked the guns, sir, and set a booby trap. When we leave the ammunition will blow."

"Well done Captain. Casualties?"

"Us? None. We caught them by surprise. They have six dead and twelve wounded. Pike has attended all of their injuries and none are life-threatening. We have bound the prisoners' hands behind them and taken their boots."

I nodded, "As soon as we hear from the Rangers then get Sergeant Heon to send the prisoners along the road north. It will save us having to watch them and might slow down the enemy."

"They will know our numbers, sir."

"That does not worry me." I looked around. Everything seemed to be under control. "Take charge Captain. Put the wounded inside the sandbags. When we blow the tunnel, they will be far enough away to be safe. I will go and speak with Williams and then check the beach. Were there any papers?"

He nodded, "Sergeant Heon has them."

"Good."

My men had taken every weapon and piece of ammunition. Who knew when we might need them. Sergeant Thorpe had taken some of the sandbags from the anti-aircraft gun and had made a barricade across the road. The two Korean machine guns, the Bren and the mortar were protected. "Happy Sarn't Major?"

"Yes, sir. Unless they bring a tank, we can handle them."

I walked over to Williams. He was closer to the beach but protected by some rocks. "Anything?"

"No, sir. I hope they are alright. If they had a vehicle then I would have expected them to have radioed."

I shook my head. "I have been in their position and you are too concerned with surviving to bother with an update. Keep listening."

I walked down to the beach. The three boats were tethered by stakes driven into the sand and were stern on. Petty Officer Flynn prowled along it with a cigar in his mouth. He smiled when he saw me, "We heard gunfire, sir. Every go okay?"

"Yes, Petty Officer. We have no casualties but they lost a few men."

He pointed north. "We heard the gunfire. On a quiet night like this sound will travel for miles sir." He was warning me that those in the next town might have heard.

"I know but now we wait for the Rangers, no matter what happens."

"The radar doesn't show anything, sir. We can take that as a good sign."

"Indeed, we can Petty Officer. Indeed, we can."

As I headed up the slope I turned. Did I detect the hint of dawn in the east? Everything had gone well so far. We now needed the Rangers. It was as I neared Sergeant Major Thorpe that I saw the flashes in the distance and the cracks of small arms fire. To the west of us, there was firing and it did not take an Einstein to work out that it must be the Rangers. Nearing the road, I estimated that they were about two or three miles away. The road they might have used turned north just two miles away. If Petty Officer Thorpe was right then we might have been heard by the troops north of us. It was time for a gamble.

I headed towards the tunnel, "Sergeant Heon, set the captives and the walking wounded marching north. Tell them that the United Nations frees them and hopes that they will not bear arms against us again."

He looked at me as though I had lost my mind. "They will fight us again, sir."

"I know, just tell them eh?"

"Sir!" He rattled off in Korean and the captives, at first incredulously and then with relief headed north along the road. They ran. There were just four men with leg wounds who remained.

"Captain Poulson, I believe the Rangers will be heading from the north. Leave Pike with the wounded and spread the rest of the men out in a skirmish line half a mile north of here. If there is firing then they will be coming in hot. The codewords are Sitting Bull and the response is General Custer."

"Sir, Sergeant Grant get the men together."

I headed down to the tunnel. Callow was smoking a cigarette. "Trouble sir? We heard firing."

"I heard firing to the north. The Rangers are on their way. Set the fuses to go off in forty-five minutes then go and give Petty Officer Flynn a hand."

Dawn would be upon us soon after the tunnel was blown. Time was running out for the Captain and his Rangers. I had just emerged when I heard to the west a dull whump. I wondered what it was. I was on my way back to the roadblock when Petty Officer Flynn huffed and puffed his way towards me, "Sir, the radar has picked up movement on the road. The operator can't determine what it is."

"It is men from the north. Tell the Lieutenant to prepare to leave. Things could get a little sticky!"

"Sir!"

"Sarn't Major! Trouble is on the way. Williams, get the radio back to the boat. The Rangers will be too busy to use it and we could use you on a Thompson."

"Sir."

It was obvious that Sergeant Major Thorpe had everything under control. "I will go and give the Captain a hand."

"No problem sir."

I took out my Colt and fitted a fresh magazine. I also fitted my silencer. I might just need it. The sporadic firing I had heard from the west was now definitely closer. I caught up with Private Harris. He did not speak but pointed west. I squatted next to him behind a poplar. I glanced right and saw a line of my men thinly spread out. I saw them because I was looking for them. I heard the sound of rifles and submachine guns. They were not American. I even saw muzzle flashes in the dark. The fact that there were no American bullets in reply was a good sign. The Rangers were evading. They knew what the North Koreans did not. They knew that we were waiting. I cocked my Colt and heard the reassuring clicks all the way down the line. We were ready.

Ahead of me, there was a movement in the trees. I heard Sergeant Grant say, "Sitting Bull!"

A relieved American voice said, "General Custer!"

"Advance friend."

It was Sergeant Steinla, "The rest are right behind me, sir. We have about three truckloads of Commies hard on our tail."

More of his men appeared and they stopped and turned. We heard the sound of a Colt in the distance. There were eight shots. Someone had emptied a magazine. Then there was the sound of a number of guns and a cry. A wounded Ranger staggered in. "They hit Ranger Harris, Sarge. The Captain is with him."

"Sergeant stay here! Captain Poulson, take charge."

I ran towards the firing. I saw muzzle flashes. I aimed at one of the muzzle flashes and fired. The phut from the gun would not be heard and the muzzle flashes masked. I heard a cry. I moved forward and saw four Koreans. They were advancing towards our lines. They held rifles with curved magazines. I let them pass. My men would take them. I was searching for Captain Rogers and whoever was left out here with him. Suddenly the silence was torn apart as my men opened fire on the four Koreans whom I had passed. The sound allowed me to move. Ahead I heard Korean voices. Just then I heard the distinctive sound of a Bren. Sergeant Major Thorpe was under attack. The Korean voices I heard also showed their surprise. I knew the sky was becoming lighter for I could see more. The light must have helped the Koreans too for I heard a shout and then the sound of their rifles. A Colt answered them with four shots and there was a cry. Captain Rogers and his wounded Ranger were less than fifty yards from me.

I saw a pair of Koreans ahead. They broke through the undergrowth and began to set up a machine gun. I rose and, running towards them, fired at them. The three shots hit them and as they fell I ran beyond them aware that the tunnel was due to blow. I kicked over the machine gun as I passed the two writhing Koreans. There were more Korean bullets. I saw four Koreans. They had an officer with them and, pointing towards some rocks and an area of shrubs, he shouted something. Even as they ran I opened fire. I emptied the Colt. Three fell and the other two looked for the source of the bullets. I drew my Luger and shot the other two.

As I neared the rocks I shouted, "Captain Rogers, Commandos coming in."

I burst through the undergrowth and clambered over the rocks. Captain Rogers and Ranger Harris were in a protective hollow. I jerked my thumb for them to come out. Turning I put my guns on the rock, took a hand grenade and, using the elevation of the stone threw it high towards the west. I dropped. Taking off the silencer I holstered the Colt and put the silencer in my pocket. I still had bullets in the nine millimetre. Harris was hurt in the leg. I saw the field dressing. Captain

Rogers hoisted him up and I put my hands under his armpits. We manhandled him out of the den and over the rock. I pointed east. "Your men are safe. Head there and I will cover you! You are half a mile from the beach." To the north, the mortars and small arms fire was intensifying. As Captain Rogers slung the Ranger over his shoulder he gave me a questioning look. "Move, Captain, we have company!"

He began to move. He had not gone ten yards when the tunnel blew. I was expecting it but the power and noise still surprised me. The air around me seemed to shake. Two Koreans ahead of me rose in surprise. I shot them in the leg and then turned to run after Captain Rogers. As the concussion from the explosion rolled over us then dust began to fall. My hearing was affected and I could no longer hear the sound of Sergeant Major Thorpe's battle. I kept glancing behind but I saw no one. We must have been two hundred yards from safety when the submachine gun shredded the leaves of the bushes behind me. I turned and resting my elbow on my knee, emptied the automatic as I turned half a circle. I took a grenade, pulled the pin, released the handle, counted to four and threw it high. I dropped to the ground and covered my ears. The grenade exploded twenty yards from me but in the air. The shrapnel scythed through the undergrowth and there were cries. I reloaded my Colt and holstered the automatic. I rose and ran after the Captain.

Dawn was breaking and I spotted Sergeant Grant as he rose, "You had us worried, sir."

I nodded. I walked with him and saw Pike and the Ranger medic tending to the injured Harris. "Captain Rogers take your men to the beach. Petty Officer Flynn will see to your embarkation. Captain Poulson, take your men and extract Sergeant Major Thorpe."

Captain Poulson said, "Sir, come on lads!"

Captain Rogers still looked in shock. "Sergeant Steinla take the Captain and men back. I will stay with the medic."

"Come on sir, these guys know what they are doing." The fifteen Rangers hurried after their Sergeant and the Captain he led.

Lance Corporal Pike looked up. "This will just take a jiffy."

I saw that the Ranger still held his M1 Carbine. He grinned, "Thanks, sir. When I am bandaged I will give you a hand."

The Ranger medic shook his head, "You big lummox follow orders for once! Getting wounded is becoming a bad habit you need to shake! Put your arm around my shoulder." He and Pike lifted the huge American and they began to head towards the beach. I could hear that the

Koreans had recovered and were moving through the undergrowth. I had two grenades left. I took them both out and hurled them into the shrubs and woods ahead of me. I threw one to my right and one to my left. I threw myself to the ground and sent four bullets into the undergrowth. Bullets came back and then the two grenades went off. I heard moans. I rose and ran down the road.

As I neared the roadblock I saw that it was all over. Haynes and Barton were already packing up their mortar and Captain Poulson was directing men to the beach. I saw in the lightening dawn that the Rangers were being helped aboard the three boats. We would be crowded.

Sergeant Thorpe pointed to the burned-out vehicles. "We took them by surprise, sir. Twenty of them headed west when the tunnel blew."

"Get the men aboard. There are still Koreans behind me. I think we have discouraged them but… any casualties?"

"Just Hope and Collins. Both were hit but not seriously. They were sent to the beach."

I saw that there were just four of us left. "Right, let's go."

We walked backwards to the beach. Once I felt the sand beneath my shoes I turned and we headed towards the boats. We had almost reached Petty Officer Flynn when he suddenly seemed to aim his gun at us. He shouted, "Down!" As we dropped to the sand he emptied the Thompson. The six pounder on 523 opened fire as did the Oerlikon. "Right sir, you can get aboard now!" I looked back and saw a knot of North Korean soldiers.

Lieutenant Drake had rigged a scrambling net over the side and we clambered aboard. Leading Seaman Wilkinson grinned as he helped Petty Officer Flynn aboard. "Just like Errol Flynn in Objective Burma!" For some reason that seemed to please the American.

As I made the deck the net was pulled up and the Fairmile put into reverse. The motor gun boat now felt like home. I clambered up on to the deck. Midshipman Brown said, "Just in time sir. I think they sent something heavier down the road. Looks like tanks." He handed me the powerful field glasses. The sun bathed the coast in a cold harsh light. Looking through them I saw T-34s. They were still two miles away but they would have made a mess of both my men and the boats if they had arrived sooner.

We spun and turned. The three boats formed a line astern and headed south and east. That course was to throw off the Koreans. As soon as we were a mile from land we turned due east to head to Dagelet. The crew were all closed up. This was the dangerous time. The Koreans would have scrambled aeroplanes and would be seeking us. Wilkinson brought me a mug of tea and a corned beef sandwich.

"Here y'are sir. It is a bit crowded below decks. Petty Officer Flynn is busy organising them."

"Thanks, Killick." I swallowed some of the tea and then devoured the sandwich. I had not realised that I was so hungry.

Lieutenant Drake was scanning the skies with his glasses. We had radar but old habits die hard. He said, without turning. "How did it go?"

"Better than we might have hoped. I have not had a chance to speak with Captain Rogers but he lost men."

"We are not out of the woods. That was a hell of an explosion! They would have heard that in Pyongyang!"

"The longer they delay sending birds after us the more chance we have."

"You are certain about the endurance of their aeroplanes, sir?"

I nodded, "I am a pilot. Dad told me that the two limiting factors in fighting aeroplanes are fuel and ammo. Ships can carry far more of both. I am not saying they won't come for us but if they do then it will be a short sharp attack and then they will have to run. Just head east as fast as you can."

He nodded, "We could allow the other two to use full speed, sir."

I shook my head, "We need the combined firepower of three boats and their men."

I finished my tea and took out my pipe. I had just got it going when Captain Rogers appeared at the bottom of the ladder. The bridge was crowded already and so I descended and we went aft to the lee of the second six pounder. "Thanks for coming for us sir. Sergeant Steinla told me."

"We never leave a man behind. Was it tough?"

"Only the last part. We stole a truck and headed towards you guys. We were unlucky. We ran into a roadblock and one of my guys panicked. They opened fire before our interpreter could try to con our way through it. We killed the Koreans but they killed the interpreter and wrecked the radio. I guess we were heard. We hadn't gone two miles before we were pursued. They had their version of a jeep with a machine gun. It killed four of my men before we destroyed it. That bought us some time. We reached the part of the road where we had to leave. We booby-trapped the truck with the bodies of our guys inside and then headed east."

I nodded, "I heard the explosion. I wondered at the time."

"We made good time and I thought we had escaped but they must have risked their vehicles in the woods. We heard them and they caught us. We delayed them with booby traps and little ambushes. We knew we were getting close when we smelled the sea. I thought we were going to make it when Harris saw four Koreans. He opened fire and he was hit in the leg in the firefight. I grabbed him and found the little hidey hole. Then you came!"

I took out my silencer. "These are worth their weight in gold, Captain. In our line of work the silencer can be the difference between life and death."

Just then, Midshipman Brown shouted, "Gun crew close up! Enemy aircraft to the west!"

I turned to the Captain, "I would get your men on deck with their weapons. This is not over yet!"

Chapter 11

Sergeant Callow met me with my Thompson. I pointed to the stern, "We can help the stern six pounder!"

Our formation meant that we were the leading ship and we would be the last to be attacked. I shaded my eyes and saw the six Lavochkin La 9s as they began to descend. They came from the west. I guessed that they had searched further south for us first. I hoped they were on the limit of their fuel. Even as I cocked the Thompson I heard the Midshipman shout. "Prepare to fire!"

The six aeroplanes were wasting no time. They had to be low on fuel. They screamed lower and lower. 256 was at the rear of our line and her guns opened first. The quick firing six pounder, behind us, began to fire. The Oerlikons joined in. The Americans and my men on the other boats opened fire. I waited along with the machine guns next to the bridge. I watched the cannon shells strike 256. Even as smoke began to pour from her the first Lavochkin exploded in mid-air. The concussion and turbulence threw the next pilot off to the side. The smoke must have put off the third pilot for his bullets and shells struck the sea.

"Open fire!"

I had fourteen men with me and we sent up a cone of lead. The Lavochkin shuddered and shook as our bullets hit it. I heard the change in the pitch of its engine. It was hurt and it headed home. The last three came swooping down in line abreast. They poured shells and bullets into 527 and 256. The quick firing six pounder hit the middle aircraft and it exploded just a hundred feet astern of 256. And then they were gone. The four survivors must have been on fumes.

Smoke was pouring from 256 and we and 527 went to her aid. Even as we went the radar rating emerged, "Sir, four patrol boats three miles away."

I saw the Lieutenant train his glasses west. "Middy signal 527 to take 256 under tow. Ask Lieutenant King to take command. We are going to slow down the patrol boats."

I turned, "Spread yourselves out on both sides of the boat. Find cover close to the bridge." This was where I needed Haynes and Barton. A mortar could do some serious damage to a patrol boat. We would have to make do with what we had. I would ask for a grenade launcher and a bazooka for our next raid. The four patrol boats were too far away for me to make them out clearly but from the information I had, they were not as heavily armed as we were. The problem was they outnumbered us and could attack on both sides at the same time. The crew all had steel helmets and they would need them. I put in a fresh magazine. I reloaded both my handguns. The Vickers K guns were both at the side. The Oerlikons, like the six pounders, were in line. The only other offensive weapons were the depth charges. I knew that the Lieutenant was contemplating using them when he sent Able Seaman Hopkins down to the stern.

Next to me, I had Harris and Campbell. Williams was next to them. Sergeant Callow and my other men were on the far side. The Americans were at the bow and the stern. It was my men who would be at the greatest risk for the patrol boats would target the bridge. I pulled the fenders closer to me. They might not stop a bullet but they would stop splinters from the wooden hull of the Fairmile D. I lay down and rested the Thompson on the fender. Once again, I regretted not having a rifle with a telescopic sight. I might not have the firepower but a bullet which took out a helmsman could win a sea battle.

The Lieutenant had slowed us down. I knew that it would take time to take the stricken MTB in tow. A slower speed might make us an easier target but we would have a stable firing platform and that was more important. We were an MGB. We had as much firepower as half a dozen small patrol boats. I peered along the side of the boat. I could see the black specks as they bounced on the water. The sea was a little choppy. If the North Koreans had any sense they would slow down but I suspected that they sought revenge for our attack on their land. I saw that the two boats on our side both had a gun at the bow. That could be anything from a machine gun to a two pounder. When the leading boat opened fire, I saw that it was an Oerlikon. It was using tracer and I saw the bullets arc. The gunner was using it for ranging. He fired twenty rounds. They fell short. The Koreans were approaching at a great rate of knots. Lieutenant Drake was very experienced. He waited until we were just over two thousand yards away. This was the most effective range for a six pounder. As he spun the wheel over he shouted, "Shoot! Shoot! Shoot!" The speed of the patrol boats brought them even closer very quickly.

The crews had all been waiting and, because of his manoeuvre, both six pounders were able to open fire. As luck would have it both guns fired at the leading boat on our port side. With the Oerlikons adding their fire the leading patrol boat exploded in a volcanic eruption of petrol and ammunition. The boat and its crew simply disintegrated. The second boat took evasive action and the rear Oerlikon stitched a line across its hull. The skipper continued his turn and the two six pounders, emboldened by their success, continued to pour shell after shell into the two patrol boats which had been on our starboard side.

The Lieutenant shouted, "I am going full circle. Small arms and K guns you will be in range!"

The two Korean patrol boats were manned by men who were no cowards and they fired at us. I heard their shells cannoning off the bridge. Had we not sheltered then some of us would be dead. The Oerlikon on one of the patrol boats disappeared under a torrent of shells and the second one had its wooden bridge raked by our two Oerlikons. When it veered to port we knew the bridge had been decimated. The two guns turned as the ship did and they continued to pour shell after shell into the two patrol boats.

As we came around the last boat, the one which had taken evasive action, was less than four hundred yards from us. "Open fire!"

Every gun from rifle to six pounder fired at what was, effectively, point blank range. Miraculously the boat did not explode but I saw blood flowing from the scuppers as the holed boat began to drift and then to slowly sink. The last two boats had had enough and they turned and headed north-west. The gun crew continued to score hits until the skipper shouted, "Cease fire!"

We turned to head after our two consorts. They had not moved. Men were still dousing the fire and trying to attach the two. I stood, "Anyone hurt?" I saw my men rise and raise their hands to show that they lived. One of the Rangers said, "Lee was hit in the leg, sir, and Jones has wooden splinters in his face."

"Pike!"

"Sir!"

The SBA and my Lance Corporal hurried along to deal with them. Automatically I changed my magazine. It was unlikely that we would be attacked again but it paid to be prudent. I walked to the stern and Captain Rogers. "I think we annoyed them a little Captain. They certainly came after us."

"Yes sir and paid the price." He looked ahead to the two MTBs. "I hope my guys are alright." I said nothing. I worried about Sergeant Major Thorpe but there was little we could do about the tragic events. They had just been unlucky.

By the time we pulled alongside to add another rope to the tow, the fire was out. Sub Lieutenant Guttridge was bandaged. He had one around his head and his right arm was in a sling. Lieutenant Drake walked to the stern to speak with the young skipper, "How is it, Richard?"

"A mess sir. The engine room bore the brunt of the attack. I have lost Chief Petty Officer Hardacre and Petty Officer Keely. Twelve others are either badly wounded or dead. Three Rangers died and two of the commandos. Sorry, sir."

"Not your fault, Richard. Do you need help?"

"I have an SBA and the Ranger medic is aboard. We will manage. It is only an hour or so to the island."

"Good man! You are safe in our hands. He walked to the starboard side. "Peter, keep it at ten knots. There is no rush. I intend to spend the night on the island while we affect repairs!"

"Yes, sir!"

Towing a boat is a tricky affair. The two captains had to work as one so as to minimise the stress on the stricken ship. Once we reached ten knots then the motion became easier. Our men and the Rangers mucked in to make tea and sandwiches. I think it was more to keep active than anything else. We kept a good watch but we were too far from Korean waters to be in any real danger. When the island hove into view I felt a real sense of relief. We landed men who took the rope and hauled 256 on to the beach. We emptied her of men. We rigged the parachutes the Rangers had used as tents. The two engineering officers went aboard 256 to see what they could do. Both sets of soldiers scavenged in the rocks for shellfish to make a stew. It was what we did. By the time it was dark we had repaired the hull of 256 so that she would not sink but the engine needed a shipyard. We would have to tow her all the way back to Dongbaek-Ri.

The officers and NCOs of our little force of raiders ate together on the beach. We were all anxious to learn from each other. "You were right about the parachute jump, sir. We lost two men before we even began the mission."

Sergeant Steinla nodded his agreement. "Yes, sir I would have dropped lower than we did. It is a little riskier but you all land together."

"Any problems with the communications centre?"

Captain Rogers shook his head, "I think they thought they were so far inland and well-hidden that they were safe. They had just four sentries. We took those out and the rest was easy. We need better intelligence about their inland defences. We should have known where the danger lay and we didn't."

"I have a feeling that was deliberate."

Sergeant Steinla growled, "You mean they wanted us to run into trouble, sir?"

"Let us just say that this mission was intended to draw attention to our presence in the eastern half of their country. Look at the response to our raids. Six aeroplanes and four patrol boats. The fact that we hurt them is just lucky. If you were the North Koreans then you would be worrying that we were the prelude to something larger."

Just then the radio rating on 523 waved to Lieutenant Drake who was also eating ashore, "Sir, it is base. A Major Hampton wants to speak to you, Major Harsker and Captain Rogers."

I laughed as I stood, "I am guessing that we have been summoned to the headmaster's office!"

Lieutenant Drake grinned, "Six of the best eh?"

Captain Rogers looked confused. I explained to him. "It is like going to the principal's office and being caned."

"Ah. What have we done wrong?"

As we climbed up the scrambling net I said, "I think the Major does not approve of our using our initiative. He assumed we would head due south."

We climbed aboard, "But that would have meant we were attacked by more ships and aircraft!"

"Exactly!"

Lieutenant Drake said, "Put it on speaker, Wentworth, and then go and get yourself a cup of cocoa."

"Sir."

Lieutenant Drake picked up the microphone. "Drake here. Over!"

"This is Major Hampton. Is everyone there? Is this on speaker? Over."

"Yes, sir. Over!"

"Where are you? Over."

"A place called Dagelet Island sir. We are making repairs. Over."

"Repairs? What is the damage? Over."

"256 was hit by cannon fire. She has lost her engine room and we will have to tow her back. Over."

"That will take too long. Burn her and come directly back. Over."

The Lieutenant was going to speak but I shook my head, "Major Harsker here. As senior officer, I have taken the decision to tow back the ship. Out!" I smiled as I turned off the speaker. "Lieutenant I took the liberty of bringing the last of the whisky on board. Let us take it ashore and drink it eh?"

Captain Rogers said, "What about Major Hampton?"

"Well eventually Leading Seaman Wentworth will come back and he will tell the Major that we are ashore. I am sure he will get the picture."

We felt safe on the island. The Koreans could not hurt us and we enjoyed a pleasant evening drinking whisky and eating seafood. It was a change from corned beef. The next day we spread the wounded between the two undamaged vessels and took 256 in tow. We had learned much the previous day. We had a hundred and thirty miles to go. And at ten knots it took us all day. Major Hampton sent over a pair of Mustangs to monitor our progress. He could not hurry us in any case.

We approached the wharf at dusk. We had radioed ahead so that 256 could be berthed close to the workshop. I suspect that it was too late for Major Hampton to venture forth. In any event, we were able to send our wounded to the mobile army surgical hospital, the MASH unit, that was attached to the base. As there had been little fighting for a day or so it was quiet. Ranger Harris was adamant that his wound would not keep him out of the war. As he was taken away on a stretcher he extended a hand, "Major, I didn't get to thank you for coming back for the Captain and me. I guess you really did earn those medals!"

"We never leave a man behind, Harris. But could I advise a little more caution when you go to war again. Otherwise, you will have an exciting albeit short life!"

I was not certain he understood what I meant for he shook his head and grinned, "If I could talk like you, sir, I would be beating off women with a stick!"

The Rangers were driven in our lorry back to their base by Petty Officer Flynn. While the men prepared the food, I sat and wrote my reports. I was keenly aware that this report would come under extreme scrutiny. I had to make certain that all of my actions and decisions could be justified. From the number of ships in the small port and the others, we had seen heading for the port of Pusan further south I knew that the balance of power had to swing in the allies' favour. As I wrote my report I wondered how that would be achieved. We ate well thanks to Petty

Officer Flynn. He took off in one of the trucks with Sergeant Heon and the two Korean drivers. He arrived back with pork chops!

The next morning, I went with the Petty Officer to meet with Major Hampton and Captain Rogers for a debrief. The journey took longer than normal as the road was choked with tanks and trucks heading north and west. We were whisked directly to the conference room and, this time, the Petty Officer was dismissed. I noticed two huge Marines on guard outside the door. Captain Rogers came in and nodded at the door, "What is with the muscle, sir? We in trouble?"

The door opened again and Sergeant Aitkens entered. She must have had sharp hearing for she said, "No, Captain Rogers; both your units did exactly what was planned. I believe that the brass, as you call them, will be well pleased. Major Hampton will be along directly. I came early to speak with the Major. Captain Rogers, if you could get yourself a coffee and close your ears then I would appreciate it."

I smiled. This was no sergeant! Captain Rogers just grinned as he walked to the far end of the room where there was a pot of coffee and doughnuts.

She sat next to me and took off her fake glasses. "I have spoken with London and they are sending someone to speak with you. I told a Major Foster what you told us. He then got back to me with another of your officers. He said he was L and he would be on a flight out as soon as he could manage it. Does that mean anything to you?"

I nodded. "I was briefed by him before I left England. It must be important if he flies halfway around the world to speak with me."

She gave me a wry smile. "Don't flatter yourself, Major. You are part of the reason he is coming and not the whole one. You are the ones in uniform who fight with guns. There are others who fight our enemies in other ways. Both are important."

"Thank you for telling me."

She nodded, "Tell me, Major, why did you volunteer?" She was staring at me as she spoke. She had stunning green eyes.

"If I am honest I didn't. I responded to a request and found myself here."

"Yet we both know that you could have refused. You are in the Reserve. There are other officers who are regulars. They could have come. I don't say they would have done a better job but they could have come."

"You are right and my wife would be endorsing everything you say. I don't know. I would rather be at home with my children and my family but there must be something in me; patriotism, loyalty, I honestly don't know. I just can't sit back and let others risk their lives. I am not being arrogant but I am quite good at this job. I like to think that I help to save men's lives while still getting the job done. I don't always please my superiors but they are not important to me."

She laughed and suddenly looked younger than she appeared. She was an actress. "You can say that again. Major Hampton was almost apoplectic with rage when you hung up on him. It was all I could do to keep a straight face."

"You were with him?"

We heard footsteps outside. She became serious again and donned her glasses. "I am part of the planning team, Major."

It begged the question, planning team for what? When the door opened I had my answer for General Douglas MacArthur walked in with Major Hampton and a covey of senior officers. Captain Rogers and I leapt to attention. The General nodded and drawled, "At ease!" He sat at the head of the table. "Sit. We have no time to waste!" Captain Rogers sat next to me. Major Hampton sat next to Sergeant Aitkens. The General took out his famous corn cob pipe. He began to fill it. He looked at me, "Major, I understand you are a pipe man too. Feel free to smoke."

It did not sound like a request, more like an order. "Yes, sir." I took out my pipe and my pouch. I was aware of the silence in the room and the fact the General was watching me. I shaved some tobacco from the bar and began to crush it into flakes. I filled the pipe loosely and struck a match. I drew on the pipe to get it going and then tamped it down. It was drawing well and I did not need to use a second match.

The General smiled, "I can see you are a real pipe man. I haven't used bar tobacco for many a year." He held his hand out. "Do you mind, Major?"

I slid the pouch and knife over to him, "Be my guest, General."

He sniffed it and his eyes widened, "Whisky?"

"Yes sir, a sailor taught me the trick in World War Two. He used rum but whisky works as well. It gives a nice flavour and keeps it moist."

"I can see. I use orange peel."

I nodded, "I would too sir but in the war, it was a little in short supply back in England!"

He laughed and filled his pipe. He pushed my pouch and knife back to me. When he had it going he nodded, "Nice tobacco." He jabbed his pipe in my direction. "This, gentlemen, is a real soldier. Forget the medals, they are show. I have read this man's record. Major Hampton might want him on charges," I saw the Major flush, "but his decisions are all sound military ones. Major, Captain, you were used on my behalf. I don't work that way. I like to look a man in the eye and tell him why he does something." He glared at Sergeant Aitkens next to me who did not flinch. "Your men were sent to make it look as though we were going to invade the east of North Korea. We aren't! But we are going to invade. The North Koreans have got us on the ropes, gentlemen. They are still pushing us back. I am sending troops to prepare defences at Taegu, Masan, and Pohang. We have to blunt the enemy attack and then attack ourselves. Your two units are our only offensive weapon. You are like the defenders of the Alamo and I am Sam Houston. You have to buy me time. You have to hit behind their lines and keep them looking over their shoulders. Task Force Smith and the Eighth Army along with the rest of the allies will hold them until I am ready to strike but you need to give me August!"

August! A whole month of raiding. My face showed my shock.

The General laughed, "There is no guile about you Major nor you Captain. Yes, I am asking for the impossible. And there is a good reason for that. The Rangers and the Commandos do the impossible every day! I promise you this, whatever you need you shall have. You both have the targets and the missions. You two have shown that you do your best even when you are hamstrung. Keep doing that for August and you will have my thanks. You, Major, will be able to go back to your family. So, what do you say? Are you my boys?"

It was weird, we both chorused, at the same time, "Sir, yes sir."

The General laughed, "Real soldiers, Hampton, real soldiers!"

Major Hampton stood, "If you would come with me Major, Captain, I will escort you back to your vehicles."

I saw Sergeant Aitkens hiding a smile as we left.

Once we were outside the Major said, "There will be a Lieutenant McKenzie who will be your new liaison officer. I will be working more closely with the General on the invasion plans." He held his hand out. "I hope there are no hard feelings, Major Harsker. I was just doing a job."

Korea

I shook his hand, "No hard feelings, Major, but there are ways and there are ways of doing a job. Honesty works with real soldiers. The General showed you that."

"Yes, well, good luck. Lieutenant McKenzie will be in touch." He scurried back into the building.

I laughed and Captain Rogers smiled, "We must be doing something right if Dugout Doug approves."

I shook my head and tapped Captain Rogers' chest, "Jack, you know in here when you have done something right!"

He saluted, "I am not sure if our paths will cross again. From the look of it, my team will be operating inland and north-west of here."

I saluted back, "You never know. Good luck Ranger."

He turned and headed for his barracks. I sat in the passenger seat and waited for Petty Officer Flynn to return. When he did come he had two privates with him and they had boxes. The three of them were laden. Petty Officer Flynn secured them with a bungee cord. I said nothing until the privates had left us. "More steak Mr Flynn?"

He stuck the stump of a cigar in his mouth and grinned. As he started the jeep he said, "I won't deny that there is food there, sir, but there is also a bazooka with rockets and two grenade launchers and grenades."

"How did you get them so quickly?"

"I went to the Quartermaster and asked. He said that whatever we wanted we could have."

I nodded as we left the compound. "I guess General MacArthur meant what he said."

For the first time since I had known him, the petty officer showed surprise. "Dugout Doug is here?" I nodded. "I carried him and his family once when we bugged out of the Philippines. I was just a young sailor then. I could still see my feet!" He nodded, "Then things will start to get done now, sir. I feel better already!"

With some of the men in the hospital, albeit temporarily, we had more room in the barracks. I sent Williams to fetch Lieutenant Drake so that I could tell him our news. With Captain Poulson and my three senior NCOs, I told them of my meeting. Lieutenant Drake shook his head. "I felt certain that you would have had at least a reprimand, sir."

"I have been lucky so far, Lieutenant. Those who have been in command of my unit have been good officers. MacArthur knows his business. Perhaps because he got up the greasy pole so quickly made a difference. Anyway, we can make sure that 256 is repaired properly and that we are fully crewed before we start to raid." I took out the next mission. "It looks like this one is just north of Pohang." Now that I had spoken with the General I understood his strategy. We were holding on to the three towns he had mentioned and he wanted to choke their supplies. Thanks to our air superiority the Koreans were forced to bring supplies down at night. They used convoys to do so. We were to ambush one.

I pointed to a bay seven miles north of Pohang. The main road south passed within a mile of the bay. Our brief was to disrupt their supplies. We had the latitude to decide where. We had done this journey before and forewarned is forearmed. "Lieutenant, we need more protection from air attack. The cannon shells cause too much damage to such flimsy craft. See if the resourceful Mr Flynn can manage to get some thin sheets of metal. The boats won't look pretty but a few sheets around the bridge will protect the helmsman and the engine room."

"Sir."

"Sergeant Major, Green in my section is capable and has learned to use explosives. I want two men from your section to work with Sergeant Callow, here, and Private Green to allow us to use two teams in the future."

"Sir."

"Captain Poulson, we have a couple of days while the boat is being repaired. We take the men out twice a day. I want us to be able to run to the road, ambush the convoy and run back! It is only one mile. I want us to be able to run, with kit, and cover one mile in eight minutes." I pointed. "There is a road."

"Eight minutes?" He whistled. "A tall order."

"We can do it. Just to prove we can I am going to set a target of six minutes for myself. Sergeant Major Thorpe and you can be at the rear. I know not all of our men will manage it the first time but if we do not stretch ourselves then we will become sloppy. See you at six a.m.!"

I had set myself a hard target but I was determined to give it my best shot. I had run a six-minute mile but that had been when I was younger and in running gear. How would I cope with a full Bergen? We had done the route a number of times. Since our last run, however, the small port had burgeoned as more men and equipment were landed. As I ran in battle dress with my crown on my shoulder we were not harassed but I knew that we caused a stir as we raced around the narrow streets. The crowds meant that we could not relax into our running. We had to keep our wits about us. I had a second hand on my watch but I had Petty Officer Flynn waiting at the barracks with a stopwatch we borrowed from 523 and a clipboard to record all of the times. My men were competitive. Whoever was last would ensure that, on the next run, they would not be. I just had to make certain that I was able to keep up a steady pace.

I ran the first half mile using a steady rhythm which would enable the men to make an eight-minute mile pace. Then I began to open my legs and to work my arms. The Bergen was a good rucksack and I had adjusted the straps to make it chafe less. I knew that some of the younger men would not have done so and they would suffer. I glanced over my shoulder after two miles and saw that I had stretched out my men but that Private Carter was the closest to me and he was grinning. Since Blair's defection, he had been a changed man as had Evans. Carter still kept to himself but he was more confident and bantered along with the others. Captain Poulson had told me that he was very steady under fire. More than that he was clever. He had potential as a non-commissioned officer.

At the fourth mile, there was a slight hill. I shortened my stride but drove at it. As it happened there was a turn there for the main road headed north and we would be heading back to the sea. I was able to see that the troop was spread out over more than half a mile. Carter was still twenty yards back and did not look to be suffering. That was the last slope and I opened my legs again as we headed to the sea. I felt better than I had expected. I checked my watch. I was on target for just over six minutes for a mile. I was not out of breath but the straps of the Bergen were beginning to rub. I needed some grease where they rubbed. I would see Flynn. I was pounding as I ran towards the petty officer. There was an invisible tape for me to break. I checked my watch and turned around. Carter was just forty yards behind and did not look distressed. Collins, Lowe and Williams were the next three in and they did the run in seven-minute mile pace. Sergeant Heon managed just over seven minutes a mile. The last ones over the line were the Captain and Sergeant Major and the two Korean drivers. They only managed nine minutes. I had not asked the drivers to do it. They had volunteered. They were bent over double and could hardly breathe. It showed the level of fitness of my men.

I nodded. "Petty Officer Flynn will post the results and times in the barracks. This afternoon we go out again. This time a shorter course, just four miles. The target is seven minutes for a mile." I saw the looks of horror and heard the groans.

Over the next two days, the team became both faster and fitter. Even the Korean drivers managed eight-minute miles. When we were not running we were preparing to attack the convoy. It was Evans and Black who were trained in explosives. Black had already shown ability with explosives and Evans was his oppo. We needed to stop the convoy with explosives. By using the two ends we had the chance to inflict the maximum damage. Carter and Collins trained with the bazooka while Hope and Campbell practised with the grenade launcher. Thanks to the General's order we had plenty of ammunition. In my odd time of quiet, I visited 256 to see how the work was progressing. Replacements arrived for the dead and we even had a couple of spare hands.

As July came to a close we heard that the fighting on the front was desperate. There were over ninety thousand North Koreans trying to retake this last corner of South Korea. The Allied forces were barely holding them. Our perimeter was still shrinking but the North Koreans were not making the rapid progress they had in the first couple of weeks of the war. There were even a couple of jet squadrons which guaranteed that we had air superiority but until the Pershing tank arrived the T-34 would out gun the Shermans and Chaffee tanks. The good news was that a freighter in Pusan was unloading M26 heavy tanks, and the British Centurion, Churchill, and Cromwell tanks. They were more than a match for the T-34.

The afternoon before we would raid I sat with Captain Poulson and my three senior NCOs. Everything was planned and we all knew what to do. 256 was repaired but we would nurse her. She had some new crew and new machinery. Both could break under pressure. "Those new tanks will make a difference, sir."

I shook my head, "I am not certain about that Sergeant Grant. North of here is not tank country. Look at the job Captain Rogers had to reach us from twenty miles inland. Their roads are not the best and it is mountainous. It is too easy to ambush tanks."

Captain Poulson picked up the latest intelligence we had. "We may get to put that to the test sir. The air force reports large numbers of tanks north of Pohang. "

"Then we will have to tell Carter and Collins that the only place to hit a T-34 is up the backside. Anything else will be a waste. I don't want to lose two lads with such potential!"

Chapter 12

We left in the middle of the afternoon. I had no doubt that there were spies in Dongbaek-Ri. They would have come in with the thousands of refugees. Lieutenant Drake had taken two of his ships out while we had been in port. Our three ships would not appear to be on a mission for we headed east until we were away from prying eyes. Then we opened up the engines and raced north. Lieutenant Drake had done this run before and he was more confident now than on the first run. The beach we had chosen for our landing was one which would be empty and deserted. There were low cliffs just behind it. At just twenty feet in height, they would not pose an obstacle to my men and might help us in the unlikely scenario that we were pursued.

There was a business-like atmosphere in the mess on this raid. All had been blooded. Everyone now had a job. That made it easier for the newer hands. They did not feel like spare parts. We would need Bergens. I had still to acquire a telescopic sight and so I just had my Thompson. There was a healthy buzz of conversation when I entered the mess. With two crews to carry the explosives, we did not have to share the weight amongst our Bergens. Campbell was already laden with his spare grenades. He was looking forward to using his grenade launcher. With three sections to care for Pike had more dressings and bandages. Williams would not need the radio and so he carried extra ammunition. We were a team. It had taken me some time in World War Two to get to the same level but I had had to put in the time as a commando, sergeant and junior officer before I could run the unit the way I wanted to. We planned on reaching the coast before dark. There was a risk we might be seen but Pohang was the nearest large place south and that was eight miles away. The troops there were fighting the South Koreans and Americans. Yeongdeok to the north was eighteen miles away. The convoy would be coming from Yeongdeok and I hoped that it would take more than half an hour for the convoy to reach us.

We blacked up. It was a ritual more than anything. It meant we were going to war. I checked my guns and ammunition for the umpteenth time. To keep myself busy I went on deck and lit my pipe. It was a warm night, even at sea. I knew we had to make the most of the good weather for when it changed then it would be dramatic. Sergeant Heon had told me how cold it was. In preparation for a harsh winter, the two Korean drivers were insulating the outside of the barracks with turf and lining the walls with cardboard. Sergeant Major Dean would not have approved but it would keep us warm. They were also gathering as much firewood as they could. Stacked inside the barracks it kept the wood dry and added to the insulation. Our three Korean soldiers were more than useful. They were an integral part of our team. I saw the Lieutenant glancing astern. He was worried about the other two boats. He felt a responsibility. The loss of life had not been his fault but he would blame himself. We had endured two air attacks. The odds were that on our way south we would have a third.

Just then we saw a flight of Gloster Meteors roaring south. They had obviously attacked somewhere in the north. I shook my head. They were fast. I had never flown one and I was not certain if I could handle one.

"If things go as we have planned them we will be away by midnight and back at Dongbaek-Ri in time for breakfast."

He nodded, "But if something does go wrong then we may have to travel back in daylight. I know you mean well, sir, but let me fret and worry eh? We are just the bus driver but these buses are all that I have."

"Do you still intend to leave the service at the end of all this?"

He nodded, "If I stayed in I would need to move to a bigger boat. If I was lucky and in command then I would have more men under me. I have found it hard enough with three crews. A destroyer or a frigate would mean even more men. I like this size of the crew but the days of the small boats are gone. Soon you chaps will go in by air. Helicopters are the thing, I hear."

I nodded, "They have come a long way since the first ones were flown in the war. I can see the advantage of them."

"Can you fly one?"

"I daresay I could have a go. They are a little expensive at the moment. We like buying Government surplus. It is good value and we know that it has been cared for. It is something for the future."

"And I envy you that. A future! You have a legacy for your children. I have nothing as yet."

"Have you not thought about buying one of these? A Fairmile could be easily converted."

"To do what?"

"They have long boats on the canals. Think bigger. This could take people in little jaunts up the rivers in France and Germany. You could manage with a crew of half a dozen. We found lots of ex-servicemen. Someone like Chief Jennings eh?"

"The Chief has grandchildren but it is an idea. Thank you, sir. It is not much of a plan but…"

Midshipman Brown came on deck, "Coast ahead sir. I have darkened ship."

"Good man, Middy. About time for your Lieutenant's exams isn't it?"

"Yes, sir. I am looking forward to it. Not that I want to leave you, you understand. It is just that a sub-lieutenant's pay would mean I could get married!"

I turned and smiled, "You have a girl Middy?"

The Lieutenant nodded, "A bonnie girl too, Janet. Far too good for Brown here." He winked at me.

"Well take my advice, Middy, marry sooner rather than later. My aunt lost her husband to be shortly before they were due to be married in the Great War. I know that she regrets it. She might be well off and have a fabulous life but she regrets that they were not married. Even a fortnight or so would have given her memories. She wonders what their children would have been like. Don't have regrets Middy. Have memories!" My pipe had gone out. I tapped it against my hand and headed down the ladder. "Time to play at soldiers again."

The darkening of the boat had told my men that we were close and they were already helping to load the Bergens on to their comrade's backs. I carried mine. I would put it on just before we disembarked. "Right lads, on deck. Sergeant Heon with me and Sergeant Callow, you bring up the rear."

"Sir."

We were still moving quickly. Behind us, the sky was darkening. Within an hour it would be dark. A bank of clouds which suggested a summer storm were also gathering behind us. Hopkins and Tyreman were rigging the scrambling net. We needed no radio and could afford to get wet. It was almost a luxury to travel in without having to worry about hidden shoals and rocks. The light was fading but the rays from the west conveniently lit the water before us. Reassuringly empty of defences, the coast grew closer. The North Koreans had been busy consolidating their grip on the towns and ports. If we did not shift them then they would militarise the coast but for the moment, just over a month since their invasion, it remained untouched. The light began to fade dramatically and I wondered if we had mistimed the attack. I guessed that the convoy of trucks would be prepared to leave and head south, safe in the knowledge that there would be no allied air attacks. The Meteors' daylight attack would have reassured them.

I saw the beach and I put my Bergen on my back. Petty Officer Flynn was at the bow with his Thompson ready. I think that he was disappointed that there was no enemy for him to shoot. He turned and made the A-OK sign. There were no rocks and the beach looked to shelve. The boat slowed as the Lieutenant took us in gently. The other two boats flanked us. The petty officer had learned his lesson. He pumped his arm to show the Lieutenant that he could stop and I ran to the bow and jumped as far forward as I could manage. The running had strengthened my legs and I landed in knee deep water. I heard a splash behind me. Those with heavy gear clambered down the scrambling net. I ran on to the beach and peered north and south. Behind me was darkness. I saw that Sergeant Heon had landed in knee deep water. The other boats had landed successfully. I pumped my arm and hurried up to the road.

I crouched at the edge of the road. There were a few houses just eight hundred yards away. Smoke rising from them told me that they were occupied. Sergeant Heon joined me and I pointed to the house. He nodded and hurried to it. I saw that we had landed just two hundred yards south of the road we would use to get to the ambush site. That was not bad. My men joined me. We would move in three sections. It made control easier. I led and ran to the road. I could see the crossroads ahead. Any civilians that we met would be friendly although those that could had fled. The crossroads was deserted. There was little cover close to the road but we knew that from the aerial photographs. The fields were full of ripening crops. As I ran along the road to the crossroads I saw that there was a drainage ditch. We could use that. By the time I reached the crossroads, the sun had set but I had the layout of the road in my head. I waited for Sergeant Callow to join me. I pointed to the road and he nodded. He would prepare the explosives. I pointed to Campbell and the ditch.

"Lance Corporal Williams take charge here. Make a position here."
"Sir!"

I cocked my Thompson and ran to Captain Poulson. He and his men were a hundred yards from me. They had the hardest job. They had to hide in the ripening wheat. The bazooka and the mortars would be the ones who would destroy the vehicles in the centre of the convoy.
"Happy?"

"Yes, sir. We found some driftwood on the beach. We have entrenching tools. We will be fine. It is Sergeant Major Thorpe who will be exposed."

Sergeant Major Thorpe was a further eighty yards away and was the most exposed. My section would trigger the ambush and Evans and Black would have to react. It might well be that they had to explode their device with some of the convoy to the north of it. That could not be helped. We had no idea of the size of their convoys. "I suggest, Sergeant Major, that you are a little bit back from the road. Your Bren and the grenade launcher will have to deal with any attack from the men in the convoy."

"We have plenty of ammo sir. We will be fine."

"I'll have a word with the young lads."

The two of them were packing their explosives on both sides of the road. I watched them as they packed stones and dirt around the field side. Sergeant Callow had taught them how to channel the force of an explosion. When they had finished they ran the detonator cable across the road and connected the second charge. Then they moved back into the field. I picked up some of the dirt, sand and grit from the road. I covered the wire. It was hard enough to see anyway but the dirt made it invisible. When I reached them they were just tightening the cables.

"Now remember, you two, that you set the charge off as soon as you see Sergeant Callow set off ours."

"Yes, sir."

"If something goes wrong then listen for Sarn't Major Thorpe. If he tells you to blow it then blow it. As soon as you have done that then get back to the boat. You two are the closest of our men to the Koreans. Do not stop until you get to the boats. Clear?"

"Clear, sir!"

I could hear, a long way in the distance, the sound of engines. The convoy was coming. I hurried back to Sergeant Major Thorpe. His men had dug a shallow trench and used whatever they had, including their Bergens, to give themselves some protection. "Sergeant Major, if things go wrong then order your lads to blow their charges and you get back to the beach. Understood?"

"Yes, sir. Otherwise, we wait for you to trigger the attack?"

"You will have a better idea than anyone when we are going to blow it. You can count the vehicles which pass you."

"Right sir."

I could not even see Captain Poulson and his men so good was their camouflage. I knelt to speak to him. "We hit them hard and run. If they have troops with them then we do not try to engage them. We have the advantage of the dark and the boats. We know that the men can be on the beach in seven minutes or less. You have the larger ordnance. Just drop all your shells until you have none left."

"Sir!"

My men were in the ditch next to the road which led to the beach. We had the shortest of runs and I would not leave until I knew that my men had escaped. "Charges set, sergeant?"

"Yes, sir."

"Private Campbell, you have the range?"

I could see he was nervous. He chewed his lip. "Yes, sir. I hope so sir."

"Listen Campbell the best man I knew with a rifle grenade was Tommy Foster from Haltwhistle. It took time for him to learn how to use it. Regard this as field training."

He looked happier, "Yes sir!"

I looked towards Sergeant Major Thorpe. I was reassured when I could not see him. Less than two hundred yards covered the three sections but I felt as though they were much further away than that. I heard a noise and I listened. It was vehicles but there was something else. I strained and then I realised what it was, it was a tank. I turned, "Sergeant Callow will the explosives take out a T-34?"

"They are across the road and in the ditch sir but I can't honestly say. The ones in the ditch will certainly take out the tracks."

An honest answer. Too late to change the plan now. "Williams, with me." I turned to Sergeant Callow. "Williams and I will have grenades. As soon as the charges have exploded then we will use grenades in the turret. The rest of you pour bullets into the convoy!"

"Sir."

Williams arrived. "Put your gun here. You and I are going to take out a tank. You need two grenades."

"Right sir."

We crawled into the ditch next to Callow and Green. I put my Thompson next to Green. He would not need to reload his own weapon. He could use mine. The tank made such a noise that the crew would be unable to hear anything. I saw it as it neared what I guessed would be Sergeant Major Thorpe's position. It was travelling slowly. The ground vibrated with the sheer weight and power of the tank. It weighed over thirty-one tons! It was dark but I could see that the commander had his body half out of the tank. In my experience, World War Two tanks were both smelly and claustrophobic. The commander was taking advantage of his rank to enjoy fresh air. We had a chance. I saw that the trucks behind were spaced at five-yard intervals. I spied at least one tanker. The rest were hidden in the dark. I nodded to Williams. Putting my mouth to his ear I said, "Wait until the charges go off. Then we mount the tank. You ram one grenade through the driver's visor and I will put one in the turret. Then off the tank and into the ditch."

He nodded.

The tank was now just thirty yards from us. I knew we could not be seen but the fact that we could see them made it feel as though we must be visible too. Sergeant Callow was behind us. I could see the wire in the ditch and so I knew where the charge lay. As the front of the tank passed the wire Callow said, "Down!" I buried my head in the dry ditch. The explosion was forty yards away but I felt the concussion whizz over my head. Then I felt the heat of the explosion. A heartbeat later I heard the explosion from the rear of the column and then the satisfying sound of the mortar as it sent shells into the middle of the column. I rose and ran. I saw that the tracks of the tank were on fire and it was slewed around. There was a fire at the rear of the column and I saw the muzzle flashes from my men's guns. The tank's commander must have been dazed and disorientated for he only saw me when I was twenty yards from him. He started to descend into the turret. I leapt up, pulling the pin on my first grenade as I did so. There was a tiny gap and I rammed the Mills bomb inside. I heard the ping as the arming handle flew off inside. I turned and jumped from the tank. Williams landed next to me and we lay down as bullets came from a vehicle in the middle of the convoy. The grenade launchers and the bazooka were picking off trucks. I heard the two grenades go off. Flames leapt from the driver's visor. The tank was destroyed. I said, "Back to your gun." Pulling my Colt, I ran back and opened the hatch of the tank. It was a charnel house. I saw that the second truck had been hit by machine gun bullets and the driver and crew were dead. I could smell petrol. The fuel tank had been punctured. I slid off the back of the tank, pulled the pin from my second grenade and rolled it under the truck. I ran back to Sergeant Callow. I counted to five in my head and dived to the ground. When the grenade went off it ignited the petrol and the truck rose into the air and burst into flames. Whatever was in it was destroyed.

I reached my men and took my Thompson from Green, "I reloaded it, sir." I raised it and looked for a target. I counted twelve trucks and a tanker. They were all on fire. I was just going to order my men to advance and finish the convoy off with grenades when Evans came racing towards us. "Sir, there is another tank!"

"Sergeant get the men back to the beach. Fall back!" I ran towards Captain Poulson. "Pull your men back. There is another tank."

"I know sir. Carter and Collins would like a crack at it though."

I looked at the two young commandos and their bazooka. "One shot and then move. Sergeant Grant, you cover them. Captain Poulson, get the rest of the men back to the beach."

"Sir."

The tank opened fire with its gun. I had no idea what the target was. The shell exploded half a mile away beyond the road. Then the cupola machine gun began to fire. It was firing blind. Firing the main gun had temporarily blinded the gunner. The M20, so-called super bazooka, was effective at two hundred yards and could penetrate side armour. The tank, which was advancing across the field towards us presented just its front. The two needed a shot at the side.

"Carter, when it turns send one at it. Hit the side when it is two hundred yards away and you have a chance. If it comes for you then run!"

"How do you know it will turn sir?"

"Because it will be trying to get at me." The tank was heading for the beach. I took out a grenade and pulled the pin. I ran at the tank. The gunner was still blinded by the burning vehicles. When I was a hundred yards away I threw the grenade and then ran towards the beach. I ran as fast as I had ever run but, even so, some shrapnel struck my Bergen. Other fragments hit the tank. I turned and fired a burst from my Thompson. I saw the turret turn followed by the tank. I jinked like a rugby scrum-half. The bullets were too high. A common mistake. I could now see the boats on the beach and my men streaming towards them. I saw the ditch at the end of the field and I dived into it just as the gunner corrected his aim. Then I heard the whoosh of a rocket and heard it explode against the T-34. I raised my head and saw that the lads had stopped it. Then a second rocket hit the same place as the first. The turret flew into the air and flames engulfed the tank. Carter and Collins picked

Korea

up their launcher and rockets and raced back to the beach. They were grinning like schoolboys. Sergeant Grant and my two men ran towards me. I stood and aimed my gun at the tank but the crew were dead. Muzzle flashes told me that there were troops with the convoy. When Sergeant Grant reached me, I followed them to the beach. They boarded their boat and I was pulled aboard.

I heard Lieutenant Drake shout, "All guns, shoot! Shoot! Rapid fire!" Our launch began to edge back into the sea. The two six pounders struck the vehicles advancing towards us. The Oerlikon shells added to the damage. As we turned Middy shouted, "Cease firing!"

We disappeared into the dark. The sea and the night swallowed us up.
"Any casualties, Pike?"
"Sergeant Heon sprained his ankle sir. I think Wilson and Hope in Sergeant Major Thorpe's section were hit by shrapnel. They were helped back but they didn't look serious."
"Good. Well done everyone."
The Lieutenant said, from the bridge, "A little reckless Major Harsker, making yourself a moving target like that."
I smiled, "I can run a bit and I knew the gunner was still blinded by the fires."
Sergeant Callow shook his head, "More like the Galloping Major!"
Private Harris began to sing the music hall song and everyone, sailors included, joined in!

"Here comes the Galloping Major
All the girls declare
He's a grand old stager
All the girls declare

That I'm the gallant major

Hi, hi, clear the way
Here comes the Galloping Major"

I was discovering that my men liked nothing better than a sing song. They might be mocking me but it was in the right spirit and I did not mind. They were my team.

Chapter 13

We reached Dongbaek-Ri almost as dawn was breaking. Lieutenant Drake had spoken on the radio to the other two captains and all was well on 256 and with the men who had been wounded. The mission had not gone as planned but my men had adapted. The two Korean drivers had kept watch all night and when they saw us arrive rushed off to brew tea. Petty Officer Flynn was the first one off the boat. I assumed that he was going to supervise the Koreans for he disappeared into the barracks. Once again I had managed to write my notes on the raid while we travelled south. With Major Hampton now elevated to the General's staff we would have to send the report to Lieutenant McKenzie. There would be no hurry and we could plan for our next raid. We would do that in the afternoon. The men needed their sleep. We could have a leisurely day. I might even manage a longer nap than was usual.

As the engines were turned off I said, "Any issues, Lieutenant?"

"Not with 523. I will check with the others but they both seemed happy enough."

"Good. Pop over this evening. You can mess with us and we will go over the next mission. Bring the other officers as well. We might as well celebrate destroying two tanks."

I was the last one from the boat. I picked up my Bergen and my gun. I would see if Petty Officer Flynn could acquire me a sight. It would have been a handy weapon to have. The tea was as we liked it. The Korean drivers had learned quickly. Sergeant Major Thorpe organised a fry up for Petty Officer Flynn produced, like a conjurer, a tray of eggs and rashers of bacon. As the oil drums were lit I took out my pipe and waved over the American. "Now how did you manage that Petty Officer Flynn? We have been out for twelve hours and the eggs and bacon weren't here last night."

He smiled conspiratorially and pointed to an American freighter. The boat had brought in food supplies. "She came in two days ago. The Captain likes his weapons. I told him that we would try to bring back some Russian guns in return for the eggs and bacon. I gave him a rifle and a Tokarev when we docked."

"But we didn't capture any today."

He smiled, "But we had a boatload from the tunnel, sir. Your lads all have spares and since the General was so magnanimous then we have trade goods! I feel like one of those guys who traded up the Hudson giving Indians stuff which was valueless and taking riches in return."

"Valueless?"

"Where will he get the ammo, sir? He didn't ask for that. Now between you and me sir I reckon before he leaves he will offer me a trade for some ammo."

I nodded, "I am glad you are on our side, Petty Officer. We have the Navy for dinner tonight. What can you rustle up?"

He rubbed his chin and I filled my pipe, "The Korean boys are good cooks, or so Sergeant Heon tells me. I will have a word with them. Perhaps something local? It might be hot but I have seen the way your Navy puts hot mustard on their beef!"

My pipe was going, "That sounds like an excellent idea."

"Leave it with me, sir and I will see if I can get some good soju."

"Soju?"

"Korean rice wine. The locals drink stuff that will make you go blind sir but I think that Sergeant Heon and his boys might know where we can get some better quality wine. It isn't really wine, sir. It is fermented from grain!"

"I leave it in your capable hands."

When the Petty Officer left us in January I would miss him. Perhaps by then, this would all be over. The General had a bold idea. I didn't know where he would invade but I couldn't see how the North Koreans could be ready. If you poke a bear then you had to be ready for the consequences.

We had rigged a second shower up while 256 was being repaired. At the moment we used the heat from the sun to warm the water. I knew that if we were still here in winter we would need to heat the water. As the sun had just risen then the water would be cold. The rest of the men were in the barracks and so I took the opportunity to have a cold shower. I used soap to scrub the blacking from my face and hands.

"Private Kang, water!" I mimed shaving. Private Kang was a fast learner and he nodded.

I didn't mind showering in cold water but a shave in cold water was beyond the pale! Showered and shaved I took a fresh cup of tea and began to write my report. I had just finished it when a young American officer appeared. He was not a Ranger. He had a crisp clean uniform and a clean-cut look about him. He snapped to attention, took off his hat and saluted, "Lieutenant McKenzie sir."

I smiled, "Sit down Lieutenant. I wondered when we would meet."

He remained standing, "Sir, Lieutenant McKenzie respectfully requests a salute in return."

I put my pipe down, "Lieutenant, if you had done your homework then you would know that the British Army only salutes when wearing headdress. You took off your cap and therefore no salute." He looked embarrassed. "Sit down, Lieutenant, you will learn that we are quite casual in this troop."

"Sir. Sorry, sir. This is my first post with responsibility."

"Just out of the Academy?"

"Sir!"

"I came up through the ranks, Lieutenant. That is a slightly tougher school than the Academy. Anyway, your timing, like your uniform, is impeccable." I pushed the report over to him. "I have just finished my report."

"Thank you, sir. That was promptly done."

"I hate paperwork and I like to get it out of the way whenever possible." I picked up my pipe and used my knife to clean away the old ash. "Do you want a cup of tea?"

"Tea sir?"

"This is the British Army, Lieutenant. Tea runs in our veins!"

"No sir, Thank you, sir." Any stiffer and he would have broken!

I nodded and began to fill my pipe. I was giving him the opportunity to relax and chat but he sat rigid in his seat. I lit the pipe. "Smoke if you want."

"I don't, sir."

"Good, filthy habit!" I leaned contentedly back in my seat. A one match pipe was always an achievement. "So what else do you do at base apart from liaising with us?"

"I compile reports sir from other units and then copy them and file them."

It did not sound like soldier's work to me but I guessed that it was necessary. "You will read Captain Roger's reports too then?" He frowned, "Lieutenant I have been on two missions with the Captain. I didn't ask anything which is secret."

"Yes sir but I haven't met the Captain. I only arrived two days ago. He is on a mission."

I nodded, "In Indian country. They are good men, Lieutenant, look after them."

"Sir."

I sighed, "Look, Lieutenant, we are having something of a celebration this evening. Why not come along. You can meet the other officers. Get to know the men you are sending out behind enemy lines."

He looked shocked, "But it is not me sir! I don't send men anywhere. I just liaise!"

"And you liaise from behind a desk where the most serious injury you could get is a paper cut. Last night my men, some younger than you, were fighting behind enemy lines and destroying two T-34 tanks. Come along and get to know us."

"Yes, sir. It will be a pleasure." His voice belied his words. "And now I had better get back to base. This report needs to be studied."

"When you return you might bring the report from the reconnaissance section. I would be interested to know what we achieved last night."

"Sir."

After he had gone I wondered at his day. He would spend all day reading the report which had taken me less than an hour to write. I had no doubt that he had clerical staff working for him. There might be many thousands of soldiers in Korea now but how many were fighting men? When he had read it and had it copied he would have it filed. He would shuffle papers around his desk and have a coffee. I couldn't do it.

I began writing two letters; one to Mum and one to Susan. I should have asked the young Lieutenant about letters from home. I would ask him at dinner. From the other side of the curtain, I heard snoring. That would be Private Lowe. He was a notorious snorer. My men took their sleep when they could. After finishing the letter, I stood. I walked through the curtains to the cots for Captain Poulson and myself. He was asleep. The next were the NCOs. Sergeant Major Thorpe and Sergeant Heon were not in their cots but the others were happily sleeping. Finally, the rest of my men were all sound asleep in their cots. The noise from Lowe was like a band saw. I wondered how the others could sleep.

I did manage an hour of sleep. When I rose I went for a solitary run, or so I thought. I heard feet pounding along behind me and saw Private Carter. "Hope you don't mind, sir. I enjoy the runs."

"You are more than welcome." As we ran I spoke to him. "When we were based in Falmouth my section and I were all in the same digs. We would run to the camp each day. I miss the runs and the chats."

It was a pleasant, not to say hot, afternoon but that was good for the sweat would cleanse our pores and the water would be warm.

"Sir, what was it like in the war?"

We ran the full circuit and I told him of my experiences. I did not dwell on the heroics such as the battle of Belleville and the race to Paris. I spoke of the sadness of losing young men like Alan Crowe. I told him of watching soldiers being executed by the S.S. I saw him take it all in. He was a sensitive soul and a thinker. That was how Blair had got to him.

When we reached the barracks the rest of the troop were sat outside drinking beer. I had no doubt that came from the freighter and the resourceful Petty Officer. Captain Poulson said, "You are keen Major."

"I enjoy running Captain. Besides, it will give me an appetite and I am looking forward to tonight's food. Is everything arranged for the barracks?"

"Yes, sir. The Sergeant Major has moved the men's cots closer together and rigged up a table. The chairs don't match but there should be enough. The lads will eat outside. Sergeant Heon has arranged for enough food for all of us. He says the two Koreans are delighted to be given the opportunity to thank us for what we are doing for their country."

After a warm shower and another shave, I put on the best uniform I had. My Number Ones had not been needed yet and this was not the occasion for such formality. I went outside and Private Harris brought me over a packing case as a seat. Captain Poulson handed me a glass of something.

"Glasses?"

He nodded to the Petty Officer who was busy with the three Koreans around the oil drum barbecues. They were about to light them. "I suspect they came from the base. Certainly, he disappeared while you were on your run. This is the local rice wine. It is not bad. Sergeant Heon made certain we were not sold hooch! Cheers, sir!"

"Cheers."

I sipped it for I wanted to know its strength. It tasted a little like dry sherry and I could taste the alcohol. I would watch my intake. It would not do to have the commanding officer paralytic.

"You met the new liaison officer, sir?"

"Young and straight from officer school. He was, shall we say, a little formal. We shall see how this evening goes. Remind me to ask him about letters. It has been well over a month since we arrived here. You would have thought they could have sent some. I know that the folks at home would have written."

He nodded. "It is not so bad for me but you chaps with families, sir. It must be hard."

It did not feel like a war zone. The fighting was more than fifty miles away. In many ways, I felt guilty until I thought about what we did. We all served, it was just the manner of our fighting which differed. The men were having a sing song. The beer did that. I saw some of the crew of the American freighter. They were lining the side and watching. Harris had the best voice. The NCO's joined in leaving the Captain and I to enjoy a pleasant drink on a late summer afternoon.

"It went better than it should have. Last night, I mean, sir."

"The mortar crew and the bazooka crew did well. I was a little busy to notice but how did the grenade launchers work out?"

"Erratic. The two lads are new to the weapon. As I recall, sir, it took us some time to adjust."

"When we get the photographs, we will have a better idea. Evans and Black did well. I couldn't fault them."

"It is amazing to think that Carter and Evans were two of the ones we worried about when we left England."

"That was Blair. The more I think about him the more I come to believe that he was deliberately planted in our unit."

"Really sir? One small troop of commandos?"

"Think about it. We were given high priority tasks. We have carried them out with great efficiency. He had more than ten per cent of our troop as potential saboteurs. Sending us to Sason-Ri was not part of the plan. Remember he and Marsh never fired their weapons. I think that if Marsh had not been killed so early then who knows what damage they might have wrought."

"Evans and Carter, saboteurs? They have both been exemplary, sir."

"Only since we got them away from Blair and Marsh. There is no point the Reds trying to do the same in an infantry regiment, there are too many men but us? Everyone is vital. Someone is coming out from London to speak with us and I will give him my theory."

"What do you think happened to Blair?"

"If I am right he is having a wonderful time being lauded as a Communist hero and if not, he is in a prison camp." I finished off the rice wine. "I hope I am wrong but I fear I am right."

Korea

Over by the barbecues, there was a whoosh as Petty Officer Flynn used some petrol to get them all going. I laughed, "Crude but effective. I shall have one more glass of rice wine and then wait until we eat."

The three boats were in plain sight and once the food began to be cooked then I knew that the officers would wander over. The three Koreans all had aprons. It looked like Sergeant Heon would be acting as a waiter. The two drivers were busy chopping using meat cleavers with the dexterity of a concert pianist. Captain Poulson handed me the wine. "Do you think we will like it, sir? What they are preparing I mean."

I knew that most of my men were conservative when it came to food. Meat and two veg was their preferred meal. Even the steaks provided by the petty officer were considered second rate compared with an English roast. Even in the war families had saved up ration coupons to have a joint once a month. It made them feel English.

"It might be a little spicy but I am going to give it a go. I think it is highly unlikely that I will travel this far east again. We only live once, Captain. Let us embrace the opportunity."

I could smell the food as it began to sizzle. I saw that they had lit all of the barbecues. We had four now and were going to use one to keep the food warm. I guessed that was the idea of the petty officer who stood supervising like some sort of maître d'. He came over to us, the inevitable cigar in his mouth and a bottle of beer in his hand, "Sir, we will serve the officers inside when they arrive. This will be a series of dishes." He shrugged, "It is the Korean style of dining, apparently. It sure smells good but it looks a little strange. We will feed the non-coms and other ranks out here." He leaned in, "If it gets a little noisy, sir, don't worry, the Sergeant Major, the Chief and I will keep good order. You officers enjoy yourselves. You deserve it."

The sun began to set. The smoke from the fires kept bugs away and it was pleasant to be outside. The four officers all strode over together. They were very smartly dressed. I guessed the Lieutenant felt he had a tradition to uphold. Sergeant Heon scurried over with a metal tray. From the engraving, I think it had come from the American Officer's mess in the base. He held out the tray as I stood, "Gentlemen, rice wine courtesy of the commandos."

They took it. As Midshipman Brown prepared to swallow it I restrained him, "Think port when you drink it Middy. We wouldn't want any accidents."

"Thank you, sir."

I raised my glass, "His Majesty and the Royal Navy!"

The men all stood and raised their bottles. There was a chorus of "His Majesty and the Royal Navy!"

I drank a little. The Lieutenant said, "The Commandos!"

"The Commandos!"

I saw the crews coming from the boats, "Shall we retire inside gentlemen?"

As we headed indoors a jeep roared up. It was driven by Sergeant Aitkens. A flustered Lieutenant McKenzie climbed out. He was going to salute and then saw that Captain Poulson and I did not have headgear but the four Naval officers did. I came to attention and he saluted, "Well done Lieutenant. Test passed."

Sergeant Aitkens climbed out. She picked a folder from the back seat, "I am afraid that the Lieutenant is a little shaken due to the journey. I am a country girl and I know how to drive. Here are the photographs you requested, sir. If I might have a word?"

I took the folder from her. I noticed that she allowed her hand to touch mine. I handed it to Captain Poulson, "If you would take this inside, Captain, I will join you a little later."

The rest of my men gave us space. She leaned in, "Quite a little home from home you have here. You make me envious. The smell of a barbecue makes me homesick."

"You are more than welcome to join us."

She laughed, "I think I might inhibit your conversation and besides," her voice became huskier, "after a glass or two of rice wine I might let my hair down, quite literally, and that would never do eh, sir?"

I smiled, "Probably not." We both understood the unspoken words which hung in the air between us.

She gave a sigh, "Ah well, ships that pass in the night. On to business. I am guessing that you will be going out tomorrow on your next raid."

"All things being equal we shall sail in the afternoon."

"Then the day after you should come to the base. There will be a visitor there from England. He is quite keen to speak with you."

"Thank you."

"Don't mention it. I shall be along later to pick up the Lieutenant." She shook her head. "His father is a general and he sees himself as a staff officer. He is not a real soldier. At least Major Hampton had fought. Good luck tomorrow sir." She came to attention as did I. Before she turned she winked.

I confess that my mind was not on the dinner. I had too much racing around a mind which was already befuddled with two glasses of rice wine. The visitor had to be L but why was Blair important enough for a member of MI6 to fly halfway around the world? As for the Sergeant… there had been an invitation in her eyes. Susan and three children made it easier to refuse but the light in her eyes had made me wonder what it might have been like.

Sergeant Heon shouted, "Just bringing in the food, sir!"

"Excellent! I am starving!" The men all stood when I entered. The table was impeccably laid for dinner. "Sit, this is supposed to be informal!"

As they sat Captain Poulson said, "I have put the photographs on your cot, sir. They look good!"

"I will look at them later."

The two Korean drivers, preceded by Sergeant Heon, entered. They bore three huge steaming platters. One had rice mixed with vegetables, one had a variety of seafood and the last was what looked like pork chops. I pointed to it, "What is that Sergeant Heon?"

"Samgyeopsal sir. Grilled pork belly. It is my favourite."

"It looks delicious. Thank you."

"Oh, there will be more sir! Hwang and Kang are enjoying themselves!"

I smiled as the three left. "Tuck in gentlemen! It seems that tonight we are eating for Britain." I glanced at Lieutenant McKenzie, "For tonight we will assume that the War of Independence never happened! God save the King!"

Even the American Lieutenant joined in as we all shouted, "God save the King!"

The evening was a huge success. Midshipman Brown was just a little younger than the American and they got on well. Captain Poulson and Lieutenant Drake regaled everyone with stories from the war. They were the sanitized ones which were fit for impressionable company. We did not mention the burning soldiers or the Roman candles when a parachute failed to open. Captain Poulson spoke of the characters we had known like Gordy Barker, Daddy Grant and Scouse Fletcher. I added details of their lives now. Lieutenant Drake told of the operations in the channel. He spoke of Chief Jennings as a Leading Seaman and the officers under whom he had served. We were honouring the memory of both the living and dead. I kept my drinking to a minimum. The American and the

Middy did not. They would both pay a price. The food kept coming long after I had ceased to eat. Kimchi was interesting and I quite enjoyed it. I had always liked pickles. By the time dessert came, mainly tteok and yaksic, both sweet rice cakes, I declined much to the disappointment of Private Kang who had been responsible for the delicacy.

I had Petty Officer Flynn bring the three of them in and we all stood, saluted and then applauded them. I thought the two cooks were going to burst into tears. When they had gone the American sailor said, "Nicely done sir. They worked hard and that means a lot to them."

I nodded, "Don't let the lads get too drunk, Mr Flynn, we have a raid tomorrow night."

"I know sir and many commanding officers would have made them have an early night. This will do them far more good. They are all getting on famously out there. There are boys sharing photographs of loved ones and addresses."

"And thank you Petty Officer!"

Just then a horn sounded. Petty Officer Flynn said to the American Lieutenant, "I think this is your ride sir."

Lieutenant McKenzie looked around as though the sailor was talking to someone else. It made us all laugh. I put my arm around him, "Come on Lieutenant. We don't want to keep Sergeant Aitkens waiting, do we?"

He waved an arm and almost fell over as he said, "What a great bunch of guys! Byeeee!" For some reason that made him and Brown giggle.

Lieutenant Drake said, "And I believe that is our cue to leave. Thank you, sir, for a delightful evening. We shall return the favour."

I nodded in a distracted way. I needed to get the American to the jeep before he passed out. The Sergeant saw me as I left and she hurried to put her arm around the Lieutenant's side. I felt it brush against me and caught a whiff of her perfume. "I take it the Lieutenant had a good time, sir?"

"Oh yes. It is a good job he doesn't have a mission tomorrow."

"I brought a pail. We will put him in the back."

I suddenly realised that he was a dead weight. He had passed out. I stopped and hauled him up on my shoulder. As I did so my face brushed against Sergeant Aitkens' face. It had an effect. I put him in the back and propped him so that he would vomit into the pail and not the seat. Instead of saluting the sergeant held out her hand, "Thank you, sir."

I shook her hand. It was soft. She squeezed my hand gently and I returned the squeeze. Our hands slid slowly apart; one red nail scored a faint line in my palm. I waved as she spun the jeep and headed out of the town. She was a resourceful woman.

    Before I went to bed I took the photographs and with a last pipe of the day looked at them. Apart from the two tanks, we had destroyed one petrol tanker and eight lorries. The photographs had been taken as they tried to salvage what they could from the other vehicles which were wrecked. For some reason, they had not bothered with the dead men. It looked as though we had managed to hit a couple of lorries containing troops. It had been successful and that was good. Soon the meal and camaraderie would be an interlude, a pleasant memory as we went north on another raid.

Chapter 14

The next raid was like our first. North of Pohang was the small port of Osan-Ri. Within a few days of its capture, the Koreans had made it into a base for a minesweeper and four patrol boats. I suspected that the boats we had fought had been from the same flotilla. They had added anti-aircraft guns. One of the reconnaissance aircraft which had taken the photograph had been damaged by the gunfire and we had no further photographic evidence. We would be going in partly blind. In many ways, it was St. Nazaire in miniature. We would strike before dawn. The three boats would damage as many of the ships as they could. We would lay charges on the minesweeper and the harbour facilities to try to make it unusable. There was a river to one side of the harbour and we had a simple enough plan. The three boats would land us on the river bank and the three boats would creep around into the small harbour. We would disable the guns and the minesweeper. Our three ships would destroy the patrol boats. We intended to sink the minesweeper and blow up the fuel. We would board our ships and escape. When we had planned it there appeared to be little which could go wrong but I knew that we did not have the full intelligence we might have expected. We would not take the mortar. Barton and Haynes would help our four explosives specialists. For the rest of us, it would be a case of fighting whoever remained.

One piece of good news we had was that Petty Officer Flynn had managed to find a telescopic sight. He brought it to me just after lunch. We were preparing our weapons and he handed it to me. When I asked him its provenance he tapped his nose. It resided in my footlocker. I would need to fit it and try it before I took it on operations.

We left at dusk and, as usual, headed east before turning north. Midshipman Brown was green from the moment we set sail. He received no sympathy from anyone on board. Many of the crew of 523 had also been rolling drunk but they showed no ill effects when we headed north. There was a good deal of friendly banter between the sailors and the Commandos. It reminded me of the times on the **'Lucky Lady'**. I had been running short of tobacco and I had to go into the village to buy some. I had little choice of tobacco for most smoked cigarettes but I bought that which they had. It was far cheaper than in England but it was loose and would dry out. Once it did so I would have to mix it with my precious bar. I lit up as we headed north into the dark. It was aromatic and I found it a pleasant if slightly hot smoke.

Lieutenant Drake was happier that he would not just be a bus driver for us. His part was the equal of ours. In theory, it was also more dangerous. He would be on the water and exposed. We knew where two emplacements were but they might have added others.

He let Brown and Jennings have the helm while we looked at the last aerial photographs. They were three weeks old. "They have two quick-firing fifty-five-millimetre guns on the two sides of the harbour. If the crews are any good, sir, then we will be matchwood."

"The one to the south is not a problem. We can assault that from the land. The other one, on the north mole, is more problematic. We have to rely on our bazooka. I think it has the range but you may have to engage it with your own guns."

He nodded. "If you can definitely take out one then it might not be a problem, sir."

"The alternative was to land some men on the north mole but that had the inherent danger of alerting the enemy. This way we will be in the port before they know it."

We had worked out that the river, although narrow, would be deep enough for it would be high tide. Each boat would land its men in succession. My team would land first. We had the most experience. Petty Officer Flynn would also be coming ashore. He knew boats and he would be with Evans and Black to help them sink the minesweeper. He was looking forward to it and was in the boat with the two young commandos. At last Evans had someone he could look up to. The warm and pleasant evening of our celebration had been replaced by a grey dawn and scudding clouds. As the day wore on the clouds increased and by the time we sailed there was a stiff wind and squally skies. The rain came in savage flurries. Len Green shook his head, "I thought Manchester had bad rain but this is a bit much sir!"

I laughed, "Enjoy it Private. It decreases visibility and men are more likely to hunker down when it rains. And it stops aeroplanes from venturing forth. We can dry off on the way home!"

As darkness fell and we used radar for our approach the squalls gave way to continual rain. We slipped our new oilskin capes on. They covered our shoulders but left our arms free. It was a good job that we had radar for we could barely see fifty feet before us and we crept in like a teenage girl who had been out too late. Hopkins was at the bow and he waved an arm to guide us towards the north bank of the river. I hurried to the bow with the rest of my men. The intention was to let the incoming tide push our stern around and then 523 could power her way out. There was a steep muddy bank. This would not be easy. I did not envy the bazooka team. As soon as I saw the water disappear from beneath the bows I leapt and landed ankle deep in mud. I pulled myself up as Sergeant Heon landed next to me and the stern of the launch swung around. It was a real effort to drag myself free but when I did I was able to reach the bank and lie flat. I could see very little save for the glow from some buildings. The port was less than a hundred yards from where I lay. I scanned the river. I could see working lights on the minesweeper. I counted three patrol boats and one small coastal freighter. They had a deck watch on the minesweeper and the freighter. That was a problem. While I waited for the rest of my men to join me I took out my Colt and fitted the silencer. Captain Poulson tapped me on the shoulder. My men were all ashore.

I pointed to the minesweeper and Sergeant Major Thorpe. He, along with Petty Officer Flynn, would deal with that. Captain Poulson and his men would take out the patrol boats and the far gun. My team, led by Sergeant Callow, would deal with the gun emplacement. As they moved off I said, "Sergeant Callow, take over the section!" I ran ahead of Sergeant Major Thorpe. There was a deck watch and I needed to give my team a chance.

The port was a jumble of ramshackle buildings which afforded me cover as I descended to the waterfront. I had my Thompson over my back and my Colt in my right hand. The rain was pounding down hard. Our rubber-soled shoes splashed in the puddles but they would not be heard. There were lights over the gangway but I also saw a glow from the bridge. There was someone there. I stopped behind a discarded packing case and I knelt. I levelled the Colt and held it in two hands. I tracked the glowing cigarette and then I saw another movement. The light from the gangway light picked out an oilskin and a rifle as a sentry started down the gangplank.

Petty Officer Flynn was no commando and he was certainly not light on his feet. He must have kicked something for the sentry looked up. Even as he began to swing his gun I fired two shots. They hit the sentry in the chest and he fell into the water. The cigarette stopped moving and a Korean voice shouted something. I suspect it was a man overboard. The delay allowed Sergeant Major Thorpe and my men close with the minesweeper. I aimed at the glow of the cigarette and fired three more shots. The glow disappeared and Sergeant Major Thorpe led my men up the gangplank.

The silence of the night was shattered not by gunfire from the minesweeper but by the crack of bullets from the gun guarding the harbour entrance. Sergeant Callow and my men had begun their attack. I jammed my Colt in my belt and swung around my Tommy gun. Bullets ricocheted and cracked around the minesweeper. Captain Poulson and his men began to fire at the crews of the patrol boats who had begun to emerge from their bunks. I kept running. I saw muzzle flashes close to the seventy-six millimetre and then heard the whump of a grenade. There was a flash and the closest seventy-six millimetre was silenced. The second seventy-six millimetre began to swing around. I saw Carter and Collins. "Get that second seventy-five millimetre!" I made sure I was not behind the launcher.

"Sir."

Collins tapped Carter on the shoulder and the rocket sped across the water. It struck the sandbags. There was a flash as it did so but the gun was undamaged. The concussion must have disorientated the crew. They did not fire immediately. The ZiS-3 could fire twenty-five rounds a minute.

"Again!"

This time the rocket struck the armour protecting the gun. The rocket went through it and exploded killing most of the seven crew and damaging the breech. "Well done! Try to hole the freighter below the water line."

"Sir!"

I heard an explosion near the first ZiS-3. Sergeant Callow had blown the gun up. I saw the three boats enter the harbour. From across the harbour came the sound of gunfire. There were more guns over there. There were a pair of 37 mm automatic air defence guns. They had a rapid rate of fire and could bring down an aeroplane. They could certainly sink any of our boats.

"Carter! Take out the anti-aircraft guns. "

"Sir!"

The three ships had all turned to concentrate their fire on the two guns but 527 was taking hits. I saw bullets strike the bridge and the MTB veered off to the side. The helmsman was gone. 523 turned broadside and the two six pounders concentrated their fire on one of the guns. It exploded in a mangled mass of metal when the shells hit the ammunition.

Korea

A rocket whooshed and the second gun followed it. I watched as 256 pulled alongside 527 while 523 raked the far side of the harbour with her guns. There were ships and supplies there. I saw some fuel erupt in a fiery fountain.

I forced myself to look away from the vengeance of Lieutenant Drake as he and his crew demolished the north side of the port. Sergeant Callow was running back down the south mole with my section. They had all survived. The pops from the minesweeper had ceased and I saw a line of North Koreans, their hands in the air as they were trooped ashore by Petty Officer Flynn. The freighter was listing. Carter and Collins had managed to hit her below the water line. When I heard the guns of 523 fall silent I looked back and saw her also going to the aid of 527.

"Sir!"

"Lance Corporal Pike get aboard the patrol boats and start their engines. I want them sunk in the harbour. Let me know when the charges are set and you are ready to go."

"Sir!"

I ran down the wharf to the freighter and minesweeper. As I passed them I shouted, "Carter and Collins, leave your bazooka there. Go and help the Petty Officer!" Sergeant Heon was still with me and he would be more use with the Koreans. "Sergeant Heon go and translate for the Petty Officer. Keep those sailors quiet!"

"Sir!"

Sergeant Major Thorpe was leading his men from the minesweeper. Private Blackwood looked to be carrying books. Lance Corporal Swift ghosted up to my side, "Captain Poulson's compliments sir. He has found code books on the freighter. He is ready to blow it when the charges arrive."

I nodded, "Sergeant Callow, Private Green, get charges aboard the freighter."

"Sir."

Just then I heard the sound of a vehicle coming from the west. It was in the distance but it sounded like one or more trucks. Most of my men were busy. The three boats were heading for the wharf. Lance Corporal Pike had moved one patrol boat already and they would be able to tie up. I looked around and shouted, Lance Corporal Williams, fetch Kenny and Burrows with their Bren."

"Sir!"

"Private Campbell. We shall need that grenade launcher of yours. Come with me!"

"Sir!"

"Sergeant Major Thorpe, destroy the ships. We have company. When we return we will be coming back hot!"

"Sir!"

My four men appeared and I pointed west. "There is something coming down that road. We have to stop it or slow it down."

There was a high lump of tree covered rock which overlooked the small port and the road from the west crossed over a small bridge. The bridge was less than two hundred yards from the basin. We had to stop them there. The rain was still falling but it was a steady rain now. The deluge had ended sometime during the battle for the port. I had not noticed. I could still hear the vehicle in the distance. I realised there was more than one. "Set your Bren up to cover the bridge approach. Build a defensive position. Campbell, hide yourself. I want you to drop grenades on the far side when I say."

"Sir!"

"Williams to the other side." We reached it and I said, "Keep watch!" I took out a few lengths of parachute cord from my battledress. I laid one booby trap across the bridge. I saw just four yards from the bridge, a partly demolished house. It must have been damaged when the North Koreans attacked and took the town. It would be a perfect place to set up a defensive position. I took the pin from a grenade and laid it beneath a loose stone.

"Sir, I can see lights!"

"Back over the bridge and watch the cord!"

"Sir!"

As I turned to run I saw the glows in the distance. It was hard to make out what it was but I guessed a lorry or two. There must have been a garrison further down the road. The exploding guns would have been heard for miles. Burrows and Kenny had found some loose stones and they had made a small wall across the end of the bridge. Their Bren peered out from an aperture. I could not see them. That meant North Korean bullets would also be more likely to miss them. When we fled, the small wall might slow down a vehicle. Campbell was hidden by the bridge parapet. "Williams to the other parapet." I dropped next to Campbell. "The range to the other side of the bridge is less than a hundred feet. I want you to start dropping grenades on the road a hundred yards from us. Any further away and you will be wasting your grenades. Keep dropping them until I tell you otherwise and listen for my commands. I will spot for you."

"Sir!"

"How many grenades do you have?"

"Ten, sir!"

"When you have fired ten then head back to the boats. We will follow you."

"Sir!

Just then there was an almighty explosion behind us. It lit the sky and, in its light, I saw the two trucks as they raced down the road. They were four hundred yards from us. The minesweeper or the freighter had been destroyed. The light from the fire faded but I had an idea where the trucks were. "Now, Campbell!"

The first grenade landed short by twenty feet. The shrapnel smashed the glass on the truck and made it swerve. "Keep them there! Open fire!" The Bren began to fire. Williams had a Thompson and he used short bursts. Campbell must have practised a great deal for the grenades popped in the air very quickly. The second one hit the rear of the truck. I saw men disgorging. The Bren and our two Thompsons made them take cover. As the second truck tried to overtake the damaged one the fifth of Campbell's grenades exploded prematurely in the air. It sometimes happened. The shrapnel joined the rain to shower the North Koreans. I heard a voice shouting orders. Men began to pour from the second truck. Most had managed to get out when Campbell's last grenade hit the truck and it exploded in a fireball which showered the Koreans as they spread out. I saw a heavy machine gun being manhandled. I should have asked Campbell to save one grenade. It was too late now.

"Campbell, back!"

"Sir."

He slid away and ran, crouching towards the basin. The first crew who tried to set up the machine gun were cut down by the Bren. Bullets from rifles and pistols zipped over our heads. They were firing at muzzle flashes. I heard bullets striking the Bren's wall.

"Just one magazine left, sir."

"Private Burrows, when Kenny has fired it you throw one grenade into the middle of the bridge and then run back to the boat. Williams and I will be hard behind you."

"Sir."

I saw men moving towards the rubble where I had left the hand grenade. It exploded. I fired a burst as Burrows shouted, "Grenade!"

He had a good arm and the grenade landed and rolled almost to the middle of the bridge before it exploded. As it erupted, blinding the Koreans, the two gunners took off like rabbits. "Right Williams, empty your Thompson and then run."

"Sir!"

He fired the last of his magazine into the smoke and the rain on the bridge. I did the same. I slung my Thompson over my shoulder and fired two bullets from my automatic. I turned and ran. Behind me, I heard a Korean voice and then a cheer. I covered twenty yards before they triggered the two grenades I had left across the bridge. I was almost knocked down by the explosion but I kept my feet. By its light, I saw Campbell. He was lying behind some fallen masonry. Had it not been for the explosion I would have missed him. He was wounded. Blood covered more than half of his face. I holstered my gun and picked him up. His hand was still gripped around the grenade launcher. I hefted him on my shoulder and ran the one hundred and sixty yards to the basin. I saw the minesweeper and the freighter had settled into the water. Buildings were burning. My men still held guns on the prisoners and Captain Poulson and Sergeant Major Thorpe had six men advancing towards me.

I shouted, "Sergeant Heon, release the prisoners. Send them this way!"

I saw Sergeant Heon shout in Korean and then the crew of the minesweeper began to shuffle in our direction. Private Harris ran to help me with Campbell. "Here sir, give him to me."

I drew my pistol and turned. I heard a pop as Private Hope used his grenade launcher. "Sir, we have done enough. Let's get the hell out of here!"

"Right, Captain Poulson!"

Sergeant Heon shouted something and Petty Officer Flynn fired his gun in the air. The thirty sailors took off and ran towards the bridge. With luck, they would slow down the Korean soldiers. We ran down the wharf to the waiting boats. I saw that Midshipman Brown and Chief Petty Officer Jennings were on the 527. The top of the bridge had been destroyed. I could see the wheel. Lieutenant Drake shouted, "Petty Officer Flynn, you are back in the navy. Take over as Chief!"

"Yes sir, with pleasure!" He slung his gun, "Prepare to cast off!"

Lieutenant Drake shouted, "All guns, rapid fire!"

Korea

As we boarded the boat every gun opened fire at the Koreans who were racing down the wharf to get at us. I had barely stepped aboard when we left the wharf. Wilkinson was at the helm and he spun the wheel as we raced along the safe channel to the harbour mouth. I saw the tops of the patrol boats. My men had sunk them. I sat down next to the Oerlikon. The raid had not gone as planned. We had thought it a milk run. Men had died.

Chapter 15

I waited until we had left the harbour and were heading south before I spoke with the Lieutenant. I had already had news that Campbell's wound was not serious. He was already being treated as a hero for his accurate barrage of grenades. It would change him. I took out my pipe and filled it. I ducked down beneath the bridge to light my pipe. I said nothing. I knew that the Lieutenant would feel the loss. Peter King had been a young and promising officer. The fact that Midshipman Brown was now at the helm of 527 told me that the officer was either seriously wounded or dead.

"Keep her on this course, Killick."

"Yes, sir."

The Lieutenant took out his own pipe. He filled it and lit it. The simple act would help to calm the officer. When he had it going he looked south and waved his pipe. "Less than thirty-six hours ago we had not a care in the world. We were eating well and drinking rice wine. Peter was laughing and joking. He was telling us about his fiancée and now he is dead. His life snuffed out by a thirty-seven-millimetre shell."

"He is dead then?"

"Him, the chief and young Hargreaves, the lookout." He shook his head. I should have taken us in quicker. They might all be alive."

I shook my head, "Don't second guess yourself. We knew that the photographs were three weeks old. Should I have manned the guns on the minesweeper and tried to destroy the guns?" He shook his head. "We all did what we were supposed to. We achieved our objective. The freighter had not unloaded and was full of ammunition. We are here to stop the North Koreans. We certainly slowed them down today. When we do the rest of the missions we might actually halt their advance. That is what we do."

"I have thought about what you said. I think I will put in my papers and find something new. I would hate for Chief Jennings to end up like Chief Petty Officer Dodds. He only had six months to go. Now his wife will be a widow and his grandchildren will never know their granddad."

I said, quietly, "And that is true of a lot of families in Britain. World War Two touched everyone. It is war."

He nodded, "Did you lose any of your chaps?"

"I am not sure. Campbell was wounded. I will get on the radio and ask the others." I tapped out my pipe. "Will you be alright?"

Korea

He nodded, "Ask Barham to make some cocoa, stoker's cocoa, would you sir?"

I headed below deck. Barham was already in the galley making corned beef sandwiches. The kettle was bubbling away. "Barham, the Skipper wants some cocoa. I'll see Petty Officer Flynn and get the rum."

"Aye, sir. Mr King's death will hit him hard. They were friends."

I saw Petty Officer Flynn emerging from the mess, "Mr Flynn if you would issue the rum ration and give a mug to Barham for the cocoa."

He grinned, "Yes sir! I like some of your traditions sir!"

Campbell was lying on the bench. A bandage covered part of his head and one of his eyes. I looked at Pike. "Don't worry sir. The bullet creased the side of his head just above the ear. He was lucky."

"Yes sir and I owe you my life."

"Nonsense. We are all a team and we leave no man behind. You get well. Those grenades of your slowed them up." He nodded. "Lance Corporal, any other casualties?"

"We were lucky sir. A couple of Sergeant Major Thorpe's men had splinter wounds. There was a lot of wood on the minesweeper. Nothing that will leave a permanent scar. It was navy who bore the brunt this time."

I went to the officer's mess. I would have it to myself until we reached Dongbaek-Ri. I took off my cape and battle dress. I reloaded my guns. That was necessary. Until we reached the safety of our port we could be attacked again. Barham came in with a mug of cocoa. He was grinning, "I don't think Chief Jennings will be happy about Petty Officer Flynn sir. He was more than a little generous with the rum!"

I sipped the cocoa. It was one-quarter rum. "Never mind. The rum will be replaced." I began to make my notes. We had another three missions scheduled. So far they had all gone remarkably well. I knew it could not last and the three deaths on 527 were a reminder of how dangerous our job was.

We reached Dongbaek-Ri before dawn. The Korean drivers had the kettle already boiling as we tied up. I strode down to 527. I saw that Midshipman Brown, although he had his first command, looked as though he would have swapped it in an instant for the return of Peter King. The Chief saw me looking at the officer, "The young gentleman did well. He will be a good skipper." He smiled, "I know, I have served under a few."

"Well done Acting Lieutenant Brown. I think that Sub Lieutenant King would be pleased that you brought his boat and crew home safely."

It was the right thing to say and I saw the glimmer of a smile pass across his face. "Thank you, sir."

Captain Poulson and Sergeant Major Thorpe were waiting for me. I nodded, "Good raid despite the losses. After I get cleaned up I need to go to base. Paul, I would like you to come with me. I want to know about the next targets. We need better intelligence. The lack of photographs could have been a disaster. I want you to get Lieutenant McKenzie to pull out all the stops."

He nodded, "Right sir."

"And the rest of us, sir?"

I smiled, "They deserve a day off. I intend to tell Lieutenant McKenzie that we will not be leaving port until we have up to date intelligence on the next targets."

After a shower, some breakfast and clean uniform Petty Officer Flynn drove us to the base. More and more men were pouring in each day. We passed a column of six M26 Patton tanks. They could handle the T-34. Petty Officer Flynn was in high spirits. "Now we can duke it out with their armour sir! I will see about replacing the grenades and rockets. Your guys handled them well, sir."

"We will leave the Sarn't Major in charge. I am not certain how long we will be." Captain Poulson threw me a questioning look. "There is someone coming from London. They were due to arrive yesterday. They want to pick my brains. That is why I brought you, Captain Poulson, to deal with Lieutenant McKenzie."

He said, "L?"

"Could be."

Petty Officer kept his face deadpan. He knew a secret when he heard one. Sergeant Major Thorpe had plenty to occupy him and we left in the jeep. We were now well known and waved through when we reached the base. I saw the sentry ring someone as we passed through the barrier. We climbed out and the Petty Officer said, "I will be back at noon sir. If you are going to be later then just let me know."

"Will do Mr Flynn."

Lieutenant McKenzie met us. He seemed a little more relaxed. "How did it go, sir?"

"We did the job but 527 lost three men."

"Sorry, sir. And how did the captain take it?"

"He was one of the ones who died, Lieutenant." His face showed the realisation that death was ever present. He had been seated next to Sub Lieutenant King and now he was gone. "You will need to get in touch with British liaison. Midshipman Brown is in temporary command but we will need more men."

"Sir." He opened the door for us to enter. "You are wanted in the conference room, Major. Perhaps if I took the report…"

I gave it to Captain Poulson. "The Captain will deal with it. He has some requests. We need better intelligence."

"Yes, sir. I quite understand. Do you know your way to the conference room?"

"Yes thank you. Captain, I am not sure how long we will be. If you and the Petty Officer need to get back to the barracks then do so. I will get a lift back."

"Sir."

There was a sentry outside the door. The MP asked for my papers and then opened the door to admit me. Sergeant Aitkens was already in the conference room along with the MI6 agent. He was wearing a full colonel's uniform. Captain Rogers was also present. Sergeant Aitkens and the MI6 agent were busy studying papers and ignored me. Captain Rogers nodded, "I hear you were out again last night."

I nodded. "We lost a couple of men from 527."

"Tough break."

"And you?"

"Slipped behind the lines to sabotage some tanks. We were lucky. We lost no one and the new guys gained experience. The fact that we are both here suggests to me that we are going to be working together again."

Sergeant Aitkens' voice was authoritative as she said, "Quite so, Captain." She gestured to L, "This is Colonel Churchill from Intelligence. He is here to brief you both."

"We are working under the British now?"

L gave the Captain a reptilian stare. "We are all here under the governance of the United Nations. As I am a full colonel then my orders are to be obeyed."

It seemed a little heavy handed to me but then the agent was not used to this sort of command structure. I guessed he sent individual agents out to do his bidding and I wondered what our role would be.

205

Korea

Sergeant Aitkens pushed over two folders. They were different in colour and that suggested, to me, that we were having different targets.

'Colonel Churchill' said, "Major Harsker will be taking a small elite group of his men through enemy lines to Uiseong-ro. It is twenty miles behind the current front and into enemy lines. You, Captain Rogers, will be travelling with him as far as a bridge which is seven miles from Uiseong-ro. Your task will be to blow the bridge and then retire south. The Major and his men will be carrying out their own mission and then making their way to the coast where one of his boats will pick him up from a beach north of Pohang and south of Yeongdeok."

Captain Rogers was about to ask something and I put my hand on his arm and shook my head. I knew there would be more to follow.

"Major Harsker, we have discovered that your soldier who defected, Private Jeremy Blair, is there along with some of the North Korean Ministry of Propaganda. You need not know how we discovered this. Suffice it to say that as much as we are being spied upon, we spy just as much on others. He is about to be revealed to the world. Our troops are holding the North Koreans and they intend this to damage the morale of the Allied forces. They have announced a press conference in four days' time." He smiled, "The fact that it will just be Eastern Bloc journalists and those from China is irrelevant. He will publicly renounce this war as an act of western aggression. We believe that he will spread fictitious stories about atrocities committed by you and your men, Major. There are many at the United Nations who will believe such lies. This war is young and the last thing we need is for such bad publicity. The fact that it is untrue does not matter. Journalists will pick up on the story and dig around. They will happily print that which is untrue. Any element of grey can be subverted. It is a distraction we can do without. In addition, we believe that this Blair is part of a red cell which seeks to undermine our armed forces."

I nodded. It made sense to me. I had been about to give the MI6 agent my views. This was an unpopular war with many. We had just finished a world war. We were just an atomic bomb away from another. The pacifists at home had grown vociferous. Some were demanding that we ban the bomb and pare down our armed forces. Atrocities by commandos would merely add fuel to their fire. I wondered how many other agents there were?

"Your mission, Captain, is twofold. Get the Major north of the river and then blow the bridge so that the Communists cannot resupply their men at the front. By blowing the bridge you will also sow confusion about the whereabouts of Major Harsker and his men." He looked at me. "Your mission is to capture Blair and bring him back."

"And if I cannot bring him back?"

The smile disappeared and the reptile returned, "Then kill him." He nodded to emphasise the point. "You will, of course, need to take your Sergeant Heon with you."

"But sir, he is not a commando."

"You will have two other men with you. Three commandos should be able to ensure that one Korean survives."

I opened the folder. There was an aerial photograph of the town and I saw a building in the centre with the North Korean flag flying. It was circled and, on the map, which came with it, was also circled. There were sandbags around the building and a gun emplacement on the roof. There were just a couple of buildings close to this one. I thought it might have been some colonial residence from the time when the Japanese ruled Korea. It looked to be a small town and hardly worthy of such a prestigious press conference. The photograph showed tanks but they were at the bridge, by the river. I saw a small track which led east. There was rough ground and I saw forests. I liked forests. We could get lost there if we had to. Captain Rogers glanced over my shoulder at the photograph. He whistled which evoked a tut from L. I saw that there were military vehicles parked at the front of the building. Most were military. I needed one of my men to be someone like Emerson. The only one I thought might fit the bill was Williams. Already I was picking my team.

"And how many men are there in Uiseong-ro, sir?"

"A battalion of regulars and half a regiment of artillery. Oh, and the crew of ten anti-aircraft guns, say another hundred men."

Captain Rogers could not contain himself, "Sir! That is suicide!"

"Which is why we are not asking you to complete this mission. Well, Major? What do you need?"

I took out a pen and scribbled on the manila folder. "We need a North Korean jeep to get up there. I will need a radio in the jeep. I want an air raid on the tank compound at midnight."

"Air attack? Isn't that risky? It is a small town and there may be collateral damage to your building or vehicle."

"People will take cover. I trust our pilots. The compound is a good half mile from the building. It gives us the chance to get in while people are running around and then get out. You need to make it in two waves. Three bombers and then another three."

"Night-time bombing is not accurate and we don't want any civilian casualties. They are South Koreans in the town."

"I told you, sir, it does not have to be. We are not talking about Lancasters carpet bombing Cologne. This will be three B-29s dropping H.E. If they fly line astern they can do it. The river is a good marker. They need to straddle the river with their bombs and it will make people take cover. That is what we want. People looking up and not down. We will need a moon." I had already read that there was a full moon in two days' time. "Apart from that, I need nothing. Oh, handcuffs. The slippery bugger will not escape again."

"So, you think you can do it Major?"

I gave him a wry smile as I took out my pipe, "Surely you must think we can or is this a suicide mission to kill Blair and then get killed ourselves?"

"That is a cynical attitude, Major."

"That is how I have lived so long. I assume the worst in all those above me!" I caught the vague hint of a smile from Sergeant Aitkens.

"We believe that your record gives us the best opportunity of eliminating this threat. In a perfect world, you would bring him back so that we can find out all that he knows and then lock him away for a very long time."

"Then we can do it."

Captain Rogers said, "You Brits are all crazy. There is just the smallest problem of getting through enemy lines." He held up his folder. "I have been reading through this and I see that we are taking just the one vehicle for the Major and one truck. How will we get through?"

"If you had read a little more closely, Captain," Sergeant Aitkens' voice was icy as she spoke to her countryman, "then you would have seen that you are using a Korean truck and there will be three Korean soldiers in the cab. We are going to pursue you with a couple of Chaffees. The Major and his men will be wearing North Korean field caps. They will help to disguise their faces. I do not think that you will have any trouble. When you blow the bridge the air raid which the Major has requested will give you cover to cross back to South Korean territory. It is the Major who is out on a limb."

Captain Rogers knew when he was beaten and he nodded. We spent a good hour going through the routes, the passwords and the various avenues for my team to escape. Sergeant Aitkens was correct, Captain Rogers did have an easier route home but he just had the one way to travel. When he blew the bridge, he would be stuck on the one road. All we had to do was to make our way east. We would have a fifty-mile drive. We could have made it shorter but that would have taken us through Cheonseong. Our route was through the mountains and the uninhabited part of the land. More importantly, it would bring us out north of Pohang and we knew both the waters and the beaches around there.

We would leave the next evening. That fitted in with the cycle of the moon and would allow the air raid to be organised. "I take it that you will brief Lieutenant Drake?" I nodded. He stood and shuffled his papers. "Then good luck. I will wait until you return here in case a debrief is necessary." He left.

Sergeant Aitkens said, "The light truck we have for you is a Gaz 67. We managed to get one with a canvas covered back. You can drive it back if you like." I nodded. "We have managed to get you another two Colts with silencers. I will bring them down to the Gaz for you. Your vehicle, Captain, is close to your barracks as are the three Korean soldiers. There are explosives being delivered tomorrow. Major Harsker will be here by two p.m. You have ninety miles to cover and you need to be at the jump-off point well before dark to allow the Major to reach his target before the air raid." She stood. "If that is all, Captain, I will take the Major to the truck."

The Captain nodded, "See you tomorrow then, sir."

I gathered my papers and maps.

Sergeant Aitkens' voice was both soft and sympathetic as she said, "He is right, you know, this could be suicide. I know that this is a British operation and I am an American but I would have thought there was another way."

I held the door open for her. "The only other way is to bomb the town and that would incur too many casualties. That is why they are holding a press conference in the south in a small town."

We descended the stairs, "You are a thinker. They could use you in Intelligence!"

"I am a man of action who thinks. We will be alright."

"We have a North Korean Officer's coat there too. Sergeant Heon will be speaking. He will play the officer."

"Good idea. Yours?" She nodded. I saw that the Captain and Petty Officer were waiting by the jeep. I waved at them. "Go ahead without me."

"Sir!"

From the grins on their faces, they obviously thought we had some sort of tryst. Nothing could be further from the truth. Whatever thoughts I might have had about this American agent were buried deep within me.

There were mechanics around the Russian built vehicle which looked remarkably like an American Willy jeep. The mechanics saluted. "All gassed up sir and we gave her a service. She is a four-wheel drive. There is a spare tyre. She has a good wheelbase and according to the specs we have has a 3.3-litre engine." He scratched his head, "Sir, what is a litre?"

"Almost two pints." I smiled, "3.3 is a little beefier than most British cars. Thank you, gentlemen. I will try to look after it for you." That was untrue, of course. We would abandon the jeep before we boarded our boat. I looked inside and saw that we could accommodate Blair. It would be cosy though. I threw my papers in the passenger seat and shook Sergeant Aitkens' hand. "Thanks. I suspect you have done all that you can to make this go smoothly."

"That is my job."

I laughed, "And we both know that is a lie. If I don't see you again then know that it has been a real pleasure to meet you and I will take your memory with me wherever I go."

She shook her head, "You Brits sure have honeyed tongues. Get out of here and get some sleep" You spend so much of the night awake you must be a vampire!" Her eyes became sad, "Keep your head down, Major! You are running out of lives!"

Chapter 16

As I was driving back I was assembling my team in my head. I would have to take Heon. I did not want to for he was not a professional but I needed someone who could speak Korean. Williams was necessary. He knew vehicles and he could operate a radio. My last man would be Sergeant Callow. He was dependable and if anything happened to me would see the job got done. I also needed his skills with explosives. L had given me one plan. I would adapt it. We had explosives left from the raids we had been on. The building where Blair was hiding was a military headquarters. We would blow it up. In the confusion of the air raid, our escape might not be noticed and they would assume that he was killed when it blew up. It would take two hours to drive the fifty miles to the coast and that assumed we met neither roadblock nor enemy.

When I pulled up at the barracks I parked it between the hut and the boats. I waved over Private Harris. "Get Carter to help you and cover this with camouflage netting."

"Sir."

The sky was still overcast and the men were inside. The weather forecast predicted clear skies beginning in the morning. I went to the table. Private Kang said, "Cup of tea sir?" He looked pleased with himself. His English was improving.

"Gomawo!"

He beamed. I had said *'Thank you'* in Korean.

I laid the papers out. "Lance Corporal Williams, could you find Sergeant Callow, Sergeant Heon, Sergeant Major Thorpe, Lieutenant Drake and Captain Poulson?"

"Sir!" He glanced at the papers, "Summat up sir?"

"Another little jaunt."

Kang brought my tea and I filled my pipe. I would ask the three men if they wished to come. I would not order someone to do what was, in effect, a one-way ticket. As they entered I could see they were curious. Williams was going to join the others until I said, "No, Lance Corporal, I would like you to hear what I say too." Sergeant Grant was hovering nearby. "Sergeant Grant, could you take the rest of the lads on a five-mile run. I will explain later."

"Sir! No problem. Come on you idle shower. We are going for a run!"

When the barracks was empty I said, "We have a new operation. We have to drive through enemy lines to this town here," I pointed at the red circle. "Private Blair is there and I have been given the task of bringing him back for punishment." They said nothing. The pipe was not drawing properly and so I poked around it with my spike. It cleared the blockage. "It is a four-man job. I will tell you my first choices. It is, however, voluntary. Say no and it will not go against any of you. I think that this is an almost impossible mission. There are more things which could wrong than any other raid I have been on."

They all nodded.

"Sergeant Heon I need someone to translate. That means you."

He beamed, "I would be honoured, Major!"

"Lance Corporal Williams I need someone with a radio and someone who knows vehicles. We have a Russian jeep!"

"Excellent sir! You have made my day!"

I could see the disappointment on the faces of the others. They knew that only one more would be selected.

"Sergeant Callow I would like to blow up a building. I need an explosives specialist."

"Then I am your man."

"We leave tomorrow afternoon. Captain Rogers and his Rangers will get us through the lines and then we are on our own."

"What do we do sir?"

"Simple, Captain Poulson. Lieutenant Drake will take you here," I pointed to the bay, "And you will pick us up. I leave those arrangements to you. We will be snatching Blair at midnight tomorrow. It will take between three and four hours to reach this point. We have a radio and if I think we are not going to make it then I will let you know. I would not wish you to put your lives in danger when there is no need for it." I relit my pipe as they studied the photographs.

"I still have no replacements for Brown and Jennings, Major."

"I know. It is up to you. If you wish to draught more men in then that is your decision. Captain Poulson will choose the men to secure the beachhead." I turned to Williams. "The Gaz 67 is outside if you wish to have a look at it. Sergeant Heon, there are four North Korean field caps and two Colts with silencers in the jeep. Be so good as to fetch them, would you? They will augment our disguise. While the others studied the map, I showed the photograph of the building. "Can you destroy it with the explosives we have?"

"Of course sir, but it will make a mess. What about civilians?"

"If you noticed they have cleared around the house. There will also be an air raid. I am guessing that the locals will have taken shelter."

"In which case no problem, sir."

"Sergeant Heon will bring two Colts with silencers fitted. They are for you and Williams. We will take Thompsons too but if we have to use them then things will have gone badly wrong. Take plenty of grenades."

"Yes, sir. Do you need me here sir?" I could see that Sergeant Callow was keen to get his explosives and detonators organised.

"No, you will have much to do."

He rose, "And a letter to write sir."

He was married. I would have to write a letter too. Was I sentencing a family to a life without a dad? I put that unpleasant thought to the back of my mind. I could afford no distractions. By the time the men had returned we had ironed out the kinks in the plan. Williams had checked the engine and was pleased. He was even more delighted with his silenced Colt. The rest of the troop knew that something was going on but they just knuckled down to the preparations for the evening meal. Captain Poulson joined me outside leaving Sergeant Major Thorpe and the Lieutenant working out which men they would take. Private Hang appeared with two tumblers filled with whisky. He pointed to Petty Officer Flynn. We raised our glasses and the Petty Officer gave a mock bow.

"I shall give you a letter tomorrow, Paul. See that Susan gets it if..."

"You will be back, sir."

"Of course, and you will give me the letter when I return and that will be an end to it. We both know that if I do not write one then it will play on my mind and might impair my judgement. I didn't get a chance to ask about letters from home, sorry."

"You had a lot on your mind." He drank half of the whisky. "I would just shoot the bastard and save yourself the trouble of bringing him back, sir."

"And it may come to that but we will try and do it by the book. The hard part will be getting into Uiseong-ro. The air raid should cover our attack and our escape. The road looks rough. It reminds me of the ones in Luxembourg. The advantage is that we can ditch the GAZ if we have to although it is four-wheel drive. If they send trucks after us we can disappear in the woods."

The Captain laughed, "Like old times."

"Yes, Captain but with a new team."

The Lieutenant came to see us before he left. "I will be there tomorrow, sir. I will get there before midnight."

"That is too early! The air raid is not scheduled until then."

"And that is why we will be there at twelve, sir. They will have watchers out as soon as the bombers are heard. I would rather be in position and camouflaged."

"Thank you, see you very early the day after tomorrow then!"

"I sincerely hope so."

I retired early. I was tired. I half wrote my letter to Susan and then wrote a complete one to Mum and Dad. I would write the rest of Susan's letter in the morning. I have never been one for sleeping late and I was up almost as early as normal. I went for a short run. It was more to clear my head than for exercise. The clouds had gone and it promised to be a lovely August morning. It lifted my spirits. Kang had a cup of tea for me when I returned and, after a shower, I felt energised enough to finish the letter to Susan. After breakfast, I began to prepare for the raid. I selected my oldest battle dress. It was devoid of medals or rank. I would wear my cap comforter. It would be hidden by the field cap. I had my two handguns and my Thompson. As I had told the others the Thompson was a last resort weapon. I planned on taking eight grenades. When being closely pursued they were a good weapon. We would not need rations but a canteen was vital. I made certain that I had no documents about my person. I had my ID tags and that was all. My wallet, photographs of my family and letters from home were in my footlocker. I did not shave. We could not travel blacked up but my beard grew so quickly that it would darken my face.

At ten I went to the GAZ 67. The others were there already. It needed to be loaded carefully. We loaded the radio first. The canvas top meant that it would have protection from the elements. Callow and Williams would be seated in the back. Heon was the officer and I would be the driver. We used the spaces under the seat for the Korean hats and the water. Sergeant Grant was resourceful and he rigged up netting around the insides of the two doors for the grenades. Similar netting held our submachine guns behind the front seats. The spare gas tank was strapped to the rear. The spare wheel fitted on the side.

Sergeant Callow spotted the obvious problem. "Sir, the GAZ is just five feet wide. Blair was a big man. How do we fit him in?"

I had already thought of this. "Pike has given me a hypodermic with the drug he uses to knock men out while he gets them to surgery. We knock him out and you two carry his body across your knees. We handcuff his hands behind him."

I could see that they were not convinced. I saw no other way of doing this short of strapping his body to the bonnet and that thought had crossed my mind! We left for the base, quietly, in the early afternoon. There was no point in hanging around. Goodbyes were perfunctory. Anything more would have been maudlin. That was not our way. We were not accorded a second glance as we drove through the small town. We looked like an American jeep. I had to show my ID at the gate and we were directed through the base to a quiet area at the rear. There we met Captain Rogers, his men and the two Chaffee tanks which would chase us. The Sergeant and the Lieutenant who commanded the two vehicles were both young and seemed keen to participate in the charade.

"We have blanks as well as live ammo sir. It will be noisy and colourful. Once we lose you we switch to live ammo and make the North Koreans think that you guys were lucky. Our unit is based at the front. We know where their positions are." He patted his tank. "These babies are fast. They don't have the thickest armour but there are no T-34s where we are going!" He took out a cigarette and lit it. "The rest of our regiment will be attacking three miles further east. The Commies will be looking there, sir."

His confidence was infectious. However, I had no intention of just relying on that. We had a large tin of tomatoes. Once we set off I intended to open the tin and pour the contents over William's lap. In the dark, it would look as though he had been gut shot. Sergeant Heon would be animated. My silenced Colt would be hidden in case things became desperate. We ate with Captain Rogers and his men. It was an opportunity for the two of us to ensure that we both knew the plan in detail. Once we began there would be no further opportunity to talk.

We left at three in the afternoon and gathered with the men who faced the North Koreans on this new front line. There was sporadic fighting as the North Koreans probed the American and South Korean defences. We hid our vehicles in a clearing to the west of the road we would be using. Captain Rogers and I headed up the road with a grizzled sergeant. He held his hand and stopped us close by a machine gun crew. A rifle squad with a bazooka team were entrenched in shallow foxholes. They had the red-rimmed look of men who were due to be relieved. We knelt next to the sergeant behind a wrecked American jeep.

"That sir, is the front line. It is just two hundred and fifty paces away. So far they haven't bothered with snipers and neither have we. That explains how we can stand here." He pointed to a T-34 tank. It was off to the side of the road. "They have men behind that tank. That was the furthest they got when they attacked last night. We are slowing them down sir. The length of that tank is the total advance in one day. Last week they were gobbling hundreds of yards every day."

Captain Rogers turned to him, "Has anyone told you what we will be doing tonight?"

"No, sir. The Colonel just said that there would be a truck, a jeep and two tanks. You guys must be crazy if you think you can break through their lines with just two tanks and a truckload of men."

"No sergeant, we do not. The tanks are going to fire at us and we are going to try to sneak through as North Koreans. Later on, in the night, if my team is successful then we will sneak back across the lines. When we come through it would be good if your men fired, just not at the road."

He nodded, "Yes sir. Then you guys are crazy but that might just work. When they attacked last night the men on foot broke through in a couple of places. It might work. I had better tell my guys what to expect."

"And before we leave we will give you passwords and responses. We don't want to be shot by trigger happy riflemen who are due some serious R&R."

"You can say that again, sir."

I took out my glasses and scanned the enemy positions. There were men at the side of the road but the road itself merely had, as a barrier, a couple of oil drums. If the North Koreans used the road to attack then they would need it clear of permanent obstacles. I turned to Captain Rogers, "I will have Sergeant Heon tell them that we were men who attacked behind the American lines and that we have many wounded. He will say that we were surprised by the Chaffees. If we don't get through quickly then we will have to fight our way through."

"We are ready for that. I spoke to the tankers, they might appear flippant sir but they know their business. They will clear the ground on the sides of the road."

"Once we are through then we will go as fast as we can. Our jeep can motor. I won't be waiting for you. We have to travel just six miles north of the bridge and I want to be in position before midnight."

The sergeant returned. "They all know, sir. Now the passwords?"

216

Korea

We moved up to the road just after dark. We waited half a mile from the sergeant and his men. The South Korean troops who were there ready to reinforce a breakthrough looked on in amusement as we donned Korean headgear and then opened a tin of tomatoes to empty on to William's lap. Sergeant Heon saw some Koreans eating and he went to ask for a cup of noodles. He came back and macerated the tomatoes with his fingers and mixed in the noodles. It looked as close to a stomach wound as I had seen. The two tanks pulled up a hundred yards behind us. "Ready when you are sir!"

I shook Captain Rogers' hand, "Good luck, Jack."

"And you sir. This will make a helluva story!"

"Then let us hope that it is me telling it to you eh? Over to you Sergeant Heon! You are in command!"

I saw him lick his lips. He was nervous. He took out and lit a cigarette. When we had been in Sason-ri we had taken the packets from the dead North Koreans. I had kept one packet. Sergeant Heon would smoke one. They had a distinctive smell. "Right sir. Drive!"

The GAZ 67 was fast. The road surface was not the best but we still gripped. The leading Chaffee fired. It seemed inordinately loud. Its machine gun also fired. As we passed the sergeant and his men they let rip at the North Koreans who responded. Passing the tank, a North Korean stepped out with a grenade. Sergeant Heon rattled out a command and the man stopped. I braked when we reached the oil drums and turned around to feign concern over Williams. The three of us had our heads down and Williams was moaning so hard I thought he was going for an Oscar! Gun barrels were pressed against us. Sergeant Heon was magnificent. The young officer to whom he spoke barely got a word in. Behind us, the guns increased their rate and I heard the truck pull up behind us. The three Koreans inside added to the shouting. Then the officer turned and shouted an order. The barrels were moved. Heon shouted to me and I nodded and put my foot down. I accelerated so quickly that we scraped one of the barrels. I drove as fast as I could. No one spoke for a while. Once we had cleared the last North Korean campfire I risked speaking. "How did you manage to convince him, Sergeant Heon?"

He laughed, "Before I taught at the University I taught in a school. I used my teacher voice. He was young enough for it to terrify him." To our right and behind us I heard the crack of tank shells, machine guns and rifle bullets but around us, we drove in a sea of blackness.

"Sir, can I get rid of this stuff?"

"Of course Williams, and I am pleased to see that you have made a full recovery."

He and the sergeant scooped the noodle and tomato mixture and dropped it out of the GAZ. We drove through the night. My worry had been that they might use the night time to send supplies and men south. We had passed the bridge and were just four miles from Uiseong-ro when I saw the dimmed headlights of a convoy heading south. I pulled over to the side so that Sergeant Heon faced the convoy. As it happened we were ignored. The convoy took twenty minutes to edge past us. I feared for Captain Rogers. They would be behind us. Would they have time to set their charges before the convoy reached them? I could not afford to worry about that. We continued north and reached the bridge over the river at ten p.m.

As the road descended to the river we saw the glow from the brazier of the guard post by the side of the road. Two light tanks, the T-70, faced south. This would be a test. We had almost two hours to find the house but first, we had to cross this last barrier. We stopped.

"Sergeant Heon you have done well but this will be a severe test. What do you plan to say?"

"When we were stopped at the front line I saw that the soldiers wore the flashes of the 82nd Regiment. They are part of the 8th Division. I will say that I am from the 82nd here to report the attack by American tanks."

Sergeant Callow shook his head, "Sounds a little thin to me, sir. Why not radio?"

"Tell them that you could not use the radio as the Americans were jamming you and you feared they could listen in."

"Might work, sir."

"I will try Major!"

"Right, let's go." I put the GAZ into gear and began to drive down the hill. I had to judge the speed right. Too slow would look suspicious and too fast might alarm them. In the end, it was Captain Rogers who saved us from an interrogation. We were less than a hundred yards from the bridge which led to the town when the sky lit up to the south of us and then there was a huge explosion. He had blown the bridge. I then heard small arms fire. The Korean sentry at the bridge removed the barrier and screamed at me. Sergeant Heon waved his arm and I put my foot down. Rather than bullets, we were waved through. I heard the tanks fire up their engines. As we neared the first buildings I slowed down the GAZ and looked around. The tanks were crossing the bridge. All around us men were rushing to vehicles. An officer came and screamed at us.

Sergeant Heon said, "Drive sir. They fear an attack from the south. We have a chance!"

We did indeed for we were the only ones heading into town and we were ignored. I had a map of the town in my head and knew that we had to be on the eastern side of the town. I took a road to the right and found myself in a deserted street. I drove down until I came to a small deserted square.

"Torch."

Williams passed me a torch and I took out my drawing of the town. We were less than four hundred yards from the headquarters. I could hear the sounds of vehicles and men as the soldiers in Uiseong-ro heeded the sounds of bugles. They were heading for the river and a defence line. They thought the bridge being attacked further south heralded an offensive from the south. They would have heard of the light tanks attacking and perhaps thought we had broken through.

"Sergeant Heon we shall have to use you like a commando. When we get to the building I want you to casually stroll along and engage the sentry in a conversation. Ask him what is going on. Find out as much as you can about the personnel in the building without alerting his suspicions."

"Yes, sir. I will try not to let you down."

I put the map away and turned north. I drove as slowly as I could. It was almost eleven by the time I reached the headquarters. One of the roads I had taken had been a dead end and I had had to retrace my steps. I saw that there were fewer vehicles than there had been in the photograph. I did not want to park at the front for there was a guard post there. Instead, I found a space by the side. I reversed in. We had made it and now we had to wait. We did not speak. I took out my Colt and fitted the silencer. Williams and Callow did the same. With that on my lap, I took out the hypodermic needle and the vial of the drug we would use. Sergeant Aitkens had managed to get hold of a small leather pouch which held it safely until it was needed. I slipped two grenades in my pockets. Sergeant Callow was the only one with a Bergen. He had the explosives and the detonators. All of us would just use pistols. Sergeant Heon's was a Tokarev.

Tapping Sergeant Heon on the shoulder I pointed to the front of the building. He nodded and stepped out. He lit a cigarette. He put his hands in the greatcoat he was wearing. I admired the Korean greatly. He was doing something which was incredibly difficult. If he was caught then death would be the only happy outcome. The North Koreans would deal harshly with what they considered a spy. We stepped out of the GAZ. I looked at my watch. The air raid would be starting soon. We needed to be in position. Callow and Williams took out a packet of the North Korean cigarettes and lit them up. I took one and lit it but I just held it in my fingers. I loved my pipe but I could not abide cigarettes. Perhaps that was because my dad and grandfather had both smoked pipes. I had stubbed mine out and still, Heon had not returned. I began to worry that he had been captured. I immediately dismissed the thought. If that was true then we would be surrounded by North Korean guards.

I looked at my watch. It was eleven forty. I heard boots on the road. Sergeant Heon turned and walked slowly towards us. He leaned in. "Many of the men who were inside have taken up positions on the river. They fear an American attack. The guard was quite chatty. They are protecting an important man. He said that there are ten men inside to protect him as well as half a dozen servants. Major, these men who protect Blair are specialists. The one outside is a conscript. The ones inside are dangerous."

That made sense. "And where is Blair?"

"He is on the first floor but the sentry told me that there is a basement in case of air raids."

"Then that is where he will be. Heon, when we go in I want you to stay outside and be the sentry. Take his weapons."

"Are you going to kill him? He is a conscript. He seems a simple man."

I shook my head, "Not unless we have to." I took out my sap. "When the air raid begins we run to the sentry. Tell him we seek shelter. He will not let us in but I will be able to render him unconscious." I turned to the other two. "If these are elite forces we take no chances. Shoot to kill. We will have the element of surprise."

"Sir." Just then I heard the faint hum in the east of aero engines. The B.29s were slightly early. Perhaps they had a following wind. It made little difference to us we would go in as soon as the bombs began to drop. I took out my sap as the engine noise drew closer. I heard an old-fashioned siren. I had not heard one since the war. We moved closer to the edge of the building. I risked a glance around the corner and saw the sentry looking up. He turned and spoke to someone inside. Sergeant

Heon whispered, "He asked someone inside if he could take shelter. He was told to stay at his post. The bombs would be for someone else." Just then half a dozen men ran from the building. They were obviously the servants and were running to one of the shelters we had passed on our way in.

That gave me hope. If the ones inside delayed going to the basement we had a chance of catching them unawares.

Anti-aircraft guns began firing from the river defences. They were firing in hope rather than expectation. The bombers were invisible and they had no searchlights. The noise of the engines grew. It seemed to be overhead. When I heard the distinctive whistling of falling bombs I said, "Let's go!"

The sentry looked petrified. Sergeant Heon shouted something to him and he shook his head. I reached him as the first bombs hit south of us. He instinctively ducked his head. I brought out the sap and smacked him on the back of the head. He fell like a sack of potatoes. As Heon took his place I slipped my sap into my pocket, took out my Colt and then hefted him on my back. I had an idea.

We ran up the steps of the colonial looking building. I had my gun at my side. I counted on the Koreans inside seeing me carry what they thought was an injured man. The tomato stain on Williams' battledress would add credence to the illusion. The house had blackout curtains and the inside was brightly lit. As we stepped in I saw four men in the hall. Another two were by a door leading down to what I presumed was the basement. All had a weapon. They were dressed in black. They saw the sentry and hesitated. I brought up my gun and fired at the four men. Callow and Williams joined me. One managed to go into the basement and lock the door. If Blair was down there then we would have to blow up the house with him inside. The five men all fell. We had fired twenty bullets between us. The silenced Colts just left the whiff of gun smoke.

I laid down the sentry by the door and ran to the stairs. I had fired five bullets. I hoped that Williams and Callow were close behind me. Outside the bombs were now exploding in greater numbers. Perhaps the second flight had caught up with the first. If so that might prove disastrous. A stick of bombs landed so closely that our building shook and dust fell from above.

I had reached the landing when the house shook and two men appeared in the doorway. Both had rifles in their hands. I fired three shots. One fell backwards into the room and I heard a shout in Korean. I ran into an open doorway. When the next two men appeared Williams and Callow both shot them. Even as they fell I ran into the room. There was Blair. Seated on the bed he had a bottle of rice wine and was smoking a cigarette. Two young Korean boys, half-dressed and looking petrified were close to Blair who was in his underwear. He had been a commando but drink had slowed his wits. Before he could react and reach for the pistol at the foot of the bed I ran and cold-cocked him with the Colt. I said to the two Korean boys, "Gagi!" I hoped it meant go. My waving arm added further information and they ran.

"Sergeant, begin to set your bombs. Williams, find a dressing gown for Blair. Handcuff him." I took out the needle. This was the part I was least confident about. I had been briefed by a doctor at the base but as I pressed the plunger I wondered if I was killing him. I saw as I put away the pouch, that there were papers and a briefcase. While Williams dressed the unconscious traitor, I put as many papers in the briefcase as I could.

"Williams, pick up Blair. It is time we were gone." I had noticed that the explosions were becoming fewer. We needed to make the Koreans think that a stray bomb had blown up their building. When I reached the ground floor I saw that the last Korean had made the mistake of venturing from the basement. Callow had shot him.

"Time to go, Sergeant."

"Sir, it might not destroy the whole building."

"It is largely wooden. It should burn but we have no time. The air raid is almost over. Williams, get Blair to the GAZ. You and Heon get in the back."

"Sir."

The two of them manhandled the overweight commando.

I picked up the sentry and dragged him outside. Sergeant Callow attached the cables and followed me out of the door. The street was still empty. We ran across the road and I laid the Korean in a doorway. There was a car in front of us. It already had rubble on it from a stray explosion. Callow attached the cables. Time was passing. I could hear explosions closer to the river. This was our last chance. Sergeant Callow nodded and then pushed down the plunger. A wall of flame leapt from the open door and then the house exploded. The car in front of us bore the brunt of the explosion and was actually moved three feet closer to the wall. When my ears stopped ringing I rose. Callow took the plunger and cables and we ran to the GAZ. Flames were leaping up the building and

Korea

the breeze fanned and spread them. The nearest building was twenty feet away. I saw burning debris landing on it. That, too, would catch fire. I threw myself behind the wheel and started the GAZ. Sergeant Callow dropped the plunger at his feet. He would discard it when we were clear of buildings. I glanced around and saw that my two men and the prisoner were jammed in the back. This would not be a comfortable ride. I floored the accelerator and we leapt on to the main road. To the south, I saw fires burning. The bombs must have hit ammunition for I heard the sound of shells exploding. I almost missed the road which would take us to the coast. It was narrow and between two old houses. I threw the wheel over and all four tyres gripped. I put on the lights. We might be seen but I needed to see the road. I knew that this was a mountainous road with few people. The drops at the side were, potentially, deadly.

Sergeant Heon asked, "The sentry sir?"

"Is safe."

Sergeant Callow said, "We should have killed him, sir. He will tell them about Sergeant Heon. He has to remember being sapped."

He was right. "I know Sergeant but Sergeant Heon was right, he was a conscript. The others were killers. Don't forget the two young boys. Should we have killed them too?"

"No, sir."

"We are taking the most unlikely of escape routes. They will search the road to the bridge. I reckon they will assume we were with Captain Rogers and his men or that we were in the building when it blew. By the time they examine it we should be at sea. Anyway, it is too late now. We just have to drive as fast as we can."

Williams was peering out of the side. "Without dropping down a precipice eh sir?"

I could not read the odometer and the speed dial was in Korean. I had to estimate our position. I had Callow take the torch and map to give me an idea of where we were. There were few road junctions and they proved to be good markers. The one or two tiny hamlets through which we zoomed were also useful.

"Cheongson is the only danger to us. We pass less than eight miles south of it. Then we have a long loop south and then northeast. If they think we are on this road then they can send men after us."

Sergeant Callow said, "That looks to be the crossroads a mile or two up the road."

"And how are you two in the back?"

"Sir, Blair stinks of cheap perfume. It is making me sick! Can we not put a bullet in his head and dump him?"

"As much as that is an attractive proposition we need him in our custody."

There was a guard post at the crossroads. We were lucky that they were not taking their job seriously for the men there were inside their hut. We were through before they emerged but, as we turned to head due south for a while I saw them as they stared after us. One of them was winding up a field telephone. There were other soldiers close by. We would be reported. We had thirty miles to go and another four hours until daylight. Would our luck hold? The last three and a half miles would severely test the GAZ as it was off-road. If we had to take to Shank's pony then we could cover that in an hour.

Behind me, I heard Williams and Heon as they moved Blair a little. They were helping their own circulation. I looked at the dial which indicated the fuel. We still had plenty and I would not need to stop and refuel. My two men in the back would like me to stop. We were in the dark and time was passing. Each mile we covered took us closer to safety and further from danger.

We descended down a series of sharp hairpins. They were very distinctive. I remembered them from the map. Sergeant Callow said, "According to my calculations, sir, we reach the river and the point at which we leave the road in just under two miles."

The track we wanted went north and east while the bridge took the road we were on south to Pohang. We turned the last hairpin. There was a checkpoint at the bridge and they had been alerted. We knew that when we saw them with guns pointing down the road. We were lucky that Sergeant Callow was quick-witted. I was concentrating on the road for I knew that the track lay close to the bridge. I was so pleased to see the bridge that I did not notice the men. Callow did and he grabbed his Thompson and shouted, "Williams, grenade!"

The muzzle flashes from the Koreans stitched a line through our canvas. The spinning GAZ threw stones at them and our sudden arrival had put them off their aim. Callow's Thompson scythed through them and I hurled the wheel to the left and the track. Williams shouted, "Grenade!" as we sped up the bumpy track. A couple of pieces of shrapnel hit the rear of the GAZ.

"Anyone hurt?"

"No, sir."

"Well done Sergeant Callow. Williams, get on the radio and tell the boat we are coming in hot."

I had to concentrate so hard on the track that I was oblivious to the conversation behind me. The tyres spun on stones and rocks. I heard a worrying crunch as a rock hit something underneath. It sounded ominous. There was an ever-increasing chance that we would have to walk. We climbed up the track which was just a rough gravel one.

Callow looked behind us and said, "Sir, I can see headlights."

"Then we are being followed. We have just three and a half miles to go."

Williams said, "The boat knows, sir and they have a defensive position. They wished us good luck, sir."

As we struggled up the hill I felt the engine hunting. What had the rock done? We had almost reached the top when it shuddered and stopped. Sergeant Callow jabbed a finger at the dials. "Sir we are out of petrol. We must have a punctured fuel tank."

"Everybody out. Heon, Williams, carry Blair and head over the rise. The bay should be less than two miles away on the other side. Sergeant, you and I will slow them down." I took the briefcase and handed it to Williams. "This is important." I grabbed grenades and my Thompson.

"What about the radio sir?"

"Can't be helped."

The GAZ was on a steep slope. The handbrake was barely holding it. I took most of the grenades out. Sergeant Callow said, "I can see the men sir. They are at the bottom of the slope, they are less than half a mile away. It looks like they have left their vehicles."

"Then we use the GAZ as a bomb. When I release the handbrake drop a grenade under the seat. We run as fast as we can over the top. We will have to slow them down." Just then bullets zipped from below us. We had been seen. "Now!" I released the handbrake and barely got my arm out in time as the GAZ rolled down the slope.

Sergeant Callow hurled the grenade and then shook his head, "I only just managed it, sir."

I could not help but watch the GAZ career down the slope. It must have hit a rock for it flew in the air and exploded. The grenades I had left inside and the spare petrol can exploded, showering the hillside in burning fuel. It made the Koreans dive for cover. I had to hope that we had taken out some officers and sergeants.

I turned and ran. It was less than half a mile to the top. We reached the crest and saw the bay before us. The boat was slightly further away than I had thought. Williams and Heon were struggling to carry the overweight commando. "Sergeant we will ambush them here. We need to buy Williams and Heon time to get him down the slope."

"Sir."

We laid our grenades before us and watched. I saw the Koreans as they were urged on by their officers. They were less than a hundred and fifty paces from us. I counted more than thirty. More appeared to be disgorging from a lorry. I took the pin from a grenade as did Callow. I hurled it high and then took the pin from a second. I sent that on a flatter trajectory. Callow did the same. The four grenades filled the air with shrapnel. We had four left. I grinned. "It seems a waste to leave these."

"Good idea sir."

We both stood and stepped back from the skyline so that we were not silhouetted. Using my long arms, I hurled them both one after the other over the top. Picking up our guns we ran. There were shouts and screams as the last grenades exploded and the shrapnel took effect. I saw that my men had almost reached the boat and Captain Poulson had men rushing up to help him. I deliberately shortened my stride so that I would not over extend myself and fall over. I saw now why my two men had taken so long to get down the slope. What passed for a track twisted and turned and was uneven.

Suddenly heavy machine gun bullets began to fill the air as our pursuers made the top of the ridge. They had tough soldiers if they could lug a heavy machine up that slope. I was ahead of Callow. I turned and saw the muzzle flashes. It would take a lucky shot to hit us but a good soldier never discounted luck both good and bad. When I heard the pop of a mortar I knew that we had bad luck. Their first shells were ahead and to the right of us. They would become more accurate. We were less than half a mile from safety when I heard Callow cry out. I turned and saw that he had been struck in the back by mortar fragments. I turned and emptied my Thompson up the slope. I slung my Thompson. "Leave me, sir!"

"We never leave a man behind!" I picked up his Thompson and emptied that too. I picked up Callow and held him before me like a baby. The mortar shells were still falling as I picked my way down the slope. All those runs had helped. I saw Petty Officer Flynn. He was just a hundred yards away. He held the Bren gun like a Thompson and was spraying the hillside behind me. He shouted, "Come on sir! Nearly there!"

I didn't hear the mortar shell which hit me. It just felt like someone had slammed a cricket bat into my back. My legs wouldn't move. I felt Callow slipping from my arms. I couldn't hold him. I saw Captain Poulson and Petty Officer Flynn as they ran towards me. I tried to speak but nothing came out. I could feel nothing. I hit the ground and the world went black.

I heard voices but they seemed far away. Were they speaking Korean? Then I was in a dark cave and I heard voices. Bizarrely they were the voices of Alan Crowe, Ken Shepherd and Peter Groves. They appeared out of the dark. They couldn't be here. They were dead. Alan Crowe held out his hand and said, "Hello sir, we have been expecting you."

All went black.

Epilogue

"Daddy, daddy come back! Daddy!" I heard Samuel but I couldn't see him. I was blind!

Then I saw a light and the light grew. I smelled new grass and then I was almost blinded by the sunlight. I shaded my eyes and when sight returned I saw Susan holding my children. I slipped into the darkness of sleep.

"Major! Are you awake?" I shaded my eyes against the bright light. I saw a nurse above me but the voice was coming from my left. The nurse hurried off. I looked around and saw Sergeant Callow. He was lying on his front and grinning. "You had 'em all scared you were going to croak. I knew you would come through. You kept moaning and I heard you say your kids' names and 'Susan', over and over again you said it. I knew anyone who wanted to get to their family so much wouldn't let a little piece of mortar fragment stop them."

I croaked, "How long was…"

"It has been three days, sir. They have operated on you three times. Once at the MASH unit and then we were whisked off in a helicopter. You were lucky, you were asleep but thanks to these fragments up my arse I had to watch the sea whizz underneath us. They brought us here to somewhere in Japan and they operated again when we got here. My operation seemed to work but they whipped you back in last night and they operated for almost seven hours." We heard footsteps and he turned around. "Ah, here he is, Doctor Frankenstein."

The doctor looked to be younger than me and when he spoke he had an American East coast accent. He sounded like he was from New England. "Sergeant, I have told you before my name is Doctor Frankenberg!" I saw that he was smiling. "I think the sooner we have you out of here the better." He turned to the two nurses who were with him. "Roll him over gently nurse so that I can examine the wound." He went to the basin and rinsed his hands. After drying them he approached me.

I winced as they lifted me. The doctor seemed pleased, "Excellent, you can feel pain!"

"I think you are right, Sergeant. This one sounds like he is used to working on monsters." His hands were soft and delicate as they probed the back of my neck.

"Back over, nurse." He washed his hands again. "Have your joke Major. From what I can gather you are something of a hero. You certainly saved your sergeant's life. You, however, came closer to death than he did. The initial operation did not remove all of the mortar shell fragments. It is hardly surprising. Some were tiny. We only discovered the last one during your last operation. It was lodged next to your spinal column. Had we not removed it then you would have been paralysed from the neck down for the rest of your life." I think my eyes showed the horror of that future. He took a small metal bowl and showed me a tiny piece of metal. "There it is. I think the last operation worked and you should make a full recovery." He looked sad, "And I dare say you will go back to playing at soldiers again." Shaking his head, he said, "I will be glad to get back to a civilian hospital. There my patients don't repeat the same mistakes which injured them in the first place. Good luck, Major Harsker."

Then he left and I felt like a fool. I had mocked him. "I am sorry that I was so flippant, Nurse. It is just the way of soldiers. When will he be back?"

"He won't. He was flown in especially for you all the way from Hawaii. General MacArthur sent for him. He is the leading surgeon for injuries of the spine."

I heard Sergeant Callow whistle, "Friends in high places eh sir?"

The nurse gave me a drink of water. "Here you are, sir. You have not eaten yet and you have had all of your liquids by drip. We have a week to build you up and then you will be out of here."

I nodded and, after I had drunk and the nurses had left, I said, "What happened to the others, Sergeant?"

"We were the only casualties, sir. When you fell it seemed to set the lads off. I could do little about it after you dropped me. They charged the Koreans and the guns on the boat helped. They were driven off. Heon, Williams and Blair didn't have a scratch. Lieutenant Drake almost blew the engines getting you back."

"Captain Rogers?"

"They got back but he lost half of his men. He tried to see you at the MASH. Captain Poulson was given the rank of Brevet Major in your absence, sir. The lads came to see me before we left. You were drugged up to the eyeballs, sir. They were all worried."

I had much to take in. I wondered where I would be sent at the end of the week. When Sergeant Callow left after two days I had the small ward as my domain. I was beginning to feel sorry for myself. I had no one to talk to and I had read all that there was on offer. I was used to an active life and this did not suit. When the door opened and I had a whiff of perfume I wondered who it could be. Sergeant Aitkens walked through the door. Except she now wore the uniform of a major and had no glasses. She smiled. "So what part of '*keep your head down*' did you not understand?"

"Sergeant, er Major…"

"It is Kathleen. I think we know each other well enough to be on first name terms, don't you, Tom?"

"Yes, Kathleen. What brings you here?"

"You. First of all, congratulations you and Captain Rogers have been awarded the Distinguished Service Cross. I don't know of too many outside of the American Armed Forces who have been awarded the medal. Secondly, they want you in Hawaii. They have taken Blair there for a debrief. Your 'L' is flying out to meet us."

"But I am a combat officer! What do I know about interrogation?"

"Nothing but you do know men and, more especially, commandos. The powers that be think that your ear might pick up in things which we do not. Consider it part of your recuperation. You will not be passed fit for active service for another three weeks in any case."

"I could go home."

I saw a flicker of pain across her eyes. "And I knew you would say that. You could but I think I know enough about you, Tom Harsker, to know that you will stay. You want to see this through. Anyway, it is out of your hands. You are still part of the American forces for a little while longer. When you are dressed I have a car waiting to take us to an airbase and they will fly us to Hawaii."

"I thought I had a few more days here."

She put her hand to her chest and feigned fainting, "My charms have deserted me! The Major would rather be bored out of his mind than spend a few days with me."

"I didn't mean that!"

"I know and besides they need the bed. They have more casualties coming in. Now can you dress yourself or would you like me to give you a hand?"

I confess I didn't know if she was joking and so I smiled and said, "I will dress myself."

"And I will wait for you outside. For the next month, Major I will be your shadow!"

I felt like Alice falling down the rabbit hole. What would happen next?

The End

Glossary

AP- Armour Piercing Shell
ATS- Auxiliary Territorial Service- Women's Branch of the British Army during WW2
Bisht- Arab cloak
Bob on- Very accurate (slang) from a plumber's bob
Bombay-Mumbai
Butchers- Look (Cockney slang Butcher's Hook- Look)
Butties- sandwiches (slang)
Capstan Full Strength- a type of cigarette
Chah- tea (slang)
Comforter- the lining for the helmet; a sort of woollen hat
Conflab- discussion (slang)
Cook-off- when the barrel of a Browning .30 Calibre overheats
Corned dog- Corned Beef (slang)
CP- Command Post
Dhobi- washing (slang from the Hindi word)
Doolally tap- Going mad (slang- from India Deolali- where there was a sanitorium)
Ercs- aircraftsman (slang- from Cockney)
Ewbank- Mechanical carpet cleaner
Formosa- Taiwan
Fruit salad- medal ribbons (slang)
Full English- English breakfast (bacon, sausage, eggs, fried tomato and black pudding)
Gash- spare (slang)
Gauloise- French cigarette
Gib- Gibraltar (slang)
Glasshouse- Military prison
HE – High Explosive shells
Jankers- field punishment
Jimmy the One- First Lieutenant on a British warship
Killick- leading hand (Navy) (slang)
Kip- sleep (slang)
Legging it- Running for it (slang)
LRDG- Long Range Desert group (Commandos operating from the desert behind enemy lines.)
Mao Tse-tung- Mao Zedong
Marge- Margarine (butter substitute- slang)

Korea

MGB- Motor Gun Boat
Mossy- De Havilland Mosquito (slang) (Mossies- pl.)
Mickey- 'taking the mickey', making fun of (slang)
Micks- Irishmen (slang)
MTB- Motor Torpedo Boat
ML- Motor Launch
Narked- annoyed (slang)
Neaters- undiluted naval rum (slang)
Oik- worthless person (slang)
Oppo/oppos- pals/comrades (slang)
Piccadilly Commandos- Prostitutes in London
Pom-pom- Quick Firing 2lb (40mm) Maxim cannon
Pongo (es)- soldier (slang)
Potato mashers- German Hand Grenades (slang)
PTI- Physical Training Instructor
QM- Quarter Master (stores)
Recce- Reconnoitre (slang)
SBA- Sick Bay Attendant
Schtum -keep quiet (German)
Scragging - roughing someone up (slang)
Scrumpy- farm cider
Shank's Pony- walk (slang)
Shooting brake- an estate car
Shufti- a look (slang)
Skiver- those who avoided conscription
SOE- Special Operations Executive (agents sent behind enemy lines)
SP- Starting price (slang)- what's going on
SNAFU- Situation Normal All Fucked Up (acronym and slang)
Snug- a small lounge in a pub (slang)
Spiv- A black marketeer/criminal (slang)
Sprogs- children or young soldiers (slang)
Squaddy- ordinary soldier (slang)
Stag- sentry duty (slang)
Stand your corner- get a round of drinks in (slang)
Subbie- Sub-lieutenant (slang)
Suss it out- work out what to do (slang)
Tatties- potatoes (slang)
Tommy (Atkins)- Ordinary British soldier
Two penn'orth- two pennies worth (slang for opinion)

Korea

Wavy Navy- Royal Naval Reserve (slang)
WVS- Women's Voluntary Service

Korea

Historical background

Royal Marine Commandos did operate in Korea. However, I have Tom and his men arriving early. The North Koreans did race through the South Korean army and by the time the Americans arrived the South Koreans and the Americans held just an 80 by 50-mile corner of southeast South Korea. The attack by MacArthur at Inchon was a masterstroke. The North Koreans lost not only all of their gains but elements of the American and Allied forces reached the border with China. Had China not intervened then who knows how history might have been altered but invade they did and the war which might have lasted months dragged into years and the peace talks lumbered on into the next millennium!

I have tried to use the names of the places as they would have been in 1950. Mumbai was Bombay then and Busan was Pusan. Beijing was Peking!

The Royal Marine Commandos and the Rangers both operated in North and South Korea. Most of their missions were behind the enemy lines. My raids are all fictitious but reflect the sort of work that would have been carried out.

'MGB 523'

By Hampton, J A (Lt) Royal Navy official photographer - Imperial War Museum Collections Search A 23877, Public Domain,
https://commons.wikimedia.org/w/index.php?curid=31021929

Radio protocol from:

Korea

https://www.globalsecurity.org/military/library/policy/army/fm/24-19/Ch5.htm

Reference Books used

- The Commando Pocket Manual 1949-45- Christopher Westhorp
- The Second World War Miscellany- Norman Ferguson
- Army Commandos 1940-45- Mike Chappell
- Military Slang- Lee Pemberton
- World War II- Donald Sommerville
- The Historical Atlas of World War II-Swanston and Swanston
- Churchill's Wizards: The British Genius for Deception 1914-1945- Nicholas Rankin
- The Korean War 1950-53 -Thomas, Abbot and Chappell
- Military Small Arms of the 20th Century- Hogg and Weeks
- Jane's Fighting Ships of World War 2
- Jane's Fighting Aircraft of World War 2
- World War II tanks- Grove

Korea

Other books by Griff Hosker
If you enjoyed reading this book, then why not read another one by the author?

Ancient History

The Sword of Cartimandua Series
(Germania and Britannia 50 A.D. – 128 A.D.)
Ulpius Felix- Roman Warrior (prequel)
The Sword of Cartimandua
The Horse Warriors
Invasion Caledonia
Roman Retreat
Revolt of the Red Witch
Druid's Gold
Trajan's Hunters
The Last Frontier
Hero of Rome
Roman Hawk
Roman Treachery
Roman Wall
Roman Courage

The Wolf Warrior series
(Britain in the late 6th Century)
Saxon Dawn
Saxon Revenge
Saxon England
Saxon Blood
Saxon Slayer
Saxon Slaughter
Saxon Bane
Saxon Fall: Rise of the Warlord
Saxon Throne
Saxon Sword

Korea

Medieval History

The Dragon Heart Series
Viking Slave
Viking Warrior
Viking Jarl
Viking Kingdom
Viking Wolf
Viking War
Viking Sword
Viking Wrath
Viking Raid
Viking Legend
Viking Vengeance
Viking Dragon
Viking Treasure
Viking Enemy
Viking Witch
Viking Blood
Viking Weregeld
Viking Storm
Viking Warband
Viking Shadow
Viking Legacy
Viking Clan
Viking Bravery

The Norman Genesis Series
Hrolf the Viking
Horseman
The Battle for a Home
Revenge of the Franks
The Land of the Northmen
Ragnvald Hrolfsson
Brothers in Blood
Lord of Rouen
Drekar in the Seine
Duke of Normandy
The Duke and the King

Korea

Danelaw
(England and Denmark in the 11th Century)
Dragon Sword
Oathsword
Bloodsword
Danish Sword

New World Series
Blood on the Blade
Across the Seas
The Savage Wilderness
The Bear and the Wolf
Erik The Navigator
Erik's Clan

The Vengeance Trail

The Reconquista Chronicles
Castilian Knight
El Campeador
The Lord of Valencia

The Aelfraed Series
(Britain and Byzantium 1050 A.D. - 1085 A.D.)
Housecarl
Outlaw
Varangian

The Anarchy Series England 1120-1180
English Knight
Knight of the Empress
Northern Knight
Baron of the North
Earl
King Henry's Champion
The King is Dead
Warlord of the North

Korea

Enemy at the Gate
The Fallen Crown
Warlord's War
Kingmaker
Henry II
Crusader
The Welsh Marches
Irish War
Poisonous Plots
The Princes' Revolt
Earl Marshal
The Perfect Knight

Border Knight
1182-1300
Sword for Hire
Return of the Knight
Baron's War
Magna Carta
Welsh Wars
Henry III
The Bloody Border
Baron's Crusade
Sentinel of the North
War in the West
Debt of Honour
The Blood of the Warlord
The Fettered King

Sir John Hawkwood Series
France and Italy 1339- 1387
Crécy: The Age of the Archer
Man At Arms
The White Company
Leader of Men
Tuscan Warlord

Lord Edward's Archer
Lord Edward's Archer

Korea

King in Waiting
An Archer's Crusade
Targets of Treachery
The Great Cause
Wallace's War

Struggle for a Crown
1360- 1485
Blood on the Crown
To Murder a King
The Throne
King Henry IV
The Road to Agincourt
St Crispin's Day
The Battle for France
The Last Knight
Queen's Knight

Tales from the Sword I
(Short stories from the Medieval period)

Tudor Warrior series
England and Scotland in the late 14th and early 15th century
Tudor Warrior
Tudor Spy

Conquistador
England and America in the 16th Century
Conquistador
The English Adventurer

Modern History

The Napoleonic Horseman Series
Chasseur à Cheval
Napoleon's Guard
British Light Dragoon
Soldier Spy

Korea

1808: The Road to Coruña
Talavera
The Lines of Torres Vedras
Bloody Badajoz
The Road to France
Waterloo

The Lucky Jack American Civil War series
Rebel Raiders
Confederate Rangers
The Road to Gettysburg

Soldier of the Queen series
Soldier of the Queen
Redcoat's Rifle

The British Ace Series
1914
1915 Fokker Scourge
1916 Angels over the Somme
1917 Eagles Fall
1918 We will remember them
From Arctic Snow to Desert Sand
Wings over Persia

Combined Operations series 1940-1945
Commando
Raider
Behind Enemy Lines
Dieppe
Toehold in Europe
Sword Beach
Breakout
The Battle for Antwerp
King Tiger
Beyond the Rhine
Korea
Korean Winter

Korea

Tales from the Sword II
(Short stories from the Modern period)

Other Books
Great Granny's Ghost (Aimed at 9-14-year-old young people)

For more information on all of the books then please visit the author's website at www.griffhosker.com where there is a link to contact him or visit his Facebook page: GriffHosker at Sword Books

Made in United States
North Haven, CT
29 April 2023